Robert Muchamore was born in 1972. His books have sold millions of copies around the world, and he regularly tops the bestseller charts.

He has won numerous awards for his writing, including the Red House Children's Book Award. For more information on Robert and his work, visit **www.cherubcampus.com**

Praise for CHERUB and *Henderson's Boys*:
'These are the best books ever!' Jack, 12

'So good I forced my friends to read it, and they're glad I did!' Helen, 14

'The CHERUB books are so cool, they have everything I ever wanted!' Josh, 13

'Never get tired of recommending CHERUB/ *Henderson's Boys* to reluctant readers, because it never fails!' Cat, children's librarian

'My son could never see the point of reading a book until he read *The Recruit*. I want to thank you from the bottom of my heart for igniting the fire.' Donna

BY ROBERT MUCHAMORE

The Henderson's Boys series:
1. The Escape
2. Eagle Day
3. Secret Army
4. Grey Wolves
5. The Prisoner
6. One Shot Kill
7. Scorched Earth

The CHERUB series:
1. The Recruit
2. Class A
3. Maximum Security
4. The Killing
5. Divine Madness
6. Man vs Beast
7. The Fall
8. Mad Dogs
Dark Sun
9. The Sleepwalker
10. The General
11. Brigands M.C.
12. Shadow Wave

CHERUB series 2:
1. People's Republic
2. Guardian Angel
3. Black Friday

and coming soon . . .

Rock War

BLACK FRIDAY
Robert Muchamore

Hodder
Children's
Books

A division of Hachette Children's Books

ISBN 978 0 340 99924 0

Typeset in Goudy by Avon DataSet Ltd,
Bidford-on-Avon, Warwickshire

Printed and bound in Great Britain by
Clays Ltd, St Ives plc

The paper and board used in this paperback by Hodder Children's Books
are natural recyclable products made from wood grown in sustainable
forests. The manufacturing processes conform to the environmental
regulations of the country of origin.

Hodder Children's Books
A division of Hachette Children's Books
338 Euston Road, London NW1 3BH
An Hachette UK Company
www.hachette.co.uk

WHAT IS CHERUB?

CHERUB is a branch of British Intelligence. Its agents are aged between ten and seventeen years. Cherubs are mainly orphans who have been taken out of care homes and trained to work undercover. They live on CHERUB campus, a secret facility hidden in the English countryside.

WHAT USE ARE KIDS?

Quite a lot. Nobody realises kids do undercover missions, which means they can get away with all kinds of stuff that adults can't.

Key qualities for CHERUB recruits include high levels of intelligence and physical endurance, along with the ability to work under stress and think for oneself. The 300 kids who live on CHERUB campus are recruited between the ages of six and twelve and allowed to work undercover from age ten, provided they make it through a gruelling hundred-day basic training programme.

CHERUB T-SHIRTS

Cherubs are ranked according to the colour of the T-shirts they wear on campus. ORANGE is for visitors. RED is for kids who live on CHERUB campus but are too young to qualify as agents. BLUE is for kids undergoing CHERUB's tough one-hundred-day basic training regime. A GREY T-shirt means you're qualified for missions. NAVY is a reward for outstanding performance on a single mission. The BLACK T-shirt is the ultimate recognition for outstanding achievement over a number of missions, while the WHITE T-shirt is worn by retired CHERUB agents and some staff.

THE ARAMOV CLAN

In April 2012, CHERUB agent RYAN SHARMA was promoted to the rank of Navy Shirt following a successful American-led operation to infiltrate a global smuggling organisation known as the Aramov Clan.

Rather than immediately destroying the Aramov network, United States Intelligence decided to take over the clan. The aim was to slowly wind Aramov operations down, while gaining valuable intelligence on dozens of other criminal groups that use the Aramov smuggling network. This covert takeover was led by a unit known as TFU, under the command of DR DENISE HUGGAN.

Shortly after his promotion, Ryan Sharma returned to the Aramov Clan's headquarters in Kyrgyzstan, posing as the son of CHERUB instructor YOSYP KAZAKOV. While TFU agents discreetly controlled the Aramov

Clan from the top, Ryan and Kazakov operated at grass roots level, picking up the kind of intelligence that never reaches senior management.

1. THANKSGIVING

November 22nd 2012, Manta, Ecuador

Manta Airport's only terminal felt like its best days were behind it. Built to serve a United States Air Force squadron running anti-drug operations, the Yanks didn't like it when the Ecuadorian government kicked them out and before leaving they'd stripped everything – from the main radar in the control tower to the benches at the departure gates.

Fourteen-year-old CHERUB agent Ryan Sharma squatted on a canvas backpack in the airport's sparsely populated passenger lounge, hearing cheesy piped music compete with rain pelting the metal roof.

Ryan had barely slept during a twenty-hour journey from Kyrgyzstan. The long flight had given him a sore throat and bloodshot eyes. A hot shower and soft bed would have been perfection, but it would be a long time before he got near either.

For the past seven months, Ryan had been based at Aramov Clan headquarters in Kyrgyzstan – known as the Kremlin. Ryan's job was to scrape gossip out of the smuggling operation's employees and family members.

The Kremlin didn't offer much in the way of entertainment and the main hangout for teens was an outdoor yard full of weightlifting equipment. Ryan had pumped enough metal to put ten centimetres on his chest. He liked the way he looked with his shirt off now, and so did the girl he'd fallen in love with.

Three aircraft could be seen through plate glass windows across the shabby lounge. It was early morning, but clouds blotted the sun and it felt more like twilight. The smallest plane was a turboprop flown by the Ecuadorian Post Office; next door was a Boeing 737 cargo jet with custard-yellow hull and the logo of *Globespan Delivery*. The company's slogan was painted beneath it: *Anywhere, Anytime, On Time.*

The third much larger aircraft loomed behind these two, standing on eighteen threadbare tyres, with flaking paint and patched-up bullet wounds. It looked badass, like it might roll up to the two smaller planes and make them hand over their lunch money.

It was an Ilyushin-76. The four-engined Uzbek-built freighter had rolled off the production line in 1975 and could swallow a truck through its gaping rear cargo door. This old bird first saw action when the Soviet Union invaded Afghanistan. Records showed the Soviet Air Force selling her for scrap in 1992, but in reality the old freighter had spent twenty years flying the world, carting everything from stolen Mercedes coupés, to Class A drugs.

Anyone could hire her if the money was right, and besides the naughty stuff the Ilyushin had dropped bags of food in earthquake zones, and made deliveries for the US military in Iraq. Over the years, the plane had worn the insignia of twenty different airlines, two national governments and the UN, but anyone smart enough to follow a paper trail of forged maintenance logs and dodgy holding companies would always have found that the real owners were the Aramov Clan.

Ryan had to block out the cheesy airport music as a low voice sounded through the invisible communication unit buried inside his left ear. 'Has she moved?'

The voice belonged to CHERUB instructor Yosyp Kazakov, currently playing the role of Ryan's dad.

Ryan looked up slightly, catching a woman in the corner of his eye. She was touching thirty, sat in a battered armchair, wearing a pilot's uniform. A cap with the *Globespan Delivery* logo on a yellow band rested on the next seat.

'Not yet,' Ryan said, putting a hand across his mouth so that he didn't look like some loony talking to himself. 'Size of that latte she bought, she's gotta need a piss soon.'

'What's she doing?' Kazakov asked.

The pilot was reading a copy of *USA Today*. She'd made it through the paper itself and now studied a wodge of advertising pull-outs. Home Depot, Wal Mart,

Target, Staples. *Black Friday Special – 40-Inch Sony $399, Two-Part Air Con $800, Complete Harry Potter Blu-Ray $29.99.*

'She looks depressed,' Ryan said.

Kazakov snorted with contempt. 'It's Thanksgiving. She wants to be home in Atlanta, watching NFL with hubby and the rug rats.'

Ryan felt a stab of guilt. What he was about to do was hopefully for the greater good. It might save thousands of lives, but this pilot was about to go through the most horrifying experience of hers.

'You really have it in for the Americans,' Ryan noted.

The voice that came back in Ryan's ear was grudging. 'You've got three brothers, Ryan. How would you feel if the Americans had sold a missile to a bunch of terrorists that killed one of them?'

Before Ryan could answer, he saw the pilot fold the crumpled newspaper and post it beneath her seat. As the woman stood, she tucked her cap under her armpit and grabbed the briefcase standing between her legs.

'Showtime,' Ryan mumbled.

He let the woman take a couple of steps before standing up himself. As he swung his pack over one shoulder, Ryan realised the woman was hurrying. Either late for something, or desperate to use the bathroom.

'Shit,' Ryan mumbled, knowing it's much harder to follow someone in a rush.

'Problem?' Kazakov asked.

'I can handle it,' Ryan said quietly, as he tried to catch up without making it too obvious.

'Try getting her in the corridor.'

'I know,' Ryan whispered irritably. 'I can't *think* with you babbling in my earhole.'

Although Manta wouldn't handle a passenger flight for another six hours, there was still a newsagent and café open and a few other people in the lounge. There was a chance the pilot might freak out, so Ryan didn't make his move until she'd walked into a deserted corridor, passed a speak-your-weight machine and was turning into the ladies' toilet.

'Excuse me,' Ryan said loudly.

The pilot assumed Ryan was speaking to someone else, until he repeated the call and tapped the back of her blazer. She looked startled as she turned, then a little irritated.

'Can I help you, son?' she asked, sounding cocky.

'I need you to listen carefully,' Ryan said, keeping his voice flat as he pulled a large touchscreen phone out of his pocket. 'I've got something to show you.'

The woman raised both hands and took a step back. Ryan's olive complexion meant he could just about pass for a local.

'*No money,*' she said frostily as she swiped a finger across her throat. 'It's bad enough kids begging on the street. Clear off before I report you to security.'

Ryan switched on the phone and turned the screen to face the pilot.

'Stay calm, don't make a sound,' Ryan said.

The pilot dropped the cap under her arm as she saw the picture on screen. It was her living-room. Her husband knelt in front of the couch, dressed only in pyjama bottoms. A hooded man stood behind, holding a large knife at his throat. On his left stood two small boys, dressed for bed. They looked scared and the older one had wet pyjama legs from pissing himself.

'What is this?' the pilot asked, trembling. 'Is this a joke?'

Ryan kept his voice firm, but felt terrible inside. 'Tracy, you *need* to keep your voice down. You *need* to listen carefully and do everything I tell you to. If you do *exactly* what I say, your husband and sons will be released unharmed.'

The pilot trembled as her eyes fixed on the photograph. 'What do you want?'

'Speak quietly,' Ryan ordered. 'Take deep breaths. Walk with me.'

Ryan pocketed the phone and began a slow walk, leading Tracy back towards the passenger lounge.

'Me and my people came on that big Ilyushin parked out on the tarmac,' Ryan explained. 'But we need a plane with flight clearance to get cargo into the USA.'

'What kind of cargo?' Tracy asked.

Ryan ignored the question. 'We've got friends behind the scenes at this airport. Right now they're loading your 737 with our stuff. You're scheduled to fly to Atlanta in four hours. You're going to take off on schedule, but once you're in US airspace, you'll put out a mayday and do an emergency landing at a small airfield in central Alabama. By the time the authorities realise what's happened, we'll have emptied our cargo and vanished.

You and your family will be released unharmed.'

'I want to talk to my husband,' Tracy said.

'You can want whatever you like, you're getting Jack shit.'

'How do I know that picture isn't Photoshopped?'

Ryan hated what he was doing, but faked a mean smile as he looked back. 'You want your boy Christian to lose a thumb?'

'You're just a kid yourself,' Tracy stuttered, as she touched a wet eye. 'Who are you working for?'

'They like to call themselves the Islamic Department of Justice,' Ryan said. 'But I don't work for them. Me and my dad are just in this for the money.'

2. SKIDS

The English weather wasn't bad for late November. A bit of a sting when the wind blew, but the sky was bright. The four CHERUB agents wore their combat trousers and training boots, but nothing with the CHERUB logo on was allowed off campus, so their T-shirts and hoodies were plain.

'Where the hell are they?' Leon Sharma asked, as he lay flat on a bench, six rows up a decaying wooden grandstand.

Ryan's eleven-year-old brother Leon was the youngest of the quartet. The other three all had a Ryan connection too: Alfie DuBoisson was one of Ryan's best mates, Fu Ning was a good friend and Grace Vulliamy had been Ryan's girlfriend. Or maybe still was his girlfriend, depending on who you asked.

'Why make us get up so early?' Leon moaned, as

he glanced at the clock on his iPhone. 'I hate waiting around.'

'Beats lessons,' Alfie said, as he lobbed a piece of gravel that bounced harmlessly off Leon's belly.

'I looked this place up on Wikipedia,' Ning said, though nobody seemed interested.

Three days past her thirteenth birthday, the broad-shouldered Ning sat near the top of the grandstand, with a view over a long tarmac straight, faded Dunlop and Martini billboards and the steel frame of a much larger grandstand which had buckled in a fire.

'I can't get my Facebook,' Leon said, scowling at a battered BlackBerry. 'Maybe they forgot about us. There's not even a mobile phone signal.'

'Stop complaining,' Alfie said, his French accent strong as his bulky frame loomed over Leon. 'You do my head in.'

'I looked this place up,' Ning repeated. 'Wikipedia says there hasn't been a professional race on this track since 1957. A Bentley went over the banked kerb, burst into flames and killed seven spectators.'

But Grace wasn't listening and Leon was unnerved by Alfie's presence.

'What you gawping at?' Leon asked.

Rather than reply, Alfie uncupped a hand and flicked a small spider on to Leon's chest. Leon sprang off the bench, flailing his arms and screaming his head off.

'You dick,' Leon screamed, swiping at imaginary spiders as he scrambled over the rows of wooden benches towards the racetrack. 'Where is it? Get it off me!'

Grace couldn't resist. 'I think it's in your hair!'

'Jesus,' Leon shouted, as he frantically flicked his hands through his hair. Then he started unzipping his hoodie and reaching up inside his T-shirt. 'Is it gone?' he screamed. 'Don't laugh, it's not bloody funny.'

Grace wore a huge grin. 'It's at least *moderately* funny, Leon.'

Alfie was howling. 'Ryan told me you were scared of spiders, but I never expected that drama.'

'I can't help it,' Leon spat.

Leon had finally convinced himself that he'd brushed the spider off, but he glowered as he stepped up the wooden grandstand towards Alfie. 'What did I do to you?' Leon shouted. 'I'm gonna smash your face in.'

But physical reality stood in Leon's way. He was an average-sized eleven-year-old, while Alfie was thirteen and held his own playing rugby with lads several years older.

'Suddenly not so brave,' Alfie said, smirking and pounding a beefy fist into his palm.

'This won't end well,' Ning shouted wearily. 'Pack it in before it gets out of hand.'

But while Leon wasn't stupid enough to throw a punch at someone who'd flatten him, he wanted revenge and Alfie's backpack lay on a bench two metres away.

'Yoink!' Leon said, as he grabbed the strap and started running.

'You'd better give that back,' Alfie roared.

Alfie was speedy in a straight line, but he was more battering ram than ballet dancer and Leon's whippy frame gained ground as he hopped across the wooden benches towards the top of the grandstand.

'See how you like it,' Leon shouted, as he flung Alfie's backpack over the rear of the grandstand into a mass of overgrown bushes.

Alfie got within a couple of benches of Leon, but his boot slid and he bashed himself.

'I will kill you!' Alfie shouted, as he rubbed his kneecap. 'Go get that back.'

But Leon was sprinting across the top of the grandstand, and when he reached the end he turned towards Alfie and gave a succession of two-fingered salutes.

Alfie realised he had little chance of catching Leon and decided to lure him out instead.

'OK,' Alfie shouted, as he stepped back towards where Leon had been lying. 'You throw my backpack away. See what I do to yours.'

When Alfie reached his target, he raised a size 7 boot and stamped down on a Puma backpack. There was a sound like a ruler snapping, and a pop of a yoghurt carton. Then Alfie took a step back and booted the backpack high into the air towards the racetrack.

'Happy now?' Alfie shouted, but he couldn't understand why Leon was still smiling.

'My bag's up here,' Leon said.

As soon as Leon said this, Ning remembered that she'd left her backpack down there. And the one she'd seen cartwheeling through the air looked awfully similar . . .

'Alfie!' Ning shouted, as she stood up.

Few girls, even grown women, would intimidate Alfie, but Ning was a former Chinese boxing champ and when she threw a punch you knew all about it.

'I thought it was Leon's,' Alfie said, holding his palms out meekly as Ning steamed towards him. 'He tricked me.'

'You started it with the spider,' Ning said, as she picked up her backpack and unzipped it. 'I told you to pack it in.'

Ning looked furious as she stared into the backpack, seeing science textbooks and a calculator smeared in yoghurt.

Ning turned back towards Leon. 'You wipe that smirk off your face and go look for Alfie's pack in the bushes,' she demanded. Then she thrust her pack into Alfie's belly. 'I don't know how you're gonna clean that out, but you'd better or you're buying me a new one.'

Ning's steely glare made it clear that she meant business. Alfie started hunting in his pockets for a pack of tissues and Leon headed behind the grandstand to retrieve Alfie's pack, but before either made much progress they were distracted by the sound of cars on the track.

'Finally,' Leon said.

Grace was now highest up the grandstand and got a glimpse over treetops at two VW Golfs - one silver, one blue - driving in close formation on the far side of the track. Tyres squealed on a tight corner as the engines grew louder.

On the final approach to the straight in front of the grandstand, the silver car in the lead put its rear end out and there was a hairy moment as the other Golf nearly clipped it before overtaking on to the main straight.

When it reached the grandstand in front of the kids, the man driving the blue car hit the brakes and threw the car sideways into a donut, throwing up clouds of choking grey rubber smoke. As it did this, the silver car stopped more sedately and a crash-helmeted driver stepped out.

'All right, boys and girls,' the driver said, as he unbuckled the helmet. 'You're all here for the Advanced Driving course?'

When the helmet came off, Ning liked what she saw. The instructor was six feet tall, in his early twenties with a solid physique. He had blue-green eyes, and blond hair just long enough for the helmet to have mussed it up.

'I expect my good buddy Mr Norris will be with us when his ego calms down and the tyre smoke clears,' the instructor said. 'But I'll introduce myself first. I'm Mr Adams, but I'd prefer it if you call me James.'

3. CARGO

Until late 2010, the Islamic Department of Justice (IDoJ) was regarded as one of many obscure militant Islamic groups mainly known for posting anti-American and anti-Israeli material on the Internet.

This changed in October 2011, when IDoJ kidnapped two wealthy American executives attending a conference in Cairo. Sophisticated techniques used during the abduction suggested IDoJ members had received Special Forces-style training.

After a video was released showing the beheading of one kidnappee, the family of the other victim defied US Government wishes and paid a ransom of several million dollars. It is now believed that this money has been used to fund further terrorist activity.

Nothing more was heard from IDoJ until March 2012 when a woman was arrested in Paris while conducting a cyber-attack on the French train-signalling system. She had proven links to IDoJ and further investigation revealed a credible plot that might have resulted in the hijacking and deliberate collision of two high-speed passenger trains.

This threat to a prestigious European target elevated IDoJ to a top priority for global intelligence agencies. However, the suspect arrested in France gave little away under interrogation and the rest of the organisation slipped back under the radar.

The next sign of IDoJ activity was picked up when the group attempted to hire a large cargo aircraft from the Kyrgyzstan-based smuggling outfit known as the Aramov Clan. Fortunately, this organisation has been under the effective control of US intelligence for some months, and we are now presented with a unique opportunity to infiltrate and destroy the IDoJ terror group.

Extracted from a CIA anti-terrorist briefing, given to the United States President, October 2012.

Ryan had been chosen to deal with Tracy's capture because he was strong enough to handle her physically, but would look less suspicious than some adult goon as he moved her around the airport.

He'd role-played at the Kremlin, with TFU agent Amy Collins acting as Tracy. Ryan's first job was to freak the pilot out with the picture and nasty mental images of what might happen to her family, but after this Tracy had to play the part of an untroubled pilot preparing for a routine flight, so Ryan moderated his voice and started acting nicer.

After taking Tracy's mobile phone, Ryan stood close by while she used a disabled toilet. She had to go to the pilots' lounge to file her flight plan, and Ryan watched her through a glass door as she checked weather data and used a PC to log her flight plan.

'You've got a missed call,' Ryan said, when Tracy came back into the corridor. 'Atlanta HQ. You need to act normal.'

Tracy nodded as she took her cheapo Android phone off Ryan. Even on a routine trip, a flight plan requires complex calculations on fuelling, weather and cargo weight. Major airlines like Globespan require pilots to e-mail flight plans to headquarters as soon as they're filed and Tracy worried that her nervous state had led to an error.

But the Globespan employee was calling about a crew problem. 'Phil Perry ate some bad crabmeat at his hotel and he's doubled over,' the woman explained. 'Luckily the local crewing agency has dug someone up. He's an Indian named Elbaz and he should be with you shortly.'

Until now, Tracy had drawn comfort from the assumption that she'd be sharing her ordeal with a familiar co-pilot. 'Is Elbaz security-cleared for flights into the USA?' she stuttered.

'Full clearance,' Atlanta confirmed. 'He's already on airport property and he has your number if he can't find you.'

'Great,' Tracy said, trying to hide her nerves. 'Is that it?'

'All good to go, Tracy. Fly safe.'

Tracy looked at Ryan as she handed back her phone. 'Do you know about Elbaz?'

Ryan nodded. 'He's working with us.'

'Is Phil Perry OK?'

Ryan only knew a few details of IDoJ's plan, but they were a ruthless bunch with no reason to keep the co-pilot alive after pointing a gun at his head and ordering him to call in sick.

'I'm sure Phil will be fine if he behaves himself,' Ryan lied. 'We'll head to your plane now. There should be plenty of spare time when we get there, I'll see if they'll let you call your husband.'

Tracy nodded as they walked side by side, crossing the little terminal in less than a minute.

'You need a pass,' Tracy said, flashing an ID hooked to her belt as they approached the doors leading out on to the runway. But the airport security officer let Ryan through with a nod.

It was getting lighter, but they still got blasted with rain as they stepped on to a paved verge and followed a striped yellow walkway towards the three parked planes.

'They've got things sewn up tight,' Ryan said, hoping that giving some info away would help Tracy to feel more in control of her own destiny. 'During quiet periods, there's only a couple of customs officers and a small cargo crew on duty here.'

'So your people bribe or threaten ten men, and you've got control of the whole airport?' Tracy said.

Ryan nodded, as he flicked his fringe back to keep the rain out of his eyes. 'I'm told they searched the globe to find an American airline flying a plane big enough for our needs into an airport small enough for a few men to take control for a few hours.'

'So the customs officer got shown a picture on a mobile phone too?' Tracy asked acidly.

'Something like that,' Ryan said, as they reached the nose of the custard-yellow Boeing. 'They don't tell me a lot; I'm not exactly senior management.'

'How does a kid get mixed up in this?' Tracy asked.

'There's enough money in this for my dad and me to start a new life in the USA.'

'Do you know what they're putting on my plane?'

Ryan pointed at the big Ilyushin. 'We picked up a bunch of military explosives in China. Apparently a piece the size of a ping-pong ball will blow up a car and we've got eleven tonnes of it.'

'And I'm flying it to America,' Tracy said, with a sob in her voice as she looked up at the sky. 'What did I do to deserve this?'

'Think about your family,' Ryan said. 'Nobody will blame you for protecting them.'

They were now within a few metres of the yellow 737 and a man was coming down a set of steps towards them.

'Has she been behaving herself?' a handsome Indian asked, when Ryan got close.

This was Elbaz. Tall, stubbly beard. He looked like a Bollywood actor, dressed in a pilot's uniform with aviator shades and bleached white teeth. He spoke with the posh English accent you pick up at the best Indian boarding schools.

'She's fine,' Ryan said.

'Have you filed our flight plan?' Elbaz asked.

Tracy nodded.

'Then get up into the cockpit and run our pre-flight checks,' Elbaz ordered.

'The boy said I might get to speak to my husband,' Tracy said, as she put her shoe on the bottom step.

Elbaz glowered at Ryan, before turning to Tracy. 'We'll see about that.

'You get back to the Ilyushin,' Elbaz told Ryan, as Tracy clanked up metal steps towards her cockpit. 'You're too young to be out here and not everyone is working for us.'

Elbaz was right, but Ryan resented his tone. He was supremely arrogant, never saying thanks, and always assuming that he was in charge.

Ryan jogged fifty metres through the gloom and walked up the cargo ramp at the back of the big Ilyushin. Most of the bulbs inside the fuselage had burned out and the smell was a mix of oil and cigarettes. Kazakov was the only man inside, sitting up in the cockpit with tired eyes staring at nothing.

'All set, Dad?' Ryan asked. After seven months undercover, calling the CHERUB instructor Dad had become second nature.

The muscular, silver-haired Ukrainian was dressed in an oil-stained string vest and battered khaki mechanic's overall. 'Explosives are all rigged. This old wreck will blow up four hours after we leave in the Globespan 737.'

'Is our crew gone?'

'They've transferred all the cargo to the Boeing. Now they're driving to the Colombian border, with false IDs and pockets full of dollars.'

Ryan studied the IL-76's filthy interior, imagining the dramas that had taken place over thirty-seven years and resenting the tiredness caused by his sleepless, deafening journey from the Kremlin.

For this one-way trip, the Aramov Clan had patched up a plane that had spent two years decaying in a hangar. It had to be destroyed where it now stood: nobody would dare crew it once the Americans learned of its role in a terrorist attack and IDoJ were too smart to leave a rich haul of forensic evidence standing in an Ecuadorian airport.

'What do you reckon on Elbaz?' Ryan asked.

Kazakov looked wary. 'Obnoxious prick, but undoubtedly impressive. His people took Tracy's family and the co-pilot without a hitch.'

'They've got everyone who matters at this airport in their pocket,' Ryan said, as he nodded in agreement with Kazakov. 'Customs waved me and the crew through. Could we have underestimated IDoJ?'

'IDoJ set up the kidnappings and organised everything here at Manta,' Kazakov said. 'But our people scouted and organised the landing site in Alabama. We'll be landing on home turf and the Feds will be waiting for us.'

Ryan knew how the rest of it was supposed to go down: the FBI would wait until the plane made its 'emergency' landing in Alabama and see who turned up to meet them. In one swoop, they'd capture Elbaz, his two companions, members of IDoJ who'd been working inside the United States, and eleven tonnes of high grade explosive purchased from a corrupt Chinese general. In Atlanta, a second FBI team would storm Tracy's home in a surprise raid, ensuring the safety of her family.

But the plan didn't feel as solid as it sounded as Ryan looked out of the open cargo door at rainswept tarmac.

'If something *does* go wrong, we'll be responsible for delivering eleven tonnes of high explosive to a bunch of nutty terrorists,' Ryan said.

Kazakov raised one cheeky eyebrow and broke into a broad laugh. 'Never liked the bloody Yanks anyway.'

As Ryan rolled his eyes at Kazakov, Elbaz's silhouette appeared in the shaft of light coming through the open cargo door.

'We're about to close up the cargo door on the 737,' Elbaz said. 'I take it you two are coming aboard?'

Kazakov stood up and nodded. 'Mrs Aramov would get cross if we lost sight of our explosives before she got paid.'

4. REPUTATION

'I've heard of you,' Leon said, as James Adams approached. 'You're the guy that started the epic food fight in the campus dining-room.'

James smirked. 'Good to know my legend lives on.'

'I bow down before you,' Alfie said. 'You're the guy that had sex in the campus fountain.'

Grace shook her head. 'No, that was Dave Moss.'

James was supposed to set an authoritative tone, but couldn't help laughing. 'A couple of my girlfriends fighting caused the food fight, but I doubt anyone has ever had sex in the campus fountain. The water's *freezing*.'

Bruce Norris was another ex-CHERUB, a year younger and a few centimetres shorter than James.

'Winner of his weight class in the campus Karate Tournament six years running,' Leon said, as Bruce approached. 'Your name's engraved on the trophy currently residing in *my* room.'

Grace tutted. 'And we'll never hear the end of that, will we, Leon?'

'All right, you know who we are,' Bruce said. 'And you saw me overtake James for a spectacular victory, but we're here to work, so shut your yap-holes.'

James took up where Bruce left off. 'This is the CHERUB Advanced Driving course. You've all learned basic driving skills, but over the next five days you're going to learn advanced techniques, both on this track and on the roads between here and campus. You'll sample a variety of vehicles from motorbikes to limousines. You'll practise skills ranging from skidpans to evasive manoeuvres and running roadblocks. This is the course that everyone wants to be on, and I'm not gonna deny that some parts are fun. But cars are *not* toys. If you don't pay attention, you, and more importantly me, could end up in A&E. So, if you mess about, I'll kick you off the course. Is that clear?'

'Yes, sir,' the kids said snappily.

'It's probably been a few months since most of you got behind the wheel of a car,' James said. 'So we'll each take two of you and you'll take it in turns driving around the track, starting off slow, then building up speed. Once you've got a feel for the cars, we'll show you a few special moves, and if you're very lucky you can finish the day with a race.'

'Leon Sharma and Grace Vulliamy, you're with me,' Bruce said. 'Fu Ning and Alfie DuBoisson get to ride with the runner-up.'

'Get a crash helmet from the back of my car before we start,' James said. 'Any questions?'

Leon's hand shot straight up.

'Go on?' James said.

'Sir, if you never tried having sex in the campus fountain how do you know that the water's too cold?'

James didn't mind having a laugh, but the kids had to respect him if he was going to get the best out of them and he wondered what a full-fledged CHERUB training instructor would have done. Before he could speak, Bruce grabbed Leon by the scruff of his hoodie and yelled right in his face.

'Tell you what, Leon. This circuit's about four kilometres. Instead of riding in my car, I think you should familiarise yourself with it on foot.'

'What?' Leon said dopily.

'Get running,' Bruce said.

James smiled at his old friend, then looked at his two pupils.

'Right,' James said, as Leon set off jogging. 'Crash helmets on, Alfie starts behind the wheel. Three laps, then Ning takes control. And try not to run Leon over . . .'

*

Kazakov armed the master detonator aboard the IL-76 and set the hydraulic rear door to close, jumping out as it began rising up towards the tail. He was last up the steps on to the Boeing and one of Elbaz's men closed the door and signalled to a member of the ground crew to pull the steps away.

Like most cargo planes, this 737 had served a couple

of decades as a passenger jet, before being converted for cargo. But although it had a few years under its belt, the beige plastics and efficient hum of the ventilation were a contrast to the brutal noise and vibration inside the big Ilyushin.

A single row of six seats had been preserved at the front of the cabin, with a sheet of dented aluminium separating them from a cargo hold behind.

Ryan had an aisle seat, with the two near-mute IDoJ men who'd been with them since they'd left Kyrgyzstan sat on the other side. Kazakov gave Ryan a reassuring look as he stepped over his legs to take the window seat, but Ryan didn't see it because he was studying the action inside the cockpit.

Elbaz might have been co-pilot, but he was clearly the man in charge. Tracy looked comfortable going through her pre-flight routine, though Ryan could only see the top of her hair and her chubby arms reaching for overhead switches.

'Tower, flight GD39, request permission for take-off. Over.'

The reply came through Tracy's headphones, so Ryan didn't hear.

'Roger that, control. Following route B to runway south.'

As Tracy pushed the throttle forwards to begin taxiing, Elbaz looked back at his comrade in the aisle seat and gave a thumbs up.

'Let's go kill some bastard Americans,' he shouted.

The flight would last around five hours, and Ryan

pulled his iPhone from his jeans and untangled his headphone cord.

'Try and get some sleep,' Kazakov suggested. 'You look like you need it.'

This was no major airport with queues of planes waiting to take off, and Ryan found himself being pushed into his seat by the force of take-off before he'd got his ear buds in.

*

CHERUB agents are supposed to blend in and act like ordinary kids. Ordinary kids don't know how to drive cars, but in dangerous situations the ability to grab a set of car keys and drive fast had kept many young agents out of serious trouble.

James' silver Volkswagen had dual controls, so that he could brake or accelerate if the driver did something stupid, and as it was a few years old the bodywork bore scrapes and dents, many of which had been crudely retouched with grey rustproofing to avoid the expense of respraying.

Ning almost added another dent as she came into a curve much too fast and put the tail out.

'I told you last time,' James shouted, as scenery whizzed by. 'Take the corner from the left, turn in smoothly and put the power on when you hit the apex.'

'Sorry,' Ning said.

'The engine's roaring,' James said. 'Change up.'

As Ning went for fourth gear, the box made a horrendous crunch and the engine raced as she accidentally put it into second.

'I'm glad it's a long time since breakfast,' Alfie shouted, as he sat in the rear passenger seat gripping the hand strap like his life depended upon it.

'Marker,' James shouted. 'Brake!'

The front tyres locked up as the car went into the next corner, but suddenly the vehicle lurched to one side. They'd just turned on to the pit straight, which meant that the car hit a metal crash barrier before it had a chance to veer dangerously out of control.

Ning screamed as the car scraped the barrier. Sparks flew and the door mirror snapped off. Below the car there was a loud drumming sound. James' heart was in his mouth, but he used the brake at his feet to gently push the car to a juddering halt.

'Women drivers!' Alfie shouted.

Ning would have punched him if hitting someone sat behind you in a car wasn't so awkward. Instead, she looked at James in a state of confusion.

'I don't get what happened,' she said. 'What did I do?'

James was opening the front passenger-side door, and looked back along the side of the car.

'Puncture,' James explained. 'Must have picked up some debris on the track and I can't really blame you for that. So, who knows how to change a tyre?'

Ning and Alfie offered up blank stares.

'Right,' James said. 'I guess that's our next lesson then. Now go put out the warning triangle so that Bruce's team don't rear-end us next time they come around that corner.'

5. CAMP

Hayneville, Alabama had a population of less than a thousand, and a tiny airstrip used by Central Alabama aviation club. The town's location at the intersection of three highways, with Interstate 65 a few kilometres east, made it a good spot for anyone wanting to land a plane and disappear with its cargo before anyone except the local two-car sheriff department could reach the scene.

Pre-Thanksgiving traffic that had choked the highway corridor through the centre of Hayneville had subsided, and now it was mid-afternoon. All over America people were home cooking turkey and waiting for the NFL's Thanksgiving Classic. But the holiday was cancelled for a forty-strong team of FBI officers, commanded by intelligence officer Dr Denise Huggan.

Huggan was an eccentric, who insisted everyone call her Dr D. She headed up a unit called TFU, which had targeted the Aramov Clan and now effectively controlled it. Despite a flowing purple dress and wooden beaded necklaces, this petite woman was as tough as the FBI officers under her command.

It was reasonable to assume that IDoJ were watching Hayneville Airport, so Dr D's team had to tread lightly to avoid being noticed in such a small town. Nevertheless, over the past week she'd sent officers into the airfield, posing as mechanics and pilots, and now the tarmac, hangars and surrounding roads were rigged with tiny night vision cameras.

She had three screens on the little desk in her motel room, and one presently showed a trio of U-Haul hire trucks rolling up to the airfield's only entrance. A camera near the main entrance followed a man jumping out of the lead truck and using a key to take a padlock off the main gate.

A female FBI agent came across the com system. 'Eyeballing three trucks with my binoculars. Opening main gate, dark-skinned, beard. Looks like they're here to meet our plane.'

'Understood,' Dr D said. 'All units keep well out of sight. IDoJ are known to be skilled operators, Special Forces background.'

As Dr D said this, she clicked an icon on one of the screens, switching from a CCTV camera at the airport to an output from air traffic control. The black and amber graphic was alive with slow moving triangles, each with aircraft IDs flashing beneath them. So far the Globespan flight from Ecuador was keeping to its slot in the civilian flight corridor and had clearance through to Atlanta's giant Hartsfield Airport.

The leader of the FBI assault team squinted at the display over Dr D's shoulder, then checked his watch. His name was Schultz, and he was plated up with body armour, with a Taser and gun on his belt.

'How long do you reckon?' Schultz asked.

'The plane will need to start losing height in about seventy minutes,' Dr D replied. 'I'd expect Tracy to deviate from course and make the mayday call shortly after, so I'd say we're looking at a landing in ninety minutes.'

'Well, my boys are all ready and waiting,' Schultz said, as he cracked a slight smile.

'Just be sure they don't move until *I* say so,' Dr D replied firmly.

*

Ning's day had been tough. Fast driving required intense concentration, her butt was numb from the car seats and her calves ached from working foot pedals. But she was a fast learner and she was starting to feel like the bashed-up Volkswagen was an extension of her body rather than some weird alien device.

Ning put the car into third and hit the gas as they rounded one of the track's sharpest corners. When you got speed and position right, the car was close to skidding off the track and the steering wheel felt light, as if the car was gliding over the tarmac.

When Ning hit the straight, she clicked the gearbox neatly into fourth and floored the gas pedal. It was dark, with the only light coming from the yellow cones produced by the headlamps and a misty orange glow from streetlamps on a nearby housing estate.

James was in the passenger seat and looked at his stopwatch. 'Very nice,' he said. 'Look for the cone, you're four seconds up on Alfie's time.'

As the speedo hit 110mph, Ning spotted the single orange cone in the middle of the broad tarmac straight. She braked hard and, once the nose was past, dropped down into second gear, reached for the handbrake and yanked the steering wheel hard left.

Ning had practised handbrake turns for an hour that afternoon, but her success rate was barely half and dread shot through her body as she grabbed the lever between the two front seats.

The combination of a tight turn and the handbrake threw the back of the car out violently. If Ning got braking and steering right and put power back on at the right moment, the Golf would pivot on its front wheels and change direction in under four seconds. But get the move wrong and she might veer off in any direction, or stall the engine and stop dead in a cloud of tyre smoke.

Twenty miles per hour was a little fast, and Ning didn't get the steering exactly right. She had to correct the steering to avoid hitting the cone as she straightened up, and there was a nasty moment as the engine choked, but she was gentle on the accelerator and nursed the car back up to cruising speed.

Alfie was in the back and didn't much mind that

Ning was inside his time. After a tough day's practice the pair had bonded and Alfie screamed and pounded his seat.

'Nailed it, Ningo!'

The final part of the run took the car off the track, down a single lane, past a line of run-down pit garages and into a car park behind the trashed main grandstand. Cones marked out a winding course, but in focusing on where she was going, Ning failed to see an old lady on the apex of the turn in.

She swerved, but not soon enough to avoid demolishing the dummy and sending a hail of polystyrene clumps against the windscreen. A large white chunk squealed as it got trapped under the car, followed by a loss of traction as it went beneath one of the rear wheels.

After clipping a couple of cones, Ning cut her speed for the final weave across the car park. She stopped at a white line, then threw the car into reverse, looked behind and reverse-parked into a rectangle marked out with bales of hay.

As soon as she'd stopped, Ning cut the engine and gasped as she tugged at her crash helmet. Sweat was running into her eyes as she put the helmet in her lap and looked across at James.

'Good news, bad news,' James said, smiling as he showed Ning the face of his stopwatch. 'The good news is that you were five point three seconds faster than Alfie. The bad news is there's a ten-second penalty for killing Polystyrene Pauline.'

'I wasn't expecting her *there*,' Ning explained, sounding a touch indignant. 'She was in a much harder position than when Alfie did it.'

James showed no sympathy as he took off his six-point racing seatbelt. 'That's kind of the point. Pedestrians can crop up anywhere. And don't worry about it. The competition element is only a bit of fun. You both did good today.'

Ning smiled as she pushed a mound of sweaty hair off her face. 'You're a good teacher.'

James had never done anything like this before and was flattered and intrigued by the comment. 'What makes you say that?'

Ning shrugged, but Alfie answered for her. 'You get the balance right. Pushing us when we need it, but not so hard that we get pissed off.'

'And you're good at breaking things down to explain them,' Ning said.

The other Golf with Bruce, Leon and Grace inside had finished its final run a couple of minutes earlier. James, Ning and Alfie walked towards them, while fifteen-year-old black shirt Kevin Sumner dashed about collecting the cones.

'All good?' Bruce asked. 'Ready to take us on tomorrow?'

James laughed. 'We'll crush you.'

'Got a people carrier waiting to take you back to campus,' Bruce said, looking at the trainees. 'Any volunteers for driving duty?'

All four kids looked at their feet.

'Now *that's* enthusiasm,' James said, smiling at Bruce.

'I'm knackered,' Leon said defensively.

'It's not physically as hard as normal training,' Grace explained. 'But mentally! Like, you lose concentration for one second and you smash a car into the wall and die.'

'Guess I'll have to drive you tired little bunnies home then,' James said sarcastically. 'And don't stay up too late because we're out here again all day tomorrow and things won't be getting any easier.'

6. BORDER

The racetrack was twenty minutes' drive from CHERUB campus, or fifteen if you were James Adams and you'd decided to show off. The four pupils belted off to the dining-room for some hot food as soon as they arrived, while James and Bruce cracked smiles as they stepped into reception and recognised the hot-blonde-in-short-denim-skirt coming out of Chairman Zara Asker's office.

'Amy Collins, bloody hell,' James said.

'Hey!' Bruce added. 'What are you doing? I haven't seen you in yonks.'

Amy grinned. 'Could ask you guys the same question.'

James pointed at Bruce. 'He's just back from uni for a few days. Zara found out I was at a loose end. Mr Kazakov is on some mission and another instructor's on long-term sick with a dodgy back, so she asked if I'd like to come back for two or three months and help out in the training department.'

'So you dropped out of uni?'

James shook his head. 'Graduated this summer. Applied for some jobs around Silicon Valley, but the job market's dead right now.'

'Is Kerry with you?'

'Nah,' James said. 'She's in her final year at Stanford. Says having me bumming around our apartment was putting her off studying.'

Amy laughed. 'So you must be twenty-one now! We're all getting old.'

'So why are *you* here?' Bruce asked.

'I was doing the classic post-CHERUB thing,' Amy said. 'You know, you leave and can't find anything else that really lives up to it. Then I got headhunted by a little American intelligence unit called Transnational Facilitator Unit – TFU.

'It's mainly anti-smuggling operations. The big stuff: people trafficking, weapons, drugs. The money's decent, and it's a small team so you're always close to the action. Plus, my two bosses Ted and Dr D are close to retirement, so there's a *lot* of potential to step up career-wise.'

'So you live in the States?' James asked.

'Dallas,' Amy said. 'Though I think I've spent ten nights in my apartment since January.'

'And what's with the Chairman?' James asked.

'There's a CHERUB agent working on TFU's biggest project. So I'm here briefing Zara on the operation, and discussing a few other situations where CHERUB agents might be useful.'

'Sounds like it's all working out for you,' James said.

'It's manic, but I'm loving every second,' Amy said. 'I'm on a flight to Dubai tomorrow lunchtime, but if you're on campus tonight us three should have dinner together.'

'Sure,' James said, glancing at his watch. 'It's six now and I've hardly eaten all day. How about I scrub up and meet you both at seven?'

Amy was fine with this, but Bruce shook his head. 'I'm going out for a drink with Bethany Parker.'

James laughed. 'Your old flame!'

Bruce acted defensive. 'You and Bethany always rubbed each other up the wrong way, but she's cool once you get to know her.'

James took a step back towards the lift and gave Amy a smile. 'See you at seven.'

When James got in the lift, he pressed six to go up to his old room, but then realised he was all grown up now, and hit number two to go to the staff quarters.

'Is it true you're James Adams?' a puffed-out little grey shirt holding a tennis racket asked. 'The guy who started the food fight and had sex in the campus fountain?'

*

Ryan had been awake for twenty-four hours, but sleep doesn't come easy when you're ten thousand metres above the United States in a plane packed with high-energy explosive, piloted by a terrorist and a woman whose family is being held at gunpoint.

His mouth felt dry as he stepped out of the cramped toilet cubicle, shaking drips off his hands, tiredness making everything blurry. Before heading back to his seat, Ryan looked through the open cockpit door. Tracy and Elbaz looked serene, lit by the clean gold sunlight that you get when you're above the clouds.

'Hey,' Elbaz said, looking back as Ryan's shadow sent a flicker across the cockpit glass. Ryan expected a rebuke, but Elbaz sounded friendly for once. 'We'll put the mayday call out in three minutes. Should be on the ground five after that, so jazz them all up back there.'

'Right, boss,' Ryan said.

Tracy looked around and seemed like she was going to say something too, but nothing came out and Ryan tried not to think about her torment as he walked back to the single row of passenger seats.

'Hey,' Ryan said, tapping the arm of the terrorist dude, who had a cheapo iPod rip-off plugged into his earholes. 'Elbaz says eight minutes. Be ready to move as soon as we touch down.'

The other IDoJ terrorist was studiously reading a Koran and gave Ryan a nod as he tucked the little blue hardback into the pocket of his linen shirt, then started feeling around the cabin floor for his trainers.

Kazakov was the only person who'd slept, same as he'd done on board the IL-76. After two tours of duty during the Russian invasion of Afghanistan, Kazakov claimed he could sleep anywhere provided nobody was shooting directly at him.

'Get up, Dad,' Ryan said.

He put emphasis on *Dad*, because it's easy to forget a cover story in the first seconds after waking up.

'Where are we?' Kazakov asked, before opening wide into a yawn.

'A few minutes from landing,' Ryan said.

As Ryan lowered himself into his seat, the plane lunged and his knees thumped the partition in front. He leaned out to look back into the cockpit, half-expecting to see Tracy fighting Elbaz for control of the plane. Instead, she was in her seat, making the emergency call.

'Mayday, mayday!' Tracy said. 'Globespan 2726 heading for Atlanta. Our left engine just had a major blow-up. Right side is spluttering and I can't get accurate fuel readings. Turning one-sixty degrees east. Emergency landing in progress. Mayday, mayday!'

Ryan couldn't hear the reply from air traffic control.

'Roger your emergency landing coordinates,' Tracy said. 'Navigation has pinpointed runway, over.'

Ryan clipped his seatbelt on and felt his guts head for his throat as the plane lurched again. 'Jesus.'

Kazakov slid a pill bottle out of his mechanic's overall and gobbled two caffeine tablets before offering them to Ryan.

'You need your wits about you and these'll keep you awake,' the instructor said.

Ryan looked uncertain. Each pill contained the same amount of caffeine as three strong cups of coffee, but they could also leave you with a serious headache when the effect wore off.

'You haven't slept in twenty-four hours,' Kazakov said firmly. 'Take one.'

As Ryan reluctantly swallowed a single pill, Kazakov turned to the two terrorists across the aisle.

'Drugs?' he asked, grinning wildly and fully aware that the two strict Muslims would be horrified at the thought of taking a stimulant.

Cotton wool cloud was passing the window and when they broke through Kazakov peered down over sunny Alabama countryside. But there wasn't as much countryside as he'd have liked to have seen and, in particular, he was troubled by the sight of a gleaming football stadium with ASU painted inside bright yellow endzones.

'What's wrong?' Ryan asked, as Kazakov stood up. 'Mind your head, we're bouncing all over the joint.'

'The last time I checked, Hayneville, Alabama had a population of a thousand and wasn't near any football stadiums,' Kazakov said, loud enough to unsettle the two IDoJ guys across the aisle.

Kazakov stepped into the cockpit and made both pilots jump as he shouted. 'Where the hell are we landing, Elbaz?'

Both pilots were concentrating on the rapid descent, and they were lined up to a runway a few kilometres away.

Elbaz turned to Kazakov. 'Last-minute change.'

'Like how?' Kazakov shouted. 'This isn't what was agreed.'

Ryan didn't like what he was hearing. He felt under

his seat and was reassured by the handle of a large hunting knife. TFU had known Tracy's plane was going to be hijacked and Dr D had arranged for an emergency arsenal to be placed aboard in case Ryan and Kazakov needed it.

'We had a tip-off that someone was watching the airport,' Elbaz explained. 'Get back in your seat. You have no cause for concern. You'll still get paid.'

Even if Kazakov was going to make a move, he couldn't do it until tyres were on the ground. Ryan glanced out of the window to see how high they were and got a view down into the football stadium. There were queues of cars rolling into the parking lot, stands filling up with spectators and a blimp floating in the distance.

'Turkey Day classic, stadium grand opening,' Elbaz shouted, sounding proud of himself. 'Every police in Montgomery will be on duty, and with that traffic we'll be long gone before they get anywhere near us.'

'Customs?' Kazakov asked.

'Nothing down there but tarmac. The whole area's gonna be turned into a parking lot for the stadium.'

An electronic voice came out of a speaker grille in between the pilots' seats. '*Two hundred metres.*'

'Sit down and buckle up,' Elbaz ordered. 'Touchdown in thirty seconds.'

'*One-eighty metres.*'

Ryan and Kazakov exchanged uncomfortable glances as the big Ukrainian clambered back to his window seat.

'Change of venue,' Kazakov said.

They couldn't discuss details with the IDoJ guys sitting close by. As the plane's wheels thumped the runway Ryan felt jazzed up. The caffeine pill was doing its job, and he was glad he'd taken it because there wasn't going to be any FBI team waiting to scoop them up when the 737 rolled to a stop.

7. HORNET

'Where's it going?' Dr D yelled, as she grabbed her mobile to call air traffic control.

FBI team leader Schultz had a laptop open on the motel room bed and was using Google Maps to check out all the local airfields.

'If it's heading for Montgomery, there's a choice of three,' Schultz said. 'Montgomery regional airport, Maxwell air force base. There's also a mothballed landing strip out by the new Hornets' stadium.'

Dr D thought for a second. 'Regional airport will have full-on security and unless they're planning to blow themselves up on landing, they'd have to be nuts to land in the middle of an air force base. So how far's the mothballed landing strip from here?'

'Twenty miles,' Schultz said, after a pause. 'But there's a football match kicking off in an hour. Traffic around there's gonna be hell.'

Bangles jangled as Dr D pounded her little fist on the desk top. 'They'll have known that,' she snapped. 'IDoJ probably has an escape route planned out, while we're stuck behind traffic rolling into a college football game.'

'I guess the U-Haul trucks coming in here were part of the deception. Do we arrest them?'

'Try and follow them when they leave,' Dr D said. 'The big question is, does IDoJ know we're on to them, or did they just change the landing site because they're super cautious?'

Schultz was about to reply when another FBI man burst in without knocking. 'It's on TV,' he blurted.

Without asking permission, the agent flipped on an old-fashioned tube TV bolted to the motel room wall and tuned a local station showing the football game.

The coverage had just started, but studio commentators were all excited about a plane that had skimmed the stadium and come within a couple of hundred metres of the blimp.

'Well I don't know what's going down,' the marshmallowy commentator said. 'But that could have been a tragedy on opening day for this *amazing* new stadium. We'll bring you all the latest on this college classic after these messages from our sponsors.'

'We need bodies up there,' Dr D said. 'Local law enforcement. There must be police at the stadium.'

'What about the two agents and hostage pilot?' Schultz asked. 'If we storm in they could be executed.'

'We've lost track of eleven tonnes of high explosive

that could kill thousands,' Dr D snapped. 'Priority one is getting that back no matter *what* the consequences. Priority two is arresting every IDoJ operative we can get our hands on.'

The FBI man looked shell-shocked. 'But . . .'

'Those are my orders,' Dr D said. 'And those orders cover your ass, so get on with it.'

*

Ryan used a double tap on the back of his ear to switch his com unit on as the plane taxied. He hoped to hear a familiar voice, but the tiny device only had a range of two kilometres and all he got was digital noise caused by interference from the aircraft's radar.

'Keep cool,' Kazakov whispered as the plane came to a halt. But a bang ripped out from the cockpit.

As Kazakov jolted, Ryan leaned into the aisle where he saw Elbaz standing with a gun. Tracy was slumped against the cockpit's side window, with the right side of her headset in bits and blood spattered on the cockpit glass.

'Why'd you kill her?' Ryan shouted furiously.

Elbaz turned with the gun and Ryan clenched, fearing he was next.

'What use is she now?' Elbaz asked. 'She's seen our faces.'

Then he flipped a couple of switches to release the cargo door in the side of the fuselage. No steps had been brought up to the plane, so one of the other terrorists pulled in the cabin door and yanked the lever to activate an inflatable emergency slide.

As the first terrorist went down the chute, Kazakov put a hand on Ryan's shoulder. 'Don't get emotional.'

'They killed her,' Ryan said, as he grabbed his backpack out of the overhead locker. 'What about us?'

'Tracy's of no value to them,' Kazakov said. 'If they touch us, they'll expect to answer to the Aramov Clan and I doubt they'll risk that.'

It was bright sunshine and touching twenty degrees as Ryan zipped down the nylon chute towards the runway. The tarmac was in decent condition, but the runway markings were peeling. Giant mounds of soil obscured their view towards the stadium and there were excavators and dump trucks lined up, ready to transform this airfield into an overflow parking lot for the new stadium and adjacent college.

On the other side of the plane a forklift with *Denver Airport* painted on the side was driving up to the cargo door. When it touched the side of the plane, six men standing on the elevated deck dived into the hold to start unloading.

At the same time a squat man with a kufi on his head embraced Elbaz and spoke with a mid-west accent.

'My brother, welcome to America!'

'Mumin!' Elbaz said enthusiastically. 'Is everything organised?'

Kazakov stepped up to the men, keeping one hand on the knife in his pocket.

'Where's my money?' Kazakov yelled. 'You'd better know who you're messing with here.'

'An FBI agent was seen at the original landing site,'

Mumin explained calmly. 'We didn't know the reason so new arrangements were made on very late notice. You will come to no harm, but I must ask you to stay with us for a short time.'

'That wasn't the plan,' Kazakov said.

'Plans change,' Mumin said firmly. 'Your money and US passports will be given to you when we reach our base. Would you rather the FBI had arrested you upon landing and you spent the rest of your life in federal prison?'

Ryan tried getting his head around the evolving situation. The plan had been for the FBI to swoop when the 737 landed in Hayneville, scooping up the explosives and everyone working for IDoJ. He badly needed sleep, but at least they had a chance to keep track of the explosives if they were travelling to IDoJ's base.

As the elevated platform lowered three pallets of explosive from the aircraft, Mumin pointed Ryan and Kazakov towards a yellow mini-van.

'Wait in the back,' Mumin said. 'Don't turn on telephones or any other electronic devices. Any radio signals can be triangulated by the FBI.'

Kazakov and Ryan stepped through a sliding door and into a shabby ex-taxi.

'Good day,' the driver said warily, as Ryan breathed the sickly citrus air-freshener dangling off the rear-view mirror.

The driver was in his teens, brown skin, with a slim build and boy's puny moustache. He didn't say another word as Ryan and Kazakov watched the plane being unloaded.

Ryan counted seven men and a woman on the cargo team. They'd clearly practised unloading aviation pallets and their rapid coordination and matching blue overalls reminded him of a Formula One pit crew.

The wind carried a cheer across from the stadium as the final battered silver container went up a ramp into the truck painted with the logo of a sportswear retailer. The tracks around the landing strip had been used by heavy vehicles on stadium construction and the four trucks crawled off over rutted ground.

When the last truck pulled away, Elbaz and Mumin hopped in the back of the mini-van, and sat facing Ryan and Kazakov. Once the sliding door slammed, the young driver set off, just six and half minutes after the 737 had stopped moving on the end of the strip.

While Mumin was handed an Uzi submachine gun by the driver, Elbaz looked at Kazakov and sounded keen to keep him happy.

'We very much wish to work with the Aramov Clan again and I'm sorry for this operational inconvenience,' Elbaz said. 'Twenty thousand dollars will be added to your fee, as an apology.'

Ryan's back jarred as they went over a particularly big pothole.

'I understand why you've done this,' Kazakov said. 'But you should have told me while we were in flight.'

'I suppose,' Elbaz said.

'Weren't you supposed to blow the 737 to hide the evidence?' Ryan asked.

'It's rigged,' Mumin said. 'But it's fuelled to Atlanta and I don't want it going off while we're close by. The blast will be triggered by a motion sensor when the first Fed climbs aboard.'

Elbaz smirked. 'Bonus casualties!'

Ryan's hands itched to turn on his phone and drop just one text to TFU, but all he could do was bide his time.

A few moments later they pulled off through a hole cut in the airfield's perimeter fencing and turned on to a four-lane highway. There was only one car in sight on this side of the median, while the other side was gridlocked with vehicles, trailing yellow flags and daubed with football slogans.

8. SWIM

Kids and staff on CHERUB campus lined up for food from the same self-service kitchen, but staff could opt to eat in a separate dining-room. The racket from kids next door was heavily muffled and there were posh touches like tablecloths, better condiment holders and usually some poor kid on punishment duty to set out cutlery and clear tables. Most importantly, adults got three glass-fronted chillers stocked with booze and a swish espresso machine.

James and Amy caught up over fish and chips. They talked about old times and shared a bottle of white wine, while James packed his chips between slices of white bread.

'I took Kerry to some poncy restaurant for her birthday,' James said. 'But it wasn't half as good as a decent butty.'

'Campus chips are the best,' Amy replied, as she licked salt off her fingertips.

Their table was by a window, with a view over downward-sloping lawns to the side of the main building. In the distance, a twelve-metre-high corrugated fence cut across the landscape, above which poked cranes working on the Campus Village site. When complete, all CHERUB agents and campus-based staff would move to the village, while the main building would be redeveloped as an education and training centre.

'I've been back to campus a few times in the last year,' Amy said. 'But I never get much chance to chill out.'

'It's cold, but I've been cooped up in a screaming car all day,' James said. 'You fancy a stroll? See what's changed.'

Amy smiled at the prospect. 'Bring on the nostalgia,' she said, as her chair grated backwards.

Amy grabbed her coat and headed straight for the exit, but James went for the chillers and opened up two bottles of beer.

'One for the road?' James asked, as he held a bottle out to Amy.

'I like the way you think,' Amy said, as she took the bottle and gently sucked the foam bubbling out of the neck.

Most kids were indoors having dinner or doing homework, so James and Amy strolled through a crisp November evening with breath curling up in front of them.

'So, do you think temporary training instructor might become permanent?' Amy asked.

James shrugged. 'It's not impossible. It depends on what Kerry wants, and if I did come back I'd prefer to work on the mission side. Making ten-year-old trainees exercise until they spew doesn't exactly push my buttons.'

'You and Kerry have been together a long while now.'

James nodded. 'Eight years on and off, but if I'm honest it's more off than on right now.'

'How come?' Amy asked.

'I got in shit,' James admitted. 'Me and a couple of maths geeks I graduated with have been making trips to Las Vegas to play blackjack.'

Amy looked surprised. 'So you lost all your mum's money?'

'Nah. We had a card counting system and made a *bundle*,' James said. 'Casino security worked out what we were up to so they banned us from Vegas. That was a slap on the wrist, but a couple of the guys had serious student loans, so we put on disguises, went back for one last trip and ended up in the city jail.'

Amy gasped. 'You went to prison?'

'Las Vegas has laws on *prohibited persons* entering casinos. You can get two years' prison time. Kerry freaked out when I got busted and called campus asking for help. We all accepted a plea bargain and got a two-thousand-dollar fine and three-month suspended sentence.'

'Heavy,' Amy said. 'At least it was suspended.'

James nodded. 'But it doesn't make job hunting any

easier when you get to that *have you ever been arrested* box on the application form.'

'Nope,' Amy said.

'Anyway, Zara was short of instructors on campus, and Kerry wanted me to stay out of trouble. So here I am.'

'Your mum left you plenty of money though,' Amy noted.

James shrugged. 'It wasn't about money. Thing is, I drove a car in a high-speed chase when I was thirteen years old. I've tangled with motorbike gangs, hung out with terrorists and banged a drug dealer's daughter in a bathtub. I think I did the casino stuff to get some of the old buzz back. The idea of nine-to-five in an office does my nut in.'

'I know what you mean,' Amy said. 'Until I got the TFU job, I had no clue *what* I wanted to do with my life.'

They hadn't been paying much attention to where they'd been strolling, but Amy and James found themselves approaching the side of the campus swimming complex. A few poolside lights shone through the windows of the main pool, but there was nobody swimming when Amy pressed her face up to a window.

'New tiles,' Amy said. 'Very swish.'

But James was thinking of something else. 'This is where we first met,' he said, as he swigged from his beer. '2003, eleven-year-old CHERUB recruit James Adams can't start basic training until his beautiful sixteen-year-old black-shirt instructor teaches him to swim.'

'You were sweet back then,' Amy said. 'That tatty Arsenal shirt with Viera on the back! They'd sheared all your hair off, you were new on campus and you acted like you were scared of your own shadow.'

'I got such a crush on you, but I felt like a nobody,' James confessed. 'You were all mature and sophisticated.'

James wasn't sure Amy heard what he said, because she'd pushed the pool's main door and stepped into a lobby. James followed, enjoying the warmth, while breathing chlorine and hearing the familiar rumble of the pool's ventilation system.

'I fancy a swim,' Amy said.

James could hear kids shrieking in the adjoining leisure pool as he studied the notices in the lobby: *No outdoor shoes. No running. No screaming. No using the pool when lifeguard is not present.*

'There'll be towels in the changing room,' James said.

Amy slid her coat down her arms and dropped it on a bench as she stepped through a pair of doors that led to poolside. James was allegedly a grown-up now, but he was still awed as he watched Amy kick off her shoes and start unbuttoning her blouse.

'You joining me?' Amy asked, as she dropped her skirt and started peeling off one stocking. 'Or do you plan to keep staring like a pervert?'

'Pervert,' James said, but he'd already started pulling his T-shirt over his head. Amy had dived in by the time James had his jeans around his ankles and the first thing Amy did was dig both arms into the water and give him a soaking.

'Mind my clothes!' James yelled. 'We've gotta walk back and it's cold.'

'Stop me,' Amy said, as she splashed again.

As James kicked his clothes bundle against the wall and dived in, Amy started an athletic swim towards the deep end. He couldn't catch up, but James eventually got Amy cornered and she looked *amazing* as she trod water in the half-light, with reflections dancing across her face.

'You've still got one sock on,' Amy said.

As James looked down to confirm that he was sock-free, Amy used the instant of distraction to try swimming out of her corner. If she'd wanted to escape she could have climbed out of the pool, but this was a game and she'd made for a gap where there wasn't one. Almost as if she *wanted* James to grab her.

James felt awkward as he got an arm around Amy's waist. He kept his grip loose so that Amy could break free, but she pulled in close and relaxed her body like she wanted to be kissed.

'Where's this going?' James stuttered. 'I had no idea you liked me.'

Amy laughed. 'Back when you were eleven? No! But a girl can do worse than James Adams at twenty-one.'

James had fantasised about Amy since he'd first got interested in girls. Kerry flashed through his mind, but this wasn't something he could turn down.

'Mind you, I've spent the last seven months living in a country where most men smoke sixty a day, bathe monthly and get their brides by kidnapping them. So my standards might have dropped a little.'

They kicked into shallower water, kissing on the mouth when they reached the side of the pool.

'Just so you're clear, there's nothing to this,' Amy said, as she broke off. 'Two old mates who fancy each other. What's wrong with that?'

'Nothing at all,' James said, as Amy's fingers dug into his back and her mouth closed in for another kiss.

9. CUT

The guy with the teenage moustache drove for twenty minutes, then ditched the old taxi in an empty high-school parking lot. He then drove on with Ryan squeezed in the middle seat of a Chrysler sedan, between Mumin and Kazakov.

An hour later, they turned off a remote highway and clattered over a mile of dirt to a farm property with a foreclosure notice and *Sale by Auction* sign by the entry gate.

Ryan didn't know agriculture, but guessed this had been a dairy farm, based on outdoor pens tall enough to hold big animals and refrigerated tanks at the side of a huge aluminium-sided shed.

Ten trucks were parked in front of a big ranch house, but these were smaller than the ones that picked up the cargo at the airport. A mobile home stood on bricks a couple of hundred metres from the main house. The Chrysler dropped off Ryan, Kazakov and Mumin there, while Elbaz and the teen rolled on to the house.

The mobile home was grotty inside, with the smell of stale piss coming out of the bathroom and a summer's worth of dead insects dotting the floor.

'It's not great, but you'll be here less than twenty-four hours,' Mumin said, before pointing at two black wheelie cases lying flat on a sofa in the bay window at the far end. 'That's what you're here for.'

Kazakov unzipped the bags and threw back canvas flaps, unveiling stacks of fifty- and hundred-dollar bills. IDoJ believed that the Aramov Clan needed this untraceable cash inside the USA to pay for clan matriarch Irena Aramov's cancer treatment. In reality, the FBI was paying for Irena's treatment and the cash was an excuse that enabled Ryan and Kazakov to track the IDoJ operation from Kyrgyzstan to the US, via China.

'Two million, cash,' Mumin said. 'Count if you like, but it might take a while.'

'I'll trust you,' Kazakov said. Then added casually, 'People who short-change the Aramov Clan don't usually live for long.'

'The remaining four point two has been transferred to your listed bank accounts in sums ranging from twenty to eighty thousand dollars,' Mumin continued. 'Your people should be able to confirm receipt shortly after the banks open tomorrow morning.'

As Mumin continued, Ryan was transfixed by the

contents of the battered wheelie cases. 'You have television and a shower. We put a couple of bags of groceries in the cupboard. I checked the microwave, but unfortunately there's no gas bottle for the cooker.'

'We're in the middle of nowhere,' Kazakov noted. 'We'll need a vehicle to take us out of here.'

Mumin nodded. 'When our vans leave, you'll be given keys to a hire car. Nobody will come looking for the car until the seven-day hire ends. Dump it when you're done.'

As Kazakov zipped the wheelie cases and tested their weight, Ryan slid his backpack down his arm and braved the evil-smelling bathroom.

'We're not locking you in, but we'd prefer it if you didn't wander,' Mumin said. 'The fewer people who see your face the better.'

'And vice versa,' Kazakov said. 'We'll shower and sleep. Maybe catch a couple of quarters of football.'

The cramped plastic toilet had yellowed with age and there was stomach-churning filth on the toilet brush. Ryan turned the tap for the shower and got a drizzle. There was a half-bottle of flamingo-pink shampoo that looked like it had been left by the previous owners and two raggedy towels that Ryan wouldn't have wiped his arse on.

When he'd finished peeing and stepped out, Mumin was gone and Kazakov was filling a titchy electric kettle he'd found in one of the cupboards.

'So how are we doing?' Ryan asked warily.

There was a chance the van was bugged, so Kazakov

set a tap running full blast and beckoned Ryan closer before speaking quietly.

'They're ruthless,' Kazakov said. 'They wouldn't have brought us here if they wanted us dead.'

'Is the money real?' Ryan asked.

'As far as I can tell,' Kazakov said. 'And they think we're who we say we are.'

'What makes you say that?' Ryan asked.

'They haven't searched us, or taken our phones,' Kazakov said. 'IDoJ are clearly hoping for an on-going relationship with the Aramov Clan, so they can't treat us like prisoners.'

'What about the explosives?' Ryan asked. 'There's been no sign of them, except the first few minutes when we pulled out of the airport.'

'We changed cars; if the explosives are coming here they'll almost certainly change trucks too,' Kazakov said. 'It takes time to load and unload, and they'll take different routes to avoid suspicion.'

Ryan nodded, as he pulled out his phone and switched it on. 'So it's unlikely they'd get here before us, but we should keep an eye out for trucks arriving.'

Kazakov had switched the kettle on and by this time it was making enough noise for him to turn off the tap.

'Do you think the FBI tracked us here?' Ryan asked.

'No way to know,' Kazakov said. 'If they did, lucky us. But we have to assume that we're on our own and act accordingly.'

Ryan looked at the face of his phone and saw the no-signal bar. 'I guess it was never likely to work out here in the middle of nowhere.'

'We've only got one bathroom,' Kazakov said. 'If I get in the shower and take my time, how about you take a stroll up to the house and try working out what's going on?'

'And if I'm caught?'

'Don't sneak around,' Kazakov said. 'Stick your hands in your pockets and take a stroll. If they stop you, just say your guts are playing up. Your dad's in the shower and you were looking for somewhere to take a shit.'

'Right,' Ryan said. 'Shall I go now?'

Kazakov shook his head. 'Give it half an hour. Rest up and give them a chance to let their guard down. Plus it'll be nearly dark by then.'

*

As the sun set in Alabama, it was 4 a.m. on CHERUB campus. James Adams was sleeping in the third-floor quarters he was sharing with Bruce when he got woken by an unfamiliar ringtone.

'Are you gonna answer that?' James shouted, as he sat up.

Single staff quarters on campus were similar to the kids' rooms on the upper floors, except there was a sliding partition between the bedroom and living area, plus a mini kitchen with oven and hob.

Bruce was on a sofa bed in the living-room and he yelled back. 'It's *your* phone.'

'I know my own ringtone,' James said irritably.

'It's coming out of *your* trousers.'

James huffed as he threw his duvet off, flicked on a bedside light and got up to investigate.

'Told you,' Bruce said, as James pulled the ringing iPhone from his jeans.

But not only did James not recognise the ringtone, he didn't recognise the name *Dr D* flashing on the screen.

James pressed the *answer* button. 'Hello?'

'Amy, it's Dr D. There's a problem with Ryan and Kazakov. You'll have to let Zara Asker know ASAP because this could turn bad.'

'Hold your horses,' James said. 'Amy's not here, but I can find her if it's urgent.'

James had no idea that Dr D was Amy's boss, but she sounded furious. 'Why do you have her phone? Who are you?'

'I know where she is,' James said, ignoring Dr D's question. 'I'll get her to call you right back.'

'How'd you get Amy's phone?' Bruce asked, once James had hung up.

James started pulling on his jeans so that he could walk down the corridor to the room where Amy was staying.

'After dinner me and Amy went skinny-dipping,' James explained. 'Amy said she fancied me, so we ended up bonking on a pile of swimming floats.'

Bruce tutted. 'Right, James. In your dreams!'

James grinned to himself, because he'd told the truth knowing that Bruce wouldn't believe it.

'How can you be so certain?' James asked.

'First, Amy's always gone for older guys,' Bruce

explained. 'Second, Kerry's got you on a tight leash, and third, you've always been a *colossal* bullshitter.'

'Well argued,' James said. But he'd lost his smile as he headed out of the door because Bruce had put Kerry's name in his head and this was only the third time he'd cheated on her since retiring as a CHERUB agent.

Amy was four doors along the hallway and the door wasn't locked.

'You've got my iPhone,' James said accusingly, as Amy rubbed her eyes. 'Someone called Dr D rang for you.'

'Shit, that's my boss,' Amy said, as she sprang up. 'That must be your phone in the charger over there.'

James picked his phone out of the charging cradle as Amy called Dr D. As the call rang in her ear, Amy made a *shoo* gesture at James.

'I'm sorry but it's confidential,' Amy said. 'Do you mind?'

10. RANCH

A double-trailer truck pulled up at the ranch house as Ryan stood by the mobile home's open doorway. He felt trapped, by their predicament and by the sweaty T-shirt glued to his back. He needed sleep badly, but he got a mental image of Tracy's blood spattered on cockpit glass every time he closed his eyes.

Kazakov knelt on the sofa at the bay window, peeking between filthy net curtains into the twilight. He caught the reflection on an aluminium air-cargo box as it got wheeled from the truck's rear trailer.

'Explosives?' Ryan asked, as he came close to see what Kazakov was looking at.

'Can't see what else it would be,' Kazakov said. 'The timing fits: half an hour behind us.'

They watched for a couple more minutes and Ryan thought he recognised some of the guys who'd been at the landing strip. Kazakov had put a TV on, but the signal was poor and Ryan took a couple of seconds to make out the news anchor on screen with a burning plane in the background.

'Did you turn the sound off?' Ryan asked.

It was an ancient set with a knob for the volume and Kazakov demonstrated by raising his beefy arm and twiddling it.

'Speaker cuts in and out,' he explained. 'Loose wire or something. I've read a couple of on-screen banners. One FBI officer dead when they tried boarding the 737, and the stadium got evacuated, in case there were further explosions.'

When the wavy TV images grew frustrating, Ryan looked out the window towards the ranch house. Elbaz was up there, out of pilot's uniform but now looking even more Bollywood in a bright pink shirt with fat collar. There was no sign of Mumin, but there were about a dozen young men and a couple of girls helping to wheel the pallets of explosive into the six-car garage beside the house.

'They seem happy enough up there,' Kazakov said.

'You think they're suicide bombers?' Ryan asked.

'Possible,' Kazakov said. 'You can park a truck full of explosives outside a building. But driving into your target at speed is usually much more effective. On the other hand, there's an awful lot of them.'

Ryan looked confused. 'What do you mean?'

'Even amongst fanatics, people don't exactly line up to kill themselves. Most suicide attacks are one or two man operators.'

'What about 9/11?' Ryan asked.

'There's an exception to every rule,' Kazakov said, shrugging. 'So it's getting pretty dark. How about I take my shower, and you go for that wander?'

'Makes sense,' Ryan said. 'But we're in the middle of nowhere and I'd bet the perimeter's guarded. So even if we find out what they're up to . . .'

Kazakov spoke before Ryan finished his thought. 'One step at a time. Get information, then we'll work out what to do with it.'

Ryan slid bare feet into his Converse, then did a double tap behind his ear to activate the com unit.

'Hear me?' Ryan asked.

'Loud and clear,' Kazakov said, after his own double tap. 'Don't overuse the com. The batteries are tiny and they can't have much juice left.'

'Gotcha,' Ryan said.

The fourteen-year-old clanked down the mobile home's front steps. The temperature had dropped with the sun and Ryan rubbed his arms as he walked towards the ranch house. The unloading seemed to be over and the bad guys and girls were heading inside.

From fifty metres out Ryan realised that the ten small trucks lined up in front of the ranch house were the same model. All had clean black tyre walls, shiny glass and none of the scrapes or dents you'd expect on a commercial vehicle.

The only difference between trucks was that they were painted in the liveries of several big US retail chains. There was a light on in the cab of a dark blue *Office Megastore* van and a tiny woman with a fat bum crawled about inside. She would have seen Ryan if she'd looked, but she was stretching for something in the footwell.

As the woman slid down from the cab, Ryan ducked behind a tree and unbuttoned his jeans so that he could say he was peeing if someone spotted him. The woman took a few backwards steps and flicked a switch on a control box, which made the truck's headlamps come on.

Her next button-push set the engine running and as the mechanic backed off further, she pushed forwards on a control stick and drove the dark blue truck twenty metres forward. After coming to an abrupt stop, the woman reversed the procedure, backing the van into its spot between the others and switching the lights off.

Ryan resumed his walk as the woman headed into the garage, and was soon within hearing distance.

'The battery wasn't rigged right,' the woman told a colleague as she headed into shafts of light coming through the huge garage's raised doors. 'It's fine now, but we need to get all the others double-checked.'

Ryan cut across the pathway leading up to the ranch. From this side he got a view between two parked vans and a section of the garage. The crew he'd first seen at the airfield were taking pizza-box-sized slabs of explosive out of the cargo containers and slicing off plastic wrapping with craft knives.

At the rear, a pair of more skilled operators sat

at workbenches, using magnifiers as they soldered components of what Ryan guessed was either the radio control system for the trucks or detonators for the explosives.

Ryan reckoned he'd been lucky, learning so much without getting within thirty metres of the house. But while it was now clear that the plan was to pack the ten trucks with explosive and use a radio control system to smash them into their targets, he didn't know what the targets were or when the attacks would take place.

He'd heard Mumin telling Kazakov that they'd be held here for less than twenty-four hours, but was that when the explosive-packed trucks were going to be sent to their targets, or, seeing as America was a huge place, was the plan to distribute the vans all over the USA and attack days or weeks into the future?

Ryan would only learn more by getting nearer to the house, perhaps picking up snippets of conversation by an open window. After cutting between the vans, he had to choose house or garage, but it was clear what was happening inside the garage, so it made more sense to approach the house with his *needing a crap* excuse.

The giant ranch house was two storeys, plus converted attic. The previous owner had apparently gone bust in the midst of a grand refurbishment project. The exterior mixed new glazing and a marble porch with areas further along where windows were boarded and foundations laid for an unbuilt extension.

The front door was on the latch and Ryan stepped in purposefully, knowing that people are less suspicious when someone looks like they know where they're heading.

There might have been people in any of the rooms, but all the noise came out of an open-plan kitchen diner. It was a no-expense-spared German job, but wires hung through holes where the ceiling lights should be.

While a $4,000 Swedish-made oven sat by the sliding doors cased in polystyrene, a lively crowd surrounded a veiled teenager who grabbed pieces of chicken from a bucket of marinade and threw them on to a line of disposable charcoal barbecue trays.

'Ryan,' Elbaz said, coming out of some sort of cupboard under spiral stairs leading up to the first floor. 'Did Mumin not ask you to stay in the mobile home?'

It came across more like a straight question than a rebuke, and Ryan had his excuse ready.

'My dad always takes *years* in the shower. Flying so long and not eating properly has done my stomach in.'

Elbaz laughed. He didn't seem like the arrogant man who'd flown out of the Kremlin with them a day and a half earlier. Ryan figured that the change was down to growing confidence as IDoJ's operation drew nearer to completion.

'Toilet's across the hall,' Elbaz said. 'Do you go everywhere with your father?'

Ryan nodded. 'My mother died when I was a baby. Since then we've come as a package.'

'And people don't suspect you're a smuggler when you've got the kids in tow,' Elbaz added.

'We've got out of a few tight spots like that,' Ryan

agreed, before pointing at the toilet door. 'Do you mind?'

'Better in there than out here,' Elbaz joked.

Ryan felt tense as he entered a large marbled toilet cubicle with the face of a young Clint Eastwood etched into one mirrored wall. After bolting the door, he sat on the toilet lid and stayed there for about as long as he'd normally take to have a dump. He made things seem real by flushing and washing his hands before exiting.

He walked across to the kitchen, with a backup excuse of wanting to thank Elbaz. But Elbaz had vanished and nobody stopped Ryan striding to the heart of the huge kitchen and standing by the central island between one of the terrorists who'd travelled with them on the plane and the moustached teenager who'd driven the taxi from the landing strip.

'Grab some chicken,' the teenager said warmly. 'It's good.'

Ryan smiled as he reached across the countertop and grabbed a paper plate and a drumstick stained with the orange marinade. After eating nothing but tinned food and sandwiches for thirty hours, fresh-cooked spicy chicken hit the spot and he followed up by grabbing two lamb skewers off a passing tray.

'I saw your money when the suitcases arrived,' the teenaged driver told Ryan.

'Not *my* money,' Ryan said, as he tried the lamb. 'Wish it was, but I'm just the delivery boy for your couriers.'

There was a lull in the conversation, and although Ryan had worked out that it wasn't going to be a suicide raid, he thought it might be a good way to open a conversation.

'So, are you mad bastards gonna be blowing yourselves up?' he asked.

The teenager scoffed at the suggestion. 'Yeah, we're all suicide bombers.'

'Sorry,' Ryan said. 'Just . . . me and my dad saw all the trucks.'

On the other side of the counter, two guys who were twenty at most recognised each other before exchanging a hug. They called one another cousin and started a *How have you been, what time did you get here* kind of conversation. Both looked Arab or possibly North African, but their accents were pure Texan drawl.

As Ryan finished his second lamb skewer the taller of the two cousins said, 'My aunt's after a sixty-five-inch LCD for Black Friday. I paid a guy to steal her car so that she can't go out in the morning.'

The other cousin laughed. 'This your aunt in Houston?'

The guy nodded. 'Rescued me from foster home when my mom went AWOL. I don't want her near any shops tomorrow morning.'

'What about her car?'

'Gave the guy a key. He's gonna drive it a few blocks. If nobody finds it before I get home, I'll tell her I spotted it on my way to visit her.'

Ryan picked up a ton of information about the two cousins, but the thing about the car was crucial: it confirmed that IDoJ would be attacking shops tomorrow morning, that at least one target was in Houston and that at least one bomber planned to be alive after the attack.

As Ryan turned to leave, Elbaz touched his shoulder from behind. He carried a foil tray stacked with barbecued meat, plus salad, rice, serviettes and plastic cutlery. However, his voice had become firm.

'It's not appropriate you being in here,' Elbaz said. 'Grab a carton of orange juice and take this tray back to share with your father. I must ask you *not* to leave the mobile home again.'

Ryan acted grovelly. 'Sorry, boss,' he said. 'I came out of the shitter and the smell of food drew me in.'

'Eat then sleep,' Elbaz advised. 'Enjoy the meat and tell your father that I'm grateful for his help.'

11. HOUSTON

Kazakov had taken a shower to give credence to Ryan's story. He was sitting by the bay window staring at the ball of his foot when the teenager got back.

'You OK?' Ryan asked.

'Splinter off the floor,' Kazakov said, his face lighting up when he saw the foil tray. 'That smells decent.'

Ryan put the kettle on to muffle sounds in case they were being bugged, and switched to speaking in Russian, a language skill that he doubted any of Elbaz's team possessed.

'Trucks are radio controlled,' Ryan explained. 'Ten altogether. I guess they'll drive them to the target, hop out and use the control unit for the last few hundred metres.'

'Makes sense.'

'Targets are shops,' Ryan said, pouring orange juice

into two glasses as Kazakov bit a greasy chicken wing. 'Looks like tomorrow. The logos painted on the trucks must be a clue about what shops they're targeting. There were also these two cousins who mentioned Black Friday. I saw it on the newspapers Tracy was reading as well. I wish we could Google to find out what it is.'

Kazakov smirked. 'Before the Internet, people had this thing called *general knowledge*. The third Thursday in November – today – is Thanksgiving. A lot of people here in the US take the Friday after Thanksgiving off work to give themselves a four-day holiday. Shops close on Thanksgiving, but open early on Black Friday and put on special deals.'

Ryan nodded. 'Like in the pull-outs Tracy had in her *USA Today*. I guess if she'd made it to Atlanta, she'd have been home in time to catch the bargains.'

'Black Friday is the busiest shopping day of the year over here,' Kazakov said. 'The malls are gonna be packed and I think it's a safe bet that's what IDoJ is targeting.'

'We've got to get a warning out,' Ryan said. 'There's a tonne of high explosive for each truck.'

'Enough to vaporise a superstore,' Kazakov agreed. 'If it's packed out, you're talking thousands of people in each store.'

Ryan nodded solemnly. 'That's like the World Trade Center times ten.'

'And we've got a guard watching us now,' Kazakov said.

Ryan knew better than to turn and look out of the window. 'Where?'

'Just caught sight of him moving in the trees.'

'Elbaz acted cool,' Ryan said. 'Gave me the barbecue, but it was clear he didn't like me wandering around.'

'Any clue on the targets?' Kazakov asked.

'Houston,' Ryan said. 'This guy was saying that he'd had his aunt's car nabbed so that she couldn't drive to the shops in Houston.'

Kazakov looked surprised. 'In that case the trucks will be leaving soon. Houston's five or six hundred miles from here.'

Ryan calculated out loud. 'Ten to twelve hours' drive at fifty miles an hour. I guess it depends when they plan to hit the stores.'

'People turn out early to catch bargains,' Kazakov said. 'They'll want to hit the stores when they're rammed. People will panic and go home when they hear about bombs in shopping malls, so all ten attacks have to be near-simultaneous for maximum effect.'

Ryan checked his watch and saw that it was about 8 p.m. local time. 'So if they want to attack a shopping mall in Houston at say nine a.m. tomorrow, the first trucks will have to leave here within the next two or three hours.'

'And who says Houston is the furthermost target?' Kazakov asked rhetorically. 'We need to get the warning out quickly.'

'How quickly?' Ryan asked.

'As long as it takes us to make up a plan.'

'Our cover's blown the moment we try something,' Ryan said.

'They'll be less suspicious if we take the money,' Kazakov said. 'Might think we were spooked by what they did to Tracy and the change of landing spot.'

'They'd still kill us,' Ryan said.

'CHERUB has rules,' Kazakov said. 'No agent is ever forced to do anything against their will. We've every reason to believe that IDoJ will let us go free because they want to keep the Aramov Clan sweet. Nobody will hold anything against you if you don't want to take any more risks.'

Ryan shook his head. 'Thousands of people could die and there's been no sign that Dr D's team knows what happened after we landed. We've got to try contacting someone.'

Kazakov cracked a wry smile. 'I was afraid you'd say that.' Then he pointed up to a skylight in the ceiling. 'They'll spot us leaving through a door or window,' he said. 'That skylight's a possibility, but you'd still have to crawl over the roof and drop down the side.'

'What if we make some kind of scene?' Ryan asked. 'Draw the guard in and twat him.'

'Could work,' Kazakov said. 'But our best bet's to look for a floor hatch. Mobile homes usually have a connection panel for water and electricity, or access to pipes under the floor.'

'Whereabouts?' Ryan asked, as he scanned the floor.

Kazakov headed for the cupboard under the kitchen sink. He opened it up and saw gas, water and sewage pipes running towards the bathroom. 'Not here,' he said.

The bulky Ukrainian was almost too big for the tiny

bathroom door. He ducked in and less than twenty seconds later Ryan heard a dramatic crack and a sound like plastic snapping.

'Lifts right up,' Kazakov said happily. 'Come look.'

Ryan headed for the toilet, but before he saw anything he breathed a stench of sewage and backed away fighting a gag reflex.

'Aww that's nasty,' he blurted.

Kazakov laughed. 'You wouldn't have lasted five minutes in the Soviet Army with that weak stomach of yours.'

Ryan hooked the neck of his T-shirt over his nose before making a second approach. Kazakov's bulk filled much of the tiny bathroom, but Ryan could see that Kazakov had somehow freed the toilet and the panel behind, making it swing into the adjacent shower cubicle on a hinge.

The gap behind the panel was deep and Ryan watched as Kazakov used a coin to turn a large plastic screw head, freeing a rectangle of flooring.

'I won't fit down there, but you will,' Kazakov said, as he rested the piece of flooring against the sink.

When Ryan leaned over Kazakov, he realised the stench was the result of a slow leak in a sewage pipe. The earth below was soaked in a brown ooze that looked like chocolate syrup.

'We're standing on brick pillars, so you can crawl under the floor and come out at the side,' Kazakov explained.

'Kill me now,' Ryan said, as he tried not to heave.

'I'll find something to lay over the worst of it,' Kazakov said, as he followed Ryan's horrified expression back into the kitchen.

'It's a good four kilometres to the highway,' Ryan said. 'I can easily run that distance, but I don't fancy our chances thumbing a lift in the dark.'

'Our phones might pick up a signal near the highway,' Kazakov said. 'But we'd be vulnerable on foot. I was thinking we need some kind of vehicle. What did you see up by the ranch house?'

'Cars,' Ryan said. 'There's no other way to get here. Most of them looked new. I'm guessing Mumin arranged a bunch of rental cars cos the owners wouldn't want their own cars to be traced back.'

'New cars have immobilisers,' Kazakov noted. 'With no tools, our best bet is to get a set of car keys.'

Ryan nodded. 'I'll crawl out and try taking the guard by surprise.'

'No time to lose,' Kazakov said. 'I'll stick a couple of sofa cushions down there. If you're careful you'll avoid the worst of the muck.'

'I'll leave my backpack for you to pick up,' Ryan said, before doing a double tap on his earlobe. 'Com check?'

'Check,' Kazakov said.

While Kazakov pulled up sofa cushions and laid them over the muck beneath the access hatch, Ryan discreetly moved around the mobile home looking for their guard.

'He's not trying too hard,' Ryan said. 'I see him sitting on a tree stump across the path. No sign of a gun, but he could be packing heat under his clothes.'

'He's probably got a walkie-talkie,' Kazakov said. 'You'll have to take him out before he gets to it.'

As Ryan nodded, Kazakov popped another caffeine pill and offered one to Ryan. Ryan baulked, but Kazakov was insistent.

'You've been awake over thirty hours. The risk from a couple of pep pills is a lot less than going into battle with your brain half numb.'

Ryan swallowed a little yellow pill reluctantly, then took a deep breath and tried blocking the stench out of his mind as he pushed his body through the hole in the ground.

12. BIRDS

The guard was only a few years older than Ryan, face lit by Angry Birds running on his mobile and apparently sulking because his co-conspirators were up at the ranch house socialising while he was out in the dark squatting on a tree stump.

IDoJ was a professional set-up, but Ryan reckoned this guy was a misguided college kid. He'd been drawn in for a big operation and probably didn't realise that a smooth talker like Elbaz regarded him as expendable.

Ryan didn't fancy killing him. A truly ruthless operator would have ripped out the kid's throat, or snapped his head around hard enough to break his neck, but Ryan didn't want a murder on his conscience, even if incapacitating him involved greater time and risk.

After crawling out from under the mobile home relatively unscathed by sewage, Ryan circled around and picked a couple of pine cones and some willowy branches off the ground. Not only was the young guard playing Angry Birds, he was dumb enough to have left the sound on and the game's upbeat music made a wildly inappropriate soundtrack as Ryan crept up behind.

'Gah!'

The phone landed in mulch as Ryan got an arm around the guard's neck. The guy was bigger, but Ryan was strong from pumping weights at the Kremlin and had no trouble yanking his victim backwards off the log and clamping his jaw to muffle a scream. Once the guard's back was in the dirt, Ryan pressed his knee on his throat and choked him out.

As soon as his body went limp, Ryan forced a pine cone into the guy's mouth, then rolled him on his back and dragged him deeper into the trees so that he couldn't be seen from the path. He tied the cone gag in place using a section of the flexible branch, then used two more bendy switches to bind wrists and ankles.

After testing all his knots, Ryan started on the guy's pockets. As Kazakov predicted there was a walkie-talkie clipped to the guy's belt. Ryan took it so that he could listen in to anything IDoJ was saying. He also took the guard's wallet and was pleased by a jangle of keys in his jeans pocket.

Ryan dumped a big bunch that seemed to be house keys and stuff, but there was a second ring with a key, a plipper and an enamel fob with a car rental company logo on. Finally, Ryan pulled out a semi-automatic pistol tucked down the back of the guard's boxers. He checked the chamber and found a full clip.

Ryan double-tapped to activate his com. 'Dad, you hearing?'

Kazakov's voice came back inside Ryan's ear canal. 'What's up?'

'I circled around, there's only one guard. He's out cold. I've got a Beretta and keys to a hire car.'

'Nice,' Kazakov said. 'Go up to the house and try identifying the car. I'll grab our stuff and be right up behind you.'

Ryan kept off the path and stayed low as he walked towards a dirt patch beside the ranch house where most of the bad guys had parked their cars. The garage doors had been shuttered, but the sliding glass at the rear of the kitchen was open and the gathering inside had turned more solemn, with a single voice speaking in Arabic.

There were a dozen cars parked on gravel alongside the house: dreary Chrysler saloons and Hyundai mini-vans, all with car rental company stickers on the rear screens. Ryan was about to press the plipper to see which car he had keys for when a voice came through the walkie-talkie.

'Daniel, where are you, my man?'

Ryan recalled the name Daniel from the ID in the guard's pocket. He was about to warn Kazakov on the com when a second message came out of the walkie-talkie.

'Daniel's been tied up,' the voice blurted. 'Tell Elbaz, get some guys down here, stat!'

Ryan grabbed the guard's walkie-talkie and keyed up, hoping that his signal would stop the terrorists from communicating.

Kazakov's voice came into Ryan's ear, sounding urgent. 'I broke some guy's neck, but he got a message out first. How's it going with the car?'

Ryan pressed the plipper and got a flash of indicator lights from one of the mini-vans. As he moved towards it, the single voice inside the kitchen had stopped and there were shouts of outrage. Mumin and two other dudes with M16 submachine guns ran out the front of the house and down the path towards Kazakov as Ryan slid into the mini-van and put the key in the ignition.

It was dark and he fumbled with the controls, wasting seconds as he studied the automatic transmission, trying to find the override switch you needed to press to engage reverse. More guys were charging out of the house with guns and a couple of them looked Ryan's way as he rolled back.

All kinds of shouts were going up. As Ryan reversed there was a blast of gunfire. He thought they were aiming at him, but the muzzle flashes were down by the mobile home.

Once he'd cleared the parking space, Ryan put the transmission in drive and squeezed the gas pedal. His only experience behind the wheel was a few short practice drives during a beginners' course on CHERUB campus and the top of the mini-van clattered overhanging branches as he turned on to the path.

He fumbled for the headlight switch as he drove past

a couple of armed guys, who fortunately assumed that Ryan was one of them. When the beams came on, Ryan had to swerve immediately to avoid two machine-gunned bodies and Mumin writhing about clutching a bloody stomach. Kazakov had apparently pulled some fancy move, grabbing one of the machine guns and taking three guys out.

Ryan shouted. 'Where are you? Are you hit?'

Kazakov came back through the com. 'Pull up beside the mobile home. I've got our stuff and I'm ready to jump in.'

Ryan was a nervous driver and turned too fast, almost tipping the mini-van over. He stopped sharp, making a cloud of dust as more shots rang out, then jumped with fright when Kazakov ripped open the passenger door. The big instructor placed a machine gun on the dashboard before hurriedly lobbing Ryan's backpack and his own luggage over on to the back seats.

As the dust cleared, some of the guys running towards them opened fire. A bullet slammed the back of the car and Ryan gasped as a wet thud sounded in his ear.

'Christ,' Kazakov moaned.

The only light came from headlamps and through two little windows down the side of the mobile home. Kazakov had been knocked down and was slumped outside the car with blood pumping out of a huge wound in his shoulder.

Ryan reached across and tried pulling Kazakov in, but he was much too heavy and Kazakov batted the arm away.

'Get the message out,' Kazakov screamed, as he rolled on to the dirt and gave the passenger door a kick to close it. 'I'll cover you.'

Ryan hated leaving Kazakov, but another bullet slammed the car and a guy with a pistol was running from the other direction. He floored the gas pedal and swung the steering wheel full right. Kazakov was flat on the ground taking shots at the men coming towards him as Ryan accelerated. A terrorist smashed into the bonnet as he steered on to the path towards the ranch's main gate.

*

James struggled to get back to sleep after being disturbed by Amy's phone, and Bruce struggled because James kept getting up to use the toilet, or run a glass of water. Just after 5 a.m., rain started pelting the windows and James peeked behind the roller blind next to his bed.

'They need to drive in the dark, in the rain and when they're tired,' James reasoned. 'Seeing as conditions are ideal and we can't get back to sleep, what say we go disturb our little driving students?'

Bruce grunted. 'I'd sleep fine if you shut up. Have you even got their room numbers?'

'No, but I can look 'em up,' James said. 'Plus it's Friday. And I'm thinking if we start early, we can finish early then cab it into town for a night of action.'

'I've heard worse ideas,' Bruce said. 'We are supposed to take them out in the wet if we can and I'm never getting back to sleep with you fidget-arsing.'

Ten minutes later, James and Bruce were dressed and

heading up in the lift. Bruce got out on six to grab Ning, Alfie and Grace, while James went to the seventh floor for Leon.

When he'd taken the short-term instructor job, James promised himself that he'd be a decent instructor like Mr Pike or Kazakov, not one of the mean ones like Miss Speaks, or former head instructor Norman Large, who'd got more enjoyment out of making trainees suffer than he should have and ended up being sacked. But on the other hand, James couldn't resist the idea of charging into some poor trainee's room and scaring the hell out of them.

'Rise and shine!' James shouted, as he booted the door of room 707, flipped on the light switch and whipped a Manchester City duvet off the bed.

The kid looked suitably horrified as he shielded his eyes. 'Who the hell are you?' he shouted.

'You've got ten minutes, Leon,' James said. 'Get your rear in gear! Put some clothes on. Grab something to eat in the van on the way to the track.'

The kid looked furious. 'I'm not Leon.'

'Don't piss me about,' James said.

'We're identical twins,' Daniel Sharma shouted. To prove his point he picked a framed photo off the bedside shelf and waggled it in the air. It showed Ryan in the middle holding youngest brother Theo, with Leon and Daniel standing on either side pulling stupid faces.

'Ahh,' James said sheepishly. 'I looked up Sharma on the system and this room came up. I didn't realise there were four of you.'

Daniel pointed along the hallway. 'You'll find my brother two doors along.'

James charged down the hallway and hit room 711 shouting, 'Right, Sharma!'

There was a piercing scream as a fifteen-year-old girl pulled her duvet up around her neck.

'Jesus Harold Christ!' the girl yelled. 'Haven't you heard of knocking?'

'Shit! I'm sorry,' James said, backing out into the corridor where Daniel Sharma stood grinning at him.

'Oops,' Daniel said, unable to hide his smirk. 'Did I say my brother was two doors *that* way? I meant two doors the *other* way.'

Meanwhile a stern-faced carer named May was storming down the hallway. 'Who's screaming . . . ? Well well, if it isn't James Adams, causing a rumpus in my hallway. Just like old times!'

The girl had put on a dressing gown and now stood in her doorway giving James evils. 'This pervo burst in on me!'

Daniel was killing himself laughing and James wagged a finger at him. 'You'd better *hope* you don't get a training exercise with me. I'll *nuke* your skinny hide!'

'You should stick to what you're good at,' Daniel teased. 'Having sex in the campus fountain, that sort of thing . . .'

James tutted. 'Who started that *stupid* rumour?'

A couple of other sleepy kids now stood in their doorways, peering out to see what all the fuss was about.

'You looking for me?' Leon asked.

Before James could answer, he was the one getting a finger-wagging off May. 'You wake up half the kids in my corridor again and I'll have your guts for garters, Mr Adams. Training instructor or no training instructor.'

'Sorry,' James said, feeling like he was twelve again.

'Show's over, back to bed,' May said wearily. But she gave Daniel an extra hard scowl. 'I've got my eye on *you*, stirring it as usual.'

James eventually found himself in Leon's room.

'What did you do?' Leon asked. 'Everyone mixes me and my brother up.'

'Don't worry about it,' James mumbled. 'It's raining out, so we're taking you on the road while it's dark and wet. See you downstairs in fifteen. If you plan on eating before this evening, grab something you can nosh in the van.'

13. PETROL

The mini-van wasn't built to go fast on a dirt road. Ryan hadn't put on his seatbelt and had to lean his head to one side to stop hitting the roof, while the steering wheel tried to jerk out of his hands. There was nobody in pursuit, but the walkie-talkie was alive with panicked voices until Elbaz came on.

'We don't know if they've communicated,' he said calmly. 'We have to assume that they have. So we move out everything that's ready to go and blow the base.'

The short-range walkie-talkie traffic started breaking up as Ryan took a left on to an unlit two-lane highway. Tarmac made driving easier, but there were vehicles faster than this mini-van in the fleet up by the ranch house and it seemed weird that nobody was chasing.

Keeping one hand on the wheel as the speedo touched ninety, Ryan buckled his seatbelt, then pulled out his iPhone. He'd have given his left nut for a couple of signal bars, but all he had were the words, *No Network*.

He looked up in time to see a monstrous Cadillac Escalade pick-up crash through the undergrowth at the roadside less than fifty metres ahead. Apparently, the cross-country route was more direct than the dirt track and huge front tyres spun in the air as the 4x4 broke on to the highway.

Ryan swerved into the opposite lane, but the Escalade still clipped the rear of the mini-van and sent him into a tailspin. The steering wheel ripped out of Ryan's hands and his body slammed the door.

Fifty different noises were going on as the mini-van nosedived off the road, and one of them might have been a gunshot. The front bumper ripped off as it caught the side of a drainage channel and Ryan thought he was about to roll, but the wheels on his side slammed back down and the shallow ditch began guiding the tyres on the passenger's side like a rail.

As he pulled back on to the road, the Escalade accelerated towards his rear end. Ryan's body jerked as the pick-up slammed in and he corrected violently to stay on tarmac. At this point the road went into a slight arc. With only basic driving skills and an inferior vehicle, Ryan didn't fancy his chances in a long chase, so he kept going straight, bouncing across the roadside ditch hard and crashing through tangled undergrowth.

The headlamps lit up a low wooden fence and he turned the wheel so that he glanced it, rather than hitting it head on. But he wanted his pursuers to think he'd lost control, so he allowed the car to roll to a halt in the hope that this would make his off-road trip seem like an accident.

An instant before the vehicle stopped, Ryan popped his seatbelt then leaned across and grabbed Kazakov's machine gun, which had dropped off the dashboard into the footwell in front of the passenger seat.

When he popped his head up, Ryan was pleased to see the Escalade stopped on the road more than fifty metres away. He'd fired an M16 in basic training, and he checked the machine gun expertly, seeing that he had half a dozen shots in the magazine and clicking the weapon from automatic to a far more accurate single-shot mode.

After hooking the gun over his shoulder and making sure the Beretta was still tucked into the back of his jeans, Ryan pocketed the mini-van's ignition keys and slid out into the gap between car and fence.

He'd seen two guys in the pick-up, though it was dark so Ryan doubted he'd have known if anyone was in the back. One guy had stepped out of the passenger's side and held a handgun like someone who didn't know what to do with it.

'We won't hurt your dad if you come back to the ranch with us,' the guy shouted.

Ryan recognised the voice as one of the blokes who'd travelled from Kyrgyzstan with him. On the road he'd felt outmatched, but Ryan felt more confident as he crept through tall grass back towards the road. His two opponents only seemed to have handguns to his machine gun, and clearly thought they were hunting a regular kid dumb enough to fall for a *we'll help your daddy if you're a good boy* gambit.

'What you gonna do out here all on your own, Ryan?' the guy shouted.

While one guy moved warily towards the bashed-up mini-van, half expecting to find Ryan unconscious at the wheel, Ryan had made it to the road and crouched between bushes, less than five metres from the front of the Escalade.

A shout went up from down by the mini-van. 'Kid's got out, but he can't have got far.'

The second man stood beside the Cadillac and spoke into a walkie-talkie that was apparently out of signal range. 'Base, do you copy? Anyone else out here?'

The other guy thought up a new way to lure Ryan out. 'You're ten miles from anywhere, Ryan, and there's a lot of rattlesnakes out there.'

The shout gave Ryan a chance to cover up some noise. He scooted over dirt to the rear of the Escalade, rolled into a firing stance and took a single shot that blew a hole in the chest of the dude by the car.

'What are you shooting, Mike?' the guy down by the car shouted, as Ryan stepped over his victim and planted his bum on the luxurious Cadillac's leather driving seat.

It felt massive compared to the mini-van and had loads of gadgets including a glowing sat-nav screen in the centre console. The driver's door shut with a solid clunk and Ryan pushed a chromed start button to get a six-litre V8 growling.

The burst of speed was a shock as Ryan took off, while the high driving position and sheer scale of this new ride gave him a sense of invincibility. The pleas of the guy he'd shot into the walkie-talkie made him fairly sure that no second vehicle was on his tail, and he had the mini-van keys so the other guy wouldn't be on his back.

But there was still a *No Network* symbol on Ryan's iPhone. He was no sat-nav expert, but he kept the car at a sensible fifty mph and gave the touchscreen an experimental tap. The map only showed a single line of road until he zoomed out to reveal an intersection at a small town a few miles ahead. The screen had a little petrol pump icon. Touching it revealed the town's gas station and a tap on the route button set off a calming female voice.

'*Petrol in six point two miles. Left turn, one point seven miles. Current range before refuelling, one hundred and fifty-seven miles.*'

It made an easy ten-minute drive and the brightly lit Texaco station was part of a little strip-mall that also had a Denny's diner, a Burger King and a Dunkin Donuts. Ryan didn't get his speed right turning off the road and scraped a metal post.

After turning at the Burger King arrow, Ryan rolled around to the back of the near-empty lot so that the Escalade couldn't be seen from the road. He picked his phone off the dashboard, saw three beautiful signal bars and found Dr D on his contacts list. As the phone rang in his ear, a tap on the side window made him jolt.

'Hidey-ho!' Dr D screeched. 'Afraid you got my

voicemail, but leave a message and I'll be on your case before you know it.'

At the same time, Ryan turned his head and saw a gun up against the glass pointing towards him. His first thought was that he'd been tracked from the ranch, but it was a woman cop and there was another huge officer aiming a shotgun across the bonnet.

'Outta the car, hands where I can see 'em,' the woman screamed.

Someone might have called in the shooting out on the highway, but Ryan thought it more likely that the cops' suspicions had been raised by his clumsy scrape of the metal post when he'd turned in.

The female cop grabbed the driver's door and pulled it open.

'Move out,' the big guy shouted.

As Ryan stepped out of the car, the guy moved around, keeping the gun trained on him. British cops only shoot when someone's life is in danger so Ryan might have made a dash, but he doubted the same rules applied at the Alabama sheriff's department.

'Face the car, hands on the hood.'

As Ryan did what he was told, the male officer ripped away the handgun tucked in the back of Ryan's jeans, and noted spots of blood on his Converse.

'Wrists,' the woman said.

'You've *got* to speak to Dr Denise Huggan of the FBI,' Ryan said. 'There's a major terrorist organisation at a ranch house ten miles from here.'

'Is that right?' the woman said disbelievingly.

'Please listen,' Ryan said.

'We'll listen to everything you've got to say at the station.'

'It'll take two minutes to clear this up,' Ryan said urgently.

As the female officer zipped on a set of plasticuffs, the male cop seemed more interested in what Ryan had said.

'Terrorists,' Ryan repeated. 'They're about to send out a bunch of trucks to blow up shopping malls. And the guy I was with got shot in the shoulder.'

'Whereabouts?' the officer asked.

But the woman interrupted. 'Check out his eyes, before you believe too much of what he says.'

The male officer dropped the Beretta into a zip-lock evidence bag then stared into Ryan's bloodshot eyes.

'Kid's as high as a kite, ain't you?' the woman said.

'I've just been awake a long time,' Ryan said. 'Please listen. You've *got* to listen. You must have heard about the plane blowing up by the stadium, it's all linked to that.'

The male officer laughed. 'Oh, was that you? Is this your daddy's car?'

Ryan was so frustrated that he gave the female officer a little shove. 'Please, just make *one* phone call. It'll take twenty seconds.'

The big dude didn't like seeing his partner get pushed. He grabbed Ryan under the arms, pulled him a step backwards, then slammed him over the bonnet of the truck before shooting a blast of pepper spray in his face.

'You wanna mess with us?' the man shouted. 'Well

now you can add assaulting an officer to grand theft auto, firearms and drugs. You got a long stretch in juvenile hall coming your way, boy!'

'Listen,' Ryan gasped, as the pepper spray burned his eyes and throat.

'I've heard enough out of you,' the officer said, as he grabbed Ryan's cuffs and yanked him towards a cop car parked in a disabled space outside the Denny's. 'Now you sit in the car and behave while I go buy a box of bear claws for the station.'

14. KAZAKOV

They'd dragged Kazakov back to the ranch house. Someone had made a half-arsed attempt to stop the bleeding by tying a coat around his shoulder, but all it had done was ruin the coat.

'Who did you speak to?' someone shouted.

Even if Kazakov had wanted to answer he'd lost control of his mouth. The people bustling around the kitchen kept doing a little leap to avoid stepping in his blood. His vision was blurring, but the lack of oxygen had brought his mind to a mildly euphoric state that made the pain seem distant.

Kazakov found himself thinking about his thirty-four-year-old son. He'd not seen Olek in decades, not even a photo. But he'd always hoped to travel back to the Ukraine and track him down when he retired.

The interrogator can't have been older than twenty

and pinched Kazakov's cheek.

'Did you send out a message? Who did you speak to?'

Kazakov could see his body, but it no longer belonged to him. His heart and lungs struggled on automatic, but his consciousness had retreated into his brain and he knew there would soon be nothing at all.

'I told you,' Elbaz shouted, as he gave the interrogator a shove. 'I'm blowing this joint. It doesn't matter if he communicated. We can't be sure, so we'll act as if he did. We're five men down, but we can still get eight trucks out on the road. So go join your partner.'

Kazakov was impressed by Elbaz. Combat had taught him that the best field commanders aren't always the cleverest or strongest. They're men like Elbaz who cut out background noise and keep functioning when plans go tits up.

'Two minutes,' Elbaz shouted, as he stood by the patio doors. Then he grabbed someone. 'Get upstairs, go room to room making sure it's empty.'

Two of the ten vans wouldn't be leaving because their crews were dead or injured. Six had already left the ranch and two remained outside, making final preparations for departure.

'Get that explosive in!' Elbaz shouted. 'Take all you need, then pull over and finish wiring up somewhere along the way.'

Kazakov watched as Elbaz stood at the kitchen counter, pushing a small radio detonator into one of the pizza-box-sized explosive wedges.

'Some secrets in that head of yours, eh?' Elbaz said,

giving Kazakov a half-smile. 'If it's any consolation, your boy Ryan seems to have given us the slip.'

Ryan being safe made Kazakov want to smile, but now his vision was changing. It was like he was viewing everything through a pair of long black tubes.

'All clear, boss,' the guy Elbaz had sent upstairs said, before turning to look at Kazakov. 'Is he dead?'

'If he's not he will be when this place blows,' Elbaz said, before breaking into a shout. 'Two minutes, people! I'm detonating as soon as my car's a couple of hundred metres clear. And if you're not in front of me, that's your tough shit.'

*

The two blocks of Chinese explosive Elbaz wired up in the kitchen were enough to vaporise the ranch house, but the real taste of the IDoJ threat came from a secondary blast in one of the explosive-packed trucks that hadn't made it off site.

Elbaz was driving out of the ranch gates and was shocked by the ferocity, while the mini-van filled with specialists who'd made bombs and rigged the remote control systems, directly behind him, had its back window blown in.

Five miles east, ground trembled and orange light flashed through a glass door as Ryan stood barefoot. He was in the lobby of a rural sheriff's department office that was little more than a prefabricated hut, with a brick jailhouse for half a dozen inmates alongside.

The sergeant behind the desk looked like the cartoon character Elmer Fudd, but was obviously smarter than the pair who'd arrested Ryan. He'd quickly worked out that an olive-skinned kid with a foreign accent, turning up in an $80,000 Cadillac with a machine gun and blood-spattered trainers, amounted to more than just some crazy lad who'd swallowed a few pills and taken the family car for a joyride.

The sergeant looked across at McVitie, the female officer who'd been at the arrest scene. 'The vacant farm this kid just described sounds a lot like Oak Ranch,' the sergeant said. 'Wouldn't you say that's roughly where that explosion came from?'

'You want me to drive up there and check it out?' the woman asked.

The sergeant shook his head contemptuously. '*Christ*, McVitie. This is not some call about a man slapping his wife. You can't send a patrol car up to check it out. We've got no idea what's up there.'

As the sergeant said this, two phones behind the desk started ringing, followed by the mobile of the big cop who'd dosed Ryan with pepper spray. Sensing that these three local cops were out of their depth, Ryan tried to assert himself.

'There's a contact on my phone called *Dallas*,' he said firmly. 'It's part of an intelligence unit that's after the terrorists. They're blowing up shopping malls, using vans painted in shop liveries. You need to get *everyone* out looking for them.'

'Where's his phone?' the sergeant asked, and then to Ryan, 'And why would you have this number?'

'I've been helping them,' Ryan said. 'I'm begging you

to ring it. If I'm lying you can put me in a cell and pepper spray me all you like.'

As McVitie retrieved Ryan's iPhone from an evidence bag, a switchboard operator was running into the room. 'Sergeant, call on the red line: Homeland Security Protocol. A Dr Denise Huggan wants to speak with whoever's in charge.'

Ryan gasped with relief. He hadn't had a chance to leave a message when he'd connected to Dr D's voicemail, but she'd clearly triangulated his phone signal and tracked him down to the police station.

The sergeant spoke to Dr D briefly before passing the handset to Ryan.

'Kazakov was shot bad,' Ryan blurted. 'I doubt he made it. It sounds like Elbaz just blew the IDoJ base, but there's ten vans packed with explosives.'

'Heading where?' Dr D asked.

'Shopping malls,' Ryan said. 'Kazakov said something about tomorrow being this amazingly busy shopping day.'

'Black Friday,' Dr D confirmed. 'We'll get everyone on it. Local cops, state police, FBI. How are you doing?'

'Haven't slept since I left Kyrgyzstan,' Ryan said. 'So pretty exhausted, but no injuries.'

'Well that's something, at least,' Dr D said. 'We've got helicopters on standby. I'm in Montgomery, a hundred miles from you. I'll get a local FBI agent to you for a full debriefing, and tell that sergeant to start looking for those trucks.'

*

After their early wake-up, James and Bruce took the four advanced driving students out to the track for some practice driving in dark and rain. But tracks can't prepare drivers for buses, cyclists, pedestrians and all the other real-life hazards, so for the second part of the morning James and Bruce led their students on to real roads in a pair of BMW saloons. Each had heavily shaded windows to hide the underage drivers.

The task was to drive quickly but safely, on A-roads and motorways, and finally to navigate a busy town centre and multistorey car park. Alfie drove the first stretch in James' car, with Ning set to pilot the return journey. After a ten-minute wait for Bruce, Leon and Grace in the other car, they headed into a pedestrianised shopping area and found Café Rouge for lunch.

James had picked up a couple of texts from his girlfriend Kerry back in California, but he hadn't been able to look while he was concentrating on Alfie's erratic driving style. He remembered to check them after he'd ordered a mayonnaise-free steak sandwich from the waiter.

Seen this weird terror thing? Dead scary!!!

James was mystified, but the restaurant had a good Wi-Fi connection and he managed to stream TV news on his phone. Bruce and the four trainees leaned in to watch the little screen in the middle of the table.

The on-screen bar said *Thanksgiving Terror* and there was a grainy, distant shot of a huge explosion, followed by a cut to live footage of a smouldering ranch house. As the newsreader spoke to a terrorism pundit, the scrolling news bar spelled out the facts:

College football game called off after plane explodes on inaugural day of Alabama stadium · Cargo pilot's family held hostage, then rescued in dramatic FBI raid · Explosion at ranch house · FBI hunting for ten explosive-packed trucks · Public told to stay away from shopping malls in Texas, Florida and six other southern states.

James was shocked, but also relieved because Kerry and his American uni mates lived in northern California, over a thousand miles from where everything was kicking off. As he sent Kerry a one-word reply saying WOW!, the presenter on his phone cut to a newsflash.

'News agencies are now reporting that a large explosion has occurred on a highway near the town of Jackson, Louisiana. Police there identified a truck fitting the description of one of the wanted vehicles. After a brief chase, suspects ran from the vehicle on foot but were apparently able to detonate the vehicle remotely. There are reports of damage to a footbridge and injuries from flying glass, but so far no information on fatalities . . . If this information is correct, it means that two trucks have been located, with eight still unaccounted for.'

'Heavy, shit,' Leon said.

Grace seemed less interested. 'There's a Hollister across the street,' she said eagerly. 'Any chance we could pop in before we get back in the cars?'

James scoffed. 'I've done enough clothes shopping with Kerry and my sister, Lauren. I've seen too many "quick pop-ins" that turn into hour-long sessions where you have to try on twenty-six garments and then walk out without buying anything.'

Ning smiled. 'That's a *highly* sexist generalisation. Although in Grace's case you're spot on.'

Grace scowled at Ning. 'Whose side are you on?'

'Mine,' Ning growled back.

Alfie made a purring sound. 'Me-ow, girls!'

The waiter came over with their drinks and their attention drifted away from the news broadcast until Leon's phone started ringing. *Campus Calling* flashed up, and the voice on the other end belonged to CHERUB's chief handler Meryl Spencer.

'I wanted to check if you'd heard about Alabama?' Meryl asked.

'Watched it on James' phone a few minutes ago,' Leon said. 'Why are you calling *me* about this?'

'Agents aren't supposed to gossip about their missions, but I know they often do and I didn't want you worrying about Ryan.'

'Ryan's in Alabama?' Leon gasped. 'I thought he was in Keer . . . Kyar-git-stan or however you're supposed to pronounce it.'

Everyone around the table tuned in when Leon mentioned Alabama. James whispered to Ning, 'Is Ryan his older brother?' and Ning nodded.

'Well it's nothing to worry about,' Meryl told Leon. 'Your brother's been through an ordeal but he's OK. Now I need you to put James or Bruce on.'

Leon handed the phone over and James spoke cheerfully. 'Hey, Meryl!'

'I need you and the kids back on campus by four,' Meryl said. 'Zara's getting everyone together in the main hall. All lessons and training are cancelled and there's going to be an announcement.'

Everyone had been called to the main hall a few times when James had been an agent. Usually it was an opportunity for the chairman to read the riot act about some behaviour problem. But that had always been first thing, or after dinner. He'd never known everyone to get called back to campus in the middle of the day.

'Is it old chairman Mac?' James asked. 'I heard he's been sick.'

'James, if I knew I wouldn't be allowed to tell you,' Meryl said. 'But it's definitely not Mac. The last I heard he was spending Christmas skiing with Fahim and some young drama teacher he met at a parents' evening.'

15. DALLAS

Two staff manned the CCTV booth in the security building and a senior controller stayed on duty in mission control, but everyone else on CHERUB campus had crammed into the assembly hall, from tiny red shirts sitting cross-legged on the floor near the stage, to kitchen staff, teachers and gardeners clumped at the rear.

The only other time James Adams had seen this many people in the hall was for present opening on Christmas morning. A ripple of anticipation crossed the space as Chairwoman Zara Asker rose three steps on to the stage. She wore a flower-print dress with a black cardigan over her arms.

There was silence as Zara tapped the microphone to make sure it was on. 'CHERUB is a family,' she began solemnly. 'Sometimes we forget the risks that young agents and staff have to take and now I must make the kind of announcement that every CHERUB chairman hopes they never have to.

'Many of you will have seen the news about terrorist activity in Alabama over the past few hours. I can confirm that one CHERUB agent and one member of staff have been involved in trying to foil the IDoJ terror plot. Both were at the Oak Ranch shortly before it exploded. The agent escaped and is now resting in Dallas, unharmed. Tragically, Instructor Yosyp Kazakov was shot during this escape and he died, either from his wound or during the explosion shortly afterwards.'

Zara paused as shock filtered through the gathering.

'Yosyp Kazakov was fifty-three years old. Born to a military family in the Ukraine. His brother died while fighting alongside him during the Russian invasion of Afghanistan, and we know that Mr Kazakov has an adult son with whom he'd lost contact.

'During the 1980s, Kazakov was selected for Soviet Special Forces work. After the collapse of the Soviet Union, Kazakov joined NATO as a defence analyst, and helped to train Special Forces in the United Kingdom, the US and many other countries.

'He joined CHERUB as a training instructor in 2007, but while most of you will remember him in this role, Kazakov's background and experience also made him useful in undercover work, including the mission on which he had been deployed for the past seven months.

'All lessons and training have been cancelled for the rest of the day. Details of a full memorial service will be announced shortly. In the meantime, carers and other staff are on hand if you want to talk about what has happened or just need—'

Zara stopped talking and made a slight sob.

'A shoulder to cry on,' she said, as she dabbed her eyes and backed away from the microphone.

Zara's tears had set off quite a few staff and cherubs and once it was clear that she couldn't carry on, Head Training Instructor Mr Pike stepped up to the microphone.

'Kazakov was a man's man,' Pike said firmly. 'Some of your memories of being trained by him might not be happy ones.'

A few restrained laughs went through the audience.

'But Kazakov wasn't cruel. He cared about the people he trained. I remember him in the instructors' hut, worrying about how he was going to get a kid past their fear of heights. I remember Yosyp spending a whole evening with a trainee who was struggling with her language assignments, even though he needed to be up at three a.m. to set up the following day's training programme. Kazakov worked you hard, but he worked himself harder, and you're *all* better CHERUB agents because of him.'

A well-muscled black-shirt girl standing near James shouted out the CHERUB training chant. 'This is tough, but CHERUB is tougher.'

She got a couple of weird looks, but then a bunch of her friends repeated the chant.

'This is tough but CHERUB is tougher.'

By the third chant, half the room was in on the act.

The chant became official when Mr Pike said it through the microphone and the next time it became a roar.

'This is tough but CHERUB is tougher.'

Burly black shirts, tiny red shirts, carers, mission controllers, chefs, tech-support, right the way up to Zara Asker, who was now at the rear of the stage with husband Ewart's arm around her back.

'This is tough but CHERUB is tougher.'

People had tears down their faces, but they were stamping their boots and making the training chant louder than they'd ever made it before.

Fu Ning remembered Kazakov's proud expression when she'd pulled on her grey shirt at the end of basic training, Bruce Norris welled up as he remembered Kazakov getting him out of bed to test the mettle of a new CHERUB recruit in the dojo, while James Adams fondly remembered working with Kazakov on his first ever casino scam.

'This is tough but CHERUB is tougher,' they shouted.

They were all sad, but the strength of the CHERUB family made hairs stand up on four hundred necks.

*

Ryan had struggled to stay awake while a young FBI special agent debriefed him on every minuscule detail of who and what he'd seen at Oak Ranch. He'd finally crashed out aboard a small business jet taking him to Dallas and remembered nothing that happened after take-off when he woke in an attic room with a Nirvana Nevermind poster on the angled wall over the bed and twenty pairs of girls' shoes lined up by the window.

He smelled grungy, and when Ryan opened an eye the camouflage backpack he'd brought from Kyrgyzstan was on the floor by the bed, plus his stained T-shirt and crusty jeans. The only things missing were his blood-spattered Converse, which he'd last seen getting dropped into an evidence bag at the sheriff station.

Ryan suspected he'd been carried upstairs to bed. He had dirt packed under his nails and blood matted in the hairs around his left wrist. Two red fingertip-shaped smudges from where . . .

He sat up in shock: *Kazakov's blood. Dead man's blood.*

The kick of grief made Ryan feel like his chest was in a vice. Kazakov had only been his pretend father, but they'd worked undercover together in Kyrgyzstan for the past seven months. They'd argued like you'd expect any adult and teenager living in cramped quarters to argue, but they'd also become friends.

Ryan also felt survivor's guilt. Maybe Kazakov would be alive if he'd made it to the getaway car quicker. Or if he'd killed the guard instead of wasting time tying him up. Or if he'd dragged the guard deeper into the bushes so that he'd been harder to find . . .

Ryan sat on the side of the bed, head between his knees, catching a vague whiff of his own armpits and feet. He'd felt this same deep hurt when his mother died. It would pass, but knowing that didn't make the moment any less desperate.

Close to tears and with no idea who he'd find downstairs, Ryan pulled his dirty jeans on and peeked out on to the landing.

'Hello?'

There was no answer, but he could hear a TV, so he headed down four flights clad in shaggy beige carpet. There was something comforting about finding himself in someone's home, even one clearly run by a man, with photos of college football teams along the stairs, a dartboard by the front door and lumps of motorbike engine spread over the dining table.

'Hey there, Ryan,' Ted Brasker said warmly.

Ted was a big grey-haired Texan, and Dr D's deputy at TFU. Ryan knew Ted well because he'd been another of Ryan's fake fathers during the first phase of their mission to destroy the Aramov Clan.

The other person in the room was Ethan Aramov. The same age as Ryan, he was the grandson of Aramov Clan head Irena. He now lived with Ted under protective custody, because his uncle Leonid wanted him dead.

Ethan was weedy and felt jealous when he saw Ryan's chest. 'You've been working out,' Ethan noted.

'You hungry?' Ted asked. 'How you feeling?'

'Like shit,' Ryan said, relieved to be amongst friends as his eyes were drawn to a huge LCD screen showing the news. 'What's the latest?'

'Ten trucks,' Ethan said. 'Two didn't get out of Oak Ranch. Four have been found without incident, one exploded killing six people at an intersection. One hit its target, ripping up half of a shopping mall in Atlanta.'

'Crap,' Ryan said. 'Lots of dead?'

Ethan shook his head. 'All the malls within striking range have been ordered to close. The only casualties were a security guard and two teenagers making out in the empty parking lot.'

'And the last two trucks?' Ryan asked.

'They're keeping us worried,' Ted said. 'The whole country's on the lookout for 2012 model GMC Savannah trucks, painted with the logos of major retailers. To have stayed out of sight this long they've either pulled into a garage somewhere or transferred the explosives to another vehicle.'

'So IDoJ still has two tonnes of high-explosive on the loose,' Ethan added.

Ryan had assumed it was morning, but the clock on the TV put the time nearer to three in the afternoon.

'That was quite a sleep,' Ryan noted. 'I need a shower, but all my clothes are *disgusting*.'

'You can borrow some of mine,' Ethan said. 'We're the same height. Only thing is my feet are smaller.'

'Guess we'll have to buy you some sneakers,' Ted said, as he handed Ryan a glass of iced orange juice. 'But it won't happen today. There's not a shop open within a thousand miles of here.'

'Thanks,' Ryan said, sipping the orange before looking across at Ethan. 'So how's Texas working out for you?'

'I'm enrolled in a nice private school,' Ethan said. 'Rules and uniform piss me off, but I've got a couple of decent mates. I've also taken up the drums and I'm the best player on the chess squad.'

Ted snorted. 'Still haven't persuaded him to try out for the football squad.'

Ryan smiled at the idea of Ethan's scrawny bod on a

football field. 'What about your grandma Irena? Have you visited her?'

Irena Aramov had controlled the Aramov Clan for more than thirty years, but she'd allowed Dr D's TFU unit to take her operation over, on condition that she was given immunity from criminal prosecution and was allowed to travel to the USA to receive an experimental cancer treatment.

'Been up to New York to see her a couple of times,' Ethan said. 'Treatment worked for a while, but she's crashing again. I don't think she's got long now. Last time I was up there she barely knew who I was.'

Ted put a hand between Ryan's bare shoulder blades and spoke firmly. 'I'm real sorry about Kazakov. He was a good guy.'

'He was,' Ryan said sadly.

'So,' Ted said, trying to break the silence, 'you still a pancake man?'

Ryan had fond memories of Ted's pancakes and edged into a smile. 'Blueberry?'

'I can dig out some blueberries,' Ted said. 'You go get yourself cleaned up. Ethan will lend you some clothes, then you can fill your face while we work out what happens next.'

16. CONFERENCE

After being interrupted for the announcement on Friday afternoon, the advanced driving course had continued through the weekend and Monday was the final day.

Ning felt nervous as she sat in front of campus' main building at the wheel of a large but badly mauled Opel saloon car. It was ex-police, with the high-vis stickers still along the side and filler in the roof where the flashing blue lights had once been bolted through.

James was in the front passenger seat, looking round impatiently with a clipboard resting on his lap. 'Have you seen Alfie this morning?'

'At breakfast,' Ning said. 'He went upstairs for something he'd forgotten, but that was *ages* ago.'

'I sent him a text,' James said, as he glanced at the clock on the dashboard. 'If he's not here in four minutes . . .'

But Alfie came charging out of the main building before James finished his sentence.

'Sorry,' Alfie blurted, as he climbed in the back. 'Got collared by my science teacher. The dickhead wants me to redo a whole bunch of work because it's *sloppy*.'

James should have been annoyed, but he'd spent plenty of time hiding from teachers who were after him for homework when he'd been a cherub.

'Who needs to know about molecules anyway?' Alfie asked. 'I've got my career all mapped out.'

James laughed. 'And what's that?'

'I'm gonna be a professional rugby player, but if that fails I'll become a porn star.'

'Very sensible,' James said, as Ning smirked.

'Oh,' Alfie added. 'And they announced on the news that the FBI raided some warehouse. Found the last of the explosives and they reckon they've busted IDoJ's top man in the US.'

'Good,' Ning said. 'Means Kazakov didn't die for nothing.'

'OK, that's enough distractions,' James said. 'Bruce, Leon and Grace left ten minutes ago. Have you both read the briefing?'

Ning and Alfie nodded.

'You're going to be tested on everything you've learned over the past four days,' James said. 'Drive fast, but *always* put safety first. Today won't be easy, but you're both good enough to pass this course.'

'Slay them, Ning,' Alfie said, as he buckled his seatbelt. 'Also, please try not to kill me.'

'Same to you,' Ning said, smiling warily as she started the engine, dropped the handbrake and pulled off in first gear.

There were often little kids running around, so campus had a strict 10mph limit. Ning rolled down the gravel path that led from the main building to the security gate, but James told her to pull over before she got there.

'What?' Ning asked.

James tutted. 'This is *really* basic. What do you do when you get into a strange car?'

'Check that the car is mechanically safe from the outside. Check mirrors, familiarise yourself with the controls.'

'Right,' James said. 'How far are we driving?'

'You said thirty miles.'

James pointed to the fuel gauge. 'Is that going to get you thirty miles?'

'Oh,' Ning said, when she saw the gauge on empty. 'Shouldn't the red warning light be on if it's that low?'

'It should,' James agreed. 'But this car is twelve years old. What did I tell you about old cars?'

'Old cars are shit,' Alfie said. 'You can expect everything to go wrong.'

'Exactly,' James said. 'The warning light could be faulty. Or the fuel tank might be brim full and the gauge itself could be faulty. But you set off without any awareness of a possible critical fuel problem.'

Ning looked sour. 'So do I lose a mark for that?'

'One mark,' James said. 'Eight more and you fail the course.'

'So, I should check the fuel tank, or what?' Ning asked.

James gave Ning a stern look. 'This is the final test. You've read the briefing, I'm not making any decisions for you.'

Alfie decided to help Ning out. 'I'll look in the back and see if there's a spare fuel can. You see if you can look into the tank and check the fuel level.'

'That's more like it,' James said, as the pair jumped out of the car. 'But make it snappy.'

Ning was back a couple of seconds later, fumbling around hunting for the fuel flap and boot release buttons.

'I'm just nervous,' she told James anxiously. 'I always mess up tests like this.'

'Funnel and petrol!' Alfie said triumphantly, as he pulled a metal can out of the trunk. 'Do I get a bonus mark for saving Ning's butt?'

'You'll have a bonus mark on your butt if you don't watch it,' Ning growled, as she unscrewed the car's fuel cap and dropped the funnel in.

*

Amy Collins passed the battered ex-police car as she made the final approach to CHERUB campus, with Ryan in the back. They parked by the helipads at the side of the main building and headed straight to a conference room on the first floor.

Chairwoman Zara Asker was at the head of a big oval table, along with husband and Chief Mission Controller Ewart Asker, Chief Handler Meryl Spencer and semi-retired Campus Psychiatrist Jennifer Mitchum.

'All the big wigs,' Ryan noted, feeling a little intimidated as he sat in a swivel chair and poured water from a glass jug.

'How are you feeling?' Meryl asked, as Amy sat across the table opposite Ryan.

'Could be worse,' Ryan said. 'I met Amy at Heathrow Airport last night. But it was late, so we booked into a hotel and drove up this morning.'

'Jet lag?' Ewart asked.

Ryan nodded. 'Kyrgyzstan, China, and then America is a thirteen-hour time shift. Then back here which is another seven-hour shift. My body has *no* idea what time of day it is.'

'Besides your disorientation, how are you feeling?' Jennifer Mitchum asked. 'Seeing your mission controller die must have been distressing. Especially after you've worked with him for seven months.'

Ryan nodded. 'When my mum died I felt *so* bad, and I thought the sadness would never end. But it did get better.'

'Yes,' Jennifer said. 'Understanding the grieving process really does help.'

'I also wonder if I could have saved him,' Ryan said. 'Like, I tied our guard up. But that took ages, and if I'd killed him I probably would have got to the car before the guard got found.'

Ewart Asker smiled. 'You can play *what if* games your whole life. Maybe if you hadn't tied the guy up, you would have got to the parked car sooner, but an armed guard could have been out there having a cigarette break and you'd have been killed when you got there.'

'Feelings of guilt are completely normal,' Jennifer Mitchum said. 'But you didn't *intentionally* do anything that led to Kazakov getting killed and that's what you should focus on.'

Ryan nodded, before Zara spoke. 'Ted Brasker tells me that you're very keen to go back to Kyrgyzstan and resume the mission. I must say, I have concerns about this.'

Ryan sat bolt upright. 'There's nothing wrong with me,' he said defensively.

'I'm not saying that there is,' Zara replied. 'But you've been away from campus for seven months. You've lost out on your education; you must have missed your friends. I know you feel that you have unfinished business at the Kremlin, but as chairman, my duty is to put agents' wellbeing first.'

Amy spoke next. 'I do think Ryan would continue to be useful at the Kremlin. I'm living on the top floor, watching over Josef Aramov and basically pulling strings to run Aramov Clan operations. Ryan and Kazakov have been feeding back really important information about the mood of people lower down the organisation.'

'There must be other ways of doing that,' Ewart said. 'Cherubs are only supposed to operate in situations where adults can't. There must be dozens of people inside the Kremlin who'd make willing snitches.'

'I have other sources,' Amy confirmed. 'But Ryan and Kazakov were the only ones I could totally trust. The mission could certainly continue without Ryan. Although as we all know, kids tend to be less cagey than adults, and Ryan has already picked up a lot of information from people he goes to school with.'

'I can *really* help,' Ryan said. 'And it's not like I'm in massive danger at the Kremlin.'

Handler Meryl Spencer looked at some of Ryan's mission notes. 'I don't want to make Ryan uncomfortable, but I can't help but feel that part of Ryan's reason for wanting to return to the Kremlin has something to do with this girl, Natasha.'

Ryan squirmed with embarrassment as everyone looked at him. 'First off, her name's Natalka, not Natasha. Second, I don't see that my love life is any of your business.'

Zara spoke firmly. 'Ryan, this meeting isn't about your love life, but it is about your wellbeing. If you have a strong emotional bond with someone at the Kremlin, it obviously affects your willingness to return to the mission in Kyrgyzstan.'

'There's not that many people my age at the Kremlin,' Ryan said. 'Natalka's nice. We hang out and stuff.'

'Would you say you loved her?' Meryl asked.

'I like her a lot,' Ryan said. 'We spent most evenings together.'

'Have you been physically intimate?' Meryl asked.

'I haven't shagged her if that's what you're thinking,' Ryan said irritably, feeling really uncomfortable discussing this in front of five adults. 'We've kissed and stuff, obviously.'

'Do you think you'd want to go back to Kyrgyzstan if it wasn't for Natalka?' Zara asked.

Everything Ryan had said up to this point was either the truth or close to it, but now he told an outright lie. 'Natalka's not that big a deal. I only want to go back to Kyrgyzstan because I want to help finish the job that Kazakov and I started.'

'OK, I think Ryan's had enough of a grilling,' Zara said. 'Here's what I think: Ryan has been away from campus for seven months and he's been through a nasty ordeal over the past week. He needs to catch up on his education and spend some time on campus.'

'No way!' Ryan blurted.

'Let me *finish*,' Zara said firmly. 'However, Ryan also has unfinished business and emotional ties in Kyrgyzstan. So he can return, but only for a *maximum* of six weeks. This should give Ryan a chance to tie up loose ends, and for Amy to find someone else to take over his role.'

'Oh, right,' Ryan said sheepishly. 'Sorry.'

Zara continued. 'When you come back to campus, you'll spend a minimum of six months on off-mission status. You need to catch up with your training and education, and spend time living like a normal teenager. Does anyone around this table have any major objections to this?'

'Six weeks is plenty of time for me to replace Ryan at the Kremlin,' Amy said.

The psychiatrist, Dr Mitchum, spoke. 'A traumatic event like the death of a mission controller shouldn't be brushed aside. I'd like to see Ryan for a couple of counselling sessions before he leaves and further sessions when he returns to campus.'

There was a couple of seconds' silence before Zara wheeled her chair back and stood up. 'OK, that's all agreed then. Meeting adjourned.'

Ewart, Meryl and Dr Mitchum filed out, but Zara cornered Ryan and Amy before they left.

'I'm really sorry if we made you uncomfortable talking about Natalka,' Zara said.

Ryan gave an awkward shrug. 'Guess you have to cover everything.'

'I'm sitting in on a video conference early this afternoon,' Zara said. 'It's a debrief on the IDoJ operation, involving Dr D and some other figures in the US Intelligence community. I know Amy will want to watch, but, Ryan, you've been so closely tied up in this that you're welcome to sit in as well.'

17. GRANNIES

James Adams and Bruce Norris stood up in the racetrack's grandstand as the trainees lined up four abreast on the start line, in matching Volkswagen Golfs.

Bruce had a walkie-talkie that linked up to all four drivers. 'Remember, two laps of the track. At the end of your second lap pull off into the parking lot, through the pit lane and follow the obstacle course.

'Look out for random hazards. You'll be docked one point for each one you hit. You'll also be docked one point for every full ten seconds that you finish behind the lead car. Now, start your engines!'

As Bruce spoke, James stepped down the grandstand holding a black-and-white chequered flag. Ning's mouth felt dry as she sat in the driver's seat, wearing a crash helmet and six-point safety harness. She was on the outside of the track, which she hoped would give her the best run into the first corner.

James stood rigid with the flag held high as the four Volkswagens revved. When he dropped the flag, Grace shot off into the lead. Ning got an OK start and tucked in behind Grace. Leon had pulled left in an aggressive attempt to get the best line into the corner, but Alfie had no intention of letting him through and tried sandwiching Leon into the pit wall.

The cars were normal diesel-powered Golfs and they'd barely reached twenty miles per hour, but the boys still had a noisy coming together. Leon kept going, but Alfie lost power and found himself rolling with a stalled engine as Grace narrowly led Ning into the first corner.

Ning caught a slipstream as Grace came off the corner and hit the straight, but as she tried to overtake, Grace swerved to avoid a polystyrene dog and Ning's only choice was to swerve the other way.

The Golf's front driving wheel lost grip when it hit damp grass off the side of the tarmac, and while a jerk of the steering got Ning back on course, she'd lost momentum and Leon had enough speed to overtake on the outside at the next corner.

Unfortunately for Leon, he was so keen to make the pass that he didn't brake in time for the following corner and Ning cut back through on the inside. Now Ning found herself on a straight, with Leon close behind, Grace four car-lengths ahead and Alfie too far back to be seen.

Three quick corners passed in a blur, but when they reached the next short straight Grace was shocked to see that two stripped-out cars had been parked sideways across the track, making a roadblock. There were two options: hit the rear of one of the cars to spin it out of the way, or divert off the main track and take a longer route on to a winding section used for go-kart racing.

They'd been taught how to ram a roadblock, but you had to slow down to no more than thirty miles per hour to avoid a whiplash injury, and even then hitting other cars wasn't an exact science. Grace decided that her advantage was big enough to take the safer option.

Ning considered going for the lead, but she'd already been deducted five of her eight points during earlier tests, and while a win might be good for her ego, her real goal was to finish within twenty seconds of the winner and not hit too many obstacles to pass Advanced Driving.

As Ning followed Grace through the twisting diversion, Leon charged the roadblock. He hit the rear of the two cars spot on, making a nice hole between them. While Leon had slowed down to crash the roadblock, Alfie took advantage of his hard work and whizzed through the gap at full speed.

Ning had made up most of her gap to Grace on the twisting go-kart section and came back on to the main track behind Grace, with Leon right on her tail. Alfie was on the outside and still last, but he had enough momentum to overtake the others if he could find a way through.

As they turned on to the main straight to complete the lap, Alfie got his nose in front of Grace, while Ning and Leon ran side by side less than a car-length behind them. Up ahead, James and Bruce and their assistant Kevin Sumner had livened things up by turning the straight into a slalom using a mixture of polystyrene grannies, cardboard mums with pushchairs and a sinister-looking dummy soldier holding a bazooka.

Grace and Alfie refused to submit the lead, but Ning was focused on passing the course, not winning the race. Knowing that she only had to finish within twenty seconds of the winner, she slowed down and neatly weaved around the few dummies that hadn't already been hit by one of the two leading cars.

Ning kept this strategy up for the next half a lap, and made it up to third when Alfie barged Grace off-track into a barrier. Grace tried to rejoin, but her front right tyre had come off its rim. Technically this meant Grace had failed the course, but Ning suspected James and Bruce would give her another shot rather than fail a good pupil.

Leon had the lead as they approached the final straight and cut into the pit lane. Alfie was almost on his rear bumper and while the boys battled, Ning smartly left a gap big enough to take evasive action if one of the lads had an incident.

After pulling under the grandstand, hay bales marked out a separate route for each car. A twisting path took Ning to a sign indicating that she had to change direction with a handbrake turn. She hadn't done one in the Golf since Thursday and made a complete hash of it, but she was sure that this was the first point she'd be docked and she only had a few hundred metres left to drive.

The final stretch was slalom between hay bales, then a long twisting reverse drive, and up a ramp into the rear of a truck. Ning clipped her door mirror as she backed into the truck, but the paintwork was already battered and the dink was so slight that she doubted anyone would notice.

Ning gasped with relief as she turned off the engine and released her safety harness, but when she opened the door, she saw there wasn't room to get out. After a moment's thought, she pulled off her crash helmet and made an ungracious exit through the Golf's sunroof, followed by a slide down the bonnet and a jump out of the truck's rear.

Leon and Alfie had made it out of their trucks in the same fashion a couple of seconds earlier, but the two boys were furious about their battle on the track and both claimed to have won. Alfie had a big size advantage, but he wasn't prepared for Leon charging forwards and belting him across the side of the head with his crash helmet.

'You're a maniac!' Leon shouted.

'*I'm* a maniac?' Alfie roared, as he dodged a second swing of Leon's helmet. 'You slammed me into that barrier at the start.'

'You got a crap start,' Leon shouted. 'You should have yielded.'

As Leon's initial bravado wore off, he once again realised that tangling with Alfie wasn't a good idea. But as he backed off, Alfie hooked Leon's ankle and swept his feet away before jumping on his back.

'You're hamburger,' Alfie shouted.

Alfie landed three hard punches on the smaller boy before Ning grabbed Alfie under the arms and hoiked him off.

'Pack it in,' Ning ordered, as she shoved Alfie away. 'You're both idiots.'

Bruce and James were also now jogging towards the scene.

'Ning, well done, you passed,' James said, as Leon struggled off the ground, badly winded but trying not to let Alfie see that he was hurt. 'You two boys *totally* lost your heads.'

Bruce screamed right in Alfie's face. 'What's the number one rule?'

'Safety first,' Alfie said meekly.

'Your driving was unacceptable,' James yelled. 'You two were so busy fighting one another, that you hit more obstacles than I'd care to count and broke safety rules too. You're both decent drivers. You should have passed easily, but instead you've made *complete* tits of yourselves.'

'We've tried to be cool with you all week,' Bruce added. 'But that madness could have caused a serious accident. We can't dish out punishment laps because we're not official instructors.'

Alfie smiled cheekily, much to James' annoyance.

'But I *can* write a report,' James said, as he poked Alfie in the chest. 'So you can both expect a call to the chairman's office at some point in the next few days.'

Grace and her Golf had been picked up in a tow truck driven by the black shirt Kevin Sumner. She looked pretty upset as she jumped from the cab with her helmet under her arm, but Bruce cheered her up straight away.

'You passed,' Bruce told her. 'We're not gonna hold a burst tyre against you. Congratulations.'

'Now we're done,' James said, glancing at his watch, then glowering at Leon and Alfie. 'Ning and Grace can drive back to campus with us. Alfie and Leon can stay here and pick up all the obstacles and hay bales. If you work quickly, Kevin *might* give you a lift after he's driven all the cars back and locked up the garage. If you're slow, I hope you enjoy the twelve-kilometre walk back to campus.'

18. POLITICS

Ryan caught up with Max Black and a few other campus mates over lunch, before heading upstairs for his second meeting of the day. While the first meeting had been personal and friendly, this one was more like an inquisition.

The campus conference room was equipped with a telepresence system. Zara saw the other participants' torsos in life-size on LCD screens along three walls of the room. It was a high-powered group, which included Dr D from TFU in Dallas, the British Intelligence minister in Manchester and the US Intelligence Secretary who was on a visit to Pakistan. The meeting was being chaired from Washington DC by Senator Madeline White. She was the head of the US Senate Joint Intelligence Committee and rumoured to be considering a run for president in 2016.

Amy and Ryan watched the meeting through one-way glass from a side room. Dr D read a brief report, summarising how her unit had taken control of the Aramov Clan and was slowly winding down Aramov operations while trying to take as many other criminal groups as possible with it.

'Approximately five months ago, a Mr Elbaz contacted an Aramov Clan representative based in South America,' Dr D said. 'He wanted to hire a freighter aircraft and crew. At this time, Elbaz did not disclose that he was working for IDoJ. However, this became apparent as negotiations continued.

'Elbaz also had links to corrupt military officials willing to sell high explosives in the People's Republic of China, and hinted that IDoJ was building a terrorist cell inside the United States. We used the Aramov Clan to help Elbaz to devise a plan, involving a freighter aircraft travelling from Kyrgyzstan. The aircraft would collect eleven tonnes of explosives in China, then travel on to Manta, Ecuador, from where Elbaz claimed he would be able to move the explosives into the United States using a hijacked cargo aircraft.

'TFU's plan was to intercept this cargo of explosives, along with Elbaz and as many members of the US-based IDoJ cell as we could lay our hands on. Unfortunately – for reasons that are still not entirely clear – Elbaz tripped us up by changing the US landing site at the last moment. This enabled him to proceed to the next stage of the operation.'

Senator White rattled a bunch of papers and spoke

noisily. 'Dr D, I think everyone here is *fully* aware of what has happened over the past few days. What I want to know, is how you thought you could justify an operation in which failure would lead to a large quantity of explosives entering the United States?'

Dr D had been in hundreds of meetings like this and wasn't flustered by the senator's aggressive tone. 'We felt it was vital to unearth the IDoJ cell within the United States. The only way to do that was to track the explosives to their arrival point in Alabama.'

'And the cost to the pilot Tracy Collings?' the senator asked. 'Her family held hostage, before she's blackmailed and then executed in cold blood. Plus two more dead FBI men who tried boarding the plane, a British agent killed at the ranch, six dead and three critical in Jackson, Louisiana. And that's *before* we mention half a billion dollars in property damage, and the incalculable economic effect of half the shops in the United States closed for business on the busiest shopping weekend of the year.'

The Intelligence Secretary interrupted. 'Senator, I think you're being very emotive. There's no need for your political grandstanding. The objective of this meeting is to understand the operation.'

'Really?' the senator asked. 'Perhaps the Intelligence Secretary could clarify for the record whether the President *personally* approved this operation?'

The Intelligence Secretary looked uncomfortable. 'The President was apprised of the operation in his daily intelligence briefing. However, it's not his job to take responsibility for, or to authorise, individual intelligence operations.'

The senator made a grumpy *humph* before resuming her attack. 'And how do you think the President's approval ratings will look, if the American public finds out that the entire IDoJ operation was only made possible by the Aramov Clan, while the Aramov Clan is currently controlled by the United States Intelligence Service?'

Zara Asker chimed in at this point. 'I think we need to calm down and look at facts. There were mistakes and sadly lives were lost. But IDoJ planned to kill at least ten thousand people in the Black Friday attacks. We lost less than one per cent of that number, and in the process captured Elbaz, killed his deputy Mumin and arrested many members of the US-based IDoJ cell. Anyone who thinks you can undertake an operation of this complexity without any mistakes is a fantasist and if you leave out emotive political arguments, the result was a qualified success.'

Now Senator White turned her wrath on Zara. 'You work in intelligence, Mrs Asker. I work in politics. The risks taken in this operation may be fine for you intelligence folks, but as far as I'm concerned when you're talking about American civilians being killed on home soil the only *acceptable* level of casualties is zero.'

Dr D spoke. 'The Aramov Clan has over seventy planes in its fleet. But there are hundreds of these old Russian planes in the sky. If we'd turned Elbaz away, he could have got his explosives from China to Ecuador using any one of a *hundred* smaller smuggling outfits. And I should remind you, every single slab of that explosive has now been accounted for.'

'More by luck than skill,' Senator White snapped. 'I've come into this meeting today with a single proposal. After this weekend's events, it is no longer acceptable for a US government department – even a highly secretive one like TFU – to run illegal smuggling operations. I propose that instead of winding down the Aramov Clan over two or three years as planned, we set a target of ninety days. If we're smart, we can produce evidence showing the Aramov Clan's links to IDoJ and make it look like the elimination of the clan was revenge for their involvement in the attacks.'

Dr D looked furious. 'Controlling the clan represents a once-in-a-generation opportunity. The Aramov Clan's transportation network is used and trusted by *dozens* of major crime syndicates. The only reason we haven't moved against more bad guys already is that we have to pace ourselves, otherwise it will be too obvious where all the information is coming from.'

The Intelligence Secretary sighed. 'As a representative of the President I reluctantly agree with Senator White. I appreciate the value of the Aramov Clan as an intelligence asset. But the Aramov operation was signed off on the basis that we were dealing with a smuggling network based in central Asia. Nobody expected it to involve terrorists turning up in Alabama on Thanksgiving.'

Dr D cleared her throat. 'If it helps, I'd be willing to resign my post and let someone else take over TFU.

We could establish new ground rules, so that no Aramov-related operation should come anywhere near US territory.'

Senator White looked less than keen. 'First of all, Dr D, after the debacle over the past weekend, I'd assumed that your resignation was *already* on the table. Secondly, you can have all the ground rules you like, but the cat is out of the bag. TFU is responsible for a partially-successful terrorist attack on US soil. The faster we tidy this mess up, the less chance there is that the intelligence service's role will become public. The Aramov Clan operation must be drawn to a swift conclusion and TFU must be shut down.'

'Would it be possible for British Intelligence to take the Aramov Clan operation over?' Zara asked.

At this suggestion, the British Intelligence minister gave Zara a filthy look, before chiming in nervously. 'The British Government are firm friends to the US Intelligence Services. But we've got elections coming up and no politician wants this hot potato dumped in their lap.'

*

The meeting rambled for another hour, but the politicians couldn't be persuaded and when the telepresence screens faded out nothing had changed.

After what the media had now named *The Black Friday Raid*, politicians were scared of what would happen if the public learned that an organisation run by their own intelligence service had hired out the plane that IDoJ used to help smuggle eleven tonnes of explosive into the

USA, and had known about the kidnapping of Tracy Collings' family before it happened.

TFU was being shut down, Dr D was being bounced into early retirement and Zara Asker was fully expecting a one-on-one telephone bollocking from her boss the Intelligence minister when she got back to her office.

The Aramov Clan's fleet of aircraft would be taken out of service and the Kremlin base shut down, though the politicians had accepted that this might not be possible within Senator White's ninety-day target.

'I feel like a naughty kid coming out of the headmaster's office,' Zara said, shuddering as Amy and Ryan emerged from behind the one-way glass. 'Everyone talks about how great democracy is, but I'd feel a lot happier if the politicians could see beyond their next set of poll ratings.'

Ryan sounded frustrated. 'But Aramov has links to every major criminal network on earth. If we shut it down, the whole operation will have been for nothing.'

'I've been saying that for the past two hours,' Zara said. 'But unless you plan on storming Parliament and staging a coup, CHERUB ultimately does what the politicians tell us to.'

Amy was upset for more personal reasons. 'With Dr D and Ted Brasker both close to retirement I thought I had a good shot at a senior job in TFU in a few years. Now I'm a junior operator, with my reputation tarnished by working for a unit that messed up and got closed down.'

'CHERUB is set to expand,' Zara said. 'The first mission control vacancy that comes up is all yours.'

Amy shrugged. 'Appreciated, Zara. But I've never seen myself back at CHERUB. I want to carve my own niche, rather than fall back on my past.'

Ryan smirked. 'If I was as hot as you, Amy, I'd marry some old billionaire and wait for him to croak.'

Amy appreciated Ryan's attempt to cheer her up, but gave his ear a flick for being cheeky. Zara was leading them back down the hallway towards the stairs when Amy's phone rang. It was Ted Brasker.

'Dr D called me in tears,' Ted told Amy. 'But I say screw the politicians. I'm getting old. I'll probably get the boot once we're done with the Aramov Clan anyway. TFU's got at least ninety days and old Ted plans to go out with a bang not a whimper. Are you with me, Amy Collins?'

'Why not?' Amy laughed. 'My career's not worth shit now anyway.'

'Pack your kit and sort your flights, then,' Ted said. 'We need you and Ryan back at the Kremlin to finish what we've started.'

19. KYRGYZSTAN

Ryan had been on the move for so long that jet lag had started to feel like the normal state of things. He'd flown from London to Dubai with Amy, but they couldn't be seen arriving together so he spent the night in a hotel before flying from Sharjah to the Kremlin on one of the Aramov Clan's semi-regular passenger flights.

It was Wednesday lunchtime as Ryan walked through the Kremlin lobby, with dirty snow dripping off his new Converse. The bar was open and fruit machines flashed, but none of the grubby mechanics and aircrew paid the blindest bit of notice as he walked to the lift. They didn't know where Ryan had been, and it would be a while before news filtered through the Kremlin that his 'father' Kazakov was dead.

Aramov crews were a tight-knit community, but while they'd drink all night and gossip about landing conditions, sources for aircraft spares and who was screwing who, they rarely told other crews where they were going or where they'd just been. Smuggling is a risky business. People might blab if they were arrested, and information on where a plane loaded with fifty million dollars' worth of cocaine is heading is worth a lot of money to someone who wants to hijack it.

Both lifts were out, but Ryan only had his backpack and didn't mind walking up three floors to his room. The Kremlin had been built for the old Soviet Air Force and military dorms had been crudely divided with wobbly plasterboard partitions. Toilets and showers were grim affairs shared between six rooms, and the lingering whiff of drains and cigarettes could only be escaped if you threw your window open. This was OK in the summer, but right now it was November and the outdoor temperature was minus four.

Despite many disadvantages, the low-ceilinged room was cosy and Ryan felt fondness as he flipped on the bare ceiling bulb. The furniture and kitchenette had a kitsch ex-Soviet feel, and he'd taken to scouring dodgy electronics stalls at the massive Dordoi Bazaar in nearby Bishkek, buying the tackiest fakes he could get his hands on.

Ryan was particularly proud of his Nanasonic bedside iPod dock, bright orange Soni television/karaoke machine and a laptop that was either Dell or Toshiba, depending on whether you read the badge on the lid or the peeling sticker on the keyboard.

The other thing Ryan always picked up in the bazaar

was big bags of scented candles. He struck a match and lit an orange one, both to clear the build-up of damp smells and as a fall-back because the Kremlin's electricity supply faltered at least twice a week.

Kazakov's stuff was everywhere and Ryan hated the idea of having it lying around. He felt sad as he split the dead man's things into two piles. Stuff like clothes, work boots and toiletries got dumped in a black bin bag. Other items like his ivory-handled cut-throat razor, a pair of snazzy Oakley sunglasses and a small plastic wallet of photos got placed into a wheelie bag. Ryan doubted there was anyone who'd actually want Kazakov's stuff, but it seemed wrong throwing out every trace of the man less than a week after he'd died.

In theory it was school time, but Ryan's girlfriend Natalka played truant a lot so he headed to the end of the hallway, hoping to spring a surprise. The odds were always against and it was Natalka's mum, Dimitra, who answered the door.

There were no female loadmasters or mechanics on the Aramov crew roster and Dimitra was one of only three female pilots. She was chunky and acted tough to fit in with the men, but she was a good mother to Natalka, and Ryan reckoned she'd been beautiful when she was younger.

While most aircrew kept their families back in Russia or the Ukraine, Dimitra and Natalka lived in the Kremlin full time. Their room was bigger than the one Ryan had shared with Kazakov and seniority meant that they'd bagged a corner space as far as you can get from the smell of shared toilets. There were also large corner windows and a balcony that was best not walked on, because the concrete was badly cracked and only corroded steel rebars held it in place.

'I didn't mean to wake you,' Ryan said, as Dimitra tied a robe around her waist.

'Oh, I'm flying out in a bit,' Dimitra said, pointing to a tatty pilot's uniform draped over a dining chair, as a coffee pot boiled on an electric ring.

Ryan hid a smile, because the tiny apartment was a good place to hang out with Natalka when Dimitra was off flying.

'Coffee?' Dimitra asked, as she padded across to the stove. 'I heard about your father. I'm really sorry.'

Ryan was surprised Dimitra knew. 'They asked me to keep it quiet,' Ryan said. 'How'd you find out?'

'I've been around the Kremlin a long time,' Dimitra said. 'I don't think many other people know. Have you got plans?'

Ryan shrugged, aware that Dimitra was a useful source of intelligence and that having her take pity on him was good for the mission. 'I made it to our fall-back liaison in New York and they flew me back here. I haven't spoken to anyone properly, but I think the Aramovs are gonna try finding some work for me. Odd jobs, you know?'

Dimitra didn't look satisfied. 'What about family? Mum, aunt, grandparents?'

Ryan shook his head. 'I think I've got some cousins in the Ukraine, but I've never met them. It's always just been me and my dad.'

'Josef Aramov is no genius,' Dimitra said. 'Hiring a plane to terrorists targeting America will bring a lot of heat down on us. This never would have happened if Irena or Leonid Aramov still ran the clan.'

'Is everyone worried about Josef?' Ryan asked.

'There's no confidence in him,' Dimitra said, as she handed Ryan a small cup of Scandinavian-style boiled coffee. 'We've lost eight planes this year. That's ten per cent of the fleet and there's talk of a breakaway group going off to work for Leonid.'

Ryan liked a milky Starbucks latte and the thick black coffee Dimitra had given him felt like acid dripping on his tongue. He knew that the eight lost planes were part of TFU's programme to slowly dismantle the clan, but Dimitra's worries showed there was a real chance that scared aircrews might return home or, worse, disappear with a bunch of planes and form a breakaway smuggling outfit.

'Has anyone heard from Leonid since his mum lopped his ear off and told him to leave the country?' Ryan asked.

'Foul man,' Dimitra spat. 'I was never close to Leonid, but he's a cunning fox. He has many friends still inside the Kremlin.'

'I heard he might be in Russia,' Ryan said.

'Then you heard more than me,' Dimitra replied, as she drained her coffee. 'I'll be back on Friday and I'll see what I can do to help with your situation. Natalka will be home from school soon, but now I must get dressed, yes?'

Ryan took the hint and went down to the lobby to wait. Natalka had a mobile, but the clan made sure there was no phone signal around the Kremlin. Ryan ordered a Coke and a plate of food from the bar. In best Soviet tradition, there was only ever one meal on the menu and today it was tomato soup, followed by a pizza that had been cooked hours earlier and then microwaved until the cheese had the texture of a dog's chew toy.

'Hey,' Natalka said, when she jumped off the school bus. She wore four layers under a huge puffa jacket, but you could still tell that the fourteen-year-old had a good figure and a cute freckled nose above her scarf line.

Leonid Aramov's eleven-year-old son Andre also said hello as he stepped down into the snow. But Ryan was only interested in Natalka.

'I'm so sorry about your dad,' Natalka said, as she stroked Ryan's hair and gave him a kiss. 'You must feel like crap.'

'Better now I'm back with you,' Ryan said, welling up as he pulled Natalka in for a proper snog.

Dimitra probably still hadn't left for her flight, so they raced up to Ryan's room. Once Natalka had thrown off her outdoor clothes, they rolled around on the bed snogging for ages, ending up snuggled together in near darkness. They listened to a gale that made the Kremlin creak while a *Transformers* cartoon played on the TV because neither of them could be arsed to stand up and hunt the remote.

'We could run away,' Natalka said, longing but not serious as she tickled Ryan's ankle with a plum-coloured big toenail. 'Your dad's gone. My mum doesn't care.'

Ryan laughed. 'Your mum's great, she loves you to bits.'

'Yeah,' Natalka said dreamily. 'But imagine if we made it to somewhere warm. Strolling in the sun, eating in nice restaurants, lying on a beach.'

'Screwing,' Ryan said, as he pushed a hand between Natalka's thighs.

She blocked the move, politely but firmly, and compensated with a kiss. 'When we get somewhere warm,' Natalka said. 'Then we'll see about that.'

Ryan was frustrated, but figured he was doing OK for a fourteen-year-old. 'They sell sunlamps in the bazaar,' he joked.

'Oh you're funny,' Natalka said, as she stood up. 'I haven't eaten. Have you got eggs in your fridge?'

Natalka had unbuttoned her jeans and they slipped down to her knees as she bent over the fridge, giving Ryan a flash of skimpy purple knickers and butt cheeks.

'Eggs,' Natalka beamed, bobbing up with an egg box in one hand while yanking up her jeans with the other. 'I'm making omelettes.'

Natalka was sexy and funny, and Ryan loved being with her, but he wasn't enjoying the moment as much as he'd hoped because he knew he had to be back on campus within six weeks . . .

20. ANDRE

Eleven-year-old Andre Aramov was the grandson of dying clan head Irena, and the son of thuggish Leonid Aramov, who'd been expelled from the clan minus his left ear after killing his sister and attempting to kill his mother.

But although he bore the clan's much-feared name, Andre had a gentle nature spawned from his mum Tamara. Both had been allowed to stay at the Kremlin when Leonid and Andre's older brothers Boris and Alex vanished into exile.

Andre wasn't the kind of kid Ryan would have chosen to hang out with, but only a dozen school-aged kids lived in the Kremlin, so there wasn't a huge choice.

Although Andre could act babyish, there were upsides to hanging out with him. As an Aramov, Andre had access to the top floor, which was hardly palatial but definitely a step up from the grimy rooms below. The fifth floor also offered fast Internet, three hundred satellite TV channels and Andre's near-infinite supply of PlayStation games.

Once they got to their teens, Kremlin kids took a relaxed attitude to attending school, but on his third day back, Ryan had boarded the school bus with Natalka and she'd accepted Andre's invite to come upstairs and watch a movie after school.

'Why'd you agree to that?' Ryan whispered to Natalka, as they crunched through snow into the Kremlin lobby with Andre racing ahead. 'After school is make-out time.'

'I'm a privilege you earn, not a right,' Natalka said, only half serious. 'Plus, there's still ten cartons of Leonid Aramov's cigarettes in the flat and I'm out of cash for the vending machine.'

Ryan tutted instinctively. He was crazy about Natalka, but her two worst traits were smoking and doing whatever it took to get what she wanted, whether it was flirting with an older guy to get drinks bought for her, or accepting Andre's invites so she could steal cigarettes.

'What are you tutting for?' Natalka said irritably. 'Keep that up and I'll give you something to tut about.'

Ryan was so into Natalka that he felt like he was being stabbed when she said something mean. But it got better when they got into the lift and she pushed her hand up the back of his coat and grabbed his bum.

'Hey, Mum, I've got company!' Andre shouted as he led the way into a top-floor apartment that was comfortable, but hardly the palatial quarters you might expect for a family that the CIA reckoned had made a couple of billion during thirty years' hardcore smuggling.

'Are you staying to eat?' Tamara asked.

Andre's mum had a slightly oriental appearance and was barefoot, in a short black dress. Looking after Andre was her whole life and she spoiled her only son with brilliant food and every toy and gadget he could wish for.

'I could definitely eat,' Natalka said, as she hooked up her coat.

Andre was already in his bedroom setting up a three-player FIFA 12 tournament and the next couple of hours passed pleasantly, with games, discreet snogging and the smell of roast duck wafting from the kitchen.

'Smells nice,' Amy said, when she arrived in the doorway.

While Ryan and Kazakov had infiltrated the clan at grass roots level, Amy had come in at the top, posing as a girlfriend for new clan head, Josef Aramov. Josef had spent most of his life as a glorified handyman around the Kremlin. But with his mother dying, his sister murdered and brother Leonid in exile, Josef was the last adult Aramov standing. TFU asked him to become a puppet leader when they took control of the clan and Josef had agreed, in return for immunity from prosecution and a new identity when the mission was over.

'I need to speak to Ryan for a moment,' Amy said. 'After what happened to his father.'

She took Ryan twenty metres down the hallway, well out of the guards' earshot.

'Settling back in OK?' she asked.

Ryan shrugged. 'Not too bad. People are edgy though. Everyone knows it was an Aramov plane that flew out the explosives for the Black Friday attacks. They're worried that the Americans will target their planes.'

'I think we can use that to our advantage,' Amy said. 'I've set up a sting. Four planes will head off to Africa filled with weapons. A UN taskforce led by the USAF will intercept the Aramov planes.'

Ryan looked wary. 'Do you know how spooked everyone is downstairs? There's talk of mutiny. Rumours that Leonid Aramov wants to set up a rival smuggling outfit, taking some of the best planes and crews before Josef runs the clan into the ground.'

'Anything more tangible?' Amy asked.

'Not that I've heard,' Ryan said. 'Kazakov used to drink with a lot of the aircrew, but I'm not that close to them. Have you checked with Dan?'

Dan was an eighteen-year-old clan dogsbody, who Amy had recruited as a spy.

'Dan says the same as you,' Amy said. 'Rumours, nothing concrete.'

'It'd be good if we could find Leonid and take him out,' Ryan said.

'He's an evil bastard,' Amy agreed. 'Leonid will cause trouble wherever he goes and I'd certainly like to track him down, but our priority is to wind down Aramov operations quickly, without tipping off other criminal groups and undermining the intelligence we've gathered on them.

'So the plan is, after four of our planes get seized by the Americans in Africa all the aircrew here will be on edge. Josef will make an announcement, saying that only the most critical operations will take place and that any aircrew who want to go home until this blows over are welcome to do so, and will receive full pay.'

'With their planes?' Ryan asked.

'Don't be daft,' Amy said. 'The planes stay here. The crews will get their pay for a few months, but they'll never come back.'

'Makes sense,' Ryan said.

'Frankly, Ryan, once this plan is in place I won't really need you here.'

Ryan gulped. 'Until Christmas, at least,' he begged.

Amy smiled. 'Don't worry, you'll get your six weeks. But don't go letting this thing with Natalka get too heavy. You've got to leave eventually and you'll wind up going back to campus with a broken heart.'

Ryan looked like he'd been slapped. 'I know we're trained to keep our emotions under control,' he said. 'But I think I'm in love with Natalka. I didn't mean for it to happen, but it did.'

Amy put a soothing hand on Ryan's shoulder. 'You're far from the first CHERUB agent this has happened to. Teenagers fall in love easily and no amount of training can get around that.'

Ryan shuddered. 'I'm trying to keep it out of my mind because I don't want to ruin what I have with Natalka by thinking about the end all the time.'

Amy didn't get her reply in because a door clicked behind them. Tamara was walking along the hallway.

'I have a lot of roast duck,' Tamara said. 'Amy, would you like to stick around for dinner?'

Amy had only had good experiences of Tamara's cooking and smiled. 'Absolutely.'

*

After stuffing themselves, Ryan and Natalka headed downstairs and Andre went to his room to watch TV. With her husband gone, Tamara led an isolated existence and seemed grateful for Amy's company. The two women shared a bottle of wine over dinner and ended up sloshed as they stood in the kitchen stacking the dishwasher.

'I know you're more than Josef's girlfriend,' Tamara said quietly.

Amy looked startled. 'What do you mean?'

'I made a stupid mistake marrying Leonid Aramov,' Tamara said. 'But I'm not a stupid person. I overheard you speaking with Ryan. I know Irena went to America for cancer treatment. Josef can barely string three sentences together and you're here to control him, on behalf of whichever government you work for.'

'I see,' Amy said. She wasn't entirely surprised that Tamara knew some of what was going on, but she was curious to know why she'd chosen to mention it now.

'You told Ryan that you wanted to catch Leonid,' Tamara said.

Amy didn't understand how this had been possible. You were either in the corridor, or you weren't, unless . . .

'Is there a listening device?' Amy asked.

'Leonid bugged most rooms on this floor,' Tamara said. 'You don't need to worry. I'm the only one that knows about it.'

'OK,' Amy said, feeling a little shaken. 'What is it you want?'

'After the Aramov Clan is gone, I'll be left with my son. I have little money and no home of my own. Leonid has wanted me since I was fifteen years old. If he's alive he'll come after me. Even when we divorced, he made me stay here because he didn't want anyone else to have me.'

'Relocating you would be possible,' Amy said. 'I'm not talking about a fortune, but new identities and enough money to get you on your feet.'

'I have family in Russia,' Tamara said. 'Mother, brothers, nephews, nieces. Even if I disappear, Leonid can find me by threatening them.'

'I don't see how we can protect an entire family,' Amy admitted.

'I know you can't,' Tamara said. 'But you want to get Leonid and I want him out of my life. I'm sure I can help you.'

Amy looked curious as Tamara picked a tub of dishwasher tablets out of a cupboard.

'Do you know where Leonid is?' she asked.

Tamara shook her head. 'It won't be that simple. But before Irena kicked Leonid out he was pressuring me to marry him again. If Leonid thought I needed help, I'm sure he'd reach out.'

'What do you have in mind?' Amy asked.

'Maybe if I was in some sort of danger, or if Leonid heard I'd been kicked out of the Kremlin and had no money. Something like that.'

'But you'd still have no way to let him know,' Amy said.

'Not directly,' Tamara said. 'Irena made sure that all Leonid's people got kicked out of the Kremlin, but she didn't know everything. Leonid was paranoid and there's a guy he used to check up on his own people, to make sure they weren't ripping him off. He's still around, and if Leonid has a spy inside the Kremlin, I'd bet on it being him.'

Now Amy sounded keen. 'So what's this guy's name?'

21. PROFILE

There were a couple of offices in use on the Kremlin's fourth floor, but nobody worked weekends so Amy called Ryan up to see her there first thing on Saturday morning. They met in a cobwebbed operations room, dominated by a vast map table on which generals had once plotted the movements of the Soviet spy planes for which the airfield had been built.

'You smell like wet dog,' Amy said, as Ryan came in dressed in squelching Nikes, with a sweatshirt over a full tracksuit.

'Outdoor weights and a five K run,' Ryan explained. 'Brutal in this cold, but I don't wanna fail my fitness assessment when I get back to campus.'

'You certainly don't,' Amy said, smiling. 'I got lazy on one of my early jobs. Had to do two months of six a.m. fitness training before I got mission-ready status back.'

'Speaking of lazy, have you swept *this* room for bugs?' Ryan asked cheekily.

Amy smiled through gritted teeth. 'My bad,' she admitted.

'We all make mistakes,' Ryan said. 'This one might even have helped us. At least I assume that's why you called me up here.'

'Igor Mutko,' Amy began, as she slid a plastic document wallet across to Ryan. 'This is the guy Tamara thinks has links to Leonid Aramov.'

There was a photograph of a typically Russian man on the first sheet inside the folder. He was in his early thirties, well built, fairly handsome, with a foppish blond fringe worthy of a boy band.

'I've seen him around the Kremlin,' Ryan said. 'Always friendly, buys a *lot* of drinks. Kazakov played poker with him a few times.'

Amy nodded, as Ryan flicked through pages of printouts. She'd dug up some of Igor's Russian military records, but there wasn't much to show apart from national service and a rejected recommendation letter for a bravery medal.

'No obvious reason why Leonid would pick this guy to be his spy,' Ryan noted.

'It's possible Igor was in the FSB – the Russian Federal Security Bureau,' Amy said. 'We can't get hold of FSB records. But if Leonid is using Igor, it's safe to assume he's good at what he does.'

'What's Igor's official job at the Kremlin?' Ryan asked.

'That's another reason why I'm convinced Tamara's

right about Igor being Leonid's spy,' Amy said. 'He draws a salary as a member of a de-icing team.'

Ryan laughed: there was a constant battle to keep the Kremlin's runway in service and stop ice building up on aircraft wings during winter. But while Kremlin pilots and mechanics were mostly Russian and Ukrainian, this menial job which involved hard labour in foul weather was done by a team of Kyrgyz peasants.

'He's nicely dressed whenever I've seen him,' Ryan noted. 'No way he's a de-icing guy. That lot only come into the Kremlin to collect their wages and they're proper rough.'

'I suppose we should have been suspicious before,' Amy said. 'But I've never been through the Kremlin payroll in detail.'

Ryan shook his head sympathetically. 'There's over three hundred aircrew based here on and off. Plus mechanics, cooks, admin, maintenance, family members. At least seven hundred people in and out of the Kremlin at different times. You can't track all of them. At least not without making it obvious that we're spying on them.'

'We need to find out how Igor gets in touch with Leonid,' Amy said. 'Communications inside the Kremlin are locked down tight: Internet restricted, phone lines tapped, no cellphone masts.'

'There's at least a hundred web cafés in Dordoi Bazaar,' Ryan said. 'More in the centre of Bishkek. And you've only got to drive a couple of kilometres out of the valley to pick up a phone signal.'

'I asked around discreetly,' Amy said. 'Igor's a man who tries to make friends with everyone, like any good spy should. Besides buying lots of drinks and letting people win his money at poker, Dan reckons he's always offering to give people lifts and he's happy to pick stuff up from the bazaar.'

'Stuff?' Ryan asked.

Amy shrugged. 'You know, one of the aircrew has been away for a few days, so he picks up groceries for when they return. Takes clothes to be dry-cleaned. He takes a few som for petrol, or lets them buy him a drink. But it's always handled like a personal favour, rather than a transaction.'

Ryan nodded admiringly. 'It makes Igor seem like a nice guy, and gives him an excuse to ask the pilots what they're up to.'

'So, I got Dan to sound Igor out, saying he needed a part for his car and asking if he was going to the bazaar any time soon. Igor said he was going this afternoon. I want you to see what he gets up to.'

'He'll be suspicious if we follow him there,' Ryan said. 'But the bazaar's so huge it'll be impossible to find him after he's arrived.'

'Already thought of that. Dan gave Igor a broken windscreen wiper motor to make sure that he gets the exact replacement . . .'

Ryan finished Amy's sentence. 'You put a tracking device inside the motor?'

Amy smiled. 'The tracker's only the size of a shirt button. It's only useful over a kilometre or so, but it should allow you to follow Igor around the bazaar without stepping on his heels. Hopefully Igor has been doing this long enough to get comfortable and fall into a routine. Maybe there's a web café Igor uses, or a bar where he regularly connects to Wi-Fi, or a spot where he makes cellphone calls. Once we find that spot, we can intercept his signals, identify his phone and e-mail accounts, and with luck that will lead us to Leonid.'

'What about searching his quarters?' Ryan asked.

'I'll get that taken care of too,' Amy said. 'Though I doubt he'll be stupid enough to leave anything obvious lying around.'

*

Three hours later, Ryan was wandering through Dordoi Bazaar, scoffing a freshly baked naan. Over two kilometres long and a kilometre across, Dordoi was the biggest market in central Asia. As well as serving locals, it was a trading hub for the entire region.

There were over eight thousand pitches. Most comprised stacked metal shipping containers, with the lower container serving as a shop and the upper one used for storage. Saturday was the bazaar's busiest day and the crowds moved at a shuffle.

Ryan felt his phone vibrate. He tucked an ear bud in with his gloved hand before answering. Natalka sounded annoyed.

'Where'd you go?' she moaned. 'It's Saturday, I thought we'd do something *together*.'

Ryan had sneaked out of the Kremlin and jumped into one of the battered taxis that usually ranked out front. He'd assumed she'd call and had his excuse prepared.

'Sorry,' Ryan said sadly. 'I was in my room thinking about my dad. I needed to get out of there.'

'Poor you,' Natalka said. 'Where are you?'

'At the bazaar. I'll bring you back a present.'

'Cigarettes?' Natalka said brightly.

'I'm not feeding your habit,' Ryan said, half-jokingly.

'I could jump in a cab and meet you.'

'No offence, Natalka, but I really feel like being alone. We'll eat together later.'

'OK,' Natalka sighed. 'My mum's not back until tomorrow. We could reheat some more of her soup.'

Ryan laughed. 'It was nice of her to think of me, but frankly I'd rather eat my own toenail clippings.'

'There's four litres of it left,' Natalka said cheerfully. 'We could probably sell it to someone who needs to paint the underside of a boat.'

Ryan was distracted by a beep from the tracking device inside his coat.

'You're breaking up,' he lied. 'I'll see if I can buy a DVD to watch tonight. Love you!'

'Love you,' Natalka said, but Ryan had already hung up.

He backed into a gap between two stacked containers, then took off one thick glove before pulling his iPhone out of his jacket. The tracking receiver in his coat pocket was connected by Bluetooth and he touched the display to open a tracking app.

Although Igor was Ryan's only target, there were two

dots on his phone's screen. Dordoi's rows of metal containers were reflecting the low-powered radio signals and his target was either two hundred metres east, or four hundred north-east. That distance would normally be a minute's walk, but in Dordoi on a busy Saturday even the most ardent pusher-and-shover got nowhere fast.

The bazaar's traders tended to clump together, so all the computer stalls were in one part of the market, all the ones selling pets in another and so on. Ryan caught a break, finding an alleyway specialising in watches and jewellery that was less crowded and enabled him to pick up his pace.

He'd been to the bazaar at least once a week in the seven months he'd lived at the Kremlin, but the rows of containers looked identical and he got disorientated every time. Beyond the jewellery area, wheeled food carts were set along one of the bazaar's main thoroughfares.

The two blips on the iPhone screen mercifully merged as Ryan closed in. The screen said he was less than ten metres from Igor. He glanced about, anxious not to walk into his target, but there was no sign of him.

Finally, Ryan noticed a sign offering haircuts. Traders commonly had family members offering an extra service, like barbering, shoe repair or a nail salon. Often these secondary trades had no connection with the main business, and Ryan spotted his target deep inside a container specialising in teddies and party gear.

Igor had a red-and-white chequered cloth draped over his shoulders as an elderly Kyrgyz man worked his blond head with fast-moving scissors. Ryan backed into the crowd, then leaned against the corrugated side of a container biting chunks of his naan, and occasionally glanced at his watch like he was waiting for someone.

Igor hit fresh air ten minutes later, rubbing a napkin around an itchy neckline before sliding his outdoor coat up his arms and merging into the flow of bodies. The tracker gave Ryan the ability to follow his target out of visual range. But Ryan needed to see what Igor was up to, not just where he was going.

After buying a large bag of fruit and vegetables, Igor grabbed tea and a pastry and ate on the move as he headed to a part of the bazaar that Ryan had never visited. The stalls here were all run by Chinese. Rather than offering actual goods, these traders were wholesalers, who filled their glass display cabinets with samples of everything from 2013 calendars to Hello Kitty alarm clocks.

The crowds were thinner, mostly men in business suits, smoking and haggling. Ryan didn't like it because people his age didn't come here. Everyone stared and he had to drop further behind Igor and rely on the tracker.

After a couple of hundred metres, the wholesale zone merged into an area where over fifty traders sold auto parts. The containers had car company logos painted on the doors and hubcaps swinging precariously from wires strung across the alleyway.

Ryan got close as Igor backed out of a container that sold reconditioned Lada spares. He was baffled when he saw Igor move while the tracker blip stayed still, but Igor was laden with bags and Ryan realised that he must have dumped the faulty wiper motor with the tracker inside, or traded it when he purchased the replacement.

Either way, Ryan now had to rely on his eyes. It would be too risky to follow Igor in visual range for long, but Ryan didn't want to go back to the Kremlin with nothing, so he decided to take a chance and follow Igor for a couple of minutes.

Igor had a backpack and two big shopping bags. Ryan realised he was heading for his old Toyota wagon. But instead of driving off, the Russian locked the shopping in the back before crossing the car park and entering a shabby café alongside the bazaar's metal-canopied bus station.

Once Ryan was sure Igor was staying, he headed inside himself. The café's strip lighting was dazzling after the outdoor cloud. There were fifty tables, but only six customers.

All were men and Ryan got a shock when he noticed a stage at the back with a couple of not-very-attractive women dancing and vaguely making threats to take their tops off. There was also a bar where more women stood about in short skirts and too much make-up. Most were so skinny that Ryan reckoned they had to be drug addicts.

Igor was at a table off to the side of the stage, speaking with another blond Russian who could have been Igor's brother, though he was bigger and had a squashed-up nose. Before Ryan could learn any more a buxom waitress came over and spoke words she'd clearly said a million times before.

'I'm Lulu your hostess, can I get you something to drink?'

'Coke,' Ryan said warily.

'Right you are, sweetie,' Lulu said, jotting something on her pad and pointing towards the bar. 'Any of our girls catching your eye?'

'I just thought it was a normal café,' Ryan explained. 'I don't have to . . . I mean, can I just have a drink while I wait for my bus?'

'Free country,' Lulu said, before crouching down and winking. 'Don't be shy. Call me if you want a girl to come over.'

'Really, I'm great,' Ryan said. 'I've got a girlfriend.'

He felt like adding, *a girlfriend who isn't a prostitute.*

Once the waitress had cleared off, Ryan tried working out what Igor and the squashed nose were up to. They didn't have much to say to each other, but Igor slid some papers across the table and a roll of money in an elastic band went the other way.

Ryan had been looking for some form of electronic communication, but Leonid Aramov had lost most of his fortune when TFU hacked into his online banking. After being bitten once, it made sense that Leonid would revert to more traditional face-to-face communication for his Kremlin spy.

'Coke,' the waitress said, as she banged a bottle and glass on the table, along with a bill for three times what it would have cost in any café that didn't have ugly women dancing about.

Ryan wanted a picture of Igor's companion. The

iPhone would be too obvious, but he had a sugar-cube-sized spy camera in case something cropped up. As Ryan raised the bottle of Coke to his lips, he simultaneously aimed the tiny camera and clicked off three pictures of the Russian.

He only just got them in time. As a belch rose up Ryan's throat from the Coke bubbles, Igor and squashed nose parted with kisses on the cheek. The big dude headed off behind the bar as Igor went for the exit. But before he made it, he took a swerve and came for Ryan.

His tone wasn't angry, but wasn't friendly either. 'I saw you in the mirror when I was having my hair cut. Then again in the parking lot.'

Ryan's guts flipped, but he kept his voice casual and changed the subject to sidestep a *was I or wasn't I following you* type conversation.

'You're Kremlin,' Ryan said, smiling with recognition. 'You played poker with my dad a few times.'

'Kazakov's boy,' Igor said, his tone warming. 'I heard what happened, I'm sorry.'

Ryan shrugged and looked down at his spitting Coke. 'Shit happens.'

'You haven't bought much for someone who's been walking the bazaar for three hours,' Igor noted.

'Gotta keep an eye on my money,' Ryan said. 'Dad left a few thousand, but I don't know when I'll get any more. Just came out to wander. Walls of my room were closing in on me.'

'And you came in here for . . . ?'

'I'd heard you could get a girl in here,' Ryan said.

'Thought it might make me feel better.'

Igor laughed. 'There's a hundred better places than this if you want a girl.'

Ryan spoke quietly. 'I'd happily pay these women to put more clothes on.'

Igor roared with laughter, then stuck a ten-som note on Ryan's table to pay for his Coke. 'You heading back?' he asked. 'You want a lift?'

'For sure,' Ryan said.

22. SQUASHED

'Igor kept asking questions about America, but I didn't give much away,' Ryan told Amy. 'Just that we lost Irena's money and I made it to the liaison in New York on a Greyhound bus.'

They were back in the map-room on the fourth floor and Amy was plugging Ryan's miniature camera into her laptop.

'Hello, stranger,' Amy said excitedly, when the first of Ryan's three photos cropped up.

Ryan moved closer as Amy zoomed in on the dude with the squashed nose.

'Know him?' Ryan asked. 'They're quite alike. Brothers maybe?'

'I don't know if they're related,' Amy said, as she used the track pad to zoom the face. 'But you remember the explosion on the beach?'

'Not something I'm likely to forget,' Ryan said, remembering the first phase of the Aramov mission.

He'd been staying at a beachfront house in California, a few doors from Ethan and Galenka Aramov. His mission was to befriend Ethan and pick up information about the clan. This ended abruptly when two goons rocked up in rubber dinghies, murdered Galenka and blew up her house. Ethan only survived because Ryan helped him escape through a window minutes before a bomb went off.

'After you ran back to our house with Ethan, I crept between the houses and got a glimpse at the two assassins as they left,' Amy explained. 'I'm pretty sure that's one of them.'

Ryan felt a tingle of excitement. This all but confirmed Igor's link to Leonid. 'How certain are you?' he asked.

'Ninety-six point three four per cent,' Amy joked. 'It's a distinctive face, but Ethan got a much better look at the assassins. I'll e-mail the photo to Ted Brasker and he can get Ethan to confirm the ID.'

'And what next?' Ryan asked.

'I'll have to try and find out more about Mr Squashed-Nose, but that'll be hard without more manpower.'

'Can we get someone in?'

Amy shook her head. 'We're supposed to be winding down the Aramov Clan. I'm gonna have a hard time getting extra agents on board for a side mission.'

'I thought Dr D was keen on catching Leonid,' Ryan said.

'Undoubtedly. But she's serving out her last weeks

before forced retirement, with the head of the CIA and the Intelligence Secretary right on her back.'

'What about CHERUB?' Ryan asked. 'Zara was *totally* on our side in the meeting.'

'Could be worth a shot,' Amy said, smiling as she realised this was a decent idea. 'You're more than a pretty face, Ryan.'

Ryan grinned, like you'd expect a teenage boy to grin when a hot girl throws out a compliment.

'Igor wants to be my new best friend,' Ryan said. 'On the drive back to the Kremlin, he wanted to know if I'd heard any gossip. I mentioned that Andre Aramov was a mate. He got excited and told me he'd make it worth my while if I heard anything interesting.'

'Good stuff,' Amy said. 'Tamara's got this idea that Leonid will reach out to her if he hears that she's in trouble.'

'So do I tell Igor she's in trouble?' Ryan said.

Amy shook her head. 'Not yet. Keep friendly with Igor, but don't push too hard or he'll get suspicious. I'll speak to Zara on campus. She's got years of experience and we need to work out how to play this. We want to lure Leonid Aramov out of hiding, but he's utterly ruthless, so we've got to do it in a way that doesn't lead to Andre and Tamara getting killed.'

*

The following morning, Zara Asker knocked on a door in the second-floor staff corridor on CHERUB campus.

'I'm in the nuddy!' James Adams shouted anxiously. 'Gimme two secs.'

James answered the door with dripping hair, a towelling robe and a dour expression.

'How's it going?' Zara asked, as she glanced about. 'You look rough.'

The room was messy, with a brown stain where a coffee mug had been smashed against the wall.

'I'll clean that up,' James said awkwardly.

'I'm more worried about what caused it,' Zara said. 'Are you OK?'

James shrugged. 'My girlfriend, Kerry,' he explained. 'She was supposed to be flying to campus for Christmas once she'd sat her last exam. Now she's saying the flight's too expensive.'

Zara looked surprised. 'If Kerry has financial problems we can look into it. CHERUB supports all its retired agents.'

James shook his head. 'I'm not short of a few quid. I'd pay her fare, no problem. It feels like she doesn't want to be around me any more.'

'There's counsellors on campus if you want to talk it over,' Zara said. 'I don't mean to be unsympathetic, but I've got a full morning and I came here to talk to you about something else.'

'Sorry,' James said, as he picked a couple of china fragments off the carpet and dropped them into a pedal bin. 'You've got four kids and a mental job. The last thing you want to hear about is my love life.'

'I've been hearing good things about your work,' Zara said. 'Ning and Alfie were complimentary about the way you handled the driving course. *Tough but fun*, apparently.

And Mr Pike says it's been really useful having you helping out with training this week. There's going to be a vacancy now that Kazakov's gone. I'd look upon you favourably if you applied.'

James nodded. 'I miss the buzz of CHERUB. I like being back on campus, but I don't think I'm cut out to be a training instructor. You need a certain meanness to put kids through basic training and I don't have it. I think the job would make me miserable.'

Zara nodded. 'I couldn't do it either. But we're looking to replace Kazakov. His role spanned training and mission control. Would you consider a role that mixed the two?'

James smiled, then nodded uncertainly. 'I think Kerry wants to stay in the US for at least a couple more years.'

'We're short-staffed right now,' Zara said. 'I'm happy for you to continue working for CHERUB on a casual basis for another month or two, but I'll need a decision early in the New Year.'

'I'll have a think,' James said.

'I know you've been helping Mr Pike with on-campus training, but there's something else I need you to do. A little side project.'

'What?' James asked.

'You know Amy works for TFU?'

'Yeah,' James said. 'She seemed to be really enjoying herself.'

'TFU is getting axed because of its role in the Black Friday attacks. But Amy wants to track down a guy named Leonid Aramov before the shutters go down and needs our help. I'll send you a briefing with the full background story on Leonid Aramov and TFU's Aramov Clan operation, but it basically boils down to this:

'Amy and I have devised a plan to find Leonid Aramov using his ex-wife and eleven-year-old son as bait. The trouble is, they're likely to encounter moderate danger and neither has any kind of combat or espionage training.'

'So, some kind of express training programme?' James asked.

'MI6 will take care of Tamara,' Zara said. 'They have an established rapid training program designed for diplomats being deployed to high-risk countries. But the only expertise in training a boy like Andre Aramov is here on campus.'

James nodded. 'So I'd be training this kid one-on-one. How long would I get?'

'Ten days,' Zara said. 'That's not enough time to significantly improve strength or fitness levels. You'll need to devise a programme concentrating on essentials. Basic self-defence moves, weapons handling, safe communication protocol. I'll get Mr Pike to help you draw up the programme, and this is high priority so you'll have your pick of resources. If you need other agents or staff on hand, they're yours.'

'Why are you picking me?' James asked warily. 'Aren't there more experienced instructors who'd do a better job?'

Zara smiled. 'First off, Amy says Andre's timid and you have a good rapport with younger kids. I made you godfather to my eldest, after all. Second, Andre's first language is Russian. His English is patchy and Kazakov was my only other Russian-speaking instructor. I'm sorry to throw you in at the deep end, but the training department is stretched supermodel-thin right now.'

23. ROAD

Eight days later

Amy set her alarm for 4:30 a.m., dressed quickly and headed from her bed in Josef Aramov's spare room to his brother Leonid's old quarters down the hallway.

Andre answered the door in pyjamas. Amy squeezed past wheelie bags and backpacks in the hallway and into a kitchen where Tamara stood at the stove warming a saucepan of milk.

'All packed?' Amy asked. 'Don't worry about what you've left. I'll make sure nobody gets in here while you're away.'

Tamara made a big fuss of getting Andre to eat a hot breakfast. 'It'll be weird British food on the plane, Andre. I know how fussy you are.'

But Andre was up three hours earlier than usual and his stomach could only handle a couple of mouthfuls.

Ryan knocked twenty minutes later and Amy gave their plan a final run-through when Andre emerged from the shower.

'It's got to look like you two vanished into thin air to maximise the drama,' Amy began. 'Hoods and gloves on at all times to minimise the chance of you being recognised as you leave. Take the stairs down, go out the rear fire exit, cross country to the stables and up the side of the valley. The ground's icy, so be careful.'

'Aren't you coming with us?' Andre asked.

'Ryan knows the way,' Amy said. 'I'm supposed to be Uncle Josef's girlfriend. Too many questions will get asked if I'm seen helping you two escape. When you get to the top of the valley, there will be a car and driver waiting. He'll have your boarding passes and British passports in false names. It's forty minutes' drive to Manas International. The British Airways flight takes off at eight a.m. We're not expecting difficulties, but an MI6 agent posing as BA cabin crew will meet you once you've passed through security. She'll take you to a VIP room, so that other passengers don't see you before you board the plane.'

'What time do we get to London?' Andre asked.

'The flight is about ten hours,' Amy said. 'But London's eight hours behind so you'll actually arrive around noon. Your instructors will meet you at the airport and take you straight to your training centres.'

Andre gave his mum a nervous glance. Ryan wondered how he'd cope with CHERUB campus, even on a training programme tailored to his needs.

While Tamara sent Andre to his room to make sure he hadn't forgotten anything, Amy backed Ryan up into the hallway.

'Stick around at the airport until the plane leaves and call me if anything goes wrong,' Amy said. 'I've got to go wake Josef up and get him to sign off the Africa plan.'

Amy was following orders to wind down the Aramov fleet. She had to move fast, but not so fast that the clan's most important clients got spooked and blew seven months of intelligence work. Over the previous ten days, she'd arranged for three planes and their crews to do legitimate humanitarian aid flights on a long-term lease. Six more had been impounded at Sharjah in the United Arab Emirates. Officially, a mechanical inspection by the authorities there had shown the planes to be unflightworthy, but actually the clan had been flying dodgy planes in and out of Sharjah for years. It was just that they'd now stopped bribing officials to turn a blind eye.

From a peak of eighty-six large cargo planes, TFU had so far whittled the Aramov fleet down to fifty. Although the Africa plan would only take four more planes out directly, they were going to be seized by the US Air Force while stuffed with illegal weapons. The aircrews would be held in a US military prison, facing lengthy sentences for violating rules on the export of US military technology.

Amy hoped this would scare the daylights out of the remaining Kremlin aircrews and give Josef Aramov a credible reason to temporarily shut down clan operations, without making his client base suspect that the entire operation had been taken over by TFU.

*

'Rough night?' Natalka asked, as she gave Ryan his good-morning kiss in the Kremlin lobby. 'You look like crap.'

'Didn't sleep much,' Ryan said, as he adjusted the school pack hanging off his left shoulder.

Ryan had been up at four, then he'd escorted Andre and Tamara through the snow with way more luggage than they needed, ridden with them to the airport, sat in a grubby terminal drinking bad coffee until the 8 a.m. flight to London was off the ground, then cabbed it back to the top of the valley.

After an icy downhill run and a trip up to his room to put on dry clothes and grab his backpack, Ryan completed his adventure just in time to ride the school bus with Natalka.

'I dreamed about you last night,' Natalka said airily, as they passed the two armed guards on the Kremlin's main door and felt the bite of cold. 'You were riding a horse with no shirt on.'

Ryan laughed. 'I bet that looked *seriously* sexy.'

'Don't get cocky,' Natalka said. 'But it wasn't bad, actually.'

They got on the bus, where a girl of eight had taken their usual seat at the back.

'You want your face punched in?' Natalka growled, bunching her fist and making the girl scuttle off.

Natalka could be a bitch, but Ryan said nothing because he enjoyed their morning bus rides. Natalka's scarf dropped on the floor, and she looped it around both their necks before cuddling up as the mostly empty bus rolled away from the Kremlin.

'Your face is red,' Natalka said. 'Did you go for one of your runs?'

Ryan shook his head. 'I think I'm getting a cold,' he lied. 'You should probably back off if you don't want my germs.'

'If it's going around I'll get it anyway,' Natalka said, surprising Ryan by moving in for a snog.

Her mouth tasted like the two cigarettes she always smoked before school. It was gross, but Ryan had learned that you can put up with a lot when you're in love.

'Mum was going bananas this morning,' Natalka said, breaking away from Ryan as the rear of the bus swung over the edge of the valley on a tight turn.

'That's hardly news,' Ryan said. 'You two fight every morning.'

'She wasn't having a go at *me* for once,' Natalka said. 'One of the other pilots screwed his landing last night.'

Ryan nodded with recognition. 'Just after midnight? I heard a bang. They even had that rattly old fire truck out, just in case.'

'Tore up his undercarriage. Three days minimum to fix it. So my mum only got in late last night, but this morning she gets a call saying she's gotta fly off to Africa.'

Ryan jolted in shock.

'What?' Natalka asked.

'Nothing,' Ryan said unconvincingly. Then to cover his tracks, 'Bet she'll be in a fouler mood when she gets back as well.'

Natalka had no idea that her mother's plane was about to pick up a load of US-made weapons in Pakistan. Halfway to Congo, Dimitra would see a pair of F18 fighters cruise up beside her plane and order her to land at the nearest US airbase. After forced landings, the crews of the four planes would be placed in military custody, charged with trafficking in classified US technology and thrown in a military prison facing thirty-year prison sentences.

For Ryan's sake, Amy had arranged things so that Natalka's mum had an earlier flight too close for her to get picked for the Africa operation, but she could only steer what went on by telling Josef Aramov what orders to give. She didn't control minor operational details, like who got drafted in if a plane was wrecked.

Ryan wondered what to do. Cellphones didn't work at the Kremlin, but if he bunked out of school he might be able to contact Amy on a landline. But even if he did that, how could they pull Dimitra off the mission right before take-off without it seeming horribly suspicious?

Natalka watched Ryan staring intently out of the window and gave him a nudge. 'Earth to Ryan? Anybody home?'

'Eh?'

'You're acting *so* weird today,' Natalka said.

Ryan looked at Natalka and imagined her face red and tear-streaked when she found out that her mum was in prison halfway around the world.

'Just . . . Sorry . . . My head's not right this morning.'

24. JOSEF

Ryan had sneaked into a school office and called Amy, but the four crews were set for take-off and there was no credible way to pull Dimitra's flight.

Kremlin kids attended a Russian-speaking school on the outskirts of Bishkek. Facilities were primitive and the building was giving way to damp and mould. Ryan sat through double maths, history, lunch, science and art, feeling like a bomb was ticking and wondering what the chances were of something going wrong with the Africa mission.

It should have been an enjoyable evening, cooking a simple supper with Natalka and curling up on Dimitra's double bed listening to music, with the grouchy mechanic in the next room occasionally slamming his palm against the wall, urging them to turn it down.

'Stop moaning, you old fart,' Natalka shouted, as she

banged back. 'I've put up with your snoring every night for the last five years.'

Ryan laughed. Natalka knelt on the bed, one striped sock, black knickers, white singlet and no bra. Ryan loved her desperately, but his mind was in faraway sky imagining F18s and Ilyushins, and Natalka's mum laid out on the runway with a camouflage-clad Yank aiming a rifle at her. The bedside clock told him that the scene he kept imagining had probably played out about an hour earlier.

'No parents,' Natalka said, as she put her head in Ryan's lap. 'You wanna sleep here?'

For all the time they'd been seeing each other, Ryan and Natalka had never actually spent the night together. Ryan wasn't sure if Natalka was hinting that she wanted to have sex. The prospect excited him, but while he was a virgin, Natalka had knocked about with some older boys. He suspected she'd had sex before, and was scared that he'd do it all wrong. And if he did, Natalka was the kind of girl who'd laugh her arse off rather than show any sympathy . . .

'I guess I could stay here,' Ryan said. 'Are we talking about . . . ?'

'No we're *not*,' Natalka said firmly, and Ryan was kind of relieved. 'My mum's got vodka though. What say we get hammered and blow off school tomorrow?'

Ryan laughed as Natalka rolled a bottle of cheap Russian vodka out from under the bed. 'Get the Pepsi and some glasses.'

It should have been great, but Ryan felt like puking.

Just after 9 p.m., the Kremlin PA started gurgling. The system was a relic from Soviet days and most of the funnel-shaped wall speakers either didn't work or had been ripped off. The closest one to Natalka's room was down the far end of a hallway by the toilets and you could barely hear it.

'What's it saying?' Ryan asked, cupping his ear. 'Something about the assembly point.'

'Probably drunks pissing about,' Natalka said. 'If it's anything important they set off the fire alarm.'

Natalka's comment coincided with the fire alarm and they both laughed.

'And there you have it,' Natalka said, a touch drunk. 'Confirmation of my genius.'

'Best move, in case it is a fire,' Ryan said, knowing it wasn't as he reached for the floor and threw Natalka her jeans.

If it was a fire, they'd have to go outside, so they put on shoes and hit the hallway pulling on their warm coats and making sure they had gloves. The fire alarm automatically locked out the lifts and they merged into bodies going down the stairs.

There was no panic, and Ryan and Natalka quickly picked up rumours that everyone was being brought down to the lobby for some big announcement.

'Nat-al-kaaaa!' a guy called Vlad said, as he rudely pushed a couple of people out of the way.

Vlad was eighteen, a fair-haired Russian. He was the son of a loadmaster and had a reputation for being not too bright.

There wasn't much to do at the Kremlin, but there was a big stack of outdoor weights in the yard out back and a lot of young guys were into bodybuilding. Ryan had bulked up there himself, but mainly used the weights for fitness and as an excuse to pick up gossip from the older guys. Vlad was at the other extreme and had reached his present size with the help of serious steroids.

'Well, well,' Natalka said acidly. 'All the bugs are crawling out of the woodwork.'

Vlad and Natalka had gone out with each other in the past. Ryan didn't know the details, but found the four-year age gap paedo-ish.

'I'm surprised you and Ryan are still an item,' Vlad said.

Vlad left his comment hanging, but resumed when Natalka didn't take the bait.

'I heard Ryan went for a stroll on Saturday. Dirty little boy wound up in the café by the bus station.'

Ryan gulped. 'You're talking out of your arse.'

But Natalka was intrigued, because Ryan *had* disappeared on Saturday afternoon and she'd given him a weird look when he'd arrived back in Igor's car without a single item of shopping.

'Which bitch did you go for?' Vlad teased. 'Scabby Su-Ling? Licey Lucy? VD Valenka?'

Igor spent a lot of time in the Kremlin bar and must have flapped his mouth when he was drunk.

'I had a Coke and I left,' Ryan said, slowing right down as more people joined the staircase from the first floor.

But Natalka looked pissed off. 'That place is way over by the bus station. There's no bus to the Kremlin, so how'd you end up there?'

'I wandered all over,' Ryan said. 'I wandered for hours.'

Vlad could see Natalka wasn't convinced by Ryan's excuse and moved for the kill. 'You can't go in that place *without* knowing what it is,' Vlad said. 'There's pictures of girls on the outside. You'd have to be blind.'

This was true, though Ryan hadn't noticed because the signs were at an oblique angle from the car park, and he'd had to stay out of sight so that Igor didn't see him. But he couldn't tell Natalka the truth.

'Those girls are *so* disgusting,' Vlad said, as Ryan tried thinking what to say. 'Half of 'em are on heroin. I don't know how you could have done the dirty there, Ryan!'

'I didn't do anything,' Ryan snapped, losing his cool. 'And you're one to talk about drugs, steroid boy!'

Vlad laughed and pointed at Ryan's crotch. 'I'm telling you, Natalka, I'd have that boy checked for lice before you let him near you again.'

'I only drank a Coke,' Ryan said.

By this time they'd reached the bottom of the stairs. The bar had been shuttered in preparation for the big announcement and the whole ground floor was packed with bodies. Ryan got a few steps clear of Vlad and looked pleadingly into Natalka's furious eyes.

'You can't possibly wander in that place without knowing what it is,' Natalka said.

'My dad just died,' Ryan said. 'I was tearing over.

I don't really know what I was doing.'

Natalka's eyes narrowed. She tried to step back, but there were too many people around. 'I know you were sad, but I can't *believe* you thought going into a place like that would make you feel better.'

Vlad had come back towards them, wearing a huge smile. 'Here, Ryan, did you pay the extra to shag her without a condom?'

Ryan was angry enough to lash out, but the crowd and the fact that Vlad had biceps bigger than his thighs held him back.

'Vlad's stirring it,' Ryan told Natalka. 'He fancies you. Who wouldn't, you're gorgeous!'

Natalka half smiled, but she still looked furious and scowled when Ryan tried a kiss.

'The entire male species makes me sick,' Natalka said, holding her hands out. '*Don't* touch me.'

'Bad luck, dirty boy!' Vlad said, giving Ryan a cheeky wink.

'Why don't you go after a girl your own age?' Ryan spat. 'Pervert.'

While this was going on, the rest of the crowd had quietened down, parting as Josef Aramov came out of the lift, with fake girlfriend Amy a step behind. Josef cut an unusual figure for the head of a billion-dollar criminal network. Tall and slim, with a long beard, dressed in jeans that had shrunk and a matching denim jacket.

When he reached the bar, Josef balanced on a padded bench and turned to face a crowd closing in to hear. Amy usually made sure Josef stayed out of the limelight because he didn't make a very credible leader. TFU had made him leader because they needed a figurehead and he was the only adult Aramov who wasn't dying or on the run. Unfortunately, this announcement was so critical that it couldn't come from anyone else.

'Four planes left for the Congo this morning,' Josef mumbled.

Half the three-hundred-strong crowd couldn't hear and there was an outbreak of shushing and bodies moving closer.

'I have received information that these planes were forced to land by fighters operating for the United States Air Force.'

Gasps erupted. Ryan looked at Natalka but she'd yet to grasp what this meant.

'The heat is on us,' Josef said dramatically, as he used a monogrammed handkerchief to wipe his brow. 'There will be a break, to take the pressure off.'

Josef left this hanging and looked down at Amy as if he'd forgotten his lines. Amy realised that feeding Josef lines would make it clear to everyone that he was a puppet. Taking over herself wasn't ideal either, but she had no choice.

'The crews have been arrested. They will be taken back to the United States,' Amy said.

Natalka finally understood and shrieked, 'No!'

There were mutterings in the crowd, and broad agreement on the cause of their problems: renting a plane to IDoJ had been stupid. Irena had made a mistake kicking Leonid out of the Kremlin and Josef should have stuck to pottering around changing light bulbs and fixing leaky pipes.

Amy nudged Josef, forcing him to speak again. 'All crews are to go home,' Josef said quietly. 'No operation until this business dies down. All aircrew collect three months' pay. Go to your families. Leave your details and you'll be contacted when this is over.'

The magnitude of this silenced the crowd. Ryan had pictured Natalka red-faced and tearful, but she was ghost-white, with shoulders trembling.

'I'm so sorry,' Ryan said, reaching out to put an arm around her back.

But Natalka shoved him away and bolted for the stairs. As the rest of the crowd broke silence and started asking questions about when they'd get their pay and how they'd be able to get home, Ryan chased Natalka upstairs.

'Natalka,' Ryan shouted. 'Don't run away. I'm here for you. I love you.'

'You're a rotten horny bastard like every other male on this planet,' Natalka screamed as she slammed the door of her room in Ryan's face. 'Leave me alone. I hate you.'

Ryan stood outside the door as Natalka began sobbing.

'Please,' Ryan said gently. 'You can't be on your own now. Maybe it'll work out OK for your mum.'

There was a huge crash as Natalka threw something heavy against the door.

25. GUTS

It was 4 p.m. in the UK. Andre Aramov had arrived on CHERUB campus ninety minutes earlier and came out of an examination room in the medical building in his underpants.

'How'd it go?' James asked, speaking Russian that was rusty from lack of practice.

'OK,' Andre said weakly, as he stepped up to an office chair with his clothes folded over the back and began pulling a vest over his head.

CHERUB was a highly selective organisation. The kids it picked for training were outgoing and had physical and mental courage. Andre was a very different creature, staring at the floor like he was scared of his own shadow.

'Can I call my mum?' he asked.

James smiled. 'You left her at the airport less than four hours ago, and you spoke to her in the car.'

'I wondered if she'd arrived at her training place yet.'

James had to make a choice. He could be gentle and try coaxing Andre out of his shell, or he could act tough and hope that Andre manned up. Trouble was, it was only a ten-day training programme and there'd be no second shot if Andre had a meltdown.

'So have you got any special talents?' James asked. 'And not stuff like touching the tip of your nose with your tongue, I mean stuff that might be useful when you're undercover.'

To make his point, James poked his tongue out and curled it up to the tip of his nose. Andre smiled awkwardly as he sat on the chair to pull his socks back on.

'I can pick pockets,' Andre said, after a moment's silence. 'My dad taught me when he wanted me to steal something off my Uncle Josef.'

'Could be useful,' James said, as he tossed Andre a plain orange T-shirt that was too big for him. 'You'll need to wear this orange shirt at all times. You're not allowed to talk to any kids you see, and they're not allowed to talk to you.'

'This place is for training kids?' Andre asked.

'Pretty much.'

'For what?'

'Same kind of thing you're doing,' James lied.

'And the different colour shirts,' Andre said, as he pulled the orange shirt over his vest. 'The little kids wear red. A lot of the biggest kids wear black T-shirts. But it can't *just* be an age thing because I've seen some younger kids in black, and some older kids wearing grey.'

James smiled. He could work on Andre's timidity, but you can't improve a person's basic intelligence and the kid clearly had a decent brain.

As James considered this, a nurse pushed a trolley into the room. Its top shelf bore two sets of sterile tweezers on a stainless-steel tray, glass mixing beakers, distilled water, stirrers, and some sachets of powder.

'Are you two ready to have your com moulds taken?' the nurse asked.

Andre looked baffled, so James explained. 'We use a miniature communication system buried inside your ear canal. It's got a range of a couple of kilometres. We'll use it during your training, and possibly during the hunt for your dad too.'

The nurse began a mixing process, tapping two powder sachets into one of the beakers. When she added a few drops of water, the compounds began to hiss and bubble.

'That's going in my ear?' Andre asked James. 'Does it hurt?'

'I've never had it done,' James admitted, as he looked at the nurse warily.

'Why not?' Andre asked.

'I've been away for a few years,' James explained. 'Deep ear com is a new system. We had to make do with lapel microphones and earpieces in my day.'

The nurse kept stirring the mixture until it stopped bubbling and formed a gloopy grey paste.

'I've not killed anyone doing this yet,' the nurse said.

'I need you both to place an elbow on the desk, then tilt your head so that it's resting nice and steady on your shoulder. Once I tip the gloop in, you need to just rock your heads *very* gently to make sure it goes all the way down. OK?'

James looked at Andre. 'Did you get that?'

'My English is as good as your Russian,' Andre said.

'James first,' the nurse said, moving forward as James tilted his head.

As the fizzing was right next to James' eardrum, the sound was deafening, and he hadn't realised the chemical reaction between the two powders had made them warm.

Andre faced James as they sat next to each other with heads tilted. Andre pushed his tongue out and tried touching his nose. James smiled, but the nurse didn't like it.

'It sets in thirty seconds,' she said. 'But if you muck about I'll have to do it again.'

'I think the nurse has a nice bottom,' James said, speaking in Russian.

The nurse didn't understand, but Andre's smirk meant she knew he'd said something cheeky. She looked grumpy as she tweezered out the set ear moulds and dropped them into sample jars.

'Free to go,' the nurse said. 'The com units should be back from the laboratory within twenty-four hours. Make an appointment for Wednesday. I'll fit them and show you how to use the system and keep everything sterile.'

*

Amy found Ryan as he headed back downstairs.

'Natalka's a mess,' Ryan said solemnly. 'She won't let me near her.'

'She's in shock, she'll calm down.'

'It's more complex than that,' Ryan said. 'That dick Vlad told Natalka that I was at the brothel by the bus station.'

Amy looked confused. 'You went to a brothel?'

'The place where Igor met Squashed-Nose.'

'Oh *shit*,' Amy said, glancing around because she wasn't supposed to be seen with Ryan. 'I'll see if there's anything I can do to help Dimitra. But right now, you need to get down to the bar and talk to Igor. After what's happened tonight, he'll be sure to head off to the bazaar and pass a message on first thing tomorrow. I want to make sure Leonid finds out about Andre and Tamara too.'

'That's where I was heading,' Ryan said. 'What's the atmosphere like down there?'

'Some people's friends have been busted and they're drowning their sorrows. The rest think they've got three months' paid holiday and they're getting drunk celebrating.'

Ryan saw what Amy meant when he got down to the lobby. People had come down for the meeting, stayed to gossip and started drinking. On a good night there were thirty people in the bar, but now every one of a hundred seats had a bum on it, with more propped on tables and armrests, and a few even spilling out into the adjoining lobby.

Igor was at the heart of it all, holding court at a large oval table covered in empty glasses and vodka bottles. Ryan had to fight his way around the back of the table before crouching and whispering in Igor's ear.

'You asked me to tell you if I heard something. Can I speak somewhere quiet?'

Igor looked irritated. 'Now?' he asked.

'It's about Andre and Tamara.'

Igor raised one curious eyebrow, stubbed out a cigarette and drained his glass in two gulps before pushing his chair back.

'Excuse me, I have a little business to conduct.'

'You want Igor to give you another lift to the bus station, eh, Ryan?' Vlad shouted.

Ryan gave Vlad the finger as Igor took him out of the bar and into a grimy spot under the back stairs.

'Five thousand som for good information,' Ryan said. 'Is that still our deal?'

'For *good* information, yes.'

'Tamara and Andre have left the Kremlin.'

Igor looked shocked. 'Pardon me?'

'I got a call,' Ryan explained. 'Andre was really scared. His mum was in tears. Apparently Josef went for her.'

Igor seemed unsure. 'Went for her how? With a knife?'

'She was crying her eyes out,' Ryan explained. 'I think maybe Josef tried to rape her. Tamara never said, but she was bawling and shit. So she had a car booked from the top of the valley, but they couldn't carry all their suitcases and I agreed to help.'

'Did they say where they were going?'

'It seemed like a big secret,' Ryan said. 'But Andre let slip that they had plane tickets.'

Igor glanced at his watch. 'What time was this? What time is their flight?'

'I expect they're long gone,' Ryan said.

'But you have to check in and wait, and do security,' Igor said anxiously. 'When did they get in the car?'

'Maybe five fifteen, this morning,' Ryan said.

Igor was anxiously tugging his fringe and Ryan knew why: Leonid Aramov would go mental when he found out that his beloved ex-wife had left the Kremlin without his inside man knowing anything about it.

'Why are you telling me this *now*?' Igor shouted.

'When I got back it was school time.'

'School,' Igor spat.

Ryan was in a shitty mood, but the throbbing veins in Igor's neck cheered him a little.

'So do I get my five thousand som now?' Ryan asked.

'Five thousand if you tell me *straight away*,' Igor said, practically foaming at the mouth. 'You waited sixteen hours, and have no idea where they've gone.'

'I didn't know it was that important to you,' Ryan said.

'Here's a thousand,' Igor said, taking a roll of money out of his pocket and peeling off a pair of five-hundred-som notes.

Ryan stared at the money with contempt. 'You didn't say anything about timing. I've betrayed my friend Andre's trust for less than it takes to buy a week's groceries.'

'I said the information has to be useful,' Igor said. 'And information is less useful if it's late, dumbass. You're lucky I'm giving you anything at all.'

'Andre's on my Facebook,' Ryan said. 'He's not the smartest kid in the world so I might be able to find out where he's flown to.'

'For that you get five thousand.'

Ryan sneered. 'I'd rather not work for people who don't keep their promises.'

Igor shook his head as he peeled off the missing four thousand and pressed it into Ryan's palm. 'You're pushing your luck,' he said, wagging a finger. 'You're just a kid. Daddy's dead. You've got no source of income and no friends around here.'

26. TRAINING

Although Andre would be training on campus for the next ten days, James had been ordered to keep him apart from other kids. So Andre wound up sleeping on the fold-out sofa in James' quarters.

When James woke on Tuesday morning, he opened one eye and saw Andre standing by his landline phone, trying to read the instructions for dialling out, with the oversized orange shirt down to his knees.

'Not been away from your mum before?' James asked, making Andre jump. 'Don't they have school trips and stuff in Kyrgyzstan?'

Andre shrugged. 'Half the kids at my school in Bishkek couldn't even afford lunch. My dad took me to Tokyo Disneyland once, but he kept losing his temper and ruined it.'

James looked at the clock and saw that it was nearly

7 a.m. 'We'd better shift. I've got the firing range booked for seven forty-five. If you dial 8, you'll get the kitchen. Tell 'em we're on seclusion status and they'll send up whatever we want.'

'What about my mum?'

'You can call her tonight,' James said. 'Once a day is enough and you'll be able to tell her about your day.'

'OK,' Andre said, picking up the receiver, but stalling before dialling 8. 'I don't know what they have.'

James shrugged. 'Cooked breakfast, cereal, juice, tea, coffee. I'm in the mood to be a pig, so order me some chocolate chip pancakes, with a side of mango slices. Black coffee and some freshly squeezed orange juice.'

'Chocolate pancakes,' Andre said, smiling. 'I've never had pancakes for breakfast.'

'Give 'em a go then,' James said, as he rolled out of bed scratching under his armpit. 'And I'll have to get you a couple of smaller T-shirts. That thing looks like a dress.'

James went for a quick shave and shower and was surprised when he came out to find a sixteen-year-old navy shirt wheeling in two stacks of chocolate pancakes.

'Jake Parker on punishment in the kitchen,' James said, smiling. 'Not like you to be in trouble.'

Jake smirked. 'And you were an angel in your day, weren't you, James?'

'Do we need to tip room service?' Andre asked.

James laughed. 'Yeah, I've got a tip for Jake. Get a new hairstyle, it looks shit.'

Jake smiled as he backed out of the room. 'Next time

I deliver your breakfast, I'll spit in it.'

Andre joined the laughter as he pulled a chair up. James sat opposite at a fold-out dining table.

'I'm gonna break you in gently,' James said, biting a triangle of pancake off his fork as Andre peeled foil from a bottle of strawberry-flavoured milk. 'I'll start you on the firing range. Then I'll take you to the dojo for some basic combat moves, then I'll put you in a car for a little drive. That should get you warmed up nicely. After lunch I'll take you out to the training compound for something tougher.'

Andre looked wary. 'Tougher how?'

James smiled. 'Let's just say you'd best pay attention this morning, because you're gonna need everything you learned this afternoon.'

*

By mid-morning Andre had shot a pistol, a rifle and a machine gun, done some basic low-speed driving on the roads around campus and worked up a sweat in the dojo. There was no time to learn complex techniques so Martial Arts Instructor Takada had devised ten ninety-minute sessions, during which Andre would be taught basic knife skills and simple hand-to-hand techniques targeting the body's most vulnerable areas.

James made sure nothing was too difficult and went heavy on the compliments. By lunchtime, Andre was sweaty-but-cheerful and he rabbited enthusiastically as he scoffed a bowl of veggie pasta in the staff dining-room.

'That machine gun,' Andre blabbed. 'Oh my god! When I pulled the trigger it was like *raw* power. And the targets exploding everywhere. What was the little gun called again?'

'That was an Uzi.'

'When can we go to the firing range again?'

'We'll go back in a couple of days,' James said. 'But it's not a major part of your training. You're going undercover to find your dad. There won't be too many blazing machine guns, unless things go badly wrong.'

Andre laughed. 'And driving?'

'Yeah, you'll do more driving tomorrow,' James said. 'Handling a car is a useful skill for emergencies. But there's going to be a lot of classroom work too: communication protocols, stuff like that.'

Andre kept talking as they walked across campus, but first sight of the basic training compound and adjacent height obstacle straightened his smile.

'Am I going up there?' Andre asked, as he eyed the wooden towers linked by poles and beams over which CHERUB agents were expected to run at full pelt.

'They wouldn't let me,' James said. 'You've only got ten days and there's about a one in six chance of an injury the first time a trainee goes over that.'

'Has anyone ever been killed?'

'Nobody so far this year,' James said, neglecting to add that nobody had died in any other year either.

By this time they were up to the barbed-wire-topped gates of the compound where CHERUB agents lived during basic training. The current basic training group were overseas and Andre found himself standing in the bare concrete dorm where they slept. The beds were made immaculately and the items in twelve kit lockers were lined up to match perfectly. At the far end of the room was an open shower, and a row of sparkling toilets with no partitions between them.

'Is this where I'd train if I had more time?' Andre asked. 'You just have to sit and crap in front of everyone else?'

James let Andre's questions hang as he remembered that his basic training had been so exhausting that he hadn't given privacy a thought. Taking a crap had just been a rare opportunity to sit still for a couple of minutes.

Andre turned when he heard footsteps, and saw a tough-looking Asian girl a full head taller than he was. James had asked her to dress scarily and she'd done a great job, all in black from military boots to the baseball cap on her head. The look was accessorised with studded leather wristbands and a half-metre wooden cosh swinging off her belt.

'This is Fu Ning,' James said. 'The thing is, Andre, I can teach you a million things. But what really matters is, can you keep your shit together when the pressure's on? I have to know you can do it when the consequences of failure are more than just having to get up and try again.'

The confident, chatty Andre from the canteen had vanished as he nodded and looked at the floor.

'Fu Ning was a boxing champion. She's also a black belt in judo and Karate. She's very fast, very strong, and she's got a *major* bone to pick with you.'

'I've never met her before,' Andre said. 'I don't understand.'

James looked at Ning. 'Tell Andre about your stepmother.'

'Kidnapped,' Ning spat. 'Tortured for two days. They also beat me, broke my toe and sprayed lemon juice in my eyes. Then when my stepmum gave up the information they wanted, they strangled her.'

'What was the guy in charge called?' James asked.

'Leonid Aramov,' Ning said.

James tapped his lower jaw. 'Now isn't that a funny coincidence?' he said, looking at Andre. 'Why don't you tell Fu Ning what your name is?'

Andre was backing up to one of the beds. 'No,' he said firmly.

'You're no fun at all!' James teased. 'Fu Ning, meet Andre Aramov. He's Leonid Aramov's *favourite* son.'

'Liar!' Andre gasped, backing up further. 'I *hate* my dad. I helped my grandma get rid of him.'

Ning knew the truth, but James had told her to act like it was a big revelation.

'Oh, you're a dead little squirt,' Ning shouted, as she ripped the baton off her belt. 'I've waited a long time to kick some Aramov butt.'

But Andre was unconvinced as he ducked behind James. 'You said you didn't want me to get injured on the height obstacle. So she can't beat me up, can she?'

James smiled. 'We can't predict how you'd get injured if you fell off the obstacle. But Ning is highly trained, aren't you, petal?'

Ning smiled and nodded. 'Don't worry, boss. I can inflict *massive* amounts of pain without doing any lasting damage.'

'Right,' James said, looking at his watch. 'So the gates of the training compound are locked. It's six minutes past two. I'm going to give you a two-minute start, then I'm going to send Ning out after you. You've got to survive for one hour. If Ning catches you, she gets three minutes to do her worst, then she has to set you free and give you another two-minute start.'

'I didn't agree to this,' Andre protested. 'I don't want to do it. I thought *you* were my friend, James.'

James nodded. 'I *am* your friend, Andre. I like you so much, that I'm not prepared to send you undercover until you've grown a pair of balls.'

'Please,' Andre begged.

'Two minutes' start . . . Now!'

Andre hesitated for a couple of seconds, but as soon as Ning took half a step forwards he bolted out of the training building like his arse was on fire.

'Ninety seconds until I release Ning,' James shouted. Then he turned to Ning and spoke in his normal voice. 'Nice outfit. I'm almost scared of you myself.'

'So what now?' Ning asked.

'I reckon Andre will spend a good thirty minutes running around in a blind panic,' James said. 'We'll watch where he goes on CCTV and I'll send you out to make some noise and give him a scare when you *almost* catch him. Then come back here. Ten minutes before the end, go out again and grab hold of him.'

'What should I do?'

James shrugged. 'Find a nice muddy puddle and throw him in. Scream a lot, but don't do any real damage.'

'Simples,' Ning said, nodding.

'Might as well put the kettle on while we're waiting,' James said, as he pulled a key from his pocket and headed for the instructors' office. 'Fancy a cuppa?'

The small office had a bank of screens, each showing the outputs from the many CCTV cameras inside the training compound.

'Look at him go,' Ning said, grinning, as she watched a black and white image of Andre sliding frantically down an embankment, then looking anxiously over his shoulder before sprinting off again. 'He's bricking it.'

James smiled, as he clicked on the kettle then opened a snowman-shaped biscuit barrel that played 'Jingle Bells' when he lifted the lid. 'Oooh, Jaffa Cakes.'

27. RUN

Ten days later

The Kremlin had become eerily quiet. Take-offs and landings had dropped from four an hour to one or two per day. It was five days until Christmas. The remaining bar staff had spread purple and green tinsel trees around the public areas on the ground floor, but these somehow made the worn Seventies decor seem even more depressing.

While any aircrew who had somewhere to go to had left, Amy wanted to create the impression that the wind-down was just for the short term. The hangars by the airfield bustled with mechanics painting and overhauling elderly planes, for a resumption of operations that would never happen.

The school bus had also been mothballed because all but four kids had left, and it was easier for the ones that remained to share a taxi. And the four kids were only ever three, because Natalka hadn't been to school since she'd heard about her mum being arrested. As far as Ryan could tell, she'd barely left her room.

'Can I come in?' Ryan asked, as he knocked gently.

Natalka didn't answer, but her door wasn't locked. The silence scared Ryan as he stepped in, half expecting to find Natalka swaying from a noose, or wrists slashed in the bathtub. The truth was less dramatic. Natalka was on her bed wearing bright orange headphones. The photo albums were out on the kitchen counter. There were scattered food tins, which looked like they'd been scooped out cold, and an eye-stinging haze of cigarette smoke.

'What the hell!' Natalka shouted, throwing off the headphones and rearing up. 'Piss off. You can't just barge in.'

'I knocked,' Ryan said, then pointed at a pair of sodden Converse that he'd deliberately soaked before coming up. 'My spare trainers are in here and these ones are wringing.'

Natalka reached across the room and flung a trainer at Ryan's body. 'Now *go*,' she shouted.

'Is the other one over there?'

'Look for it then,' Natalka said, sighing and pointing to the mound of tangled sheets kicked off the end of her bed.

Then she turned to face the wall and buried her head in a pillow. Natalka was only wearing a nightshirt and Ryan couldn't help staring at her legs as he closed in to hunt for the trainer.

She was dead sexy, even with hair that hadn't been combed in a week. Ryan had been in despair ever since she'd dumped him. He couldn't bear coming home from school each night and sitting alone in his room, remembering Kazakov being there and thinking about Natalka. He'd started taking long runs around the airfield in the dark, pushing himself until everything was blotted out except muscle pain and a fight for breath.

'Got it,' Ryan said, as he grabbed the trainer. 'Would you like me to clean up? Take the tins out and put them down the rubbish chute.'

'Who are you?' Natalka asked, still staring at the wall.

Ryan's heart fluttered, sensing that she might be ready to make up. 'I'm a guy that cares about you,' he said.

But Natalka snorted. 'Cut the crap,' she said. 'I've remembered the first time I saw you.'

'Down in the lobby, my first day of school.'

'No,' Natalka said, as she sat up. 'I've been doing a lot of thinking these past few days. When you first turned up with your dad, I had this weird feeling I'd seen you before. And I just remembered: Ryan Brasker.'

Ryan gawped. Brasker had been his alias on the first part of this mission, when he'd befriended Ethan Aramov. He tried to hide his shock and figure how Natalka could possibly know that name.

'You need some air, Natalka,' Ryan said. 'Take a shower, go for a walk. I'm not saying you're losing it, but . . .'

'I was helping Ethan Aramov find out if Leonid had murdered his mum. He was getting information on how to hack computers off a friend in California. I only glimpsed the picture on Facebook once and I only made the connection last night. You looked familiar because I'd seen your photo on Ethan Aramov's Facebook page, before you ever arrived at the Kremlin.'

Ryan shook his head, keeping his face calm but panicking on the inside. At least his Ryan Brasker identity had been wiped, so there was no question of Natalka getting proof.

'You're imagining things. You've been in this room for days churning stuff over and over in your mind.'

'What else did you lie to me about?' Natalka said, keeping an eerie calm.

'You're grieving,' Ryan said firmly. 'Memory isn't perfect. Half the time you can't remember where you put your keys down the night before, but suddenly you're accusing me of being some other person who you glimpsed in a Facebook photo six months ago. You've barely left this room in ten days; you're eating junk food out of tins. It's not good for you.'

'You're a shit,' Natalka said. 'I *really* liked you – loved you actually – but you lied about everything.'

'Take a shower, put a dress on, go and get a proper cooked meal from the bar,' Ryan said. 'I know you're sad, but this isn't good for you.'

Natalka looked uncertain for a second before turning angry again. 'You've got your trainers. Now get out of here.'

Ryan backed into the hallway with his fingers looped through the laces of his trainers. He leaned a shoulder to the wall and let out a big gasp.

Natalka's grieving mind had stumbled precariously close to the fact that he was a spy. Ryan and Kazakov had first been sent to the Kremlin when TFU was desperate to get any kind of access. Nobody had considered that Ryan would keep this role up for more than a few weeks, or that Ethan might have revealed details of his secret friend Ryan Brasker to anyone else.

The good news was that Natalka's rambling story about seeing her ex-boyfriend's picture on Facebook eight months earlier didn't have much credibility given her current mental state. Ryan knew he ought to tell Amy about this security breach, but her most probable solution would be to insist that Natalka immediately be sent back to live with her aunt in Kiev and he couldn't bear the idea that he'd never see her again.

*

When Ryan got to his room, he scoffed a couple of pieces of fruit, then changed into the cotton tracksuit and mud-crusted New Balance that he used for running. After tuning the Voice of America on a tiny shortwave radio he'd bought at the bazaar, he jumped the stairs three at a time and burst out of a Kremlin side entrance on to the footpath towards the airfield.

As Ryan ran, the Voice's 5 p.m. news bulletin announced that thirty-two male aircrew and one female pilot had been charged in front of a US military tribunal convened at an airbase in Poland, while in Louisiana the US President had attended a memorial service for those who'd died in the Black Friday attacks.

'In a press briefing, a presidential spokesman refused to be drawn on whether further military action or arrests were expected in relation to the Black Friday terror raids . . .'

Eighty minutes later Ryan came back to his room and a voice in the dark scared the crap out of him.

'Jesus,' Ryan gasped, hoping for Natalka but seeing Amy reach out and flip on his bedside lamp.

'Nice to see you too,' Amy said, then sounded more alarmed as she saw that Ryan's tracksuit leg was ripped and blood pooled in his sock. 'What happened?'

'It's nothing,' Ryan said, still catching his breath from the run. 'I was on a steep track coming down the side of the valley and I lost my footing.'

'That's *not* nothing,' Amy said, pointing to a tatty armchair. 'Sit down and take your sock off.'

'Don't make a fuss,' Ryan said irritably. 'Why were you sitting in the dark?'

'Because the less we're seen together the better, and people might know I was waiting for you if I left the light on.'

'You know what blood's like,' Ryan said, as he sat down. 'It always looks dramatic, but when you wipe it off the cut's the size of a pinhead.'

Ryan winced as Amy rested his foot on the edge of the bed and started peeling off his sock.

'I'm getting worried about you,' Amy said.

With the sock down and his tracksuit leg pulled up, Amy had revealed a bloody mass of grazes going up to the knee.

'You're not to run down the valley in the dark any

more,' Amy said. 'Run in daylight, or stick to the airfield perimeter.'

'OK, Mom,' Ryan said acidly.

'I think you're depressed,' Amy said. 'I have to consider your welfare as well as the mission.'

'I've been happier,' Ryan said. 'Natalka dumped me and Kazakov was a grumpy sod but I got fond of him. But don't worry. I'm not gonna jump off a balcony or do anything else that makes you look bad.'

Amy walked to the kitchenette and hunted around for a piece of clean cloth to wipe his leg down. 'Christ, Ryan, you need to clean this sink. Is that pee I can smell?'

'It's a long way to the toilet in the night,' Ryan explained. 'There's bleach under the sink.'

'I'm not your cleaning lady,' Amy said, as she ran cool water on to a tea towel, then knelt at Ryan's outstretched foot.

'Oww!' Ryan hissed, as she started mopping off the worst of the blood.

'I could probably find an excuse for you to go away for a few days,' Amy said. 'Spend Christmas with your mates on campus. Get this dreary place out of your head.'

'I'm fine,' Ryan said, liking everything about Amy's idea apart from the fact that it would take him away from Natalka.

'Ryan, you're pouring sweat, your feet are blistered. Pushing yourself like this has got nothing to do with passing your fitness assessment when you get back to campus.'

'I've been here eight months,' Ryan said firmly. 'You're planning to have this whole place closed down in a few weeks. After everything I've been through, I think I have the right to stick it out to the end if I want to.'

Amy shook her head as she inspected the grazes. 'There's nothing that needs stitching, but it's below freezing out there. What if you'd slipped and knocked yourself out? You'd catch hypothermia before anyone found you.'

'OK, stop nagging,' Ryan said. 'I'll run laps around the airfield. I'll finish the mission here, then I'll have at least six months on campus. I'll hang with my mates, see a counsellor, do some training and try not to think about Natalka.'

'Ryan, you're a good kid,' Amy said. 'You know you can talk to me about anything?'

'Sure,' Ryan shrugged. 'So why were you waiting for me?'

'Tamara and Andre have nearly finished their training,' Amy said.

'How's Andre coping?'

'Not too bad, apparently. So once you've showered and put that muddy kit in a bucket for a soak, I need you to find Igor.'

Ryan had expected this and nodded.

'Tell Igor you've finally had a reply to the Facebook message you sent Andre. Say they've been staying in Dubai, but they're running out of money and don't know what to do.'

'Igor will ask me to pressure Andre for more details,' Ryan said.

'Of course he will,' Amy said. 'And your motivation needs to be clear, so ask him for more money. Tell him you want twenty thousand som if you manage to get an address for Andre and Tamara.'

'That'll piss him off.'

'Almost certainly,' Amy said. 'But if you make it too easy, Igor might get suspicious.'

'OK,' Ryan said, as he got out of the chair and hobbled towards a towel balled up on the floor. 'It's nearly seven. He's usually down in the bar by now, so I'd better shift if I want to catch him before he's had too much to drink.'

28. RAPPORT

'I'm in the car with James now,' Andre said, speaking to his mum Tamara on his mobile. 'I've just got this final thing he wants me to do. So how's your training been going?'

He was in the passenger seat, as James steered a CHERUB-owned Mercedes coupé around a tight corner and cruised past restaurants and pubs packed with office workers celebrating Christmas. After ten days in which they'd spent every waking hour together, James and Andre had formed a bond but were also slightly sick of each other.

'I can't believe your instructors gave you Sunday off,' Andre told his mum, before taking the phone away from his mouth and scowling at James. 'My mum says she got a day off.'

'Wouldn't have minded a Sunday off myself,' James

said, as Andre listened to something on the phone.

Andre looked at James. 'My mum said to tell you: *thanks for looking after me.*'

'Tell her that I look forward to meeting her at the airport tomorrow.'

'She heard you,' Andre said, as James stopped at a pedestrian crossing.

'We're almost there,' James said. 'You'd better hang up.'

The street of bars and restaurants had turned down-market and they drove past mini-cab offices, takeaways and a betting shop. James took a right into an alleyway with garages, beyond which the graffiti-strewn walls of a housing estate stretched into the distance.

'See you tomorrow, Mum,' Andre said brightly, before hanging up. Then, looking out of the window, 'What a dump. It's like being back in Kyrgyzstan.'

'One last chance to prove all that you've learned,' James said. 'And for the first time, you're on a real operation. Keep your head and everything will be fine.'

As James said this, he reached across, flipped the glove box open and grabbed a police radio.

'Tell me *exactly* what you're going to do,' James said.

'You told me already,' Andre said.

'I know, but I want to know that you've memorised it.'

Andre smiled confidently. 'I go up the steps behind the garages. There's a shopping concourse, but all the shops are derelict. The dealers hang out in an alleyway beside the boarded-up travel agency. I go up to the guy—'

'Which guy?' James interrupted.

'Joachim.'

'And if Joachim isn't there?'

'His lieutenants are Gabriel with the wispy beard and the guy with the double chin they call Pugs. If any of those three are around, I give them the message. If none of them are around, I keep on walking.'

'Good,' James said, reaching behind his ear and doing a double tap to activate his com. 'Testing, one, two, three.'

'Loud and clear,' Andre said. 'One, two, three.'

James spoke into the police radio. 'This is unit six. I've got the juvenile with me. Are you in position, over?'

A crackly blast came back through the speaker. 'Good to have you on board, mate. One of our guys did a quick recon. Joachim and Pugs are around. Police units in position.'

'Right,' James said. 'Sending my boy in now.'

James dropped the police radio in his lap and smiled at Andre. 'Keep it safe, because I'm gonna look a proper Charlie if I get you killed on our last day together.'

Andre nodded as he opened the car door.

'It's no parking here,' James said. 'I'll meet you by the playground on the other side of the estate in ten.'

As Andre jogged off towards the concrete steps, James clicked the Mercedes into reverse and backed out of the alleyway.

To minimise the risk of prosecution, well-organised drug dealers use a system where one person takes money and the buyer then walks to a second dealer who hands over the drugs. This second dealer only holds one or two packets of drugs at any time, and is fed by a third dealer who holds the main stash of drugs at a secret location nearby.

For the cops to successfully take out a gang of drug dealers, they need to arrest all the dealers and grab the main drug stash in one swoop. Andre's job was to help the cops make this link. After hopping up the steps, he broke into a jog along an alleyway and got his first sight of the dealers across a hundred metres of cracked pavement and trashed street furniture.

'Three guys,' Andre mumbled. 'Joachim is there.'

'Nice,' James said. 'Be confident.'

Joachim was a beefy mixed-race guy, aged nineteen. He'd been convicted of drug offences, but never anything serious enough to get jail time. Pugs was fat and got his name because he was into dog fighting. One of his pit bulls was tied to a bike rack in front of the boarded-up travel agency. Ten metres further along was a nervous-looking lad in an Adidas tracksuit. He was the guy who passed off the drugs, holding a single plastic bag of heroin and keeping a couple more tucked into an exhaust vent in the wall of a former dry cleaner's shop directly behind his position.

'Are you Joachim?' Andre shouted, trying to sound confident, but close to spewing.

Andre's heavy Russian accent made him sound exotic in these parts.

Joachim took a step forward. 'Who are you?' he shouted aggressively. 'Sayin' my name. Who gives you the right to say my name?'

Andre acted breathless, like he'd been running for longer than he really had. 'I'm Sergei's nephew,' he lied, referring to a high-level dealer who ran the drug trade in these parts. 'A bunch of Slasher Boys rushed him at the snooker club. They're out in force. Uncle Sergei told me to run down here and warn you.'

Joachim didn't look convinced. 'Sergei never mentioned any nephew.'

'I'm staying for Christmas,' Andre said. 'I live in Moscow.'

As Pugs started untying his pit bull ready for a possible getaway, Joachim went for his mobile.

'His mobile was hanging up in his jacket when they stormed the club,' Andre said, knowing that Joachim wouldn't get Sergei because the cops had blocked his phone. 'I'm getting out of here. Uncle told me not to hang around.'

'No reply,' Joachim said, looking at Pugs and pointing at Andre. 'You ever seen this kid?'

'Nah,' Pugs said. 'But he speaks exactly like Sergei and I'm not chancing if there's any taste of Slasher Boys. They tortured that crew in St Albans. Ripped out their toenails and made them eat 'em.'

Joachim pocketed his phone, then looked across at Vince. 'Slashers in the area, mate. We're closing shop.'

'Shall I go tell Reggie?'

'Yeah,' Joachim said. 'Just my dumb luck. Shut down when there's Christmas money on the street.'

Pugs tugged his snarling pit bull and followed Vince. Andre walked a few paces in front, heading off to meet

James on the other side of the estate.

'We'll leave the stash,' Joachim ordered.

Pugs turned back, shaking his head. 'That's all our Christmas gear. You want it out of our sight when there's Slasher Boys on our turf?'

'All right,' Joachim said reluctantly. 'Fetch it. Then we're outta here.'

The cops couldn't let themselves be seen coming and going, so officers had been positioned inside boarded-up shops and the derelict flats above them since before dawn.

Vince shouted something through a doorway fifty metres off the concourse. Thirty seconds later, he came out with a backpack over his shoulder and another guy jogging behind holding an even bigger load. The instant these two joined up with Joachim and Pugs, the cops pounced.

Andre was twenty metres clear of the scene, but couldn't resist a glance back as cops clambered off rooftops and pulled up graffitied metal shutters.

'On the ground,' someone screamed. 'Down, down!'

The cops had all the angles covered. Only Pugs made a run for it and he got less than ten metres before a swinging police baton took his legs out. But while Pugs was flat on the ground getting his arms wrenched behind his back, the pit bull slipped from his grasp.

The animal took an almighty bite out of a policewoman's arse, but a colleague beat it off with his baton. He tried grabbing the lead, but the dog was too strong. The animal snapped, but another baton swipe made it yelp in pain and bolt off down the alleyway.

'Ripper, down, boy!' Pugs shouted, police locking cuffs on the dealer's wrists as he called after his dog.

Andre had begun walking again when he heard the powerful dog steaming his way, its metal chain clanking along the pavement behind. There was a chance the animal would run straight past, but it wasn't a chance Andre wanted to take and he started to run.

In a blind panic, Andre reverted to his native Russian and screamed into the com, 'There's a pit bull chasing me!'

James sounded alarmed. 'Stand your ground, but don't look at it,' he ordered. 'Whatever you do, don't run or it'll think you're prey.'

'Too late for that,' Andre gasped, as he rounded a corner and found himself belting down a footpath between wooden fences, with Ripper getting nearer.

'I'll radio the cops,' James said. 'They're nearer than I am.'

But Ripper was closing too fast. The tops of the fences were high, but Andre was approaching two stacked recycling boxes. He jumped on them, grabbed the top of a fence and tried pulling himself up.

It was a struggle and Ripper crashed head first into the boxes, knocking them down and spilling recyclables along the alleyway. Pure terror gave Andre the shot of energy needed to pull his legs up and swing over to the other side.

As Ripper jumped at the fence a couple of times before picking a fight with a plastic ketchup bottle,

Andre found himself on a patio covered with broken toys and an abandoned washing machine.

The patio doors were closed but not locked, and he stepped into a lounge with presents stacked around a tree and a woman in a nurse's uniform holding a coffee mug and a pack of Hobnobs.

'You thieving little sod!' she screamed.

Coffee hit the carpet as Andre made a lunge, but the nurse pinned him in the doorway.

'I'll have the cops on you.'

She tried bundling Andre on to a sofa as James' voice sounded in his ear. 'Where are you, mate? Are you OK?'

Andre managed to grab a porcelain cottage off a shelf and swung around, clonking the nurse over the back of the head. He then stumbled down a short hallway and opened the front door. He was at the front of a housing block, with a set of steps leading down to a main road.

'James, where are you?' Andre gasped, looking back and seeing the nurse coming out on to her doorstep, hair messed up and one hand clutching her head.

James blasted his horn. Andre tracked the noise and began racing towards the silver Mercedes rolling up to the kerb at a bus stop fifty metres away.

'You OK?' James asked, switching off his com as Andre sank into the seat beside him. He slammed shut the door and clutched his hands to his chest as James pulled off fast enough to make the rear tyres squeal.

'My god!' Andre said. 'That dog was a monster. If it had got me . . .'

James smiled. 'Always best not to dwell on things that

might have happened. The cops sound happy and you didn't get your arse chewed off. That's not a bad result for a beginner!'

29. RAT

Once Andre was over the shock of being chased by Ripper, he spent most of the ride back to campus exuberantly recounting what he'd been through.

'That guy, Vince. The cop that grabbed him was huge! He got totally body-slammed. And it was a big backpack. How much do you reckon the drugs were worth?'

'Hard to say,' James said. 'But they're only street dealers so probably not more than a few thousand quid.'

'Will they get long prison sentences?'

'I dunno,' James said. 'Joachim probably will, because he's got previous.'

They were on a dual carriageway with less than five kilometres to go.

'So there's definitely no more training?' Andre asked.

James shook his head. 'You can pack your bag when we get back to my room. Then we'll have dinner and you probably shouldn't sit up too late because we're heading off to the airport at six in the morning.'

'I might actually miss you, James,' Andre said softly. 'You taught me heaps, but I'll probably never see you again after tomorrow.'

James smiled. 'I was worried that you weren't tough enough, but you've done really well.'

They were coming up to a McDonald's when James' head got turned by a highly distinctive Dodge Challenger, finished in bright orange with a big number 94 painted on the driver's door.

'Quick diversion,' James said, slowing down hard enough to make the driver behind blast his horn, and then taking the slip road into the restaurant.

'Are you hungry?' Andre asked. 'I thought we were gonna eat on campus.'

'I'm not here for the food,' James explained, as he pointed at the Challenger. 'I happen to know the owner of that orange monstrosity.'

'Monstrosity!' Andre gasped. 'It's *awesome*. Like the coolest car I've ever seen.'

James pulled up, got out and led Andre through automatic doors into the McDonald's.

'I need you to shout,' James said. 'Say, "Oh my god, someone's smashing up that orange car."'

Andre looked wary. 'Is this another one of your tricks?'

'It's a trick, but not on you,' James said. 'Just do it before we get spotted.'

'Someone's smashing up the orange car!' Andre shouted.

Quite a few people looked around and James ducked behind the table with the straws and serviettes on as an eighteen-year-old blonde came storming towards the doors.

'What did they do?' the girl growled to Andre. 'I'll kick their ass!'

Andre was lost for words. As the girl stormed out into the parking lot to check the car, James raced up to the table where the girl had been sitting and started eating her fries.

'Chips, Andre?' James asked.

The girl came back into the restaurant, looking angry and embarrassed because quite a few people were staring at her. She wore jeans and Converse All Stars, with an oversized plaid shirt instead of a coat.

'Is she your girlfriend?' Andre asked.

'Sister,' James explained, giving a little wave as the girl stormed towards him. 'Hey, Lauren, how's it going?'

'You utter bastard!' Lauren said, slapping James' hand away from her chips. 'I'll get you back for that.'

'Your car is mental!' Andre told her.

Lauren smiled. 'My boyfriend got it for my eighteenth birthday,' she explained. 'Six point four litre V8, five hundred horses, good for 175mph. Thirsty on the petrol, but it's bloody great fun!'

'To be fair, *I'd* probably have sex with Rat if he got me one of those,' James said. 'So where is Mr Millionaire Boyfriend anyway?'

'He's gone off for a big Christmas piss-up with his uni football mates. I'll pick him up at the station by campus tomorrow afternoon and tease him about his terrible hangover.'

'It'll be like old times,' James said. 'Christmas on campus. But right now I've gotta sort this little guy out, so I'll see you back there later.'

'Nice to meet you, Lauren,' Andre said politely. Then, once they were almost back to the Mercedes, 'Your sister's fit, James.'

James cracked up laughing. 'I think you'd be biting off more than you could chew with her, mate.'

*

It was gone eleven when Ryan tracked Igor down. The Russian had been for a meal in town and rolled into the Kremlin bar with three women from the admin department and a couple of the last remaining pilots.

'Farewell!' one of the pilots spat, hardly able to stay upright as he stumbled into the table. 'We're all buggered. Buggered!'

'Here's to the scrapheap,' the other one added.

Amy was trying to keep up the pretence that the clan had only suspended operations, but many people weren't convinced and airlines wouldn't be queuing up to employ middle-aged pilots who were only certified to fly forty-year-old cargo planes.

As always, Igor was buying the drinks and Ryan caught him as he reached the bar.

'I got a message from Andre,' Ryan said. 'We need to talk.'

Igor smiled. 'Gimme a second. I'll cast off these miserable sods and be right with you.'

Igor bought Ryan a Coke and carried a tray of drinks across to his dining companions before returning.

'Dubai,' Ryan said. 'That's all Andre said, but I'm going to keep pushing. Tamara's almost out of money and I get the impression they're getting desperate. Speaking of which.'

Igor smiled and went down his pockets for five thousand som.

'I want twenty thousand if I find out where they are,' Ryan said, as he pocketed the money.

Igor grimaced, then smiled. 'If you find that out, it's worth twenty thousand,' he said.

Ryan swigged his Coke as Igor went back to his companions. His grazed leg still hurt and he planned to head upstairs to bed, but that changed when he caught Natalka's reflection in his glass.

She'd left her room like he'd suggested; showering, grooming and dressing in white pumps and a skirt so short it could have moonlighted as an elastic band. She looked amazing, but walked like she'd had too much to drink and only stayed upright because Vlad's steroid-pumped arm was holding her up.

Vlad deliberately took stools at the bar close to Ryan. 'Vodka,' Vlad said. 'Double rum and Coke for the lady and a lemonade for the little boy.'

Ryan shook his head with contempt. The barman took the hint and didn't pour his lemonade.

'Hello, Ryan,' Natalka said, slumping over the bar and giving him a limp wave. 'I'm having fun with Vlad. He's got really big muscles and he's not a liar!'

Natalka giggled as Vlad pushed the double rum and Coke at her. 'A toast,' Vlad said. 'To the most beautiful girl on earth.'

Ryan felt like he'd been stabbed as Natalka downed her double, then pulled Vlad in for a snog. When Natalka broke off, she caught Ryan's eye and gave him an evil little smile.

'I haven't been with a proper man for ages,' Natalka said.

'Reckon it's past your bedtime, Ryan,' Vlad said. Then to the barman, 'Another double for my girl.'

The barman wasn't convinced this was in Natalka's best interests, but Vlad's diet of steroids made him aggressive as well as strong. He wasn't a guy you could easily say no to.

Ryan didn't want to admit defeat and leave, but rage and jealousy chewed him up as Vlad tugged up the back of Natalka's skirt. Anyone who cared to look got a view of her bum as he scooped her easily off the stool into his lap.

'Drink up,' Vlad told Natalka. 'I've got two hundred Dunhills for you in my room.'

Ryan baulked, certain Natalka would get more than two hundred cigarettes if she ended up in his room.

'Where you going?' Vlad asked, as Natalka slipped off his lap. 'You're my girl.'

'Piss,' Natalka said, before setting a wobbly course across the cigarette-scarred carpet.

Vlad turned towards Ryan once she was out of earshot. 'I'm gonna be banging that tonight. How's that make you feel?'

Ryan tutted. 'She's fourteen. You must be *really* proud of yourself.'

'God only puts tits and arse like that on the earth for one reason,' Vlad said, giving a wink. 'She can have little Vlad babies!'

'The amount of steroids you do, I'm amazed your balls haven't shrivelled completely,' Ryan said.

Ice cubes chinked as Ryan drained his Coke and jumped off his stool in disgust.

'Sleep tight, baby boy,' Vlad said.

Ryan shook his head as he crossed the bar and headed for the stairs. Part of him wanted to go to bed and try to forget everything, but he loved Natalka and felt responsible because he was the one who'd told her to get out of her room.

Although Ryan had done a ton of combat training on CHERUB campus, he'd seen Vlad bench press 240kg and do sets of bicep curls with dumbbells that he couldn't even lift off the rack. If Ryan was going to take Vlad on, he had to knock him out fast. Steroids make you super-aggressive and a guy that strong can cave your head in with a few punches.

Ryan needed a weapon, but his window of opportunity began to close as Natalka stumbled out of the toilet into Vlad's arms.

'I'll look after you, baby,' Vlad said, feeding an arm around her back to hold her up.

Natalka had been drunk when she arrived at the bar and Vlad forcing two double rum and Cokes down her neck had left her near comatose.

As Vlad waited for the lift up to his third-floor room with Natalka, Ryan raced upstairs still trying to think up a plan. He was on the last landing when he noticed a sand bucket and fire extinguisher.

The extinguisher was a big chrome job, marked *Expiry 2006*. But while its fire-fighting ability was questionable, Ryan only cared about its weight. By the time he'd picked the extinguisher up and stepped through double doors into the third-floor corridor, the lift was on its way up.

Natalka was coughing as the doors opened and Vlad sounded furious as he shoved Natalka out of the lift.

'Puked on my best shirt, you dumb slut,' he snarled.

'I didn't mean it,' Natalka said weakly.

'Might have to punish you for that.'

Natalka was coughing and groaning as Vlad grabbed a handful of hair and shoved her towards his room. The waft of Natalka's boozy puke coming from the lift made Ryan heave, but he managed to stifle it.

'Hey, big man,' Ryan shouted.

The instant Vlad turned Ryan lunged, belting him in the face with the end of the fire extinguisher. Natalka screamed and slid down the wall as Ryan booted Vlad in the guts, making him crumple forward.

Despite the head shot, Vlad remained conscious and he grabbed Ryan's ankle and pulled him down. He swung a huge punch, skimming Ryan's head and smashing his fist through the plasterboard wall. As Vlad tried pulling it out, Ryan scrambled forward and knocked his opponent out with an elbow to the head.

As Ryan rolled off he realised he was spattered with blood, and chunks of puke off Vlad's shirt. Natalka leaned forward and started retching as Ryan stood up. When she finished she gave Ryan a weird look. Gratitude? Hate? Ryan couldn't read it and her head went limp before she could speak.

'Natalka?' Ryan said, gently pinching her cheek to see if she was conscious.

He tucked hands under Natalka's armpits and groaned as he lifted her floppy body off the floor and threw her on to his shoulder.

'Christ you're a lump,' Ryan told himself, as he tried not to heave from the smell of her boozy sweat. 'Let's put you to bed.'

30. AIR

James was beat after ten days working with Andre, so his sister Lauren offered to help out and take the early drive to the airport in her Challenger.

They met up with Tamara and the MI6 officer who'd led her training at a Pret A Manger in terminal five. Andre was pleased to see his mum, but then got sad when it was time to go. He sneaked off to a gift shop to buy James a fancy box of mints, then welled up as he hugged James before passing through the security barriers for his flight to Dubai.

'Sweet kid,' Lauren said, once Andre, Tamara and their MI6 escort had disappeared. 'But I never felt like buying any of my training instructors presents. You must be too soft.'

'Andre's smart, but real CHERUB training would break him in about two hours,' James said. 'Sweetie?'

James tipped some mints into Lauren's palm.

'So when's the love of your life flying in?' Lauren asked, as they started strolling back towards her car.

'Kerry's staying in the States,' James said. 'We've not been getting on too well.'

Lauren smiled. 'Who'd she catch you in bed with this time?'

'Nobody,' James said indignantly. 'And why does everyone think I'm some kind of sex maniac? I'm a normal bloke with normal appetites.'

Lauren tutted. 'You're a good-looking bloke. Women flirt and you tend to say yes if you think you can get away with it.'

'Half the kids on campus seem to think I had sex in the campus fountain.'

Lauren smirked. 'Cool! That was my rumour.'

'What?' James gasped. 'Why'd you do that?'

'I was bored,' Lauren said airily. 'You know when you're a bit drunk and you just make some gossip up to keep the conversation going?'

James laughed so hard he had to rub a tear from his eye. 'I miss having you around.'

'My uni's only an hour from campus,' Lauren said. 'If you do stay in the UK you'll see a lot more of me.'

'That'd be cool.'

'So are you and Kerry fighting, or is it worse than that?'

James shrugged. 'Can't say for sure. We've been together so long there's not the same spark. I don't know if that's a problem, or if it's just what happens to a relationship after a few years.'

'Surely she's not spending Christmas on her own?'

'She hasn't told me anything, but there's this guy Mark who she's been meeting for coffee and stuff,' James said. 'I half suspect she'll be Christmasing with him.'

'Heavy,' Lauren said.

'I threw my breakfast at the wall when I first found out she wasn't coming for Christmas,' James said. 'But the more I've thought about it, the more chilled I've got. Me and Kerry have grown apart. Zara's offered me a job on campus and I think I'm gonna take it.'

By this time, they'd gone down an escalator and reached the platform for the monorail out to the short stay parking.

'And what about you?' James asked. 'Rat, uni, other stuff?'

'First term at uni's been good. Rat's happy, though some of the guys he hangs out with are annoying. I miss being a cherub, but who doesn't?'

*

Amy had given Ryan the login for the fast Internet connection on the fifth floor and he felt down as he used his iPhone to look at a picture on his Ryan Sharma Facebook page. His best mates, Max and Alfie, had posted a pic of themselves dressed in Scream masks and Santa hats, with Alfie's yucca plant draped in tinsel between them.

Max, Alfie & Doris wish everyone a very Merry Christmas and a splendiferous 2013!

It was funny, but it also made Ryan feel lonely. He'd been scared that Natalka might puke in her sleep and choke, so after wiping her face and putting her to bed he'd found a blanket for himself and spent the night in an armchair watching over her.

The knock at the door was gentle, but Ryan had been to his room to pick up Kazakov's gun, in case an angry Vlad came to and went on the rampage. He kept it within reach as he opened the door.

'How's Natalka?' Amy whispered.

'Dead to the world,' Ryan said, stepping back relieved.

Amy walked into the room and pushed the door shut quietly. 'Vlad's dealt with,' she said.

'What do you mean?'

'Vlad's father's taken him to the hospital in Bishkek to have his head stitched. They were already preparing to leave, so Vlad can come back to the Kremlin to pick up his bags, but that'll be it.'

'Thanks,' Ryan said.

'Do you know if Vlad's got any close mates who might cause trouble?'

Ryan shook his head. 'Vlad's not popular. He was friendly with Andre's big brothers, Boris and Alex. But since they got kicked out with their dad, he doesn't really hang with anyone.'

'Makes it easier for us if no one cares that Vlad's gone,' Amy said, before glancing across at Natalka to make completely sure she was still sleeping. 'More importantly, we've now got information on Leonid. You were right about Squashed-Nose, he is Igor's brother. He's got friends at the Russian embassy in Bishkek and he's been using their secure channels to send messages to Leonid Aramov.'

'How'd we pick that up?'

Amy smiled. 'That kind of information is above my pay grade, but the Aramov Clan has long had close friends inside the Russian Government. I'm guessing the CIA can decode Russian diplomatic traffic. The messages are being routed to Mexico.'

Ryan looked perplexed. 'I thought he'd be in Russia, or maybe United Arab Emirates.'

'Who didn't?' Amy said. 'But Mexico makes sense, given the current situation there.'

'How so?' Ryan asked.

'Our sting operation meant we got almost all of Leonid's money, but we didn't take his knowledge. Leonid knows pilots, corrupt officials, weapons manufacturers. Mexico is embroiled in a vicious turf war between drug gangs battling over smuggling routes into the USA. It's probably the nastiest and most prolonged drug war there's ever been anywhere. Now, imagine turning up in the middle of that environment, with expertise in smuggling and contacts who can supply large quantities of weapons.'

Ryan nodded. 'Leonid's connections would be *priceless*. And having no money hardly matters because the drug cartels can pay millions to someone who'll supply what they want.'

'Leonid Aramov may be a psycho,' Amy said, 'but he's no fool.'

'So do we know where in Mexico?'

'TFU headquarters in Dallas is working on some leads for me,' Amy said. 'But for now, our best hope remains that Andre and Tamara will lead us to him.'

'Igor seemed pleased when I spoke to him last night,' Ryan said.

'I'll bet he was,' Amy said. 'In one of the decoded transmissions, Leonid threatened to cut Igor's throat if he didn't find out what had happened to Tamara.'

'Andre and Tamara must be airborne by now,' Ryan noted.

Amy nodded. 'James Adams called me a while back to say their flight left on time. They'll arrive in Dubai this evening. Ted Brasker will meet them. He's sorted out accommodation in a hostel used by migrant workers. Once we've confirmed that Andre and Tamara are in place, you can go and tell Igor that you've been into the bazaar and chatted to Andre online in a web café. Then you give him the address where they're staying.'

'What do you reckon will happen then?' Ryan asked.

'The messages we intercepted between Igor and Leonid confirm what Tamara said: Leonid still has extremely strong feelings for his ex-wife. Tamara will say that she ran away because Josef Aramov was pressuring her into having a relationship with him. She'll say she needs money and a place to stay. With luck, Leonid will reach out to his damsel in distress. As soon as Tamara and Andre get to wherever Leonid's staying in Mexico, they'll let us know.'

'So once I've told Igor the address?'

'Your job will be done,' Amy said. 'If anyone notices

that you've gone, we'll say you went back to the Ukraine to live with a relative. Flights will be booked up at this time of year, but I might still be able to get you back on campus for Christmas with all your mates.'

Ryan looked longingly towards Natalka. 'You said I could stay here to the end if I wanted to.'

'You've got it bad for her, haven't you?'

'I know I've got to go back,' Ryan said sadly. 'Natalka doesn't even like me any more, but when I think about never being able to see her again, I feel like blowing my brains out.'

Amy half smiled, but picked up Kazakov's gun. 'You won't need this now you know Vlad's gone.'

'Love sucks,' Ryan said, smudging a tear from the corner of his eye and staring up at a ceiling stained by water leaking from the floor above.

Amy smiled. 'I wish there was something I could say to make you feel better, but I'm not gonna sugar-coat it. You're gonna go back to campus feeling like crap and nobody on earth can do a thing about it.'

31. FEET

Natalka woke with a thudding hangover. She showered before throwing on a fake Armani polo shirt and cut-off jeans. It was early afternoon when she invited herself into Ryan's room, barefoot and puffing on a king-size cigarette.

'So . . .' she said, before blowing a plume of smoke.

Ryan tried not to sound excited, but an involuntary grin gave the game away.

'Heard of knocking?' he asked.

Natalka gave a shrug and spoke softly. 'I opened one eye in the night and you were in my mum's rocking chair, watching over me.'

Ryan put the book he was reading down and sat up. 'Choking to death on your own vomit's not a good way to die.'

'Can I sit?'

'Free country,' Ryan said.

Natalka could have sat at the dining table, but she sat on Ryan's bed, with her knee almost touching his outstretched foot.

'Don't I get an I-told-you-so lecture?' Natalka asked.

'I've done my share of stupid things,' Ryan said.

'Brave boy taking on Vlad,' Natalka said, blowing smoke Ryan's way before dropping the last of her cigarette into a glass of water on the bedside table.

It was a perfect Natalka moment: knowing that Ryan hated smoking, but absolutely confident that she could get away with it. To Ryan's surprise, she then grabbed his foot and rested it on her knee.

'A lot of guys have ugly feet. Cracked nails, hairy toes. Yours are cute. Like a little boy's feet.'

To show her point, Natalka raised Ryan's foot up to her lips and kissed his big toe.

'Random,' Ryan said, flattered as he laughed and looked at his feet. 'Your feet aren't bad, but they're not your best bit.'

Ryan inhaled Natalka's odours of cigarettes and shower gel as she swung a leg up on to the bed and straddled his waist. He felt blissful, looking at cleavage inside the unbuttoned polo, with a little diamond pendant spinning just above the tip of his nose.

'So what's my best bit?' Natalka asked.

Before Ryan could decide between saying *personality* or, more honestly, *tits*, Natalka saved him the dilemma by lowering her head for a passionate kiss. It was always great when they kissed, but this was the best ever because until two minutes earlier he'd thought this would never happen again.

*

Dubai's government likes to portray the city-state as an upscale desert paradise of posh shops, beach resorts and high-rise towers. But less than ten per cent of the Emirate's population are natives. Menial jobs from builder to hotel maid are done by low-waged workers brought in from poorer countries like Iran and Pakistan.

Andre and Tamara's background story was that they'd fled from the Kremlin with little money, so after a comfortable business class flight from London, the pair found themselves staying in a warren of tiny four-storey apartment blocks. They'd been designed for couples, but rents were high and most were shared by eight to ten workers.

Although the pair had a room with a bare concrete floor to themselves, the previous occupants' smell lingered in the foul squat toilet and stained mattresses piled in one corner of the living area. TV, telephone and air conditioning were all coin-operated and there was constant background noise. Shouts and moped engines competed with ringing mobiles, bhangra music and La Liga highlights.

Andre stood by a cracked pane of glass, looking down two floors at a line-up of dark-skinned women, dressed in pink maids' outfits and cooking stew on an open fire in the courtyard.

'Get away from the glass,' Tamara said. 'You'll attract attention.'

Andre backed off and saw that his mother was going through the stack of mattresses. 'There's a couple that are not so bad and they've left us new bedding.'

'Was your instructor nice?' Andre asked.

Tamara shrugged. 'I learned a lot, but he was a cold fish. Went home to his family at five thirty every day. I don't think he cared who I was, or whether I'd be dead in two weeks.'

'James was really cool,' Andre said, as he strung together a couple of Karate moves that ended with an unbalanced roundhouse kick. 'You should have seen his sister's car. She's got this mental Dodge Challenger. There was no traffic on the roads when we set off this morning and she was blasting it.'

Tamara smiled. 'You're really taken with this James. I think *James* has been every third word out of your mouth since we left London.'

Andre laughed. 'I've never met anyone that cool before. I'd love to be like that when I'm older.'

'James, James, James, James, James, James, James,' Tamara teased, as she threw her own Karate kick and blew a kiss. 'I'm starting to think you've fallen in love with James.'

Andre was impressed with his mum's kick. 'You're not half bad.'

'My instructor said I was a natural,' Tamara said. 'I did ballet when I was a girl. It's not so very different.'

'Guns were my favourite,' Andre said. 'And driving. James let me take a Mercedes up to about a hundred mph.'

'Pow!' Tamara said, giving Andre enough of a kick

on the butt to send him stumbling forward over one of the mattresses.

She then switched from Karate to WCW mode, moving to jump on top of Andre but giving him heaps of time to roll out of the way.

'Narrow escape from the big fat pudding!' Andre said, giggling as his mum hit the springy mattress, making him bounce upwards.

'I'll give you fat pudding, Andre Aramov,' Tamara said, as she reached across and tweaked Andre's ear before licking her lips to give him a deliberately soggy kiss on the cheek.

'James was cool,' Andre said, wiping mom spit on his shirtsleeve before giving her a kiss back. 'But I only love you.'

They ended up lying next to each other on the grubby mattress. Andre studied ants crawling around a grimy light fitting. Someone had amused themselves by melting the plastic shade with a cigarette end.

'I can never be free until your dad is dead or in prison,' Tamara said. 'When this is over, we'll find some place close to my family. You'll go to a better school, not like that shit heap in Bishkek. You're easily smart enough to be a doctor.'

'Blood makes me feel faint,' Andre said.

Tamara laughed. 'I don't care what you do, as long as you work hard and you're happy. Amy promised they'd look after us. A house, my own little car. Maybe a job doing hair, or waitressing. I don't want anything rich or fancy. Just you and me, having a normal life.'

An e-mail from Amy made Ryan's phone vibrate and his head poked out from under the bedclothes. The afternoon had been amazing; they'd curled up under Ryan's duvet, snogging and feeling each other up until Natalka's hangover forced her back to sleep.

Ryan read the message: *Andre & Tamara in place. Igor back from market.*

Ryan had never wanted to stay in bed more. The sun was bright enough to pierce the sheets and he took a longing look at Natalka's breasts before rolling out gently, careful not to disturb her. Life felt unbelievably good as he pulled on jeans. He could even see what Natalka meant about his feet being cute and he wore a huge smile as he pushed them into his Converse.

Natalka moaned and hooked a finger through a belt loop on Ryan's jeans. 'Why go?' she asked softly.

'I'll be right back,' Ryan said. 'I owe Igor for some stuff he got me in the market.'

'He won't be in the bar until later.'

'He's expecting me,' Ryan said, throwing Natalka her cigarettes and lighter before pulling a plaid shirt up his arms and grabbing keys, wallet and a notepad off the worktop beside the sink. 'Go back to sleep.'

He gave Natalka a goodbye peck and did up his shirt buttons as he walked downstairs to the bar. Igor had two women with him, but lit like a flashbulb and excused himself when Ryan appeared.

'There's only one thing you want to see,' Ryan said happily, as he flashed a square of folded paper.

'And twenty thousand things I want to see.'

'Not here,' Igor said. 'If people see me passing you money they'll ask why.'

Igor led the way into a gent's toilet that was just a stinking metal peeing trough. The taps were disconnected and the sit-down toilets had been blocked since before Ryan first arrived at the Kremlin.

'How'd you get it?' Igor asked, as he looked at the number and address written on the ruled sheet.

The move to the toilet and Igor's tone made Ryan suspect he was about to get stiffed for the twenty thousand som.

'How'd you get the address?' Igor repeated.

'Andre's a video games nut,' Ryan explained. 'He had a delivery of new games from some website in China. I offered to post them on.'

'So you can still get access to the fifth floor?' Igor asked, as he began counting out five-hundred som notes. 'How'd you get past the guards?'

Ryan shrugged. 'They know I was Andre's mate. I guess nobody told them to stop letting me through.'

'Interesting,' Igor said. 'Who's up there?'

'Two guards on the lift, two on the stairs.'

'I mean who lives there.'

'Sorry,' Ryan said. 'As far as I know it's deserted, apart from the room at the end where Josef lives with that blonde.'

'Amy,' Igor said. 'You know her?'

Ryan shrugged, as Igor passed the twenty thousand over. 'Amy's said hello. She ate with Tamara a couple of times when I was visiting Andre.'

'It's odd,' Igor said. 'That Amy appeared out of nowhere. Before that, Josef never showed any taste for women. Not even when there was a warehouse full of Korean girls at the far end of the runway.'

'Didn't he meet her in Dubai or something?' Ryan asked. 'I heard she was a stripper, or a prostitute, or something.'

Igor laughed and gave a little thrust of his hips. 'She's a honey, for sure. If Josef's paying her, she's worth every penny.'

'I'd totally bang her,' Ryan agreed.

Igor's tone got more serious. 'You haven't got a lot of options with your father dead and this place going to shit. But I heard how you handled Vlad.'

'My dad taught me to look after myself,' Ryan said. 'It's no big deal taking a man down if you belt him with a fire extinguisher before he even knows you're there.'

'How would you feel about heading up to the fifth floor for me?' Igor asked.

'For what?' Ryan asked.

'Silenced pistol,' Igor said, making a gun with his fingers. 'I'm told there's a back corridor that the Aramovs use to go between apartments. So you go into Tamara's place, hole up for a few hours. Then you wait for Josef and Amy to fall asleep in one another's arms and *bang, bang.*'

Ryan knew that Amy and Josef didn't share a bed, and wasn't surprised that Igor wanted them dead. Leonid Aramov was a jealous man, who'd hate the idea that his brother had tried to seduce Tamara. Second, Leonid didn't know that TFU now controlled the clan. As far as he was concerned, Josef's death would create a power vacuum and enable him to return to the Kremlin and get back control of the family business.

'You'd be well looked after, Ryan,' Igor said.

'I'm not exactly overwhelmed with career options,' Ryan said. 'There was talk of Josef finding me odd jobs, but I've heard nothing so far.'

'Keep me posted on anything you hear and I'll be in touch.'

Ryan was intrigued by what he'd heard, but he was also annoyed. He'd now have to go and tell Amy about Igor's proposal, when all he wanted to do was strip and slide back under the covers next to Natalka.

32. CALL

Andre knew it was coming. Nobody else had the number, but he still shuddered when he grabbed the ringing payphone and heard his father's voice.

'Andre?'

The line was faint. A slight delay indicated that the voice came from far away.

'Dad? Is that you?'

'No, it's Father Christmas,' Leonid said. His tone was bitter, because the last time Andre saw his father, he'd sided with his grandma Irena against him. 'How are you?'

'OK, I guess,' Andre said. 'Where are you now?'

'You'll find out. I guess you've grown?'

'It's been a year,' Andre said. 'Haven't measured though.'

There was an awkward pause as a father and son who

didn't think much of each other hunted for words.

'Put your mother on,' Leonid said finally.

'Hang on.'

Tamara placed a reassuring hand on Andre's back as she took the receiver.

'Leonid?' she said, faking surprise. 'How did you find us here?'

'I found you,' Leonid said. 'That's all that matters. I tried your mobiles when I heard that you'd left the Kremlin.'

'I've got a new number,' Tamara said. 'You paid the contract on our old phones. The SIMs got cancelled when the payments bounced.'

Leonid made a kind of growling noise. 'So is it true what I hear about Josef?'

'I'd rather not talk about it,' Tamara said, changing to a higher pitch to make it sound like she was distressed. 'You'll just get angry.'

'I've a right to get angry,' Leonid roared. 'My brother harassing my wife, while some blonde whore is sharing his bed.'

'Ex-wife,' Tamara corrected, unable to hide her bitterness. 'You traded me in for a nineteen-year-old.'

'My head was in a bad place back then,' Leonid said. 'You were always the one, Tamara. How many times did I ask you to remarry?'

Tamara seethed as she remembered that Leonid and his cronies had regarded abusing the North Korean women the Aramov Clan trafficked to Europe as a perk of their job. But she had to keep the anger in check if she was going to pull off this plan and clear Leonid out of her life.

'I missed having you around,' Tamara lied.

'I'm told you're short of cash.'

'Josef let me have one credit card, but I've maxed it. We stayed in a hotel the first few days, but now we're at this horrible place. Andre can't sleep because of the noise. He's not going to school and there's needles on the stairs.'

'If I'd known I'd have helped sooner. But I know now, so you don't have to worry.'

'You have money?' Tamara asked.

'My mother stripped most of what I have,' Leonid said. 'But she let me keep enough to tick over, and I've done OK for myself since.'

'Even a few hundred dollars,' Tamara pleaded.

Leonid laughed. 'Princess, you're not staying in that horrible place alone. You belong with me.'

'Where's that?'

'I can't say, but you'll like it.'

'I . . .' Tamara said. 'What about Andre?'

'What about him?'

'I'm talking about what happened with Irena,' Tamara said. 'You told Andre you'd have him killed.'

'He's a boy,' Leonid said, after a pause.

Tamara raised her voice. 'I've always loved you, Leonid. But you lay one finger on that boy . . .'

'He's my flesh and blood,' Leonid said. 'Of course I was angry at the time, but I love Andre as much as I love you, or Alex, or Boris.'

'So how does this work? How do I get to you?'

'It'll take some working out,' Leonid said. 'Especially with Christmas in three days. Don't stray too far from your apartment and be ready to leave at short notice.'

'Right.'

'Better not stay on the line longer than I have to,' Leonid said. 'I love you, Tamara. Tell Andre not to be scared and that I love him too.'

'Right,' Tamara said. And then after a few seconds' thought and a fake sob, 'I love you too.'

Tamara looked at her son as she put the receiver down.

'What did he say about me?' Andre asked.

'He said he forgives you and he loves you.'

Andre snorted. 'I'd have more faith if that hadn't come from a man who murdered his sister and poisoned his mother.'

'I know,' Tamara said softly. 'But your father knows he'd lose me if he ever did anything to you.'

'He won't go nuts at me straight away because he won't want to upset you, but once he gets comfortable.'

'I know,' Tamara said. 'But we'll only stay long enough to get some idea of what he's up to. Then Amy's people will deal with him and we can start our new life.'

'I might change my name to Kobe for my new identity,' Andre said, trying to lighten the mood.

Tamara looked mystified. 'I've never heard that name before.'

'Kobe Bryant,' Andre explained. 'He's like the most famous basketball player in the world.'

Before Tamara could answer, a cheapo Nokia tucked into Andre's backpack began vibrating. It was Ted Brasker.

'You both did great,' Ted said warmly.

'Did you trace my dad's call?' Andre asked.

'Came out of a data-centre in Russia,' Ted said. 'Which means he was routing via the Internet. My headquarters in Dallas will do some more work on it, but it's almost certainly untraceable.'

'You still think he's in Mexico though?'

'Absolutely. But it's frustrating that we've not been able to narrow it down to a town or province,' Ted said. 'Your dad has associates in Sharjah and Dubai. It'll take him a day or two to sort out false documents for you and travel plans to Mexico, but now that he knows where you are there's a chance he'll send a minder to collect you, or put you under surveillance if he's in any way suspicious.'

'Right,' Andre said.

'So you and your mum *must* remember your training. Leonid is too suspicious for you to travel with a covert tracking device or any other equipment. It's a near certainty you'll be told to abandon your mobile phones and Wi-Fi devices because they can be tracked down. If you can find a way to communicate with us en-route to Mexico that's great, but don't take any kind of risk. The important thing is to get to Mexico safely, and let us know where you are shortly after you arrive.'

'Got it,' Andre said.

'I'll try and be on the ground in Mexico before you

arrive, but it's a big country and we don't know where you'll be heading. So it may be a day or two before I'm there covering your backs.'

33. WORK

Tamara wanted to treat Andre on Christmas Day, but couldn't splurge because Leonid had been told they were desperate for money and he might be having them watched. It would have been impossible to hide presents in their tiny room, but Dubai was an Islamic state so everywhere was open and the pair took a short taxi ride to a mall.

They ate a modest turkey dinner on an indoor terrace overlooking shops, straddled fake jet skis in an amusement arcade and came away with some posh chocolates and a few bits of extra clothing. Andre was depressed by the thought of a fourth evening lolling about in their dismal room with no video games and no English or Russian language stations on the TV.

He was squatting on a mattress, feeding laces into a new pair of trainers, when he caught a whiff of smoke. It was wafting from a window on the next level down and he took the bolts off their door and stepped out on to the balcony, which ran the length of their floor.

As more residents joined Andre on the balcony, men on the next level down tried dousing the flames with water buckets.

Andre shouted back through the open front door, 'Mum, I think it's serious.'

A few people had decided to head for the stairs, but others stood around, hoping things would calm down before they had to leave their rooms. Thickening smoke and the eruption of a fire alarm changed the mood and Tamara had angst in her voice as she tapped Andre on the shoulder and handed him a backpack. They kept everything packed, as per Leonid's orders.

'We'd better take this,' she said. 'It's all we've got.'

As Tamara grabbed a larger pack, Andre dashed back inside and picked up his watch, the Nokia phone and a carrier bag from the mall. The smoke was dense enough to taste as they merged into a crowd heading for the staircase.

At ground level, caretakers were running towards the block, pulling on fluorescent fire-marshal vests. The escape routes had been designed for two or three people per apartment, but with up to ten in each, the stairs quickly jammed.

Everyone seemed content to shuffle until there was a loud bang, most likely the bottle from an unauthorised gas stove. Andre found himself crushed and panicked as everyone pushed down the stairs. A few men in construction gear discovered that they could exit more quickly by swinging on to an overhang and sliding down a pipe.

Eventually Andre reached the bottom step, with his mum a little behind and a fire marshal herding everyone to an assembly point in the courtyard of an adjoining block. When the pair arrived, they turned back and stood watching burgeoning flames, amidst a group of Pakistanis whose matching polo shirts bore the logo of a company that installed elevators.

'Andre, Tamara,' a man said softly. 'Don't look around. Someone may be watching us.'

Andre glimpsed back instinctively and saw a black man in a grey blazer and sunglasses. He had the slim build and high cheekbones of an Ethiopian, or Kenyan.

'My name is Kenneth,' the man said, speaking English with a strong East African accent. 'I have a blue Saab parked at the end of block six. Give me thirty seconds. When you meet me I'll be at the wheel with the engine running.'

Smoke now wafted out of doorways on the next floor up, and people recoiled as a second gas bottle exploded. Andre was shocked by the realisation that this fire had been set to create confusion and enable them to get away without being observed.

A pair of fire engines were closing in as Andre and Tamara set off. The Saab was unlocked; they both got in the same rear door, with Andre scrambling across to the far seat, and Kenneth pressing the accelerator pedal the instant the door closed.

They had their packs and bags on their laps as Kenneth took a couple of quick turns, then hit a main highway and doubled back towards the smoking building to ensure they weren't being tailed.

'My detector informs me you have one mobile phone,' Kenneth said. 'I'm afraid I must dispose of it along with any laptops or Wi-Fi devices you may have. I will stop momentarily to arrange our luggage. We must then drive for many hours.'

'How long?' Andre asked, doing the talking because Tamara's English was poor.

'Your first flight leaves from Doha in Qatar in sixteen hours. If the traffic is good, I have arranged a hotel at the airport where you will have an hour or two to take room service, shower and make yourselves comfortable.'

As Kenneth said this, he pulled back on to the highway, but immediately cut across the oncoming traffic and rolled into a parking lot. They pulled up in front of an apartment complex that was slightly nicer than the one they'd just left. Kenneth hopped out and posted Andre's phone and Tamara's iPod into a storm drain, then he opened the trunk and packed their luggage away.

Back in the car, Kenneth passed a brown envelope and a paper bag from a posh deli through the gap between the front seats.

'I couldn't find Russian food, but I hope this is to your satisfaction. I must also ask you to check the passports. It is important to memorise the spelling of names, dates and place of birth and your address details.'

Andre rested the bag of cakes and sandwiches on the leather armrest as Tamara ripped the envelope. She quickly glanced through a travel itinerary taking them from Doha to Amsterdam and then on to Ciudad Juárez in Mexico. Andre reached out and grabbed a Czech passport with a three-year-old photo of himself inside, along with visas for Qatar and Mexico.

Andre was no expert, but the documents were either real or extremely good fakes. As he studied the passport, Tamara unzipped a clear plastic pouch, which contained other ID such as a Czech driver's licence and credit cards. Some of these items had been scratched and worn, because customs officers get suspicious if all your ID looks brand new.

'How long to Mexico?' Andre asked, as he picked the itinerary sheet off Tamara's lap.

The time differences made it tough to work out when they'd arrive in Mexico, but the Saab's sat-nav screen was estimating fourteen hours to Le Meridian hotel in Doha. Then it was a six-hour flight to Amsterdam and thirteen more from there to Ciudad Juárez.

'Thirty-three hours,' Andre groaned. 'And that's before you include check-ins, stopovers and hold-ups.'

Tamara smiled. 'And your cheap-ass father has booked us in economy class the entire way.'

*

James was bloated from a classic Christmas lunch and tipsy from three glasses of wine as he squelched across soggy campus grass in wellies. Sister Lauren, her boyfriend Rat and long-standing mates Bruce Norris and

Kyle Blueman were also in the group, along with thirty other past and present CHERUB agents, some senior CHERUB staff and a dozen little red-shirt kids.

For the previous eighteen months, a large area of campus to the east of the main building had been sectioned off behind a twelve-metre-high fence. CHERUB kids were also barred from a two-hundred-metre exclusion zone around the fence in case they were spotted by construction crews working at a high level.

But today was Christmas, so the construction workers were at home and Zara Asker had announced that supervised groups could be taken through an opening in the fence for a first glimpse at the future of CHERUB campus.

'Christ, it's huge!' James said, as he ducked through the opening and followed his sister into a queue for yellow safety helmets.

CHERUB campus had evolved from a disused village school and a few temporary huts when the organisation was founded in 1945, but Campus Village was the biggest construction project in the organisation's history.

'We're a little over two years from scheduled completion,' Chairwoman Zara Asker announced, her yellow wellies slurping in mud as she led the group along a curved track. 'Eventually fifty houses will give us accommodation for three hundred agents. Six kids will live in each house, with a communal lounge and kitchen space downstairs and three private bedrooms first and second floors. Each bedroom will have its own separate bathroom and a quiet study area.'

James was at the rear as the group reached a circular mud patch, with the half-built village stretching off down three branching alleyways. The buildings nearest to his position were barely out of the ground, but some of the buildings further away were already watertight and there was an open area nearby stacked with mounds of lumber and breeze blocks.

'This is not a playground!' Zara yelled, ripping into a couple of little red shirts stamping in a puddle. 'If you two want to spend the rest of Christmas Day sitting silently in my office, you're going *exactly* the right way about it.'

The chairwoman then returned to her gentle spiel. 'As well as expanding the number of agents CHERUB can take, the idea of Campus Village is to create a proper family atmosphere, with agents living in proper houses instead of long, impersonal corridors. Each house will have a small outdoor area, where you can hang out and have barbecues. Larger gaps between houses will have basketball areas, a playground, and the entire area will be cycle friendly.'

'Will we be able to have pets?' one of the red shirts asked.

'At the moment, qualified agents can't have pets because they can't be looked after when they go on missions. However, if six agents are living in a house it's unlikely that everyone will be on missions at the same time, so we're considering allowing each house to have a dog or cat.'

There were eight little kids in the tour group and they

all seemed really keen on this idea.

'The ground and first floors of each house also have full access for people with injuries or disabilities.'

'What about carers?' a navy shirt asked.

'Carers will have separate offices where you can drop in. They'll also have full access to each house, so don't go thinking you can lock them out and throw a wild party.'

'Boo!' someone said.

'When will it be ready, Mrs?'

'2014 hopefully,' Zara said. 'If the project stays on schedule, the village will open in time for CHERUB's seventy-fifth anniversary. We're trying to get the Queen to cut the ribbon. Phase two of the project will involve demolishing the education block, building new staff quarters and refurbishing the main building as an education and admin facility. That will take until 2016.'

'Do you think they'll have fixed the leaky roof in the mission control building by then?' James asked.

Zara smiled as the rest of the crowd laughed. 'That roof will be the death of me! But I'm glad to say that the village uses good old-fashioned pitched roofs, not bits of curved aluminium that cost three grand each and fall off every time there's a stiff breeze.

'Now, you're all welcome to go off and look around, but this is a building site so don't touch *anything*. Don't venture off the marked paths and I warn you now that anyone who throws mud will find all their Christmas gifts being shipped off to the nearest charity shop.'

James followed Lauren and Rat at a slow stroll as

excited red shirts started belting off, pointing at houses and saying which one they wanted to live in when the village opened.

'It's impressive,' Kyle said, doing a 360 while anxiously trying to avoid getting mud on anything except his boots. 'Homely without being twee, modern without being sterile.'

Lauren nodded in agreement. 'I really liked my room when I lived on campus, but this new set-up makes the main building look kinda shit.'

'These trousers are dry clean only,' Kyle shouted anxiously, as a grey-shirt boy and girl chased by, flicking mud off the back of their boots.

As James buried gloved hands in his jacket and set off up a gentle slope towards the top of the village, he felt his phone vibrating. It said *International* on the display.

'Happy Christmas, James,' Kerry said.

James smiled as he settled on a half-built wall. 'Hey, how's it going? Did you just get up?'

'It's ten o'clock here,' Kerry said. 'Just had my shower and stuff.'

'You're on your own?'

Kerry sighed. 'I had dinner with Mark last night, but he's driven up to his grandma's today.'

'That's crappy,' James said, though he couldn't resist rubbing it in because he'd all but begged her to come back to campus for Christmas. '*Everyone* apart from you is here. Lauren, Kyle, Bruce, Rat, the twins. Gabrielle's around, though I've not spoken to her. I'm a little drunk, and we're squelching around looking at Campus Village.'

'Sounds fun,' Kerry said. 'I bought a ticket for a Christmas dinner thing at the university, but I might just bum around the apartment.'

James felt a bit sorry for Kerry, but he didn't know what to say, and she spoke again after an awkward pause.

'I was thinking about Zara's job offer,' Kerry said. 'It's the right step for you. You should take it.'

'What about the right step for *us*?' James asked.

'Sometimes . . .' Kerry began. 'Sometimes I think I still love you as much as ever. But . . .'

Kerry was saying nothing, but somehow James understood exactly what the *but* meant.

'I don't know how we got to this place,' James said.

'I think we should live our lives and see where we end up,' Kerry said, sounding a little tearful.

'Yeah,' James said. 'Well you at least try and have a good day, yeah? I'd better catch up with Lauren and the others. We've only got ten minutes to explore before Zara brings the next group in.'

34. BOXING

'It's kind of beautiful in the sunset,' Ryan announced, as he turned slowly with arms held out wide.

Christmas Day sun was setting and the thick frost in the valley around the Kremlin had taken on an orange hue.

'And the air's so much better now. When the planes were coming in and out, you always had that petrol smell clinging to the back of your throat.'

While Ryan eulogised, Natalka stood a few steps further up the valley, wearing a scowl and a thick purple ski jacket. The end of her cigarette glowed red and smoke wafted from her nostrils as she spoke.

'I'm freezing. Let's go back.'

Ryan snorted. 'We've barely walked a kilometre.'

'And what's gonna happen in the next kilometre?' Natalka asked. 'Will magic bunnies jump out of the snow and grant me three wishes? I don't think so. I'll just get more bored and more bloody cold.'

'All right,' Ryan said. He sounded annoyed, because although he was nuts about Natalka, when you did stuff with her you did what she wanted or nothing at all. 'So we just go back to your room?'

'The outdoors is shit,' Natalka said, flicking her spent cigarette away. 'I need a buzz. Get some booze, get shit-faced. Play max vol music until the neighbour bangs on the wall.'

Ryan laughed. 'First off, the guy in the next room left for Uzbekistan two days ago. Second, don't you ever worry about your drinking? The last time you got hammered, you almost got raped by Vlad.'

'But you'll protect me now,' Natalka said, putting on a syrupy voice.

'How do you know I won't take advantage of you?'

'You could have done that three nights ago,' Natalka pointed out. 'You're a *nice* boy.'

'You make nice sound like a bad thing,' Ryan said, as Natalka came towards him.

'I like guys who are a bit scary,' Natalka said. 'Danger turns me on.'

'I did beat Vlad's face in with a fire extinguisher,' Ryan pointed out. 'That wasn't nice.'

'True,' Natalka said, rewarding Ryan with a kiss before setting off down the valley towards the Kremlin. 'And I think it might be fate.'

'What's fate?' Ryan asked.

'Well, your dad died, then my mum got busted.

And here we are, two little orphans with sod all except each other.'

Natalka was a couple of paces ahead and her bum looked great. Ryan wished it really was just the two of them. No plots or plans. Looking out for each other, instead of a relationship based on lies.

'Maybe when I go back to my aunt in Russia you could come with me,' Natalka said.

Ryan laughed. 'I'm sure your aunt will love it when you rock up with a boyfriend. Besides, I'm Ukrainian. I wouldn't be allowed to live in Russia.'

'I hate my aunt,' Natalka said. 'I'm so pissed off that my mum wrote her a letter. She should have just left me here.'

'I don't wanna talk about going away,' Ryan said, before giving Natalka an almighty two-handed shove into a bush at the side of the path.

'AAARGH!' Natalka screamed, as she emerged from tangled branches with snow melt running down her back and enormous wet patches around her knees. 'Bastard! What was that for?'

'Just being nice,' Ryan said.

Natalka's mock scowl and wagging finger made Ryan laugh. 'I'll get you for that, Ryan. When you're least expecting it.'

'Oh, I'm so scared,' Ryan said.

'You know what'd be cool?' Natalka said. 'We should go up to the fifth floor. Rob the shit out of Josef Aramov and then run away together. I bet he's got Rolexes, and gold, and stuff.'

'You're crazy,' Ryan scoffed. 'The Aramovs own every cop within fifty kilometres. We'd be lucky to last an hour before Aramov security tracked us down, beat the living shit out of us and dumped us out in the snow.'

'Nice boy,' Natalka teased.

Ryan tried giving another shove, but Natalka dived out of the way. He lost his footing and ended up doing the splits.

'Oww,' Ryan yelled, clutching a strained thigh muscle as Natalka howled with laughter. She offered him a hand up, but then pulled out and turned it into an up-yours gesture.

When Ryan finally got up under his own steam, he pulled Natalka in close for a snog. By this time they were within sight of the Kremlin lobby and when they broke off they raced each other and stood giggling in the lobby as they pulled off gloves and scarves.

'Let's never do the *walk* thing again,' Natalka said.

Ryan was back into the range of the fifth-floor Wi-Fi, and as there was no other signal around here, he knew that the vibration coming from his phone had to be an instant message from Amy.

'Cold always makes me pee,' Ryan explained, leaving a trail of wet boot prints as he strode across the near-empty bar to the gents'.

There was nobody else in the evil-smelling space and he pulled the phone out and read a short e-mail message.

I'm on 5, get up here ASAP.

'I've got a job lifting some boxes,' Ryan told Natalka when he'd stepped out. 'Odd jobs for the Aramovs are my only source of dough, so I'd better jump to it.'

Natalka shrugged like she didn't care and went inside her coat for another cigarette as Ryan headed up to the fifth floor. He wasn't supposed to see Amy unnecessarily, even now that the Kremlin was almost empty. He found her in a small bedroom which was part of Josef Aramov's quarters.

'Going well with Natalka?' Amy asked, sounding surprisingly forceful.

'Happy Christmas to you too,' Ryan said cheekily. 'What's pissed you off?'

Amy formed a flat palm and gave Ryan a gentle jab in the ball sack.

'Hey!' Ryan yelped. 'What the hell was that?'

'Three things that earn you automatic expulsion from CHERUB,' Amy said, getting close and glowering into Ryan's eyes. 'What are they?'

'Willingly taking Class A drugs, revealing the existence of CHERUB and underage sex.'

'And which one do you think I'm concerned about right now?' Amy asked.

'I've not done anything with Natalka,' Ryan said. 'Well, I've done a lot of things, but not sex.'

'That's good,' Amy said. 'Because Natalka's really vulnerable right now. You've been with her 24/7 over the last few days and this is a friendly warning to keep your pecker in your pants.'

'She's not even a virgin,' Ryan said.

Amy made a flat palm and Ryan jumped back with his hands cupped over his crotch. 'Stop that,' he gasped.

'You're a nice guy, Ryan,' Amy said. 'But I'm *not* joking about this. You're only fourteen and I'm responsible for your welfare. Natalka's also fourteen and has enough problems without you knocking her up.'

Amy let go and Ryan stepped back indignantly. 'Why does everyone keep saying I'm a nice guy?' he shouted. 'I'm not *that* bloody nice.'

Amy looked confused, but changed the subject.

'I've also got two bits of news that aren't related to your raging hormones. First off, we've got a termination date: January 9th. A team of demolition experts are going to land here on the sixth. They'll blow this dump, plus the planes, the runway and just about anything else within a half-mile radius. Secondly, there's new info on Leonid.'

'What info?' Ryan asked.

'Remember a lawyer named Lombardi?'

It took a couple of seconds before Ryan nodded. 'He was the guy Ethan Aramov tried to contact the night his mum got murdered.'

'That's him,' Amy said. 'TFU headquarters has tracked down more communications by Leonid Aramov using the Russian military network. It seems Lombardi has been wiring twenty thousand dollars a month from a bank account in Nevada to a Mexican bank. The Mexican account is in some random name that we assume Leonid is using for cover, but more importantly, the Nevada account tracks back to a company owned jointly by Leonid and Galenka Aramov.'

Ryan looked confused. 'But I thought Lombardi was

Galenka Aramov's lawyer.'

'He was,' Amy said. 'But apparently, Lombardi also does work for Leonid and while we thought Galenka and Leonid Aramov had no dealings with one another, they apparently jointly owned a holding corporation with assets worth at least twenty million dollars.'

Ryan thought out loud, trying to remember a boring campus lecture on businesses and fraud. 'Holding corporations exist solely to own shares in other companies, usually as a way of avoiding tax or hiding the real owners. So what does this mysterious holding company own?'

'We don't know that yet,' Amy said. 'And it's Christmas Day, so TFU only has a skeleton staff on duty in Dallas. The holding company's accounts and legal paperwork are filed in the state of Delaware, and their records bureau is closed until tomorrow morning.'

'Can't we just pull Lombardi in for questioning?'

Amy shook her head. 'He's a lawyer, and a respectable US citizen. That means Lombardi has no obligation to give details of his client's affairs. We certainly can't arrest him based on vague suspicions that he's wiring money to Leonid Aramov. Dr D would like to put Lombardi under surveillance, maybe have someone conduct an illicit search of his office, but her bosses are on her back and she could lose her pension if she breaks too many rules.'

'Can't we just kill Leonid once we know where he is?' Ryan asked.

'We could,' Amy said. 'But we're an intelligence

organisation not a death squad. And taking out one person is pointless if it just means Leonid's associates, or one of his sons, takes over his dirty dealings. But I'd bet my life that Leonid's up to something appalling in Mexico, and once Andre and Tamara locate him, I doubt it'll take us too long to work out what that is.'

35. JUÁREZ

Andre and Tamara reached Doha with a few hours to spare and left the Middle East on a Boxing Day morning flight to Amsterdam. After the six-hour flight there was a five-hour layover, and without euros or a credit card all they could do was sit at the departure gate, watching rolling news and getting cups of water from a drinking fountain.

When he sighted a man snoozing on a chair with his mobile and glasses resting on a newspaper beside him, Andre took the next seat. After waiting long enough for everyone to assume they were together, Andre grabbed the handset. Tamara looked about anxiously as her son flipped it open and sent a text to a number Ted Brasker had given him:

Flight KL310 AMS to CJS.

Fifteen hours later their 777 was losing height over a

sprawling metropolis. The northern half was El Paso, Texas. A million people, mostly living in estates of large red-roofed houses, bisected by arrow-straight highways. The southern half was Ciudad Juárez, Mexico. The area around the border was dominated by flat-roofed industrial buildings while its two million souls were packed much tighter than their American cousins.

From his window seat, Andre could see roads merging towards the border crossings, with cars queuing ten lanes thick to get across. He turned to his mum, smiling because a gruelling forty-hour journey was almost over, but also anxious about what he'd find when he got off the plane.

Tamara's backpack didn't appear on the baggage carousel, but neither of them spoke Spanish and they had no onward address so they decided not to report it.

They had no arrival instructions and didn't know what to expect as they got the entry stamps on their passports and stepped into a chaotic arrivals lounge. After the fire at the apartment and the slightly sinister Kenneth with his mobile phone detector, Andre expected some kind of subterfuge, but after a second a voice he recognised spoke his mother's name.

'Tamara!'

Leonid Aramov looked very different. His Russian thug look, with tight jeans and leather jacket, had been replaced by a crisply tailored suit. He'd lost weight, tanned in the warmer climate and changed his crop for shoulder-length hair to hide the ear that his mother had cut off.

'You look well,' Tamara said, managing a smile as

she hugged her ex-husband.

After the hug and an awkward kiss, Tamara backed off. Andre got a jolt of fear when he caught his father's eye. Everyone had assumed that Leonid would forgive his betrayal in order to get back with Tamara, but can you be certain about anything when you're dealing with a man who killed his sister and poisoned his mother?

'You're starting to look like a man,' Leonid said, but changed tack when he sensed Andre's nerves. 'I know you loved your grandmother, but I love you also. No grudges?'

Leonid held out his hand and Andre shook it. 'No grudges,' Andre agreed.

'My car is near,' Leonid said, as he took Andre's pack. 'Is this all you have?'

'I lost a bag but I thought it better not to report it,' Tamara said.

'Absolutely,' Leonid said. 'You can wash and sleep. Tomorrow we'll go shopping to replace your things.'

'I know you took a risk, reaching out to us,' Tamara said, as they began walking.

'You've always been my special one,' Leonid said, almost making Andre gag.

But while he was being all smiley for Tamara, Leonid reverted to type as they stepped out of the shabby terminal and got blocked by a couple of raggedy teenagers offering to carry their bags. He swept his hand, threatening a slap, and yelled something in Spanish which made the pair scuttle off.

'You have to be firm,' Leonid said. 'There's street

scum everywhere here.'

The multistorey lot was notable for metal grilles and an armed guard who checked their parking ticket before letting them enter.

'I thought we might be picked up by a guard or something,' Andre said.

'I keep my life small here,' Leonid said. 'No big organisation. No bodyguards or flunkies, or stress like I had at the Kremlin. In a few months I'll be done with my business here. Out of the game for good, I hope.'

'What will you do?' Tamara asked.

'Write an autobiography,' Leonid said, clearly joking. 'Charity fundraisers . . .'

Andre had spent his early years craving moments when his parents acted normal. He still found the happy families fantasy soothing, even though he'd grown out of believing it could really happen.

'I can't see you like that,' Tamara said, as Leonid put his arm around her back.

Andre felt awkward, because for all the planning nobody had really discussed what would go on when his parents got back together. Leonid had bullied and scared Tamara and refused to let her leave the Kremlin after he divorced her, but they'd once loved each other and Andre often sensed that his mother didn't hate Leonid quite as much as she claimed to.

Leonid's car was a Lexus, notable for bulletproof glass. A twenty-minute drive took them through busy traffic to a gated apartment complex with lush gardens behind CCTV and electrified fencing.

After an underground garage full of Mercedes and Bentleys, a lift took them to a large duplex apartment with a long plunge pool. Curving steps led from this balcony into a communal garden with huge palms shading an Olympic-sized swimming pool.

'Better than the Kremlin, eh?' Leonid said, as he threw an apartment key down on a kitchen island the length of a car. 'Though interior décor's not my forte!'

Andre saw what his father meant as he looked beyond the sleek kitchen into a double-height living-room. The selection of indoor palms looked like they'd been shot up with an airgun and the only furniture was half a dozen beanbags and an extremely fancy multi-gym plonked right in the middle of the floor.

'You can use the gym,' Leonid joked to Andre. 'Bulk up like your brothers. Speaking of which, Boris, Alex, stop being rude. Get out here and say hello.'

Seventeen-year-old Alex came out first, his well-muscled frame clad in football shorts and a tight grey vest with blobs of pink ice cream down it.

'Tamara, squirt,' Alex said, smiling at his stepmother but apparently less keen on Andre.

Twenty-year-old Boris came from a room upstairs, tying a gown around his waist and trailed by a beautiful dark-skinned girl. Andre's half-brothers were both graduates of the Kremlin's teen bodybuilding cult and had regarded Vlad as one of their few close friends.

'Look what crawled out of the dung heap,' Boris said, as he came down an open glass staircase glowering at Andre.

'Hey,' Leonid shouted. 'None of that, you hear? Andre is flesh and blood. This is a fresh start for us.'

'He betrayed you,' Boris shouted, as his massive physique loomed over Andre.

Andre knew he couldn't back off if he was to have any chance of winning his brother's respect. 'You're not as big as you used to be, Boris,' Andre said. 'Can't get the good steroids out here?'

Leonid got between his two sons as Boris closed on Andre.

'Don't start,' he told Boris. 'I made a decision. You're old enough to leave, so you either live under my roof and respect it, or piss off.'

Boris scowled. 'He was disloyal and you can't paper it over, just because you're soft for his mother.'

Boris was way bigger than his father, but Leonid had no hesitation in stepping up and giving his oldest boy a slap.

'Go back upstairs, screw your Mexican whore,' Leonid shouted. Then he looked at Alex. 'Take Andre up to one of the spare bedrooms. Find him some towels and bedding.'

Alex was hardly an ideal big brother, but he'd been known to take on vaguely human qualities when he wasn't under Boris' influence.

'You been OK?' Alex asked, as Andre followed him to the staircase.

Andre didn't want to be a thug like his brothers, but it always pissed him off that they were tough guys, while the genetic lottery had left him chubby and small for his age. This jealousy got rammed home as he followed Alex's ripped torso to the upper level.

'This room's OK,' Alex said, as he took Andre into a spacious room with en-suite shower, built-in wardrobes and a double bed with bare mattress. 'Dad picked up some extra bedding for you and your mum. It's in the utility room at the end of the hall.'

Andre looked out of the window and saw that his room had a depressing view of air conditioning units and maintenance sheds.

'Be careful around Boris,' Alex warned. 'He had a big crush on a girl in Kyrgyzstan. He lost her when we got kicked out of the Kremlin.'

Andre felt like reminding his brother that they'd been kicked out of the Kremlin after Leonid killed their aunt Galenka and tried to kill their grandma. But Alex was offering rare crumbs of brotherly love, so he didn't push it.

'I'll steer a wide berth,' Andre said.

Alex pointed to the TV. 'You still a video game head?'

'Pretty much,' Andre admitted.

'Thought so,' Alex said. 'I rigged my Xbox up under there. I've not touched it for ages, so you might as well make use.'

'Thanks,' Andre said. 'All I had for entertainment in Dubai was old *Simpsons* episodes.'

'I'll leave you to shower and whatever,' Alex said.

Alex's friendliness was a pleasant surprise. Andre wondered if his brother had fallen out with Boris, or had maybe just become isolated, living in a strange country where he didn't speak the language.

Andre kicked the door of his room shut and started undressing, smelling reminders that he'd been in the same clothes for three days solid. But he was intrigued by the possibilities of the Xbox and before going into the shower he turned it on, anxious to see if it was linked to the Internet. After picking the Xbox Live option, he typed in his account and password and clicked *log on*.

There was a long wait, but Andre punched the air as his home screen started loading. He selected the messenger box and picked a friend called Slava, which would actually connect him to TFU headquarters.

Where are you? flashed up.

There was no keyboard, so he took a couple of minutes to type the name of the apartment complex using a control pad. Seconds after he'd pressed *send*, Alex knocked on the door.

'I'm getting undressed,' Andre said, as he grabbed a remote and flicked the TV to a random channel.

'I've seen your flabby little bod before,' Alex said, as he stepped in. 'Forgot to say. Don't use your login on the Xbox, or your Facebook and stuff on the iPad downstairs. Dad reckons someone could track us down just from a login.'

'Right,' Andre said. 'Guess that makes sense.'

Andre smiled to himself as he deleted his login details from the Xbox, switched the TV to a channel showing Spanish cartoons and headed for the shower. He'd told TFU where he was, and that was all that mattered.

36. LISSON

'So, I take it you didn't just invite me up here to smack me in the balls again?' Ryan asked.

'Aww, stop making a fuss,' Amy said. 'Tough kid like you can handle that.'

Ryan smirked. 'I ought to report you for child abuse.'

'Report me all you like. I'm out of a job when I get back to Dallas anyway.'

It was Boxing Day evening and Ryan was in the big planning room on the Kremlin's fourth floor. 'So why'd you call me up here?' he asked. 'I can't hang about, I've got Natalka downstairs, ready for some hot steamy sex.'

'Don't push your luck,' Amy said, though she couldn't help smiling. 'I thought you'd like an update. We've had one quick contact with Andre. Now we know where he is, we're going to send someone out to liaise with him.'

'Ted Brasker?' Ryan asked.

'That was the original plan,' Amy said. 'But the silly arse did his back in. So we need a replacement, and as our operation to find Leonid hasn't exactly been given approval at the highest level, we're having trouble finding anyone else at TFU willing to put their career prospects on the line.'

'What does *hasn't exactly been given approval* mean?' Ryan asked.

'Officially, Dr D is supposed to report to her bosses at the CIA before launching any new operation,' Amy explained. 'She's blurred the issue by claiming that finding Leonid is part of the mission we're on here.'

'So is it, or isn't it?' Ryan asked.

'Well, our job *is* to wind down Aramov Clan operations. You could argue that finding Leonid is part of that remit, or you could argue that sending a mother and son off to Mexico to find someone who was kicked out of the clan six months earlier is completely separate.'

'Politics,' Ryan said dismissively. 'Life would be so much easier if they just left us alone to get on with our jobs.'

'True,' Amy said. 'But it'll never happen.'

'And did we get anywhere with the Lombardi thing?' Ryan asked.

'The information management team in Dallas has been digging. Ethan's mum, Galenka Aramov, and his uncle, Leonid Aramov, set up a holding corporation called Vineyard Eight. They each owned fifty per cent of the corporation and Lombardi was the only other company director.

'Vineyard Eight bought up a satellite navigation company called Lisson Communications. Lisson built navigation systems for US military vehicles and was one of the first companies to market in-car navigation. But their sat-navs never cut it and Galenka and Leonid bought a company that was nearly broke.'

'Why buy a company that's no good?'

'It was a big risk, but the Aramovs did well out of it. Galenka sold off the navigation division to a larger rival, but Lisson retained a lot of valuable patents.'

'I've never exactly got patents and trademarks and stuff,' Ryan admitted.

'Basically, if you invent something you have the right to *patent* your invention. Then you can either stop people from copying your idea, or charge them money for the right to use it. Lisson Communications did a lot of research into navigation technology and owned some very important patents. Now, every time someone makes a GPS system, Lisson charges the manufacturer one point three cents for using its patents. That doesn't sound like much, until you realise that over a billion phones and other GPS devices are manufactured every year.'

'So they make a lot of money?'

'Galenka and Leonid paid sixteen million dollars for Lisson back in 1999. They sold assets worth at least six million, and Lisson now generates ten million dollars a year in patent revenues.'

'I could live off that,' Ryan said.

'Lombardi's law practice handles Lisson

Communications' legal business. They're also used by Galenka Aramov's computer security company, which has continued to do nicely since she died.'

Ryan laughed. 'So our buddy Ethan is a rich bastard?'

'Certainly is,' Amy said. 'But it looks like a dead end as far as our investigation is concerned. All it shows us is that Galenka and Leonid Aramov pooled some of their money and made a shrewd investment.'

'Lombardi has been sending money to Leonid Aramov under a false name though,' Ryan noted. 'That must be illegal.'

'But I'd be astonished if a clever lawyer like Lombardi hasn't been moving the money in a way that makes it impossible to trace it back to him.'

'So we're back to relying on whatever Andre and Tamara find out in Mexico?' Ryan asked.

Amy nodded. 'And that's a dangerous business. We're giving them two weeks max, then we'll pull them out whether or not they find anything incriminating on Leonid.'

*

Apart from kids on punishment or in basic training, every cherub got a holiday between Christmas and New Year. After taking Boxing Day off, James got roped into driving a bunch of kids down to London for ice skating and shopping on the 27th.

Two girls were over an hour late getting back to the meeting point, so it was ten when James drove the minibus through campus' main gate, and he had a headache because his charges had been rowdy all the way home.

James wanted to go up to his room and crash, but he'd had a text telling him to get straight to the mission preparation building on his return. Ewart Asker was waiting. He was CHERUB's head mission controller and husband of chairwoman Zara.

'How were the sales?' Ewart asked, as he sat behind a large glass-topped desk.

It had been nine years since James arrived on CHERUB campus as a twelve-year-old recruit, and Ewart had probably changed more in that time than any other staff member. Back then, Ewart was a junior mission controller, with pierced ears and ripped jeans. Now he had four kids, a receding hairline and a bit of a gut.

'The less said about my day the better,' James said. 'I had two grey-shirt girls in tears when I said I'd report them for being late back to the bus, the motorway out of London was jammed and the kids didn't shut up the whole three and a half hours.'

Ewart laughed. 'And it wasn't so long ago that you were one of those kids bouncing around on the bus driving me mad.'

'Makes me feel old,' James admitted.

'So, how's your Spanish?'

James looked confused. 'The only time I've used it the last few years is when me and Kerry go to this little Mexican place near Stanford campus. But I'm sure I can get by.'

'You hit it off with Andre, didn't you?'

'He's a good kid.'

'A senior TFU agent called Ted Brasker was supposed

to liaise with Andre and Tamara when they got to Mexico. Unfortunately, he slipped on a step at his Dubai hotel, and he's zonked on painkillers for however long it takes for his muscle to de-spasm. So, we're looking for someone with varied field experience, who speaks Russian and Spanish. A rapport with young Andre would be an advantage and ideally we needed this person to be in position about six hours ago.'

'Sounds a lot like me,' James said warily.

'Normally we'd have a team of three controllers on something like this,' Ewart said. 'But to start with it'll be you and an undercover DEA agent who knows the turf. Brasker will join you when his health improves.

'The situation in Ciudad Juárez is precarious. We don't know what Leonid Aramov is up to, but we do know there's a major drug war taking place. The police are so corrupt that the president gave up on them and deployed the army on the streets. I've already prepared some detailed briefing documents and I'll e-mail you some more. Technically, you're not a mission controller yet, so I can't just send you. You have to agree.'

'If that's where you need me, I'll go,' James said, breaking into a slight smile. It was more than three years since his last mission as a CHERUB agent had ended and he'd missed the buzz of working undercover.

'I looked into scheduled flights, but the only way to Ciudad Juárez is via Amsterdam or Atlanta. Both routes involve long layovers and won't get you in for more than a day. But I can have a long-range business jet pick you up from the nearest RAF base.'

'When?' James asked.

Ewart glanced at his watch. 'I can have a plane fuelled and waiting in two hours. Go pack a bag. I'll make up a kit of surveillance equipment and get someone to create a diplomatic passport so you don't get searched when you arrive in Mexico. We've got a passport machine here on campus now, so that'll only take about ten minutes.'

Ewart slid a wodge of paperwork across his desk. 'Take this lot for in-flight reading. And you look beat, so I'll have one of the black shirts drive you out to the airfield.'

37. WARS

PART 1 OF 6: MISSION BACKGROUND AND
SUMMARY

INTRODUCTION
With 110 million citizens, Mexico is the world's 11th most
populous country. Its 3,600-kilometre land border with the
United States is one of the world's longest, and over a million
people cross between the two countries every day. The length of
the border has always made it difficult to police, despite the US
Border Agency spending more than $10 billion per year doing so.

From the 1970s to the mid-1990s, most of the cocaine smuggled into the United States was brought in by air or sea by powerful drug cartels based in Colombia. As the influence of these cartels grew, they expanded, growing huge quantities of marijuana and forming links in the Middle East that enabled them to supply heroin.

When US President Reagan came to power in 1980, he declared a 'War on Drugs'. Although the billions spent in the drug war did little to change the quantity of drugs available on America's streets, the creation of the DEA (Drug Enforcement Agency) and increased anti-drug patrols in the air and at sea made it increasingly attractive to smuggle drugs overland from South America to the USA via Mexico.

As US military and DEA operations in South America gradually diminished the power of the Colombians, a new generation of cartels began springing up in Mexico. By the early 2000s, the Mexican cartels had outmuscled their Colombian forebears and began taking control of drug production as well as smuggling.

In Mexico itself, half a dozen cartels battled over smuggling routes. The most contested territory was along the country's northern border with the USA. Brutal street battles between rival gangs turned Mexican border towns such as Tijuana from popular tourist spots for Americans into desolate no-go areas.

At the same time as American tourists stopped coming, corporations who ran factories in northern Mexico to produce cheap goods for the US market began closing them because it had become cheaper to produce goods in China and Vietnam. This collapse of industry and tourism, combined with a wave of drug money, created a perfect storm of violence, corruption, unemployment and poverty.

A police officer earning $6,000 per year could earn the same amount per week in bribes from a drug dealer, and officers who resisted found the drug gangs threatening their families. With corruption reaching the highest levels of Mexican politics and law enforcement and a murder rate seventy times greater than the USA, it is now predicted that some areas of this once rapidly developing country are on course for total collapse.

MILITARISATION

Besides an extraordinary level of brutality, another characteristic of Mexico's warring drug cartels has been the use of heavy weaponry and military techniques.

Examples include a Mexican Special Forces unit that defected en masse to work for a drug cartel. The soldiers then executed the cartel's leaders and took control themselves. Thousands of rural peasants have been kidnapped, forced to dig smuggling tunnels under the US border and then murdered when the job is done so that they cannot reveal the tunnel's location.

When Mexican President Felipe Calderon came to power in 2006, he quickly realised that police in many border areas were so corrupt that the drug gangs were running the show. More than 45,000 Mexican soldiers have now been deployed on anti-drug smuggling operations inside their own borders. In response, the drug cartels have become increasingly militarised in their fights with the government and each other.

Ciudad Juárez

Lying on the US/Mexican border, midway between the Atlantic and Pacific oceans, Ciudad Juárez and its twin city El Paso on the US side of the border have seen some of the most vicious fighting of the Mexican drug war. The three crossings between the two cities are among the busiest on the whole border. More trucks pass between the US and Mexico via Ciudad Juárez than at any other point, making it a prime spot for drug trafficking.

At various times smuggling through the city has been dominated by three different cartels, but after years of bitter fighting both inside cartels and between them, there is currently no clear picture of who controls what.

The city has also been particularly badly hit by the collapse of Mexican industry. Although the centre of town is relatively safe during daylight hours, the entire city is dangerous at night and outlying industrial areas where poverty and unemployment rates are above 50 per cent should be considered absolute no-go areas unless accompanied by a guide with excellent knowledge of local conditions.

Aramov Clan Involvement

During the 1980s, the Aramov Clan worked in close partnership with the Colombian cartels in flying heroin from the Middle East to South America or the Caribbean. The volatile situation with rival Mexican cartels, and US military presence in Afghanistan where most of the world's heroin is produced, caused clan matriarch Irena Aramov to step back from large-scale heroin smuggling in the early 2000s.

However, the clan continued some drug smuggling operations for Mexican cartels, and is believed to have sold mortars and *other heavy weaponry to the Mexican cartels.*

LEONID ARAMOV

When Leonid Aramov was disowned by his mother and forced to leave Kyrgyzstan, it was assumed that he would retreat to Russia or the Middle East. Although we currently have no idea what Leonid Aramov is up to in Mexico, he has no ties to the country and some kind of involvement in the drug war seems to be the only explanation for his presence.

Leonid does not have the cash or manpower to take on the Mexican gangs. It is most likely that he is using his extensive global contacts to obtain heavy weapons for the warring cartels.

MISSION STRUCTURE & GOALS

Leonid's former wife Tamara and youngest son Andre have agreed to work for TFU (Transnational Facilitator Unit) and are now living with Leonid Aramov in a luxury apartment complex in an affluent suburb of Ciudad Juárez.

The mission controller's goals are as follows:
1. *Travel to Ciudad Juárez and liaise with DEA agent Lucinda Alvarez.*
2. *Safely make contact with Andre and/or Tamara Aramov.*
3. *Try and establish what Leonid Aramov is doing in Mexico.*
4. *If it is safe to do so, take action against Leonid, either alone or in conjunction with Mexican authorities.*
5. *Given Leonid's volatile personality and the dangerous situation in Ciudad Juárez, Andre and Tamara will be pulled out after two weeks, even if no progress is made with the mission goals.*

38. CONTACT

Most locals thought it insane to use the communal pool in fifteen-degree weather, so Andre had it to himself. He wasn't a strong swimmer, but swimming was something he always enjoyed and as he wasn't enrolled in school and had no friends within five thousand kilometres, a few lengths were his best shot at a break from his family.

A fifth length was over-ambitious, so he pulled to the side of the pool and caught his breath at the two-metre marker. A man's legs coming along the poolside put an image of Boris in his head, but this dude wore the khaki shorts and green polo shirt of the apartment complex's maintenance and cleaning crews.

'James,' Andre gasped, before looking back to see who was around.

'Swim back to the shallow end,' James said, speaking fast because their encounter had to look casual. 'I've slid a com set and a few other things in the pocket of your robe.'

'Right,' Andre said.

'And stop glancing around. If anyone asks, I asked you if the pool was hot enough.'

James backed away from the pool, grabbed the handles of a janitor's cart and started moving. The pool was in a large rectangular garden, with individual staircases feeding from several dozen apartments. It seemed idyllic, until you noticed that every staircase had been beefed up with steel gates, spiked grilles, CCTV and occasionally an armed guard.

Although Leonid's apartment didn't have a guard, there was a chance he had associates living in other apartments who did. The brief conversation with Andre might have got their attention and even with a cap on, James' blond head and fair skin made him distinctive in a country where a more Latin appearance was the norm.

A stringy old creature taking a jog blocked James' path. She pointed and spoke angry Spanish too fast for James to keep up with.

'Are you hosing out my rubbish area today?' she snapped. 'I reported the dead rat three days ago and nobody has been near.'

'I'm new,' James said, shrugging and trying to sound thick. 'I'll ask the supervisor.'

'You guys were keener when you knocked for Christmas tips.'

'I just started today,' James said. 'I'll find disinfectant and a shovel.'

'Make sure you do,' the woman snapped, before setting off again.

As the old battleaxe jogged off, James was aware of Andre climbing out of the pool fifty metres behind. He sped up the cart, rolling it back the way he'd come, going through swinging black doors into a bare concrete storage area filled with pool chemicals and gardening kit.

After reaching down into the cart's tool area and retrieving his automatic pistol, James tucked the gun into the back of his shorts and peered into the supervisor's office. The grey-haired man was slumped across his desk fast asleep. The spray James had administered would keep him that way for at least another half hour and he hoped he didn't get caught sleeping on the job.

Four flights of musty stairs, a door and a twenty-metre walk took him to a mesh gate at the rear of the apartment complex. After hitting a button to unlock the gate he walked fifty metres over badly cracked paving and jumped into the front passenger seat of a VW camper van.

A frizzy-haired Mexican-American named Lucinda Alvarez sat in the driver's seat. She was a DEA field agent, who knew as much about Ciudad Juárez and its drug wars as anyone, and Dr D had called in a favour to get her temporarily assigned to TFU.

'Did you make contact?' Lucinda asked.

'Three hours of nothing,' James said. 'As I was about to give up, Andre comes strolling out in a beach robe and swimming shorts. The com only has a range of a couple of kilometres, so best if you drive somewhere just out of sight.'

As Lucinda set the camper's elderly diesel engine clattering, James stepped between the front seats into the rear compartment and squatted on a skinny foam mattress covered with a crocheted blanket. He pulled the gun sticking into his backside, then peeled off the green polo shirt he'd stolen from a locker in the storage area.

As Lucinda came out of the alley into slow-moving traffic, James found a backpack filled with espionage gear and grabbed a tiny receiver and a circular Perspex box with his com unit inside. Dropping it into his ear was a delicate operation that had to wait until Lucinda drove a few hundred metres and parked in an alleyway behind an abandoned pharmacy.

'Andre, you hear me? Andre?'

James repeated the call a couple of times before Andre spoke in a panic.

'Gimme a minute, I'm drying off.'

'Find a quiet spot, make sure nobody can hear you talk.'

'I'm in my bathroom,' Andre said. 'There's two closed doors between me and anyone else.'

'Great,' James said. 'So how's it been?'

Andre ignored the question and spoke exuberantly. 'I'm so glad it's you. I was told it was gonna be this old guy called Ted.'

The gushing tone made James smile. 'I think you're gonna be the founder and sole member of the James Adams fan club.'

'Journey was shit,' Andre said. 'It's been three days.

I tried finding another way to communicate, but there's no landline and I couldn't get my hands on anyone's mobile.'

'We've got com now,' James said. 'And there's a tiny cellular unit in the pocket of your robe as well. It'll work wherever you can get a phone signal.'

'It's not been too bad,' Andre said. 'Dad's being sickeningly nice to my mum because he wants to get inside her pants. Alex is acting human. Boris is still a massive dick, but spends all his time with this Mexican called Silvia. It's actually kinda funny when you hear them screwing in his room.'

James smiled. 'Any clue what your dad's up to?'

'He's definitely got stuff on,' Andre said. 'Like, he's been across the courtyard a couple of times for meetings with this guy in apartment seventeen. And he's got a little office set up and he's always on his phone. He tries speaking in Spanish, but he's really bad at it and you hear him losing his temper when people don't understand.'

'And your mum's OK?'

'So so,' Andre said. 'Dad's taken us into town a couple of times, bought me clothes and a bunch of games for the Xbox. But he's changed the wireless password so I can't go online any more. Mum's wary, because it only takes a tiny thing to set him off and he beat her up untold times when we were at the Kremlin.'

'Your main job was to lead us to him,' James said. 'And that's done. First sign of anything bad, we'll whip you out of there.'

'I'm pleased you're back in touch,' Andre said.

'We need information,' James said. 'There are hundreds of cellphones inside the apartment complex. We haven't been able to pick out your dad's and your brother's phones, but once we do, we can listen in to their calls. It would help if you got hold of their numbers. If getting hold of the phones is tricky, see if you can find a bill or any other paperwork lying around.'

'There is one thing,' Andre said. 'I know my dad's a liar, but he keeps talking about leaving soon and starting a new life with us. And I've heard my brothers talking about what they'll do when they leave.'

'Any idea where or when?' James asked.

'No idea where, but it's soon, I think,' Andre said. 'My dad had his office door open when I walked past and he was dumping papers in this massive shredder. And he's usually really messy, but all his stuff is kept in a couple of file boxes.'

James was intrigued, and also worried. They'd only just tracked Leonid down and the last thing they wanted was for him to disappear before they got any evidence.

'Do they ever leave you on your own?' James asked. 'The key to whatever Leonid is up to will be in his office. He's wary of computers, especially since we hacked him and stole most of his money. Papers in his office are our best shot at finding out what he's up to.'

'I could probably say I'm sick and stay home when they go out to dinner or something,' Andre said. 'But there's a big lock on the office.'

James wished he'd trained Andre in lock picking, but

it's not a technique you can master on a ten-day course.

'OK,' James said. 'It would be good if you could get in the office, but don't take any risks unless you run them by me first.'

Lucinda shouted a reminder from up front. 'Sat-navs.'

'Oh,' James said. 'We had one other idea. If you get a chance, go down to your dad's car, or your brothers' if they've got cars, and check the sat-navs. We're trying to work out what gang Leonid's working with and if we know where your dad is going for his meetings it would be a major clue.'

'Will do,' Andre said.

'Anything else you want to ask?'

'I'm good,' Andre said.

'Now we're in touch, I'm going to try and find a room to rent nearby,' James said. 'So speak to me on the com any time you like, and remember what I said: no big risks without running it by me first.'

39. STAIN

Ryan watched through the balcony windows of Natalka's corner room as sun set over the Kremlin's runway. It was like old times, with a tang of jet fuel in the air and five roaring planes lined up for take-off. And while the last big departure had sent four crews to their doom, this group faced a more positive future.

Kremlin mechanics had worked over Christmas, cannibalising parts from eight of the clan's most modern freighters, to make five models in decent condition. For the first time on record, Aramov planes had been fitted with new tyres, modern navigation equipment, and most importantly, each engine had been modified with a hundred-thousand-dollar hush-kit, which enabled them to pass strict noise regulations enforced by most wealthy countries.

Over the years, Kremlin mechanics had disguised

planes with liveries ranging from the UN to the Vietnamese Air Force, but these five now legitimately bore the silver paintwork and red crescent logo of an Islamic medical charity.

The story Amy sent around the Kremlin was that a wealthy benefactor had leased the planes and crews for charity work. But there would soon be no Aramov Clan to pay, so the planes were effectively a donation. Extra cash to pay crews, fuel and maintenance for the next ten years had also been donated out of the millions seized from Leonid Aramov.

It was rare that a CHERUB agent got to see a simple, direct example of the good they did and Ryan felt quite emotional as he watched the first plane take off. Two were heading to Europe where they'd be converted into mobile hospitals, providing medical care and minor surgery in remote regions. The other three faced less glamorous but no less worthy futures ferrying food and medical supplies to disaster zones.

But while Ryan was happy, Natalka looked sour.

'I bet it's another trap,' she sneered, as she stood by the kitchen worktop painting black varnish on her thumbnail. 'They'll get screwed over like my mum did.'

Ryan had barely been out of Natalka's sight in the week since they'd got back together. He was sick of her cigarettes and negative attitude. But while spending so much time together drove him nuts, their time was running out and the prospect of not being with her made him feel even worse.

'They'll sort something out,' Ryan said. 'Your mum'll be OK.'

Natalka lobbed a half-eaten pack of biscuits at Ryan's head. 'Stop saying dumb shit to make me feel better.'

'Have you called your aunt yet?'

'I hate her guts,' Natalka said. 'I'm staying here with you.'

Natalka had no idea that demolition crews were arriving to blast the Kremlin to smithereens. Ryan wasn't sure whether it was better to know that your love affair is doomed like he did, or live in ignorance like Natalka.

'I've got an errand to run for Igor,' Ryan said. 'I'll be an hour. Two at most.'

'You're always up to something,' Natalka said, narrowing her eyes.

Ryan picked up the biscuits and placed them back on the worktop beside Natalka. 'I'm bringing money in,' he said, as he hunted the carpet for his Converse. 'And you're in a mood. I can't say anything when you're like this.'

'See if they've refilled the Marlboros in the ciggie machine,' Natalka said.

Ryan tutted as he closed Natalka's door, knowing what she really meant was *buy me a packet of cigarettes*. But all thoughts of Natalka were out of his head by the time he reached his own room. He tucked a small .22 revolver in the waistband of his trousers and pulled a hoodie over his head to hide the bulge.

Igor was down in reception, looking hung over. Ryan didn't speak to him, he walked past Igor's armchair in the deserted bar and mouthed, *Five minutes.*

After getting Natalka's cigarettes from the vending machine, Ryan took the lift up to the fifth floor. Amy had told the two security guards that he was coming. He stepped into Leonid's old apartment, and breathed a weird stagnant smell, coming off something Tamara had left rotting in a cupboard.

Amy was barefoot in a nightshirt. 'Morning,' she said. 'Everything OK?'

'Natalka's miserable,' Ryan said. 'Is there really nothing we can do about her mum?'

Amy laughed. 'Dimitra spent ten years as a pilot in a heavy-duty smuggling ring. We can't get her out because you've got the hots for her daughter.'

'We fitted her up though.'

'On that one last mission,' Amy admitted. 'But what about all the drugs, guns and weapons she smuggled in the decade before that?'

'Can't we at least try—'

Amy cut Ryan dead. 'You need to focus on Igor,' she said firmly.

'I signalled him at the bar,' Ryan said. 'He'll be coming up the back stairs in a minute or two.'

'Better get going then, hadn't you?'

The Kremlin's five floors were all linked by stairs, but the Aramovs had fixed it so that everyone accessed the top floor via a single lift. There were always two armed guards on duty at the fifth-floor lift exit and the armoured stair door could only be opened from inside.

Ryan moved to this door, which was located at the

rear of a small room that had once housed Irena Aramov's nurse. After a couple of minutes squatting on a single bed, he heard Igor's knuckles tap the outside.

As Ryan yanked the heavy door, Igor pulled a huge pistol fitted with a silencer and scope.

Ryan grinned. 'Are you sure that's big enough?'

Igor shrugged. 'It'll make a mess of Josef Aramov, that's for sure.'

'What about the girl?'

'Leonid doesn't give a shit about Amy,' Igor said. 'He wants Josef dead for messing with Tamara. But I don't want her running around screaming her head off until I'm well clear, so if she's there I'll kill her too.'

'Pity,' Ryan said. 'Amy's got fantastic tits.'

Igor stifled a laugh. 'I really like you, Ryan. It's a shame about your dad, but you're a survivor.'

'Especially with a hundred thousand som in my pocket to get me and Natalka out of here.'

Igor took the hint and pulled a roll of money. 'You'll have to trust me, there's not time to stand around counting it.'

'When's your flight?'

'I've got time,' Igor said, avoiding a direct answer. 'So how do we get up to the other end without the guards on the elevator seeing us?'

Ryan led Igor out of the nurse's room and across Irena Aramov's lounge. The large space was full of ornaments and family pictures that hadn't changed since she flew to the US for cancer treatment. A sliding glass door threw in a blast of cold as Ryan opened it. When the curtain was pulled back, he revealed three balconies stretching the length of the building, each separated by half-metre gaps.

'It's icy,' Ryan warned. 'But Andre told me Alex and Boris used to jump them all the time for a dare. The third balcony ends at the entrance to Josef's apartment. I've already crept up there and made sure it's unlocked.'

'The guards didn't notice?'

'The guards are used to me,' Ryan explained.

'You'd best leave,' Igor said. 'Once news gets out that this ship has no captain, things could get pretty nasty. Looting, chaos.'

'I'm already packed,' Ryan lied. 'We're heading for the bus station.'

As Ryan walked back to the nurse's room, Igor moved out on the first balcony. The gap between the first and second balconies was half a metre. The handsome Russian snapped sheet ice off the rusted railings before hopping across.

Igor took care not to look down until his foot was flat on the springy plastic of a snow-covered garden chair. As he hopped off, he had no idea that Amy had rigged a heat-sensitive detonator to 250 grams of plastic explosive packed into an outdoor light fitting.

The blast hit Igor at shoulder height, blowing a large hole in his neck. As the first mist of blood erupted, the upper half of his body sprawled across the metal railing, then teetered momentarily before the weight of his torso dragged his legs over.

Igor's end was messy. He was briefly impaled on anti-bird spikes before a sheet of snow thrown loose by the blast gave him a final nudge to the ground. Amy had shaped the charge so that the explosion funnelled out and hit Igor like a punch, but the shock wave still shattered several windows and dislodged large quantities of snow on the Kremlin's roof. The snow sheets piled on top of Igor until only his dead right arm poked out of the mound.

40. WIRE

Andre wore jeans and a smart black going-out-to-dinner shirt as he rode a lift from the basement car park to their third-floor apartment. Leonid had a tailored cashmere suit unlike anything he'd ever worn at the Kremlin, while Tamara was in a shoulderless black evening dress which Leonid bought for more money than most Mexicans earn in six months.

'I've left my wallet in the car,' Andre said, as he patted an empty back pocket.

He'd told Tamara that he'd contacted James and given her a com unit, but she didn't know what he planned to do now and she instinctively acted like a sensible mum.

'It'll still be there tomorrow morning,' she said. 'You need to go to bed.'

'But if someone sees a wallet on the car seat,' Andre

said, 'they might smash the windows.'

Leonid had a bottle of wine in his belly and broke into a jolly laugh. 'The bullet-proof windows?'

But Tamara had cottoned on and put a persuasive arm around her ex-husband's neck.

'Give him the keys, you know he's a worrier.'

'Lock it up properly,' Leonid said, passing Andre the keys to his big Lexus.

Leonid and Tamara stepped out as Andre pressed the button to ride back down to the basement. It was a posh garage, with air conditioning, neat yellow markings and the parking bays covered with green rubber like a school gym. Occasionally you'd even see an elderly cleaning lady down on her knees scrubbing away tyre marks.

Andre pressed a button on the keys to unlock the limousine. The armoured door weighed a quarter tonne, so when he touched the handle, motors whirred to save him the effort. After snatching his wallet off the back seat, Andre clambered between the front seats. He gave the sat-nav screen one touch, then a double touch behind his earlobe to activate the com system.

'James, can you hear me?'

'Loud and clear, Andre.'

'Sweet,' Andre said. 'I wasn't sure I'd get a signal down here. I'm in front of Dad's sat-nav and I'm scrolling through addresses. Have you got a pen to write stuff down?'

'I'm recording,' James said. 'Just read 'em off.'

Andre read out the sixteen recently used addresses saved in Leonid's sat-nav. None of them meant anything to James, but Lucinda knew Ciudad Juárez well and hopefully the locations would give clues about what Leonid was up to and who he was working with.

'Nice job,' James said, after the last address. 'But you've taken longer than your dad's expecting. Have you prepared an excuse?'

'This car park's a maze,' Andre said. 'I'll say I walked the wrong way and couldn't find the car. I'll be going to bed when I get upstairs, so I'll say goodnight.'

'Don't let the bedbugs bite,' James joked. 'I'll leave my com in all night, so don't be afraid to call if you need me.'

Andre double-tapped to shut off his com, checked the car was locked and headed for the elevator. As he got close he heard footsteps behind. The deserted garage was spooky and he jumped when Boris came around a corner.

'Baby brother!' Boris said. Then he got much closer and sounded menacing. 'Alone at last, eh, titch?'

'Piss off,' Andre said, backing away.

Boris plucked Andre off the floor with one massive arm and slammed his back against the lift doors.

'Painful?' Boris asked, as Andre groaned.

Boris dropped Andre from a metre and a half and sunk the heel of his huge Nike basketball boot into his gut.

'Leave off,' Andre groaned, feeling like his restaurant meal was about to make a reverse trip as Boris ground his heel in.

Andre thought about the weak spots James had taught

him, but he was pinned and none was in reach.

'Don't think Dad's forgiven you,' Boris growled. 'Once we get to the Caribbean, Dad'll be back with your slut mum. He'll *never* forget that you betrayed him and I'll beat your arse every day to remind you.'

Andre had tears welling. 'Why are you always such a dick?' he shouted. 'I never did anything to you.'

'I like putting people in pain,' Boris said. 'Especially you.'

A chubby security guard had seen something on CCTV and was waddling over, one hand on his holstered gun.

'Only me, pal!' Boris shouted, as he stepped off Andre. 'Messing with my little bro here!'

The guard looked concerned as Andre staggered to his feet, coughing. But Boris was a monster and the guard would be putting his job on the line if he pulled a gun on a tenant.

'You're too rough with him,' the guard said, before tutting and turning back to his booth.

Andre dreaded what would happen when the elevator doors closed, so he started scrambling up the stairs, gasping for air and with tears streaking down his face.

Boris made an echoey shout after him. 'Run all you like, titch. I've got years to catch up with you.'

*

Andre didn't want everyone to see he was crying, and he didn't want James knowing either. He yelled goodnight to his parents and limped straight upstairs. He lay awake for ages, clutching an aching stomach and fantasising painful deaths for Boris.

More than anything, being humiliated by Boris made Andre mad. When he was sure everyone had gone to bed, he went down to the kitchen and grabbed a bottle of mineral water from the fridge. The light coming out of the doorway lit up the marble-topped counter. His mum's heels were on the floor, but more disturbingly so were her stockings and the expensive dress.

It didn't take a genius to work out what had happened. Tamara and Leonid had both been quite drunk when they left the restaurant, but it was less clear if his mum was a willing participant. Leaving the fridge open for the light, Andre checked his mum's stuff. The dress wasn't ripped, her bag and two half-drunk glasses of red stood on the countertop. Nothing suggested a struggle, but Leonid was strong and so it was still no certainty.

After dumping the half-drunk bottle in the kitchen bin, Andre held his stomach as he went back upstairs. It was past 1 a.m., but he could hear Boris playing Call of Duty in his room. Instead of heading back to bed, Andre turned right. The room his mum had been using was empty and he moved up to the double doors of the master bedroom.

One was slightly ajar. All the bedclothes were in a mound, there were roses everywhere and candles that had mostly burned out. Leonid and Tamara were entangled on the bed, naked and asleep. There was also a half-drunk bottle of champagne, and Andre realised that his dad had paid someone to come in and set up a whole *flowers-champagne-candles* deal while they'd been at the restaurant.

Seeing his parents in bed together made Andre feel horrible. Part of it was the gross-out thought of them doing it. But he also felt uneasy, because for all Tamara's protests that she hated Leonid, she'd never tried to leave the Kremlin. She'd done Leonid's laundry, cooked amazing meals and often ended up in bed with him. Even when Leonid slapped her about, Tamara would say that it was her own fault for winding him up.

Fear accounted for some of what Tamara did, but there also still seemed to be a basic physical attraction and Andre always felt betrayed when he saw a sign of it.

The bedroom scene was a lot to take right after the beating from Boris, and he felt like crying again as he backed up to the door. A hand waggling in the dark gave him a start. He feared Leonid waking up, but it was his mother's small hand making a come-here gesture in the flickering candlelight.

Andre caught a smell of sweaty bodies as he stepped up to the bed, embarrassed at being so close to his mum naked. Leonid had fallen asleep with his body resting against Tamara's and a hairy arm sprawled across her stomach. She was anxious not to wake Leonid up, so she silently mouthed to Andre while gesturing with her free arm.

Andre realised she was pointing to the top drawer of a cabinet on Leonid's side of the bed. He stepped over his dad's trousers and a mound of cushions and saw his mum making a *shush* gesture as he neared the drawer.

Mercifully, the drawer was on a smooth runner. Andre looked inside and saw Leonid's main bunch of keys. It's tough to grab keys without making any noise and the chinking felt like church bells as Andre clutched them in his hand.

Andre didn't need the hint, but Tamara was making a *go, go* gesture as he backed out. Boris loudly cursed at his video game as Andre darted down the hall to his room, and a relieved gasp set off a painful reminder of what his oldest brother had done to his stomach muscles.

After flipping on a bedside light, Andre worked out that there were two keys that let you into the apartment, a burglar alarm fob, two small keys that looked like they opened a desk drawer or filing cabinet and a large gold key that had to be for the office.

Andre felt a bit sick as he tried remembering what James had taught him. The first rule was to be sure where everyone was. Leonid was sleeping off food, booze and sex and it was unlikely he'd surface much before lunchtime. Alex and Boris were trickier. They wouldn't emerge for the toilet because all the bedrooms had ensuites, but there was still a slight chance one of them would come downstairs for a drink or a snack.

Andre didn't think this would be a major problem because he'd make sure both brothers were upstairs when he walked past their rooms, and if they came down later he'd be behind the locked door of his father's office.

T-shirt and boxers weren't ideal for concealing stuff, so Andre pulled on jeans and pocketed his dad's keys and the tiny cellphone James had given him.

He'd guessed right about which key opened the office and he pushed the door closed silently behind himself. The main light might shine around the edges of the door, so he flipped on a small desk lamp and aimed the beam behind a stack of files. Then he pulled back his earlobe and did the double tap that activated the microtransmitter in his ear canal.

'James?'

It took a few seconds before James answered, half yawning. 'What's the matter?'

'I'm mentally scarred after seeing my parents naked. The good news is, I'm in my dad's office.'

James sounded anxious. 'You should have spoken to me first. Are you sure you're safe?'

'I've got time,' Andre said. 'My brothers never come in here. And my mum will warn me somehow if Dad moves.'

'I'm setting up to record what you say,' James said, as Andre heard a noise like bedsprings creaking in his ear. 'You wouldn't believe the dive I'm staying in. I've got mice and cockroaches.'

'So where do I start?' Andre said. 'I've got two locked file boxes, but I think the little keys on my dad's bunch open them. There's a laptop and there's a bunch of stuff on the desk.'

'Recording now,' James said. 'Remember where everything was before you start moving things about. Let's assume that your dad won't trust computers again in a hurry. Take me through the papers on the desk first.'

'There's a stack of messages on light blue paper. They're in Russian. They're on the edge of the desk near the shredder. I guess he hasn't got around to shredding them yet . . . Oh, there's something else I forgot to tell you. Boris let slip that the place Leonid plans to move us to is in the Caribbean.'

'Interesting,' James said. 'If that's true, it rules out any plans for a return to the Kremlin. Are there other papers near the shredder?'

'There's a big stack,' Andre confirmed.

James thought for a couple of seconds. 'I reckon anything lined up for the shredder is going to be fairly interesting. It's most likely recent, and there must be a reason why he's bothering to shred it.'

'Right,' Andre said, as he moved around to the pre-shredder stack at the edge of the desk. 'There's about twenty messages. *RX 145·710* . . . And it's all banks of numbers.'

'Code,' James explained. 'Almost certainly his Russian friends. We're already decoding their messages at source, so don't get bogged down with them.'

'The next batch look like receipts,' Andre said. 'Bausch Chemical, three thousand dollars. Houston Drilling Supplies, eight thousand four hundred.'

'Could be digging a tunnel,' James said. 'Skip for now, we can come back later if we don't find anything juicier.'

'There's some big papers,' Andre said. 'Like designs for some sort of rocket. A mortar maybe?'

'Weird,' James said. 'I guess someone wants technical

details of a weapon he's trying to sell.'

'Looks like it's called PGSLM,' Andre said.

James found the initials oddly familiar. He'd not heard them for eight years, but when he placed them, he almost fell off his bed: *Precision Guided Shoulder Launched Missile*.

When James was thirteen, he'd worked with his sister Lauren, busting a kid out of a maximum-security prison as part of a convoluted plot to track down a woman called Jane Oxford. Oxford was suspected of stealing a batch of advanced shoulder launched missiles, each one fitted with a guidance system that made it accurate enough to fly through a bathroom window from a range of five kilometres. James and Lauren had succeeded in finding Jane Oxford. But while she'd been sent to prison, the missiles were never recovered.

'You might have struck gold,' James said, trying not to let his excitement filter through and disrupt Andre's concentration. 'Tell me more.'

'A lot of the writing is in Spanish,' Andre said. 'I can't understand it, but there's notes on the edge of the plan in my dad's handwriting: 74 x PGSLM @ $325,000 = $24.05 million.'

James' first thought had been that Leonid had somehow unearthed the six guided missiles that Jane Oxford had stolen ten years earlier, but apparently, Leonid had access to seventy-four of them.

'OK,' James said. 'Maybe I can drop a camera when you go swimming and you can photograph some of the documents, but for now I want you to go through and try to find anything referring to PGSLM.'

'Why's that so important?' Andre asked.

'A PGSLM is about the size of a regular mortar. But while a mortar takes a skilled operator to hit a tank from three hundred metres, PGSLM is a smart weapon that uses GPS and terrain mapping. Suppose you're a drug dealer and you want to wipe out the boss of a rival gang, or the local chief of police. You no longer need to go storming into enemy HQ with a dozen men, all guns blazing. You just need to know where your enemy is. You tap in the coordinates and launch your missile from the other side of town.'

'Sounds nifty,' Andre said, as he started flicking through the papers. 'OK, let's see what else I can find out.'

41. PUZZLES

Andre read James more documents about PGSLM and stumbled on details of bank accounts held by Leonid under false names. After ninety minutes, James told Andre to go to bed, then he typed up a short report and uploaded the audio recordings of everything Andre had said to TFU headquarters in Dallas.

The information manager on duty passed everything on to Dr D, Ted Brasker and Amy Collins. As Amy wasn't directly involved in the Mexican side of the operation the e-mail sat unopened in her inbox as she spent an afternoon on her laptop, organising logistics for the final plan to destroy the Kremlin.

When Amy opened the message, she was intrigued by the fact that Leonid was planning a $24-million deal to sell guided missiles to a Mexican drug gang. But things got really interesting when she decided to do a

Google search to find out a bit of background info on the PGSLM.

The search tool on Amy's Chrome browser used a mixture of Google's database and Amy's previous searches to guess what she was looking for. When Amy typed PGSLM into the search box, the dropdown box offered the option to search for *PGSLM Lisson Communications*.

Amy was surprised as she hit *search*. After a bunch of adverts, the first link took her to a fifteen-year-old story from a defunct stock market magazine.

LISSON COM GOLD TURNS TO RED INK AS SAT-NAV INNOVATOR DROPS 73% IN ONE DAY'S TRADING

The article had been published a few weeks before Leonid and Galenka Aramov used their holding corporation to buy Lisson Communications. The in-depth article ran to two thousand words. Most of it told a story Amy already knew, about how Lisson had been brought to the verge of bankruptcy by disastrous sales of a new generation of in-car navigation units.

But the journalist had clearly done detailed research and deep within the article was a brief reference to another setback Lisson suffered in its military division. The company had apparently been involved in bribery allegations after a failed bid to develop guidance technology for the US Army's latest generation of PGSLM shoulder launched guided missiles.

It seemed like a mighty coincidence that Leonid

Aramov part-owned a company that had worked on the PGSLM missile, and was apparently now in a position to sell seventy-four of them to a gang of Mexican drug smugglers.

Amy's cellphone didn't work inside the Kremlin, so she routed an Internet call to Dr D, using TFU's secure communication network. When Dr D didn't answer she tried Ted Brasker, but it was Ethan who picked up the phone.

'Amy,' Ethan said. 'Long time no speak. How's it hanging?'

Amy thought it best not to go into the fact that her day had begun by blowing Leonid Aramov's Kremlin spy off a fifth-floor balcony and just said, 'Not too bad.'

'I take it you want Ted?'

'Is he there?'

'He is,' Ethan said. 'But he's on muscle relaxants for his back and they leave him a bit spaced out.'

'I'll try talking to him anyway.'

Amy heard some yelling and a mini row between Ethan and Ted's college-aged daughter Lyla on whether to wake Ted up. But eventually the familiar Texan drawl came down the line and he didn't sound too bad.

'Boredom's weighing me down,' Ted said. 'The US government's got rules coming out of its ass these days. I'd rather be working, but I can't go near headquarters till the doc signs a piece of paper.'

Amy heard Lyla mutter, 'You can barely walk, Dad,' in the background.

'Your joints get fragile in extreme old age,' Amy

teased. 'I've read the e-mail from James Adams and I think I've found a connection between Lisson Communications and the PGSLM missiles.'

Once Amy had explained everything and Ted had yelled at his daughter to fetch his laptop and reading glasses, he resumed speaking.

'Lisson Communications had three directors,' Ted said. 'Galenka Aramov is dead; Leonid is our target; the third director and company secretary was their lawyer, Lombardi. If anyone knows how Leonid Aramov came to be in Mexico selling seventy-four guided missiles, it'll be him.'

'True,' Amy said. 'But Lombardi's a lawyer. If we arrest him, he'll keep his mouth shut and pull every legal trick to stop us questioning him or searching his property. And when we do question him—'

Ted interrupted brusquely. 'We have to get information *before* Leonid sells these missiles, banks his twenty-four million and disappears.'

'Andre gave James the impression that it's not long until Leonid pulls off the deal and moves to the Caribbean.'

'Legal methods won't get anything useful out of Lombardi within our timescale,' Ted said. 'But seeing as I'm getting bounced into retirement when this is over, I'm prepared to take a few risks.'

'You could lose your pension,' Amy warned.

'I *could* go to jail,' Ted said. 'But I've got my Marine Corps pension and my Marine Corps spirit. I may be an old geezer with a bad back, but I will not let a smartass lawyer and a bunch of due-process bullcrap stop me from making one last attempt to do the right thing.'

Amy laughed. 'You could always defend yourself by saying the back pills are making you loopy.'

'And besides all this missile nonsense, I'll bet Lombardi knows more than we do about why Leonid killed Galenka. I've got fond of Ethan since he's been living here. That guy deserves to know the truth about his mother.'

'So I'll leave this with you?' Amy said.

'Ted's on the case. And don't you go worrying about your next pay check either, Amy Collins. You're a good agent and I've got plenty of friends.'

*

Ethan Aramov, previously Ethan Kitsell, now lived in Texas as Ethan Brasker. He'd set the alarm for an early start on the last Sunday of 2012, met up with two school friends and spent the day at a speed chess tournament in central Dallas.

'No trophy?' Ted said, when Ethan got home mid-afternoon.

'Finished eighteenth out of seventy-four,' Ethan said cheerfully. 'Which isn't bad, because I was one of the youngest and there were six grandmasters in the field.'

'Did you get beaten by that nine-year-old again?'

Ethan smiled. 'That little smartass wasn't in my pool, but he beat my mate Josh and finished about tenth.'

'You'll get him one day,' Ted said, keeping one hand on his painful back, as Ethan moved into the kitchen and grabbed a Dr Pepper from the fridge.

Ethan laughed and shook his head. 'Your faith is encouraging, sir, but that kid's a prodigy.'

Texas was warm even in December and Ethan had unbuttoned his shirt and stepped through to the living-room where he was surprised by the two enormous men on the couch.

'Joe and Don,' Ted explained. 'Ex-professional wrestlers. A couple of recent vehicle felonies will be overlooked, provided they help us deal with our pal, Lombardi.'

The two giants made Ethan feel exceptionally puny as they offered crunching handshakes.

'Chess,' Don said thoughtfully. 'That's the game with the horsey that moves like an L.'

'You got it,' Ethan said, deciding it was best not to tell a man with a spiked fist tattooed on his neck that the piece was actually called a knight.

'So I've scrounged up an FBI jet at Fort Worth,' Ted said. 'The plan's fairly unsophisticated. We should get to California by about ten tonight. Then we drive out to the vineyard where Lombardi's spending his Christmas vacation. We knock on Lombardi's door, tell him you're Ethan Aramov and that you want to know the truth about Leonid and your mother. If he's any less than forthcoming, Joe and Don will use their persuasive skills to make him open up.'

*

As Ethan and Ted set off, James checked the spyhole in his dingy rented room and was pleased to see Lucinda on the other side of the door.

'I'm not responsible for the smell in here,' James told her, as she stepped in. 'It was like that when I got here.'

'I'll believe you, millions wouldn't,' Lucinda said cheerfully. 'Heard any more out of Andre?'

'Nothing worth knowing,' James replied. 'He's stuck home playing video games. Pissed off that his mum and dad are being all lovey-dovey. Though it looks like Tamara's mainly doing it to help our cause.'

Lucinda nodded. 'Tamara's attracted to him. A lot of women go for the Neanderthal look.'

'Does that include you?' James asked.

He was trying to be funny, but Lucinda glowered at him. 'What if it was the other way around?' she snapped. 'If you were undercover and you slept with a female target, it would be a big joke. *Ha, ha, I nailed the bitch!* Why can't a woman enjoy sex for its own sake? Why must a woman who has sex either be a victim or a slut?'

James had already worked out that Lucinda had a short fuse, but this was a strong reaction even for her.

'OK, don't bite my head off.'

'I'm not mad,' Lucinda said. 'You're a bit of an asshole, that's all. The good news is, I stopped at the market and bought you gifts.'

She passed James a carrier bag, which contained bug spray, and half a dozen mousetraps.

'Chocolate or peanut butter makes the best bait,' Lucinda said.

As James inspected a plastic trap, Lucinda unrolled a map on the bed. It was made from sheets of A4 paper, printed off Bing Maps and crudely taped together.

'I plotted the sixteen locations from the sat-nav in Leonid's Lexus,' Lucinda explained. 'Airport, shopping malls, a big industrial unit up near the border. Most interesting, there's two locations out of town, close to the secure compound of the Talavera Brothers. I'd guess that's who Leonid is selling his missiles to.'

'Can those guys afford twenty-four million?' James asked.

'They're a new force here in the north. They're muscling in on the smuggling routes and have powerful southern groups backing them,' Lucinda said. 'I also found a report on an anonymous blog about a large explosion, taking out the leader of one of the Talavera Brothers' main rivals about ten days back. The report describes witnesses seeing a missile corkscrewing downwards, taking a right turn over the heads of a security detail and slamming through the front window of a restaurant where the victim was having lunch.'

'Sounds *exactly* like a missile using GPS and terrain mapping,' James said. 'Leonid probably gave them a sample for a test firing. But why are you looking at anonymous blogs?'

Lucinda liked reminding James that she knew more than him and tutted contemptuously. 'Newspapers here print stories about politicians donating money to charity, cute baby competitions and gossip about TV celebrities. Print any real news, or even mention the names of the main gangs, and you'll get your head hacked off. Everyone reads blogs for the real news, but god help the writers if the gangs work out who's behind them.'

'Such a nice country you have here,' James said, smiling.

'I'm American, so go screw yourself,' Lucinda replied.

42. CAMPER

Ted was OK lying on his back or standing up, but sitting for a long time was painful and he was hurting as he came down six steps out of a small jet. They were at Sonoma County Airport, in the heart of California's wine country.

After picking up a hire car, they headed for Lombardi's house. There was nobody home, but fortunately Lombardi liked to portray himself as an upstanding citizen. He didn't flip cellphones like a crook would and TFU headquarters triangulated his position to a fancy seafood restaurant back in town.

Joe did a reccie and sighted Lombardi, his wife and his two pre-teen daughters. They were part of a big group, acting loud as they scoffed seafood platters and $200 bottles of wine.

'Your man's drinking plenty,' Joe said, as he leaned

into their hired mini-van speaking to Ted, Ethan and co-thug Don. 'Toilets are up the back of the building. I can take him, stick a hood over his head and push him out the fire exit.'

Ted nodded, as he sat in the front passenger seat scrolling through maps on his iPhone. 'Try not to knock him out, we need him lucid.'

It was a good plan, but it didn't work.

'Lombardi must have a bladder like a racehorse,' Ted complained, after an hour.

Inside, Joe reported that the diners were on coffee and dessert. When Lombardi stepped out into the night, he still hadn't been to the toilet. He looked a little drunk and had a sleepy eight-year-old daughter in his arms. His more sober wife took the wheel of their Audi Q7 and set off for home.

'What now?' Ethan asked.

Ted had just popped another pill for his back and Ethan reached around the headrest and tapped his shoulder.

'Ted,' Ethan said firmly.

'Oh . . .' Ted said, rubbing a palm in his eye and breaking into a big yawn. 'Guess it'll have to be the house. After they've put the girls to bed.'

Ethan was worried. Joe and Don were no masterminds and Ted was way off par with the back pills blurring his mind. Joe waited until a couple of minutes after Lombardi left and then drove down unlit country roads to his vineyard.

They spent an hour parked up near the house,

watching bulbs flick on and off as the family settled down for the night. Twenty minutes after the last light, Joe and Ted approached the house. It was a large wooden building that had been maintained in authentic condition. This was helpful, because the traditional sash windows were easily forced, and Ted found himself stepping through a window on to a parquet floor that caught the moonlight.

Under California law homeowners are entitled to shoot burglars, so Ted and Joe kept guns poised as they moved up a creaking wooden staircase. Joe entered the master bedroom first, nudging Lombardi's foot and making sure that the gun was the first thing he saw as he sat up in bed.

'Shut up,' Joe ordered. 'Don't wake your girls.'

'Watches and jewellery are at the back of the wardrobe,' Lombardi said, raising his hands as his wife gasped fearfully. 'I'm insured up the ass, so I don't care. Just take it and leave us in peace.'

Ted flicked the bedroom light three times, to indicate that Ethan should come in. Don would stay back in the car, in case they needed to make a quick getaway.

'I'm not here to steal,' Ted said, as he heard Ethan running up the stairs. 'I want you both to sit up. Keep hands on heads where I can see 'em. I've got a young man who's keen to meet you, Mr Lombardi.'

Lombardi looked stunned when Ethan walked in. The pair had never met, but Lombardi had seen pictures of Ethan when he'd worked with his mother.

'Young man, there's no need for this,' Lombardi said,

trying to turn on the charm. 'We can have a meeting in my office. There are a lot of unresolved issues regarding assets you inherited from your mother.'

Ethan tutted. 'You think I care about assets? Why did Leonid Aramov kill my mother?'

Before Lombardi could answer, Joe barked at his wife, 'Next time that pretty little hand moves off your head, I'll smack you out.'

'I was your mother's lawyer,' Lombardi said softly. 'Galenka trusted me. That's why she gave you my details and told you to call me if anything ever happened to her.'

'So you never worked for Leonid as well?'

'No.'

'What about Lisson Communications?' Ethan asked.

Lombardi couldn't hide his shock that Ethan knew about this.

'When you prepared the accounts for my mom's estate, you never mentioned Vineyard Eight,' Ethan continued. 'Nor Lisson, nor the fact that she owned half of it. And you've been paying money to Leonid Aramov in Mexico, as well.'

'This is . . . It would be more appropriate to fix an appointment and discuss these matters at my office in the New Year.'

'No, *now*,' Ethan said. He wasn't used to this kind of confrontation and felt like he was acting in a school play. 'My mom died and you tried to rip me off. What was the deal? Did you and Leonid split my mom's shares?'

When Lombardi didn't answer, Joe swung his massive arm and punched him in the throat. He then grabbed Lombardi by his long slicked-back hair, yanked him out of bed and splayed him over a dressing table.

'Truth or death,' Joe said menacingly.

'Leonid's down in Mexico trying to sell missiles for twenty-five million,' Ethan said. 'So go back to the beginning. Tell me the whole story about Lisson and PGSLM.'

Lombardi had been winded by the throat punch and fought for breath. He hesitated for a second, but started waving his arms as Joe pulled back a huge fist for a second punch.

'OK, I'll talk.'

*

James tried to stay in range of Andre and Tamara in case something happened. But Lucinda hadn't identified all the locations Leonid had in his sat-nav's memory, so when Andre went to bed after a dull day hanging around the apartment they decided to take a ride in the old VW camper and check them out.

The city was eerie at night. Traffic flowed freely on all the major roads, and until you pulled off them the only signs of a drug war were the army patrols making random stops at intersections. Ciudad Juárez was full of old VW campers and Beetles, but carjackings weren't restricted to flash vehicles and Lucinda told James to keep his gun in his lap.

The first few locations they checked out were fast-food restaurants and a gym that they guessed either Boris or Alex had considered joining. The final spot was way out in the industrial zone near the border. A raised highway took them through some of the city's poorest areas, filled with grim apartment blocks and street signs full of bullet holes.

The turn-off took them into an industrial park, full of identical one-storey manufacturing units. Some still bore the unlit logos of big corporations, or their outlines etched in the dirt where they'd been taken down. The few that were still operational had chimneys venting strong smells and lines of ex-California school buses that were used to collect workers from distant apartments.

'Here,' Lucinda said, pointing a well-manicured finger at a large unit.

It was no different to ten other units they'd passed since driving off the highway. Pale yellow light shot out of skylights in the flat roof and there were a couple of cars in the parking lot. James pulled out a little video camera and held it low as they rolled past slowly.

'Storage?' Lucinda asked. 'For the missiles?'

For once, James enjoyed superior knowledge and he sounded smug. 'A PGSLM is designed to rest on your shoulder. You wouldn't need this. You could probably store seventy-four of them in a double garage.'

'Other weapons?'

'Leonid's cash-poor,' James said. 'I can't see why he'd have a massive warehouse full of weapons. Even if he did, why store them in a city where there's a dozen heavily armed drug gangs who'd want to steal them?'

'So what then?'

'Not sure,' James said. 'You can see the border from here and one of the invoices on Leonid's desk was from a drilling equipment company.'

Lucinda nodded. 'The DEA *has* found border tunnels up to two kilometres in length. But Leonid has no use for a tunnel.'

'Unless it's someone else's tunnel and Leonid came out here to collect something,' James suggested.

A couple more turns took them to the end of the industrial park. The road widened into a big turning circle, beyond which sewage works sat behind a mesh fence.

'Damn,' Lucinda said, as she turned the camper.

Four white spots lit up on the roof of a big Mitsubishi pick-up, blinding them both.

'Cops?' James asked.

'Private security,' Lucinda said, squinting into the light as a man leaned out of the pick-up, making a signal like he wanted them to pull over.

'Gun it,' James urged. 'By the time they turn around . . .'

Lucinda laughed as she stopped the van. 'This old box is only good for sixty miles an hour. Try not to speak, you look like a Yankee and your accent is terrible.'

Lucinda was all smiles as the armed security guard stepped up to their van.

'We just came off the highway,' Lucinda said. 'It's late, I got the wrong turn.'

'Why'd you slow down going past unit eleven?' the guard asked. 'Who sent you up here?'

'I just pulled off—'

The guard cut her off as he peered into the van. 'There's a big sign *Industrial Park*. You don't come down here by mistake. Is that a camera?'

'I can't believe your bullshit!' Lucinda shouted.

The guard waved back to his colleague in the pick-up and grabbed a radio hooked over his shirt pocket.

'You need to step out of the van, both of you.'

James decided it was time to act. He undid his seatbelt, flung his door open and rolled out to the ground. Before the guard could react, Lucinda elbowed him in the face. While she flung her door open and jumped out to kick him in the head, James took two excellent shots. The first blew out a front tyre on the pick-up. The second was aimed at the passenger side of the front windscreen, shattering the glass and forcing the second guard to dive for cover.

Lucinda ripped off the gun and radio of the guard at her feet, then jumped back in the van and put it in gear. She started rolling and James hopped into the moving van, letting the forward momentum slam his door.

As they sped off – although speed was a relative thing in this ancient camper van – the guard inside the Mitsubishi tried to ram them as they came past. The van came close to toppling as the bulky Mitsubishi smashed the rear end. Lucinda's swerve kept them on four wheels, but also sent them careering into a mesh fence around one of the deserted units.

For once, the vehicle's lack of speed counted in its favour and they simply bounced off the fence, enabling

Lucinda to steer back on to the road. The guard's radio had dropped into the footwell and they could hear his colleague frantically yelling for backup.

The pick-up couldn't pursue with its front tyre shot out, but any other modern vehicle would have no problem catching them up. James kept his gun poised, expecting something to charge out of the blackness every time they passed a slip road.

He felt more optimistic as they approached the park entrance and Lucinda had two wheels off the ground as they took a tightly curving slip-road back on to the highway.

'That *really* spiralled,' James said. 'Jesus Christ!'

Lucinda pointed her thumb back towards the border. 'In the USA, you get murdered, there's a big investigation. Over here, thousands of murders, no honest cops. People can kill you and not get caught, so in a situation like that, guards see something suspicious and take you out just to be on the safe side.'

'They'd have killed us?' James asked.

Lucinda was still keeping a wary eye in the rear-view mirror. 'Only after torturing us for a few days, to see who we are and what we know.'

There was no sign of anyone behind them on the highway, but Lucinda took the next turn-off into a residential neighbourhood just in case.

'I'll have to lose this van,' Lucinda said. 'If those guards are well connected, there'll be a five-thousand-dollar reward out for anyone who spots us.'

'How soon?' James asked.

'I'm not driving it home, for sure,' Lucinda said. 'We'll park in the centre of town and get separate taxis home.'

43. LOMBARDI

After bursting into Lombardi's bedroom and slapping him around, Joe shoved the lawyer into a wing-backed armchair.

'There's a lot we already know,' Ted warned. 'The first time I catch you in a lie, I'm gonna go wake up your daughters.'

Lombardi and his wife exchanged frightened looks before he began speaking.

'In the Nineties, Lisson Communications put in a bid to design and build the PGSLM,' Lombardi said, still croaky from the throat punch. 'Defence contracts usually go to bigger fish, but Lisson bribed a general and a senator. When the truth came out, Lisson got fined and the CEO had to resign.

'Even worse, Lisson knew guidance systems, but had no expertise in missiles. The project went over budget.

The Defence Department pulled the plug and re-awarded the PGSLM contract to another company.

'Shares in a company are based on what people believe its assets are worth. Lisson would never win another government contract after the bribery scandal, so the stock market valued Lisson's defence business at zero. But Lisson had been close to perfecting its guided missile, and Galenka Aramov knew the technology was worth millions to a foreign government or a terrorist group.

'But all Galenka's wealth was tied up in her security business. Her mother wasn't interested in investing but Leonid had made money for himself and Galenka offered him a partnership.'

'So where did you fit in?' Ted asked.

'I had to set up the Lisson deal so that nobody realised it was being bought by the Aramovs. At that time, nobody was predicting that billions of mobile phones would have GPS navigation chips built in. That part of the business made Lisson far more money than anyone ever expected it to.'

'So what was the problem between Leonid and my mom?' Ethan asked.

'Your uncle and mother each owned half of Lisson Communications,' Lombardi explained. 'Leonid wanted to load all the info on to hard drives and make a fast twenty million bucks selling it to the Chinese, Indians or whoever offered the most cash, but Galenka saw something grander. Her idea was to complete the PGSLM design and manufacture it herself. She predicted sales of several thousand missiles per year at a quarter million dollars per missile.'

'Billions of dollars,' Ethan said admiringly. 'My mom was a crook, but she was a smart crook.'

Lombardi shook his head. 'Even with millions in US government research money, Lisson was struggling to manufacture the missile. Conducting a covert programme to build the missile was tough and instead of a fast profit, Leonid got drawn into a project that sucked up millions of dollars.

'By 2003 the US Army had the first functional PGSLM missiles from the company that took over Lisson's development contract. The design was closely based on Lisson's original and Galenka paid an expert thief called Jane Oxford to steal a batch of functioning PGSLM missiles. But even with a functioning missile, Galenka still had a mountain to climb.'

Ethan looked confused. 'Surely she could just copy it?'

Lombardi laughed. 'I own a toaster, but that doesn't mean I know how to build a toaster factory. Money got so tight that Galenka was working on the stolen missiles in a workshop in the basement of your California beach house.'

Ethan had seen his mum spend hours in a locked basement room at his old home, and she'd never hired a cleaner because she didn't like having strangers snooping around.

'Fast-forward to 2011,' Lombardi said. 'Leonid had grown increasingly violent and erratic. When his mother got sick, she became wary of handing exclusive control of the Aramov Clan to Leonid. She reached out to Galenka, who by this time ran a highly profitable computer security business.

'I don't know all the details, but by the time she died Galenka had perfected the missile guidance technology, and set up a production facility capable of producing missiles as good as the US-built originals.

'For Leonid this was a *complete* nightmare. Instead of taking the clan over like he'd always imagined, Leonid would become junior partner in a business run by his sister.'

Ethan nodded, and finished the story for himself. 'Uncle Leonid's ego couldn't take that, so he had my mom killed and blew our house up to stop anyone else finding out about PGSLM.'

'What about the production facility?' Ted asked.

'What about it?' Lombardi asked.

'Location?' Ted asked. 'Suppliers, logistics, finances?'

Lombardi shrugged. 'The less I knew about the illegal stuff the better. But as Leonid Aramov has surfaced in Ciudad Juárez with missiles to sell, that's where I'd start looking.'

Ethan felt strange. It was satisfying to finally understand why Leonid had killed his mother, but he'd always pictured her as someone who'd broken away from her family and succeeded as an honest businesswoman. But apparently the only thing separating his mum from the rest of the Aramovs was the scale of her ambitions.

'One thing I still don't get,' Ethan said. 'If the factory

can make missiles worth billions, why risk everything by selling seventy-four missiles to drug smugglers right on the factory's doorstep?'

'Leonid's a thug, not a businessman,' Lombardi said. 'He arrived in Mexico with a few thousand dollars and begged me to wire him some money. Based on past behaviour, I'd say that once Leonid's sold the missiles he'll have enough money to pack up the production line. Then he'll sell it to whichever defence contractor or government makes the highest bid.'

*

Getting thumped and sneaking around his dad's office meant Andre had barely slept the previous night. He slept solidly until his big brothers rolled in from a nightclub at 5 a.m. After fifteen minutes trying to ignore their racket he peeked out of his door to see what was going on in the open-plan kitchen and living-room below.

Alex and Boris both had company, though based on the women's attitude and tarty dress it was the kind you had to pay for. Latino pop came out of a music channel as the quartet stood around the kitchen counter snorting cocaine. After a couple of lines each, they moved back towards a pile of beanbags and started stripping off.

Andre made a mental note never to sit on any of the beanbags downstairs again as he got back in bed and tried blotting out his brothers' sex noises. The sounds made him uncomfortable and he kept hoping that Leonid would emerge and tell them to shut up. But the master bedroom's double doors were apparently too well insulated.

Once the women took their money and strutted out on their high heels, Andre went back for another peek as Boris and Alex sprawled out in the open-plan living area, naughty bits on display as they slugged half-bottles of Jack Daniels.

'I'm gonna ask my girl to marry me,' Boris said.

Alex snorted with laughter, making the golden bourbon drizzle down his chin. 'You soft shit!'

'I'm gonna go all sweet on her,' Boris said. 'Tell her I *love* her. Tell her to pack her bags and come to the Caribbean with me. Then when we get to the airport, I'll tell her I was joking.'

'That'd be *so* funny,' Alex said, as he pulled himself up and started staggering around looking for his trousers.

It irritated Andre that Alex could be OK, but never when he was under Boris' influence. As Alex struggled to get his legs through trouser holes, Boris swaggered across to the dishwasher, opened the flap and started taking a huge piss inside it.

'Madman!' Alex said, howling with laughter as he grabbed the handrail and started walking up the stairs. 'I'm going to bed. My brain's fried.'

'Nice present for the cleaner,' Boris laughed, shaking off as he scooped some of his clothes off the floor and followed Alex up the stairs.

Andre ducked behind his door as his brothers staggered past to their rooms. He heard Alex's shower come on as he stepped on to the landing and looked down to survey the wreckage. Besides the bottles, clothes, dustings of white powder and the streak of piss dribbling out of the dishwasher, Andre was delighted to see Boris' car keys lying on the floor beside his jeans.

44. TRINIDAD

Andre was towelling off in his room when he noticed a green light flashing on the tiny cellular receiver that James had given him. He grabbed it off a bedside chest and pressed the device's only button before holding it up to his ear.

'Everything OK?' James asked. 'Is your com broken?'

'I've been in the shower,' Andre explained, as he glanced at a bedside clock and saw a coincidence: 12:31 p.m. and 12.31 as the date on the line below it. 'I'll tweezer it back in a minute.'

'How are you holding up?'

Andre grunted as he sat on his bed. 'My brothers are *such* evil shits. Boris is talking about dumping his girlfriend before we go to the Caribbean. And he pissed in the dishwasher.'

'What a gent,' James said. 'But you're not gonna have

to put up with either of them much longer.'

'I hate it here, but I'm not giving up,' Andre said firmly. 'Mum and Dad went out, Boris and Alex are wiped from last night, so I went down to the garage. I got a bunch of addresses from the sat-nav in Boris' car. Plus there were some papers in there, relating to a house purchase in Trinidad.'

'Sounds interesting,' James said. 'But we think we've cracked the case already. You finding out about the PGSLM thing joined up a lot of dots for us. We sent your cousin Ethan with some heavies to rough up a lawyer who's been wiring money to your dad. He gave us the whole story and one of the addresses in your dad's sat-nav led me to an industrial unit. It's got serious security and we're fairly sure that they're building PGSLM missiles there.'

Andre gasped. '*Building* them!'

'Long story,' James said. 'I'll be able to tell you face to face soon. I've spoken to Dr D and she's agreed that you and your mum should be pulled out as soon as possible.'

'We'll have to sneak off together,' Andre said.

'Any idea when your mum's back?'

'They didn't leave all that long ago,' Andre said. 'They were going shopping and they were talking about seeing a film. They'll definitely be back by ten, because there's some firework display in the courtyard. Boris was fuming because Dad said he wanted us all here, seeing in the New Year as a family.'

'Some family,' James joked. 'The only thing is, until we actually get into the factory, we can't be a hundred per cent sure that we've found the place where they're making the missiles.'

'How will you get into the factory?' Andre asked.

James laughed. 'The place was a fortress. It certainly won't be me. I'm guessing they'll have to hand the operation over to a Special Forces unit.'

'One other thing,' Andre said. 'Does a PGSLM come in a kind of giant cigar-shaped tube?'

'Yeah,' James said. 'Remember the plans you saw the other night?'

'There's a golf trolley in the storage room under the stairs. But my dad doesn't golf, so I took a look inside and I'm pretty sure it's a missile.'

'I'm sure there's a lot of people who'd like to examine that,' James said excitedly. 'They'll want to strip it down, and see who's been selling parts to the Aramovs.'

'Want me to wheel it out to you?' Andre asked.

James thought Andre was joking and didn't answer.

'Well?' Andre repeated.

'I might have trouble getting access to the pool again,' James said. 'That caretaker I knocked out will remember me.'

'You don't need to sneak around,' Andre said. 'My brothers are trashed from last night and my parents won't be back for hours. I'll buzz you into the building and give it to you at the front door.'

'But your dad will notice it's gone,' James pointed out.

'Not if we leave soon after they get back. It's not like Dad's gonna come home on New Year's Eve and randomly decide to go look in some golf bag stashed at the back of the utility room, is it?'

'If you're sure,' James said.

'My brothers will wake up eventually. How soon can you get here?'

'I'm a two-minute drive away,' James said. 'Call it ten by the time I've got shoes and stuff on.'

Six minutes later, James stood outside the apartment complex's glass atrium. Once Andre buzzed him in, he walked fifty metres across seriously bouncy carpet and found Andre waiting by the front door of the apartment.

'All right, mate?'

'So far so good,' Andre said, as he slid a long black tube across the kitchen tiles to James in the doorway.

'I won't hang about,' James said, as he grabbed a thick nylon strap and swung the missile over his shoulder. 'When your mum gets back, tell her you've got to leave first chance you get. And don't start packing, or do anything else that'll give the game away.'

'Who you talking to, squirt?' a tired-sounding Boris shouted from up on the first-floor balcony.

'Collecting for the blind,' Andre shouted, shutting the door in James' face.

'Tell the prick I'll blind *him* if he comes here again,' Boris shouted, as James hurried down the hallway with the black missile pod weighing on his shoulder.

When he got back out front, James fed the missile through the side window of a VW Beetle that was even tattier than the camper he and Lucinda had abandoned in town the night before.

He worried as he drove, because he'd seen police checkpoints all over town and the sinister black pod was exactly the kind of thing that would arouse suspicion. But he made it to his dingy room without any hassle and sent a mouse scurrying between floorboards as he thumped the missile on to a wobbly dining table.

After sliding three catches and opening the clamshell pod, James found the missile and launcher in factory-fresh condition, wrapped in a Styrofoam bag printed with multilingual warnings. *Can cause serious burns. Read instructions before use.*

The PGSLM was 16cm in diameter and 120cm long, with a bullet-shaped nose and a sophisticated vectoring rocket nozzle at the other end. The shoulder launching tube and numeric control pad were disposable, so their construction had more in common with a cheap toy than something you'd expect to find on a quarter million dollars' worth of military hardware.

James had updated TFU headquarters in Dallas before meeting Andre and had a message on his phone to *Call Hao-Jing at Sonic Aviation Consortium (SAC)* as soon as he got hold of the missile.

SAC had taken over design work on PGSLM after Lisson Communications lost their contract. Hao-Jing had been the chief software engineer on the project at both companies.

'I doubt Galenka Aramov altered any of the software code she downloaded from the six stolen missiles,' Hao-Jing explained.

'Why not?' James asked.

'It worked, so why change it?' Hao-Jing asked. 'If the software is the same, you should be able to access the missile's logs. I've e-mailed you a program. Install it on your laptop, then enter #406 on the missile control panel. Provided the Wi-Fi on your laptop is turned on, you should see a network called PGSLM in the Windows communication settings.'

James smiled. 'Are your missiles Mac friendly?'

'No,' Hao-Jing said humourlessly. 'But we are working on an Android app.'

James took a few minutes to boot his laptop and install the PGSLM control software. He jolted with shock when he tapped #406 and four stabilising fins shot out the back of the missile.

'I can't fire this thing accidentally, can I?' James asked.

'Not without a six-digit firing code,' Hao-Jing said. 'In the right-hand side of the PGSLM program window, you should see a menu item called *Programming*. Click on that, and type *TLL* followed by the *F9* key.'

When James hit *F9*, a selection of hidden engineering menus popped up in a row below the main toolbar.

'Click where it says *Log*, and then tick the *On-screen mapping* button.'

James did what he was told and got rewarded by an on-screen map marked with location pins going alphabetically from A to S. On the right-hand side was a list of times and dates, along with details of where the missile had been at various stages of its life. James immediately saw that the first four entries, which were called *Test 1*, *Test 2*, *Orientation*, and *1st Power* had all taken place twenty months earlier.

'Can you see what I'm seeing on your screen?' James asked. 'Judging by the map pins, the missile was first switched on inside an industrial unit I visited last night.'

'That's exactly what it means,' Hao-Jing said. 'The US Army demands that all smart weapons are traceable. A PGSLM logs its own location every time it's switched on or off. If you programme in the right settings, it'll automatically download software updates and send you an SMS if the on-board diagnostics discovers a fault.'

'Cool,' James said, still unnerved by the fact that he had a solid rocket booster and forty kilos of high explosive on his dining table.

Before he could say any more, James heard a click and a much higher voice on the line. 'James?'

'Hello?' James said curiously. 'Hao-Jing?'

'Your call was being patched through TFU headquarters,' Dr D explained. 'I've cut Hao-Jing off. You're now speaking with Dr D.'

James had only spoken to Dr D once before, and that was barely long enough to establish that she had weird mannerisms and a voice like a violin lesson.

'You've been doing a fine job down there,' Dr D began. 'Picking up a working missile makes winding the mission up way simpler.'

'How so?' James asked.

'Get Andre and Tamara out of Leonid's house,' Dr D said. 'Then I'll get Hao-Jing to programme the coordinates of that industrial site into your missile. Drive to within four kilometres and press the launch button. If they're handling explosives in there, one shot should be enough to wipe out the whole factory.'

James was shocked. 'But I thought they wanted to strip the missile down, to check out Galenka's design and see who's been supplying her with components.'

'I'd love the luxury of doing that,' Dr D said. 'But your mission is in a grey area, somewhere between barely authorised and completely illegal. If I explain to my bosses that I've run this anti-Leonid operation there will be a major shit storm. I don't much care about myself, but I'm trying to find future employment for Amy and a lot of other people at TFU. It's best for them if my bosses aren't running a big investigation into who knew what about an unauthorised operation.'

James realised the sense in this, and also that an inquiry might reach across the Atlantic and lead to trouble for Zara Asker, or even himself.

'Right,' James said. 'That'll destroy the production line, but are we sure the seventy-four missiles Leonid is selling are being stored there?'

'It's not ideal if they're not,' Dr D said. 'But I'd rather have seventy missiles in the wild than a factory capable of producing thousands of them.'

'And if I blow up the factory, won't Leonid just walk away?'

'Your job will be to get Tamara and Andre safely out of Mexico and blow up the factory,' Dr D explained. 'Lucinda will deal with Leonid. She knows everyone who matters in Ciudad Juárez. She can get a rumour circulating that the missiles are dangerously defective, or that Leonid is planning to rip the Talavera Brothers off. If he makes it out of Mexico alive we'll make sure they know where he's moving to.'

James laughed. 'Let the bad guys do our dirty work, eh?'

'Exactly,' Dr D said.

45. LOOT

Andre didn't like being home with his brothers and spent the rest of the afternoon hiding in his room. Boris was too hung over to torment him and his only problem was being stuck in his room, bored off his head and anxious about making a safe getaway with his mum.

It was half six when Leonid and Tamara rolled up. The building concierge carried in beer and champagne for the New Year celebrations, while Tamara stood at the kitchen counter, pulling takeaway burritos and rice out of a carrier bag and plating it all up.

'No cooking tonight,' Tamara shouted. 'Get it while it's hot.'

Andre was starving and sat on a stool at the kitchen counter, stuffing his face as the rest of his family gathered around.

'Got a little announcement to make,' Leonid said, as

he took Tamara by the wrist. He raised her hand, showing off a large diamond engagement ring. 'We'll be getting married in a few weeks, when we hit the Caribbean.'

Andre offered congrats, secure in the knowledge that it would never happen. Alex didn't seem to care, but Boris looked furious.

'Why buy a cow when you're milking it already?' Boris asked.

Alex smirked. Leonid faced Boris off, but had to finish a mouthful before he could speak.

'While you're under my roof you respect Tamara like you'd respect your own mother,' Leonid blasted.

Boris laughed so hard he spat rice over the floor. 'You beat *my* mum and threatened to kill her if she ever tried to contact us.'

'Don't you *ever* mention that bitch,' Leonid growled.

Andre was less than a metre from the standoff. Leonid had age and authority, but Boris was physically stronger and neither wanted to back down.

'Eat your food before it gets cold,' Tamara said.

Leonid shot his burrito into the bin and stormed upstairs, slamming the bedroom door and yelling, 'Why do I even try with this family?'

Boris gave Tamara a mocking grin as he took a second burrito and scooped more rice on to his plate. As he bit into it, Leonid stormed back to the top of the stairs and flung a wodge of pesos over the railing.

'Money,' Leonid shouted to Boris. 'That's all I am to you. I tried making a happy night for us, but you can't say one nice thing. So take my money. Go and party, or do drugs or whatever it is you want. I don't give a shit any more.'

'Dad, stop being so dramatic,' Boris said, as he nonchalantly bit his burrito. 'At your age you'll have a heart attack.'

Leonid pulled a silenced pistol from the back of his trousers and sent Boris diving for cover as he shot a beanbag a couple of metres behind him.

'Out,' Leonid screamed. 'Show me respect when you come back, or don't come back at all.'

Boris crashed his plate on the countertop and raised his hands. 'I'm outta here.' Then he looked at Alex. 'You coming?'

Boris had a magnetic pull on Alex. After running back and forth to pick up the scattered pesos and grab clothes and keys, the two young thugs headed out with a slam of the main door.

'When we get to Trinidad they're getting their own place,' Leonid said, as he came downstairs. 'They're spoiled brats.'

He gave Tamara a kiss, then put his arm around Andre's back and gave him a gentle squeeze.

'I've been hard on you because you're not tough,' Leonid told Andre. 'But you show respect, and you've got more brains than those two screw-ups combined.'

Andre hated his dad, but on some basic level he still craved his affection and his smile was at least fifty per cent for real.

Tamara did what she always did and soothed Leonid's

temper. After pecking him on the cheek, she spoke in her calmest voice as she poured whisky into a tumbler.

'Forget the boys and this takeaway shit,' she said. 'Take this drink and go have a nice relaxing bath. I'll clean this up and cook you a nice bloody steak.'

Leonid smiled, and made a gesture like he was blocking Andre's ears.

'Why don't you come join me in the bath?'

'Eww!' Andre said.

'Run the bath and you might get lucky,' Tamara answered.

Leonid looked a much happier man as he tucked bits of cooked pepper in his mouth, before heading back upstairs.

Andre was still vaguely disgusted at how vigorously his mum had thrown herself into her new relationship with Leonid. 'Engaged?' he said irritably, once his father had disappeared behind the double doors.

Tamara raised her ringed finger and spoke in a much more abrupt tone than she'd just used on Leonid. 'This cost forty thousand dollars. That's two years of college for you.'

Andre smiled as his mum touched his shoulder. 'Have you spoken to anyone on com?'

Tamara nodded. 'I spoke to Lucinda briefly when I went to the toilet.'

'I think we should leave after the New Year fireworks,' Andre said. 'Dad will probably go straight to sleep, and I doubt Alex and Boris will be back much before three a.m.'

Tamara's eyes narrowed. 'But this isn't what we agreed with Amy Collins.'

'We've found Dad and they've worked out where the missiles are.'

'I don't give a damn about missiles,' Tamara said. 'I agreed to do this because I wanted your father out of our lives for good.'

'But they'll get him after,' Andre said.

'Leonid's clever and I want to be *sure*,' Tamara said, shaking her head. 'Turn on your com. Tell James to be ready to pick us up in fifteen minutes, but *don't* say anything else. Then go to your room and pack up. One bag, only the important stuff.'

'What are you going to do?'

'What I should have done a long time ago. Now do as you're told and get upstairs.'

Andre felt shaky as he headed to his room. It came through in his voice when he spoke to James on the com.

'What's up?' James asked.

'Nothing,' Andre lied. He'd considered telling James the truth, but loyalty to his mum outweighed his friendship with James. 'Just be ready to meet us in fifteen minutes. Alex and Boris are out, my dad's about to have a bath. He's always in there for at least half an hour, so we'll make our move.'

'If you're certain,' James said warily.

Andre switched his com off, then grabbed his only backpack. He stuffed in as many of the new clothes and trainers Leonid had bought for him as he could, plus a couple of Xbox games and the Omega watch and gold chain he'd been given for Christmas.

When Andre stepped back into the hallway, Tamara was walking into the master bedroom. Andre crept up to the double doors and watched as his mum picked Leonid's pistol off the bed and expertly opened the chamber to make sure it was still loaded.

'Are you in the bath?' Tamara asked, using her sweetest tone.

'Come and join me,' Leonid said. 'I'll make it worth your while.'

'Close your eyes,' Tamara said. 'I've got a surprise for you.'

'What is it?'

Tamara kept the gun poised and gave a girlish laugh as she approached the bathroom. 'If I told you, it wouldn't be a surprise.'

Andre opened the bedroom door a few centimetres to get a better view.

'Get that lovely arse in here,' Leonid said, laughing.

'Keep 'em closed or you'll get zip,' Tamara teased, as she stepped into a luxurious bathroom with a sunken oval bath set in its centre.

Leonid's eyes shot open when he heard Tamara clicking the safety off. The bulky silencer was over a metre from his face: near enough that you can't miss, but too far to make a grab.

'What's this?' Leonid asked, grabbing the sides of the tub and making a big splash as he sat up.

Andre crept into the bathroom doorway as his mother

spoke, with the gun slightly trembling.

'This is for all the times you slapped me around. For punching me unconscious. For raping me and breaking my jaw. For every night I sat on my own, knowing you were *partying* with fifteen-year-old Koreans. For the eighteen stitches when you smashed a vase against my back. But most of all, this is for saying that you'd torture and kill our son if I ever left the Kremlin, or looked at another man.'

'Tamara,' Leonid said. 'I love you.'

Tamara shook her head. 'Well you've sure got a funny way of showing it.'

Andre gasped as his mum pulled the trigger. A wave splashed against the tiled floor as Leonid's body spasmed. After that it was surprisingly neat, with blood draining out the back of his head turning the water pink.

Tamara hadn't realised that Andre had crept in. Her hands and blouse were splashed with blood. She had a tear running down her cheek, but didn't speak like someone who was crying.

'I told you to pack,' Tamara said. 'Are you OK?'

Andre nodded. 'I'll live.'

'Then do as you're told,' Tamara said. 'While I shower, you grab a bag. There's Rolex watches and cash at the back of the wardrobe. Get my jewellery as well.'

'Amy said her people would look after us.'

Tamara sounded extremely cool as she yanked her bloody top over her head. 'I'd rather have too much money than not enough. If James asks, Leonid tried pulling me into the tub with him while I was trying to leave and I had to shoot him. I won't hear while I'm in the shower, so you'd better take the gun, just in case your brothers come back.'

'What'll happen to them?' Andre asked, as Tamara unzipped her skirt and headed for her own bedroom.

'I don't really care, but they're not that bright. They'll wind up dead or in prison.'

'Right,' Andre said, impressed and a little scared by his mum's sudden ruthlessness.

'Get going then,' Tamara said, smiling as she undid her bra.

It took less than five minutes for Tamara to shower, spray deodorant and don a tracksuit. Andre waited for her by the front door, surrounded by a wheelie bag and two backpacks.

'You've got everything?' Tamara said, as she tousled Andre's hair before taking the gun off him.

Andre assumed they'd be walking out and meeting James at the front, but Tamara led him down to the basement and they drove out of the underground garage in the big Lexus.

James was sitting in the Beetle looking towards the apartment entrance and got a surprise when Tamara rolled up alongside and blasted the horn.

'More room in here,' Tamara said.

James had his own bag and the missile in the little Volkswagen, so while he hadn't thought about using Leonid's car, he was grateful for the extra space and there was never any harm in being bullet-proofed while riding around Ciudad Juárez in the dark.

James threw the missile and his backpack on the plush rear seat and told Tamara to head to the highway and follow signs for the US border.

'Leonid's dead,' Tamara said coldly. 'Is anyone likely to have a problem with that?'

'He went for my mum,' Andre added.

James half smiled. 'Intelligence services aren't supposed to go around assassinating people, but I can't see anyone being too upset.'

Tamara had only ever driven on the relatively quiet roads around the Kremlin. Her driving was erratic and she clipped a couple of kerbs before James told them to leave the highway and park at the gates of a construction site.

Hao-Jing had programmed the factory coordinates into the PGSLM. After resting it on the roof of the car as the missile's computer booted up, James transferred it carefully on to his shoulder, making sure he had it positioned upwards, with twenty metres of clear air in front of him.

With the missile balanced, he used his free arm to tap in the launch code – which was a factory default 000000. After that he pressed a red pre-launch button, which set a hydraulic pump hammering in his ear. After twenty seconds the pressure light came on and he squeezed the launch trigger.

The first second of the flight was powered by compressed air. This gave the missile a chance to clear its launch tube before the rocket came alive with a sharp crack, blinding light and enough heat to suck moisture out of the air in James' next breath.

The rocket-powered missile shot upwards, accelerating to four hundred metres and 1,100kph in under ten seconds. At this point the rocket only had enough fuel to run for twenty seconds, but that was enough to fly up to five kilometres, then make a corkscrewing downwards glide and accurately hit a target the size of a sofa.

James lobbed the lightweight metal launch tube over the building-site fence and had one leg back inside the Lexus as a huge bang erupted four kilometres away.

'Hell yeah!' Andre shouted, as he turned back to give James a high five. But James looked uneasy. 'What's the matter?'

James didn't answer until the boom of a secondary explosion ripped across the city.

'How many people were in there?' James asked. 'Hopefully just a few security guards, but it might be a lot more if they're still producing missiles.'

James' phone started ringing as Tamara started driving. It was Dr D.

'CIA had an infrared satellite camera targeting the site. Congratulations, James, it looks like the factory's been ripped out of the ground.'

James ended the call quickly because Tamara was pulling back on to the highway and needed directions. Once they were on course, James went into his backpack and handed Andre a pair of US passports.

'One for you, one for your mum,' James explained. 'I've got to make one quick call to get this car cleared for the priority channel. The border's less than three kilometres. I've booked us a hotel in El Paso and with any luck we'll be in our rooms in time to see in the New Year.'

46. GIRLS

Word of Leonid Aramov's death reached the Kremlin a few days into 2013, but from a population that once topped seven hundred, less than thirty were there to hear the news. The last aircrew left the following day, flying three dilapidated planes to a breakers' yard in India, before taking commercial flights onwards to uncertain futures in Russia and the Ukraine.

A dozen-strong American demolition crew arrived hours later. Only a small team keeping the runway de-iced and a few Aramov security men stood watch as they began drilling holes and filling them with sticks of dynamite.

The Kremlin was built of prefabricated concrete sections that the experts predicted would collapse with minimal explosives. The real work was in destroying the airfield, tearing up metre-thick runways so that nobody could resume operations from this near-perfect smuggling den.

Ryan's mission had ended with Igor's death, but Amy stuck to her word and let him stay on, marking his time with Natalka, counting in days, hours, then minutes. The night of January 9th was a blizzard and he sat up cuddling Natalka and hating the sight of her two packed wheelie bags by the door.

Ryan ought to have been looking forward to campus. To his mates, to paintballing, Xbox tournaments, corridor parties, football matches and trips to the mall. But all he could think about were the little details of Natalka that he'd never see again.

Her walk, her nose. The split green Converse where a little toe poked out the side. The cigarette burns on her pillowcases. Natalka thought Ryan was going to the Ukraine to live with a distant cousin. She thought they'd stay in touch, but Ryan was forbidden from contacting anyone he'd met while working undercover. Natalka's text messages and e-mails would bounce off dead accounts and, no doubt, that would poison her memory of him.

'Don't come to the airport,' Natalka said.

Ryan had counted five and a half hours until he saw Natalka for the last time, but not going to the airport cut it down to three and he felt like he'd been kneed in the guts.

'I want to,' he gasped.

'No big scene with everyone watching,' Natalka said. 'I want to say goodbye properly, in private.'

She'd started pulling her jeans on, and Ryan realised he'd never see her legs again. Falling in love with Natalka was one of the most amazing things that had happened in his life, but losing her like this was excruciating.

'You're sure you don't want me to come?' Ryan asked, hoping the lift would break down as they trundled to the ground floor.

The fruit machines still blinked in the bar, but they'd not eaten a coin in days. As a fourteen-year-old whose mother was in prison on the opposite side of the world, Natalka couldn't fly on any reputable airline without a chaperone. The balding man who shook her hand in the lobby wore the logo of Russian national airline Aeroflot on his lapel.

Ryan choked up as Natalka followed him to a blue Mercedes, with her wheelie bag cutting lines in the fresh snowfall. He was horrified at the idea that she'd get straight in, but Natalka turned back for one final hug.

'I got you these,' Ryan said, as he pulled two packs of cigarettes out of his hoodie. 'The last Marlboros in the vending machine.'

Natalka swept hair off her face and looked determined. 'I'm giving up,' she said, as she cracked a smile that would live in Ryan's head for as long as he breathed. 'I've heard those bloody things can kill you.'

*

'Kerry?' James said warily, as he stepped into a hallway.

The small detached house was less than a mile from Stamford University's main campus and had been James' home for the past two and a half years. After tapping in the burglar alarm code he picked a bunch of flyers and letters off the bristle mat, then gulped as he stepped through an archway into an open-plan kitchen/living area.

There were marks on the carpet where Kerry's bookcase had been. Shelves half empty where her CDs belonged and no pots hanging from the rack over the hob. The tap had been left dripping and as James leaned over to shut it off, he saw a note held on the fridge door by his *Viva Las Vegas* magnet.

James' handwriting was a scrawl even when he tried hard. He'd always admired Kerry's perfect letters, and the circles she drew to make dots above her *i*s.

James,

I'm sorry about last week's fight on the phone. I'm sure we both said things we didn't really mean.

I've cleared my stuff out. I think I've done it right, but if I've taken anything you think is yours, let me know. I've also taken heavy stuff like saucepans and laundry detergent because you can't ship that back to the UK.

I know I said I'd be around, but Mark and I have decided to go away for a few days before term starts.

I don't think I'll ever completely stop loving you, but

we fell in love when we were twelve and now we've grown apart.

Kerry
XXX

P.S. String, tape and scissors in left-hand kitchen drawer. I bought too many boxes and heaps of bubble wrap. It's in the garage. I'm all cleared out, so use whatever you like.

James put the note down and looked around the room. It sparked a hundred memories, from snuggling on the couch the night he and Kerry moved in, to cops charging in to break up his graduation party and the big stain on the wallpaper from the time Kerry lobbed a ketchup bottle at his head.

James had a flight back to the UK booked for the following evening, so he only had a day and a half to pack up his stuff, ready for collection by an international removals firm. He'd barely slept on the flight from El Paso to San Francisco, but reckoned he'd end up sleeping for half the day if he lay down, so he headed into the garage to grab some boxes.

He smiled when he saw his black leather jacket, hanging up alongside the Harley Davidson that he'd bought himself after his most successful trip to Vegas. Shipping the bike back to the UK and paying import taxes would be too expensive. He'd already arranged for a dealer to sell it on commission, but he reckoned one last ride, cutting across the university campus and grabbing steak and eggs with strong black coffee at a little diner he knew, would kick his body clock into gear.

The garage door had always been a pain and he had to give it a good kick to get it whirring. It took a while getting gloves and jacket on, but he wasn't planning to ride far enough to bother with his full bike leathers.

James had inherited plenty of money from his mum and made more scamming the blackjack tables in Vegas. He'd already been online sorting out the big Triumph he was going to buy when he started his new job on CHERUB campus, but there was something unmatchable about the combo of California's broad highways and a big low-revving Harley.

The old girl who lived next door was coming out on to her front lawn and James gave her a friendly wave as he rolled the big bike down his front drive and opened up the throttle. A minute later he was up an on-ramp and cutting across highway lanes, hitting 85mph with January chill blasting up his cuffs and morning sun on his back.

47. STAR

One of the demolition men had decided to cut the red star off the Kremlin roof and take it home for a souvenir. Ryan roamed the offices on the fourth floor and found an aluminium model of a Soviet-era spy plane that he thought would look cool in his room on campus.

Baser instincts took hold when someone broke the lock off the Kremlin bar and set free crates of whisky and vodka. Demolition crews and Kremlin staff all joined the fun and Ryan spent his final night in Kyrgyzstan getting absolutely smashed and head banging to Led Zeppelin until 3 a.m.

Amy was worried about the amount he'd had to drink and walked him up to a spare bed on the fifth floor where she could keep an eye on him. He fell asleep sobbing helplessly for Natalka and woke up with the first proper hangover of his life.

'I know you feel like shit,' Amy said. 'Sadly you can't have a lie-in because they're blowing the building up in four hours. More importantly, you reek of booze, you've rolled in mud and they've already cut the gas. So unless you want a cold shower, you need to get your arse in gear.'

'I want Natalka,' Ryan moaned, pulling a cushion over his head. 'Cancel that, I want to die.'

Amy whipped the cushion and blanket away. 'What's Zara going to think of me if you arrive back on campus looking and smelling like an alcoholic dosser?'

'Leave me alone.'

'I *told* you to stop drinking at ten o'clock,' Amy said. 'I've got no sympathy. Now move it before I kick your arse.'

As Ryan trudged towards the shower feeling extremely queasy, a team of men were loading Josef Aramov's personal possessions into a lift. Since there was nobody left to see him, Ryan showered, then went down to the third floor wearing a pink towelling robe that had belonged to Tamara.

Over the previous ten days, Ryan had gradually moved all of his stuff into Natalka's room. He'd laid out a set of clothes for the journey home when he'd packed the previous afternoon and he pulled them on before looking out of the window.

The last remnants of the Aramov fleet had been herded around the maintenance hangar and wired with explosives. On the runway stood a pair of modern Airbus 320s. One a passenger plane, one a cargo jet which was presently being loaded with a mixture of Aramov Clan archives, personal possessions and demolition equipment. The Airbus' engines were ticking over to prevent them from icing up, but they were eerily quiet compared to the elderly Russian jets Ryan had got used to.

A tentative cup of tea and a stale piece of naan bread settled Ryan's stomach. A lot of stuff was being taken out of the building and after letting two crammed lifts go by, he decided to slide his cases downstairs to the lobby.

By this time the heating had been off for several hours and with single glazing and cracked walls, the Kremlin's usually stifling interior was starting to chill. Josef Aramov made a jokey announcement, but became emotional as he neared the end of it.

'The Kremlin hotel will be closing its doors in fifteen minutes. Guests wishing to stay longer should be warned that their rooms may explode.'

Amy and Josef emerged from the elevator together, keeping up the pretence that they were a couple. At the same moment, Ryan thought of something and bolted back towards the staircase.

'Hey, what's up?' Amy asked. 'You feeling OK?'

'Just remembered, there's a bag of Kazakov's stuff still in my room.'

'Is it important?' Amy asked.

Ryan shrugged. 'Maybe they could send it to his son or something. It's nothing amazing, but it seems sad to leave it here.'

'Go on then, but hurry up.'

The demolition crews were working down from the top floor, linking up the detonator fuses before going into every room making sure it was clear. Ryan had to dart in front of one of them as he bolted to his room. After grabbing the case with Kazakov's stuff in, he walked to Natalka's room at the end and caught her smell one last time.

'Come on, hoppit!' the demolition man shouted.

Ryan had already checked everywhere to make sure he hadn't left anything behind, and he choked up as he thought about all the times he'd spent with Natalka. She was probably at her aunt's house in Russia by now . . .

'Hey, are you deaf?' the demolition man shouted, accompanying his words with furious gestures because he'd assumed Ryan was a local and only spoke Russian or Kyrgyz.

The burly demolition man looked surprised when he saw Ryan's tears.

'I'm going,' Ryan said sadly.

Down in the lobby, Dan had arrived. The burly eighteen-year-old had been promised a new start in the USA if he agreed to help TFU infiltrate the Kremlin. But he looked almost as sad as Ryan when Amy approached him.

'Everything OK?' Amy asked.

'I wish I could take my Lada,' Dan explained. 'I parked it near the top of the valley with the keys in the ignition. I just hope someone takes good care of it.'

Amy smiled as she opened a document wallet and

handed Dan a US passport. 'We're flying to London,' she explained. 'Then you, me and Josef will fly on a commercial flight to Dallas where I'll spend some time helping you to sort out your new life.'

By this time the demolition crews had cleared the upper floors and the demolition man who'd seen Ryan a few minutes earlier spoke impatiently in bad Russian. 'Ladies and gentlemen, I need everyone and their luggage to start walking to the plane. Thank you.'

As Ryan threw his luggage on to a waiting cargo trolley and began an icy walk towards the two jets, Josef Aramov stayed back to hand the de-icing crew their final wage packets, before giving them hugs and telling them to get well clear of the valley.

The cargo plane was taxiing for take-off as Ryan boarded his ride home. It was a regular passenger Airbus, chartered for the final evacuation. There were less than thirty passengers for the hundred-seater, so Ryan had three seats in which to sprawl out and nurse his hangover.

The demolition team were the last to board, beaded with sweat as they stood in the aisle stripping hard hats and orange overalls. Normally the demolition team would stay behind to monitor their explosions and clear debris, but blowing up large buildings without government permission is as illegal in Kyrgyzstan as in any other country and none of them wanted to be on the ground when the authorities worked out that someone had taken out an entire airbase.

Take-off from the cramped valley landing strip involved a twisting climb through a gap between two peaks with less than fifty metres' clearance for the wings of a large jet. Having a rock face skimming past the windows as you took off always gave Ryan the willies and he was a happy boy when he saw clear blue sky, secure in the knowledge that he'd never make that manoeuvre again.

Clearing the peaks was also the signal for the demolition crew to trigger the detonation. The pilot had planned a flight path so that they could view the explosion from a safe distance and as the demolition team gave a bawdy countdown, everyone charged towards the windows on Ryan's side of the plane.

'Five, four, three, two, one . . .'

Nobody heard zero because the bang was overwhelming. As the Kremlin's prefabricated sections collapsed inwards, sequential explosions punched huge holes in the runway, before a final blast took out a dozen aircraft, maintenance sheds and the refuelling facility.

'Wow,' Dan said, looking back at Ryan in the row behind.

'I think I saw a boulder fly up and smash into your car,' Ryan joked.

Dan smiled, but knew exactly how to get Ryan back. 'I bet some Russian boy is banging Natalka already.'

The smoke and flames continued billowing out of the valley, but the Airbus was still climbing and the view blotted out as they rose through the first layer of cloud.

48. SAD

Nothing unified CHERUB campus like a karaoke night. The little kids chased in and out of the main hall, drinking too much fizz and getting rowdy. Tween girls took things seriously, dressing up, practising their songs and making up dance routines. By their teens, everyone had decided that karaoke nights were uncool, but still got up on stage and belted out songs in an ironic kind of way.

James had signed a bunch of papers in Zara's office a few hours earlier. His contract defined his new job as *staff grade three*, which meant he got a room on campus, an unimpressive salary and had to spend at least six months working wherever he was needed, be it in training, care, education, or missions.

For his first night on duty James was supervising the karaoke. He was still knackered from the trip to the

USA and he lost the will to live as he saw a bunch of seven-to-nine-year-old boys moving en masse towards the boys' toilet.

The fact that every one of them was holding an empty beaker gave their intent away. James waited by the bathroom door while the sextet filled their cups with water and giggled about who they planned to throw it at.

'Oh no you don't!' James shouted, making the boys jump as the first pair emerged into the hallway. 'Empty the cups in the sink. Then you can either go back inside and act sensibly, or you can go back to the junior block and go to bed.'

'They're just drinks,' a chubby little lad said, giving James baby-fawn eyes and a butter-wouldn't-melt expression.

'I'm really thirsty,' another boy added, downing half his cup to make the point.

'Behave or bed,' James repeated.

So the boys filed back to the sinks and sulkily emptied their beakers. As they did this, one muttered under his breath.

'At least I didn't start a food fight in the canteen.'

And as the six boys giggled, another covered his mouth and blurted, 'Or have sex in the campus fountain.'

This reduced all six boys to fits of laughter. James had to assert his authority or these kids would run rings around him forevermore, but if he overdid it he'd look like an arse and his punishment would get reversed by a more senior member of staff.

'First of all, that's just a stupid rumour started by my

sister,' James said huffily. 'Secondly, you've splashed quite a lot of water on the floor. If I can see any of you in five seconds' time, I'll be sending you to the cleaning cupboard to get a mop and clean it up.'

The boys got the hint, binning their containers and scrambling back into the main hall. James was about to follow them when three ten-year-old girls started screeching out Beyoncé's 'Crazy in Love'. The sound reminded him of an angle grinder and he decided to let the hall survive unsupervised for a few minutes while he grabbed some air.

Even in January, the hall got muggy when there were a lot of bodies inside and James headed out of an open fire exit and up a few steps. He stood in front of the main building, staring towards the fountain and trying to think of a way to get Lauren back for starting the sex rumour, when he noticed a kid sitting at the fountain's edge.

The kid looked upset and when James stepped up, he saw that he resembled Leon Sharma, who he'd taught on the advanced driving course a couple of months earlier.

'You must be Ryan,' James said.

Ryan nodded, but didn't speak because he was choked up.

'I know you've been on a long mission,' James said. 'So I'm guessing it's a girl, outside chance of a boy if you swing that way.'

'Girl,' Ryan said, as he wiped a dewdrop of snot from the end of his nose.

'Been there,' James said. 'Hurts like hell, doesn't it?'

Ryan smiled slightly. 'Are you James Adams?'

'I might be,' James said, as the pair shook hands.

'Ever fall in love on a mission?' Ryan asked.

'On my first ever mission it was Joanna,' James said. 'I was only twelve, but I used to hang out with her after school and it felt so perfect. Then there was April. I didn't exactly fall in love with her but she was hot. My fourth mission I spent a summer night sleeping on a rooftop with a chick called Hannah. We watched the sun come up and it was beautiful. And then there's Kerry Chang, who I've kind of loved since I did basic training with her.'

Ryan pointed towards the fountain. 'Was she the one—?'

James cut him off and sounded irritable. 'My idiot sister started that rumour. Put your hand in the water for two seconds, it's freezing. Plus it's all lit up, and there's like sixty bedrooms looking down on you.'

'Pity,' Ryan said. 'It's a good rumour. So you're still with Kerry?'

James shook his head. 'We lived together at uni for the last three years, but she's dumped my arse for a history undergraduate called Mark Lee.'

'Does breaking up hurt less once you're used to it?' Ryan asked.

James shook his head. 'It's like an elephant kicked you in the nuts, every single time.'

'How long does it last?' Ryan asked.

James laughed. 'I'd say you've got about two weeks of

serious misery and crying yourself to sleep at night. Then about a month of quiet desperation, and after that you'll just think about her once in a while and feel sad. That's not exactly scientific, but it's how breaking up usually works for me.'

'Sounds like crap,' Ryan said.

'Unless you plan on becoming a monk you'll have to live with it,' James said. 'And look on the bright side: your Aramov Clan mission was a monster hit. I did missions where I took bad guys out, but have you any idea how rare it is that you actually dismantle an entire criminal organisation?'

'Got my black shirt,' Ryan said, as he stretched it out to show James. 'All my mates are well jealous. I should be rubbing it in, but all I can think about is Natalka.'

'We're gonna be together after your post-mission holiday,' James said. 'I'm running the advanced driving course and you're second on the list of eligible candidates.'

'Ning and Leon said it was awesome,' Ryan said, cheering up a bit. 'Could have done with some better driving skills in Alabama a few weeks back.'

'I should get back inside,' James said. 'I don't want my first karaoke night turning into a riot. If you're feeling depressed, don't be scared to come and talk to me. Just don't ask me for any advice on future relationships, because I've been going out with girls for ten years now and frankly I still haven't got a clue.'

Ryan smiled as he got off the edge of the fountain and started walking after James. 'My mates Alfie and

Max are in there. They're basically immature idiots, but they're no worse than sitting out here freezing my arse off.'

'That's the spirit,' James said.

'I do feel better now I've spoken to you,' Ryan said. 'Thanks.'

Ryan was going to say something else, but as he reached the open fire door at the back of the hall, an eight-year-old ambushed him with half a bucket of freezing water. After gasping from the cold, Ryan looked down and saw his littlest brother Theo lobbing the bucket away before squealing and belting back inside.

'You little shite,' Ryan shouted.

He moved to give chase, but then looked around at James who had a wet leg where the water had splashed off the ground. Soaking a member of staff was serious and Ryan didn't want his youngest brother getting into trouble.

'He only meant to get me,' Ryan said.

'Don't sweat it,' James said, as he shook the bottom of his jeans. 'Go have fun chasing your little brother. And when you catch him, make sure you tickle him till he pukes.'

EPILOGUE

The following updates were written shortly before the publication of this book, in July 2013.

THE ISLAMIC DEPARTMENT OF JUSTICE (IDoJ)
Following the Black Friday attacks and subsequent arrest or killing of more than twenty IDoJ members, it was hoped that the organisation's back had been broken. However, intelligence sources now believe that while IDoJ's American presence was all but wiped out, the group's Mumbai-based leadership was untouched and has been able to use the notoriety gained after Black Friday to raise a significant war chest in order to fund future attacks.

Following his arrest, the pilot ELIJAH ELBAZ is currently awaiting trial inside a Supermax Federal Prison.

He refused to cooperate when questioned about IDoJ activity and is expected to spend the rest of his life in prison.

THE ARAMOV CLAN

The two and a half year mission to destroy the ARAMOV CLAN was one of the longest and most complex in the history of CHERUB. Not only were the clan's smuggling operations completely halted, information gathered while the clan was being controlled by TFU led to further operations against many other criminal organisations with which the Aramovs worked.

Of the clan's fleet of more than eighty aircraft, fifty-two were destroyed or sold for scrap, eleven were sold on to new owners, while seventeen were donated to humanitarian organisations. Some of the money seized from the clan will be used to keep these humanitarian planes flying. The rest of the $600 million fund was retained by TFU and eventually folded into the US Intelligence Service budget.

Following the destruction of the Kremlin, Kyrgyzstan's government lodged a protest at the United Nations, claiming that US agents had illegally infiltrated its territory and destroyed the former Soviet airbase. The American Ambassador to the UN dismissed these claims as 'a fabrication', and 'utterly ludicrous'.

Former clan head IRENA ARAMOV succumbed to cancer and died at a private nursing home in the United States.

Her only surviving child, JOSEF ARAMOV, was with his mother during the last weeks of her life. Josef was given immunity from criminal prosecution in return for his cooperation after TFU took the Aramov Clan over.

Josef now lives in Philadelphia under a new identity. He was allowed to keep a personal fortune of around $5 million and used some of this money to purchase a small appliance repair business.

ANDRE ARAMOV and his mother TAMARA ARAMOV returned to Russia. Tamara has begun working part time in a jewellery shop owned by her uncle. Andre has been enrolled in a fee-paying school. He is doing well in all his classes and briefly had his first ever girlfriend.

ETHAN ARAMOV formerly ETHAN KITSELL is now fully settled living with TED BRASKER in Texas. He inherited assets worth over $50 million from his late mother Galenka. This money came from the legal side of Galenka's business operations and will be placed in trust until Ethan reaches adulthood.

BORIS and ALEX ARAMOV used plane tickets and ID purchased before their father's death and flew to Trinidad. Two months after their arrival, Boris Aramov was arrested following an altercation in a nightclub during which a French tourist was savagely beaten.

Boris is currently awaiting trial in a Trinidad jail. Alex was arrested shortly afterwards when a search of their apartment unearthed a cache of illegal steroids, used for bodybuilding. No criminal charges were brought against Alex, but his real identity was discovered and he was deported back to Kyrgyzstan.

It seems that neither Boris nor Alex had access to significant amounts of money. This has led authorities to believe that Leonid Aramov did not complete the sale of seventy-four PGSLM missiles and that they were inside the factory when James destroyed it.

Lawyer PAOLO LOMBARDI is under criminal investigation for money laundering, fraud, and illegal share deals relating to the purchase of Lisson Communications. This highly complex case is unlikely to come to trial before 2014, but if convicted Lombardi faces up to six years in federal prison.

Clan flunky DAN has settled into a new life, with a new identity, in the United States. Amy Collins set him up with an apartment and a part-time job in a Texas gym. He is currently learning English and studying for a high school diploma at community college. He hopes to start a college degree in September 2014.

NATALKA had a difficult time settling with her aunt in Russia. After several months, she ran away and spent a period living on the streets. Following an arrest for shoplifting, Natalka's aunt refused to take her back and she has been placed in one of Russia's notoriously tough reform schools.

Natalka's mother, DIMITRA, is currently in a United States military prison awaiting trial. On-going arguments over the legality of the arrests of the four Aramov Clan aircrews mean that her trial is unlikely to take place until 2015, and there is a possibility that she will eventually be released without charge.

TFU
Despite the undeniable success of TFU's Aramov Clan operation, this short-lived branch of the US Intelligence Service was not given a reprieve. TFU's main investigations were either closed down or transferred to other departments at the end of March 2013.

TFU Director DR DENISE HUGGAN (DR D) accepted early retirement from the Intelligence Service and has taken a part-time role as a lecturer on Intelligence and International Affairs at the University of Texas in Dallas.

All investigations into Dr D's conduct of the IDoJ operation were dropped upon her retirement.

Deputy Director TED BRASKER is currently on long-term sick leave following an operation on his back. He has not been assigned to a new position within US Intelligence and is expected to retire once he returns to health.

Ted has also taken formal steps to become the full-time legal guardian of Ethan Aramov.

AMY COLLINS turned down an offer to return to

CHERUB campus and work in the mission control department. Following a written recommendation from Ted Brasker, Amy accepted the offer of a place on the FBI's twenty-week training programme. Amy has now taken full US citizenship and is expected to qualify as an FBI special agent in October 2013.

CHERUB

Although YOSYP KAZAKOV's death was confirmed through DNA traces, his body was largely vaporised in the explosion at Oak Ranch. A monument to Kazakov is being created in the chapel on CHERUB campus and the main street of the Campus Village will be named after him.

Chairwoman ZARA ASKER has announced that she plans to step down and take a less demanding job when the Campus Village project is finished in 2016. Her husband EWART ASKER is currently the favourite to succeed her as chairman.

JAMES ADAMS completed his six-month probationary period as a member of CHERUB staff and has been promoted to grade four. His ambition is to work as a full-time mission controller, but currently his job remains split between the mission control and training departments.

James has purchased a new Triumph Thunderbird motorbike, which he regularly rides on the roads near campus.

He had no contact with KERRY CHANG for four months, when she called in tears and announced that she'd split with her new boyfriend. The former couple are back on friendly terms, but James has been working on campus while Kerry is finishing her degree in California. Kerry plans to visit campus after her final exams at the end of July.

FU NING has continued to excel as a CHERUB agent and received her navy shirt following a short mission.

After his soaking RYAN SHARMA caught up with little brother Theo, carried him across campus and dumped him in a muddy puddle on a football pitch. Over the following months he slowly got over the loss of Natalka, but still felt sad that he couldn't get in touch with her.

After his long mission in Kyrgyzstan, Ryan spent the first half of 2013 on campus, catching up on his education and training. Ryan is still best friends with MAX BLACK and ALFIE DUBOISSON. GRACE VULLIAMY continues to be his occasional campus girlfriend.

Following a fitness assessment and satisfactory reports from all of his teachers, Ryan will return to mission eligible status on August 1st 2013.

CHERUB

PEOPLE'S REPUBLIC
Robert Muchamore

Twelve-year-old Ryan is CHERUB's newest recruit. He's got his first mission: infiltrating the billion-dollar Aramov criminal empire. But he's got no idea that this routine job will lead him into an explosive adventure involving drug smugglers, illegal immigrants and human trafficking, or that his first mission will turn into one of the biggest in CHERUB's history.

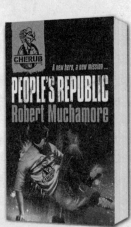

OUT NOW

Also available as an ebook

www.cherubcampus.com

Hodder Children's Books

GUARDIAN ANGEL
Robert Muchamore

Ryan has saved Ethan's life more than once. Ethan thinks he must be a guardian angel. But Ryan works for CHERUB, a secret organisation with one key advantage: even experienced criminals never suspect that children are spying on them. Ethan's family runs a billion-dollar criminal empire and Ryan's job is to destroy it. Can Ryan complete his mission without destroying Ethan as well?

OUT NOW

www.cherubcampus.com

Hodder Children's Books